THE SWORD AND

a novel by Mark Bradford

Alchemy

Printed in the United States of America

Second Printing, 2020

ISBN: 978-1-7336622-3-9

Library of Congress Control Number:2019918678

markbradford.org

1.4

DEDICATION

To those that have gone to the edge and dreamt they returned.

ACKNOWLEDGMENTS

Ludovico Einaudi - Divenire
Enigma
Steve Jablonsky
Alan Silvestri
Jerry Goldsmith
Escala

and

Those have that been with me though my journey.

THE SWORD AND THE SUNFLOWER

PRONUNCIATION GUIDE

I find that when reading words one is not familiar with it is commonplace for the mind to fill in the pronunciation. I also find it equally common that the pronunciation the mind comes up with is often times different than the author intended—some would say better.

Lest you experience this shock when finally hearing these words I present to you a pronunciation guide.

The caveat is that I default to you in the event that you like *your* pronunciation better than the one I provide here. Though I am the author you are the reader, and I find that you have the final say as far as pronunciations are involved.

Unless we meet in person. Then we can argue.

As per the Guide to simple American pronunciation markup[1].

Stojan: Stoh JHAHN.

Anastazja: Ah nah STAH zhuh. Also, AH nah

Lucjan: LOO shehn

Budziszyn: BOO Dih Shehn.

Oliwier: Ah Lee WEER

Dagmar: Dag MAHR

Talana: Tuh LAH nah

Poliska: Poh LEE skah, also POH lah

Amira: Uh MEE ruh, also Uh MEER Uh

---

1 https://en.wikipedia.org/wiki/Wikipedia:Pronunciation_(simple_guide_to_markup,_American)

THE AGREEMENT

"Do you know the origin of your name, bishop?"

It asked of him—with a voice that was an entire chorus—and the tower resonated with the sound. The voice spoke firmly, and gently. It whispered and yelled. It was many, and one. And it would make any man mad to listen to it, but it did not this day.

Perhaps because he already was.

Lucjan spoke back into the statue.

"I know many things. And many things have changed. Some information can be trusted; oth…"

"Light bringer."

The voice interrupted, almost laughing, as if revealing the final line of a very elaborate joke.

Lucjan closed his mouth, not sure how to feel, not sure what the voice wanted by this statement.

"I see."

"You are named after the one that attempted to bring light to your people."

Lucjan stared into eyes of stone. They did not blink.

“He failed.”

“I will not fail!” The bishop replied immediately, thinking this was a challenge, or perhaps that it was suggesting his namesake caused him to be destined to fail.

“We have a deal and you are bound by it.”

“Yessss…” The voice drew out the single syllable and the walls shook with it. It affirmed what Lucjan said but was also perturbed. Was there anger, or was it hate he heard?

“Seek the assassin and pray once again.”

Lucjan knew there was nothing it could do, but he was also in a precarious position. He had harnessed lightning in a bottle months ago. He had done the impossible—the saint was in his keeping and would provide all manner of knowledge and power.

But it had also alerted him to a danger with an augury. Lucjan would be struck down in a mere week. A great warrior—one known about the land— would visit him in his very tower and strike him down.

The saint could not protect him, but could provide a means for a proxy to do so.

The assassin. But this would not be a simple case of pitting one fighter against the other.

“Nay, the warrior is much too powerful. The assassin could not defeat this warrior. He would be… helpless.”

The voice had told him this almost a month ago and with it had lead him to a scroll—a scroll that would foretell the prophecy. There was a problem though—Lucjan’s ability to translate the ancient language was marginal at best, and he was running out of time.

The voice would do what it was asked but *only* what it was asked. It could not provide information, or translate the scroll. Or rather, it provided its own information, when it wished it. Though it was in his service it could only act based on the specific prayers of Lucjan.

And it could not tell him what to pray for.

This he found profoundly annoying.

The scroll had been before him for many days, and he had focused all of his efforts on translating it. Often times he wondered if it simply said he was doomed, spelled out his death... but thoughts of that ilk were quickly washed away by his pride at being so powerful as to be part of an ancient prophecy.

He had accomplished much and his accomplishments had justified his actions—every one of them.

He was indeed an important part of the church as a whole. Perhaps one day he would be a Saint.

Day and night he worked at the document until finally he translated it.

"Strike at the warrior when n'er be more weak
Motion is set when ye find what ye seek"

Once again he prayed and his audience was granted. He described what had been translated, and he asked specifically for help in sending someone to this warrior when they are at their weakest.

He just needed a warrior—one that was ruthless, a killer. One that was single-minded in purpose and would not fail him.

A simple mercenary would not do, nor would a barbaric fighter of some kind. He had considered freeing a prisoner to do the bidding. Even the strongest of warriors had their limits. Lucjan needed more than just skill. He needed something else—or an individual weighed and found wanting.

He needed someone with no heart, because their heart had been taken from them.

THE BILL COMES DUE

A tall dark figure in the doorway— a literal silhouette—stood silently. The hood of his head almost touched the top of the door frame. For minutes he remained, observing, thinking, reviewing. When he felt he had waited long enough, he cleared his throat.

The smaller man in the room was justifiably startled as he turned around —almost dropping his teapot.

The black figure blocking out most of the light in the door did not move, making it all the more startling.

He squinted his eyes in an attempt to make out features of the visitor, but he needn't have tried for he was aware of the stories, and knew the bill had come due. It was him. His hawk-like features, his height, and his deftness made it clear.

Weakly he placed the teapot back upon the table—its cover almost shaking off in concert with the man's quaking hands.

"I'll be right with you."

His eyes darted from the doorway to his bedroom door and back again. Seeing no movement or acknowledgement he stole away to the bedroom and in a moment had returned to the entry room. The black figure was no longer in the doorway and this caused him to clutch his coin purse harder while moving his head to and fro to survey the small room.

He was alone.

The man closed his eyes, his fear was visible in his face and he mouthed ever so quietly, “Saints preserve me.”

“They will not.”

At once he opened his eyes—widely, to see the source of the voice.

The tall man stood in front of him, mere centimeters away. He was dressed in light wraps of an umber color -dark browns and blacks. The wraps were misleading because under them was a thick leather and fine chain armor. The man was exceptionally thin so one was taken off guard at how well he was protected. Or so went the stories.

His expressionless face revealed nothing, as his brown eyes looked into the eyes of the much shorter man.

The bag of coins was slowly offered forward as the man said, “So… it is done?”

The burden of the coins was quickly removed from the frightened man as the other replied.

“I would not be here if it were not so.”

Relieved and saddened the man realized his hand was still outstretched, sans wealth. He withdrew it to his side.

Not sure what to do next he nervously looked upon the stranger he had just paid.

“Is… is it true?”

Silence. The coin bag was already gone, but the man was immobile.

The smaller man continued, feeling slightly confident now, and not knowing what to do to dispel the murderer he had just paid. Was there something he needed to say? Would a ‘thank you’ make him go away?

“Is it true what they say about you…? About the village?”

There was no response from the tall man, and his gaze was almost painful.

"All those people, in one day?"

The smaller man detected no remorse, no sadness. He looked into the eyes and saw no reaction—just cold hard brown eyes staring back at him. It was akin to looking up at a wall that at any moment could fall upon the viewer. One did not walk right up to it and look, and wait for the fatal collapse.

He realized he was not only looking up at the wall, but he was poking and prodding it. The questions were ill-advised at best. His eyes widened as he realized what he was doing.

Before he could do anything else he felt a sharp piercing in his side—the point of a dagger. It bit into his flesh. It was quite sharp.

Looking down then back up again he started to shake his head, as if to say he meant no harm and was only curious. His eyes spoke for him.

"You have paid me," the voice in his ear said. "I've done what you asked. If someone wishes the same of you and pays, your fate will be the same. There is always someone with more money than you."

The dagger was withdrawn and with that the man left as quickly as he came.

Slowly the terrified man placed his hand upon his side where the dagger had once been.

Taking a deep breath he started to close his eyes in a silent prayer when he heard the voice speak one last time.

"And the saints will not preserve you."

THE BISHOP'S OFFER

"Tell him they are dead."

This was all the stranger would say when greeted at the doors. The small building had a house proper and a large steeple. To the surrounding villagers it was a vestige of the ancient times, and rumors abounded that a saint rested there. Most believed they resided in cathedrals and this was too small to contain them. However, they learned quickly that a bishop had taken residence recently, called forth for servants and staff, and begun some unknown work.

The servant had answered the door and the five-word sentence was all he received. After some fumbling, and half-expressed sentences he eventually closed the door and ran to find his master. He did not invite the stranger in.

This rudeness was not overlooked by the visitor.

After much time had passed the door opened to empty stairs, a setting sun and a cool breeze. But no visitor. Not that he would have expected him to stand out in front of the doors all evening waiting. Most would, but the likes of this man certainly would not. The servant muttered to himself and eventually closed the doors. He continued muttering as he looked at the floor, walking through the opening in the elongated chairs that made up the main entry room.

He imagined the long chairs filled with people, come to hear a bishop speak, or even to witness the appearance of a saint. The glass windows that lined the walls were now dark as the sun was setting, but the array of candles were lit.

There was much commotion lately and the bishop ordered him to light the candles three nights in a row. This was only done when a saint was to be present, according to legend as repeated by the bishop.

Whether the saint had actually appeared was another thing entirely—for all the fear and things the bishop had told him, he wasn't sure if any of it was real. These were remnants from a darker time a thousand years ago. It was the Year of All Saints, 1221, and that calendar had changed on the second coming. If the calendar was right 1,221 years ago the world was turned upside down. That's all he knew and all he cared to know, and fought as much as he could not to learn anything else from the bishop.

"Did you tell him?"

The servant practically jumped onto the raised dais at the front of the entry room. It was the stranger, sitting in the front.

The man grabbed his heart, and walked over to the stranger.

"Yes. He will see you now."

"Just like that?"

"Yes?"

The servant so much as asked, as he was confused over the entire exchange. He knew nothing save for the fact that men had been sent to request the presence of the stranger, and that the stranger was in fact the renown killer of men and women, the Butcher of Budziszyn, the fallen captain of the guard who systematically murdered almost a hundred people that day—if the rumors were to be believed.

And here he sat, calmly, his sword unsheathed and used as a cane between his legs.

"Please follow me?"

Once again the servant's tone was inquisitive, as he mused the man would do what he pleased, and that the language between them was just a formality.

The man rose to his full height, his sword already sheathed, and stood behind the servant. He walked swiftly towards the door before the man could enter too much of his personal space. Risking rudeness he passed through the door and did not hold it. Up the stairs he went, eyes half-closed as he murmured to himself.

—

"I am here because a man who can afford the four dead men can afford me."

In the center of the room stood the bishop, in his purple robes with one hand upon an adorned staff. It looked too heavy to carry around and was clearly just ceremonial. It wasn't clear to the servant why he had it out. It was clear to the stranger; it completed his outfit and was there to impress him.

"So you killed them… all?"

Silence from the newcomer. Behind the visitor now, the servant started to back out slowly, only to freeze in place by an outstretched finger pointed directly at him. It was not a spell, but simple fear that held him in place. The bishop returned his hand to his side, and awaited the answer to his question.

The tall man nodded.

The four men had been expensive. The bishop spent good money to find men ruthless enough to go after the stranger. Though it took them some time they were no match for him. Killing them was unexpected as he thought them able to bring the killer to him. This turn of events was even better—not only had he already proven his worth but he'd delivered himself.

The bishop smiled and almost giggled with a sound a child makes when presented with his favorite toy.

"I have a job for you."

The man's head barely moved, but he surveyed the room. It was small, with adornments of gold and purple. A sculpture stood in the room facing away from him. From what he could see of its back, it was a depiction of some sort of large bird; its wings folded tightly in. Or perhaps it was a person with wings and wearing robes. The large item of stone was difficult to discern due to the darkness. It was positioned oddly in the room, as if to hide it or place it in storage.

This was the first such statue the stranger had seen that was not in pieces. In fact, even the debris of them were hard to find.

"The money," was all he said.

The bishop's face changed a bit, some of the glee seeping out of his voice.

"I'm sure far far more than you've ever been paid. In fact it is enough to buy your own land."

"It is not enough."

"Excuse me?" The bishop's head tilted at the quick response. Surely the man joked, but he had not smiled, had not reacted.

"What mean you by this? I haven't given you the…"

"You are too anxious. This means the amount you offer is well within your means, and well below what you can afford."

The bishop started to speak but was cut off.

"You flaunt jewels and giggle like a child, but the grave look in your eyes speaks of no price being too high."

The bishop inhaled slowly as his face became hardened. The stranger was right. He would indeed pay any price to have this deed done—his life depended on it. There was more to this man than he expected or liked. He would not have the upper hand.

"What do you want?" The bishop asked without humor.

"What do you offer?"

Again the bishop's eyes became narrow, with suspicion and anger. Was this man in league with the warrior? Was he the warrior that had come to kill him? Was this what the prophecy foretold of?

I have spelled out my own doom by inviting this murderer into my inner sanctum.

The panic in his chest was starting to erupt into his facial expression.

He spoke quickly and with much venom.

“I offer you enough monies to buy a plot of land equal to mine.”

At this proclamation the servant’s eyes went wide—he was stunned. The bishop was giving this man something only a royal would bestow. To be given a plot of land such as this was tantamount to being made a baron. One who received it would attract his own servants, militia and even an eventual village.

But did the bishop posses this much? He might, but this would be all he possessed. His master had many failings. A lack of greed was not one of them. He would never give up more than he could easily afford. Something was wrong.

Many moments passed.

“Show me.”

The bishop raised an eyebrow in response, and gripped his staff tighter.

“I can show you the gold, and jewels.”

With that he swept his staff about, as if the stranger was to guess where they were located.

“You are afraid to retrieve them lest I discover the location, return later and simply take them.”

“You assume much.”

“I assume nothing.”

The stranger was impossible to read. True to the stories it seemed he simply did not care. There was really nothing that would motivate him save for the right price. What someone like him did with these monies was something the bishop hadn’t figured out.

And what of the right price? What did he wish to purchase?

“What is it you want, exactly? Spell it out for me, stranger.”

The assassin took a deep breath and without much hesitation spoke.

"I seek enough monies so that I may travel far away and take up residence where no one knows of me, does not recognize me, and give me no cause for further harm."

As the bishop was about to respond he finished.

"To them."

"Thank you, I understand you now."
The man in the purple robes visibly relaxed. He even smiled. The servant watched as he thought for a minute.

"I commit to you more than enough monies and the means to travel a great distance and take up residence where no one will know you."

He was practically ticking off the points in his mind.

"This is a substantial amount of monies, and I will have this for you upon your departure—I swear to All Saints that this is true."

"When?"

Again a question said more like a statement. This pleased the bishop. He'd done it.

"Tomorrow morning. I will have the monies for you."

"I'll return at sunrise. If all is not as described I will leave…"

He turned back to the servant who seemed startled he knew he was still there. Looking him in the eyes he finished.

"…and take compensation for wasting my time."

The effect this had on both men was completely opposite the other. The bishop seemed delighted while the servant was terrified.

The stranger left without a word, deftly moving past the servant who was almost blocking the door.

The servant turned his now-pale face to look over at his smiling master.

"Now, you and I have much to do."

The servant just nodded. It had been a difficult night.

—

That night the bishop would not sleep, but spend it preparing and praying to his patron saint—the saint that had foretold of this, the saint that would provide the means of the assassin's departure.

The saint he had bound by extraordinary means to do his bidding, and almost nothing would ever change that.

A LION DEPARTS

The scents had changed. This was the first perception Stojan experienced. He was in a daze—as if waking from a dream. His eyes were closed or perhaps there was nothing to see. Try as he might his focus was limited and all of his effort was to gain some sort of bearing, but without his sight and even a sense as to his position he was helpless to do nothing but struggle and wait.

There was no up or down; he had no sense of where his hands were and could not feel the weight of his clothing or pack. There was just blackness, and the smell of a forest—a stark difference to the cold air of the tower.

Had he been drugged? Was this the result of a joke and was he now bound in a dungeon at the base of the tower, to be tortured for some unknown reason?

He had arrived as promised the next morning and this was his fate.

He could not become angry but instead was oddly disconnected from what he was experiencing. He felt at once exhausted and free—free of his body.

This prison of nothingness would suit him and his mood. Perhaps this was his final resting place. For all of his sins he would be rewarded with blackness, and nothing. Or perhaps Stojan the Ghost was more fitting and he would roam the land surrounding a great cathedral like the old stories explained.

The rustle of a leaf. Sound.

The first sound he experienced was rustling of leaves very nearby. Then suddenly the feeling of standing, having legs and then arms. He was upright.

He felt the sensation of weight and could now see light—first just grey and then slowly color seeped in. The scene had greens, browns and blues but was turning on and off every so often.

He was blinking.

He grabbed the nearby brown object and was able to remain standing. The tree obliged without issue.

He could now see around him, and turned his head to survey the surroundings. His head obeyed but everything moved slowly. He felt prone and very susceptible to engagement. Though he could now see, things were still in a fog as if he was surrounded by a semi-transparent cloud. To him it stunk of a sorcery dark and evil.

And it was all taking too long for his liking.

He shook his head to be freed of the effects but that resulted in him staggering and almost losing his balance. Grabbing the tree with his other hand he caught sight of a man. He was chopping wood nearby. Stojan watched and hung onto the tree—like a drunk in hiding trying to sober up. He held on and embraced the stability.

The man was middle-aged and wore the garb of a blacksmith. He was clearly a brute of a man whose height rivaled that of his observer. Though Stojan might be an inch taller, the man's girth was impressive.

He was chopping wood on top of a stump with an oversized and awkward-looking axe. It was short and thick.

Stojan had arrived very nearby and was less than ten meters away, at the edge of the tree line that abutted the yard. A small half-height wooden fence marked off the back of the property. Clearly it was decorative as it wouldn't keep out man or beast.

The man chopped rhythmically. He seemed tired, and irritated and periodically looked up at the sky. It seemed the oversized axe was becoming heavier and heavier. He removed his apron and continued.

Stojan watched closely and remembered the words of his employer:

"You will be sent to a warrior when at their weakest point. Strike then and your job will be completed."

He instinctively looked down at the forest floor next to him. His payment had not traveled with him. Taking a deep breath for what seemed like the first time in ages he stumbled, tripping on a branch that resulted in a loud snap. He was still very groggy and didn't yet have control over his faculties. So awkward was his stance he could do nothing but hold onto the tree as he leant out in plain view of the man. Stealth was not an option it seemed.

Startled and in mid-strike the man looked over towards the source of the sudden sound, and as if it had a mind of its own the axe continued downward.

Their gazes met just as the man's eyes widened in shock and surprise. Their eyes locked and a moment was stretched over centuries as his face turned from surprise to pain to sadness. He then turned from Stojan to look down with apprehension. Stojan's eyes followed the man's gaze and saw the source of the pain. The end of the axe's swing had carried it not into the awaiting wood, but into the man's leg.

He had chopped deeply into his own thigh.

Dropping the axe completely the man took a weak step backwards, stumbled and fell upon the earth.

Blood could be seen—even from this distance—as the woodcutter's heart did its best to dutifully pump regardless of the large gash it now encountered.

Stojan knew the man would be dead in minutes. His uncharacteristic clumsiness upon arrival had caused the man to be distracted, at exactly the worst moment.

The assassin, perhaps the best in all of Poliska, known for his lack of conscience, his skill with the sword and his unwavering commitment to the kill had struck again.

But this time with a twig.

Death would be probable but not certain, he realized. He must strike a final blow, the final blow he was sent to deliver, as promised. He looked around to make sure they were alone lest his final blow be interrupted by a passerby or even an animal.

Weakly, the man screamed something and just as Stojan was about to approach, movement appeared from within the doorway behind him.

He stopped to assess it and what he saw gave him greater pause.

A child no older than 14 rushed out, her blonde long hair arriving shortly after her. Her eyes found the blacksmith and the look of horror on her small, flawless face made Stojan freeze. Her focus was on the injured man and hadn't seen the new visitor.

Perhaps it was the aftereffects of the unconventional and distasteful way he arrived, perhaps it was something else, but the sight had a far greater impact on him than it should have.

He felt a sinking, and a pulling, and a clarity. He saw the scene with depth and everything surrounding it was out of focus.

Before he knew what he was doing he was running towards them, swiftly.

The girl had knelt down next to the big man and her hands were covered in his blood as she tried to press the wound closed. She was terrified.

Stojan leapt over the small fence and landed on his knees next to them. The girl looked up and just said "Help him. Help us, please!"

Her voice was imploring, and sweet and filled with infinite sadness. Stojan looked back into the great blue eyes, so similar to the man he now held.

He took off his pack and said to her—"A sheet, a towel, a rag, anything…"

She leapt up and ran into the yard to grab something from the line.

Stojan held the man's head in his hands and could feel it becoming heavier and heaver as the man's life drained away into the grass.

His big blue eyes looked into Stojan's as he spoke.

"Thank you…"

With that he slumped even further and gently closed his eyes.

The man had smiled—ever so slightly, but he had smiled when he looked upon the stranger that had come to kill him.

Stojan stared at the face of the man, then through him as his eyes stared, like those remembering an old deep memory.

The girl had returned—so quietly that Stojan had not heard her.

Was he so distracted, or still feeling the effects of travel? No one snuck up on the assassin. Ever.

She was kneeling and clutching a sheet in her tiny hands. She placed a hand upon the man and looked at his face. Slowly Stojan's eyes moved to rest upon her, her eyes, her face, her hair. She looked familiar and strange at the same time. The bright sunlight on this beautiful summer day reflected off her blonde hair, her fragile features and the blood that was everywhere.

It felt like time had frozen for him—that all things held in the balance. But instead of the stoic certainty the assassin had relied upon for years, he was strangely confused. His understanding of this moment and about his surroundings was absent. He felt out of place and unable to apply the rules he had created for himself.

There was no anger, no callousness. He felt no hatred, no coldness. He felt lost—lost without the protective barriers of hate, resentment and apathy.

He looked again into her eyes—his confusion and surprise showing quite visibly on his face—and any ruse he could have come up with would not have bested the look of pure shock and concern on his face.

All the armor, the practice, the dedications, the walls created by death, the weapons—none of it could protect him from the vulnerability he felt at this moment. He was laid bare.

She cried softly at the death of her father.

STOJAN AND ANASTAZJA

Stojan had dug much of the grave but the girl insisted she do some of the work. Her strength was surprising for someone so small. Though her frame was delicate she was not overly thin, but instead showed a density of muscle that could only come from consistent strenuous physical exertion. It was exceptional.

He learned her name was Anastazja. He thought it a beautiful name, and upon hearing it, made even more ethereal by her voice.

When the grave was dug and finished Stojan planned to move on for many reasons.

"You say you knew him?"

Stojan lifted a crate of items as he talked. They'd been cleaning up for much of the day.

"Yes, I knew of him more than I knew him," he half-lied. It was one of many. He found himself putting considerable effort into lying as little as possible to her. There was still a part of him trying to understand the situation he had been thrust into.

"He seemed to know you…" Her eyes did not meet the man's when she talked as she preferred to focus on the work instead.

Stojan nodded an unseen nod.

"...the way he looked at you," she finished.

The big man had indeed. And the gratitude in his eyes were misplaced. Had the axe not killed him the assassin surely would have. So why thank him? What was he thankful for?

"My father has helped so many people, and in the past sometimes created weapons. He must have created one for you?"

Another box was lifted, moved and placed on a shelf. Instead of answering Stojan questioned Anastazja instead.

"Has he taught you the trade?"

She put down the item she was holding, stood upright and turned.

"Oh yes, indeed he has."

Her gaze was strong, and she carried an intense certainty in her eyes, one he could not quite attribute to a blacksmith apprentice. There was something more. Her confidence seemed absolute.

She took a deep breath and her stance changed. "In three days we will have the funeral and the townsfolk will pay their respects."

This would not do. His job was done and he was not returning. Surely the sickly fog that had brought him here would return him? Or was it up to him? How far was the tower on horseback? Regardless of how he would return he was without his payment—he'd been tricked. He could hear the bishop laughing and the sight of the assassin disappearing, fading away, as his substantial payment remained. How many others had the bishop duped in this manner? Surely if the payment never accompanied the traveller one could send many to do their bidding.

The blacksmith farmer was outside of a small town. Stojan found it odd that his shop was not in the town proper, but perhaps it wasn't because he was so specialized? Or a farmer-turned-blacksmith? Or perhaps he was in retirement? From what he had seen it looked like this blacksmith produced fine goods, but mostly of utility—fencing, implements and the like. No weapons were displayed.

But someone in a large group from the town would surely recognize him. Though stealth was part of his job, his stature, skills and deeds were well known across much of the local land. Regardless, word of a very tall thin man appearing at the death of a well known blacksmith would travel fast. He had to move on, and quickly.

“I will be moving on tonight when we are done.”

She again spoke without looking, a small amount of surprise in her voice.

“You travel at night? And you will not attend my father’s funeral?”

She was speaking quickly, slightly panicked. She stopped at stared at a crate.

“I have business to attend to…” He had almost said ‘in the city’ but realized he didn’t know what city was nearby, let alone what town there were technically in. He had no bearings.

As he was forming his next lie she walked over to him.

Standing closely she looked up. He could feel her presence. There was a tangible warmth around her. Unlike the cloud of disorienting fog that had brought him here, this was an inviting cocoon of something else. It welcomed him, and provided a wholeness he’d not felt in some time.

Again he saw the face of perfection, the tiny gentle form, the blonde hair that flowed down her shoulders like a golden waterfall.

“But I don’t want to be alone.”

He almost whispered, “You have no family that can stay with you?” He knew the answer.

“No.”

She did not elaborate.

She was so familiar to him—this girl he had never met. It was then he realized that of all the battles he had fought, with stealth and strength and cunning he had always won. Not this day.

This time he was not the victor. The assassin had lost.

ASSASSIN IN RESIDENCE

“It’s just up ahead!”

The excited voice belonged to a small man of slight build—his brown/ blonde hair was in a bun and the object of his excitement was a small farmhouse ahead whose yard had been converted for use of a blacksmith.

“Shh!” his companion struggled to keep up.

They had been walking for a bit and the promise of what lay ahead seemed too good to be true. It was.

They’d learned that a well-known blacksmith lived here. He had retired but still created a weapon upon request from time to time. Rumors were that he had created some very fine weapons and perhaps had some in storage. It was a public secret that he resided here alone with his daughter.

Now word had reached them through a customer that had come to make payment on an item, just yesterday. He’d found the girl, sad and distraught. She’d already buried her father and was alone to handle his belongings and estate. This included some very unique items. Or at least some gold. And, there was the girl.

The leader turned his head back. “Don’t worry, it’s just up ahead, through these…”

“Ronaz?”

He stopped. His friend was not there. He took a few paces backwards and turned his body to match the direction of his feet.

He was alone.

He spun around, surveying the area. The sun was just coming up and he heard nothing. They were a long way from the path that cut through the trees. Their best bet of arriving undetected was from the back and the protection of the forest. Their horses were latched far away.

"Ronaz..?" His voice much quieter this time, the leader implored his friend. "I'm not… I do not feel like playing games… This… this is not funny."

He froze.

The cold blade under his chin extended outward at least a meter. The pain in his side was shocking but was probably only a warning. Mere centimeters and it would be fatal. He was like a statue.

The voice that spoke was both gruff and smooth, like a fine coffee that was left out all day and become bitter. One could still sense the flavor and depth but it was no longer drinkable.

It said only two things, spaced apart by two hours:

"You will never return here, you will never speak of this to anyone or I will find you and kill you, your family and everyone with any meaning to you."

And:

"Thank you for your contribution."

The leader of the band of two thieves never saw the source of the voice, and was only privy to being walked back towards his horses, bound tightly about the arms and torso just like his companion. He and his partner did not look back lest one or both of them lose their lives right there on the spot. They walked for some time, were deposited face down in the grass and were relieved of their horses. When they did finally muster the courage to look up they indeed found the horses gone.

After much comic rolling around on the ground they were eventually able to line up their hands to untie each other. This took far more time than expected and included much exclamations, blame and yelling. They were exhausted, freighted and defeated. The stranger left only this additional rope, their packs with food and their lives. He'd removed everything else—horses, weapons, monies, and dignity.

—

"You are up early."

It was Anastazja's way of saying *good morning*.

Stojan agreed to spend the night. And the next, and finally for the funeral. Each day he could not say no, and leave her alone. The thought of it was uncomfortable, and he still needed to get his bearings.

He used the latter to explain the former.

He agreed to stay but would not stay in the house. The blacksmith's bedroom was to be left alone out of respect, the girl's room was not an option. Instead he slept in the barn in a loft, and found it both comfortable and advantageous. Learning that the house was potentially under scrutiny of those that would prey on it made the barn an incomparable vantage point.

For the funeral he would risk being recognized. If he was he would simply leave and make his was back.

"You are not familiar with Budziszyn?"

"No. I have not gone into town. I was only here to see your father."

"And Warwick?"

"I have not traveled there."

She cocked her head slightly.

"Surely you've heard of it—it is a large city many kilometers away."

"Of course, though I have not been there either."

It was then that Stojan finally had some sense of where he was, though he did not believe it. If the closest city was Warwick then he was hundreds of kilometers from the bishop's tower. The prayers that had

brought him here were indeed powerful.
It would take much time to return, but he would. A part of him wanted payment; a part did not.

He wanted answers though. There were things that were not right, and he sensed there was more that he would discover.

The most confusing was the weather. Though never having been here, he did not think the weather should be so different. In all of Poliska the weather was essentially the same. There were rumors of lands that experienced snow year round, or cold when it was hot.

But when he left it was the end of summer, and here it was much warmer, as if summer had just begun. It was not unheard of for some extra warmth to make itself known, and the seasons sometimes expanded and contracted. Nor would it be shocking if the cooler summer's end had a reprieve and offered a few weeks more of heat before giving into fall.

It was most certainly the latter that was happening. Yes.

"I would like to travel there."

So lost in his musings he paused to catch up. "To… ?"

"To Warwick." She put her hands on her hips. "That is where the Cathedral of Saint Wiktor is."

Again, silence as Stojan struggled to catch up.

"You are interested in this cathedral? I have no interest in the saints."

His lack of interest made her all the more curious. She repeated his statement as a question. "You have no interest in the cathedral? In the saints?" She was genuinely confused as the position seemed to place him in the minority.

"Which is your patron?"

"Young lady, I have no patron."

He shifted his weight a bit.

"But we do have an agreement—the saints and I."

"Oh? All of them?"

"They have no interest in me and the feeling is mutual."

She looked both disappointed and curious.

Stojan shared these very feelings that day.

———

Though out of touch for the three years he had hid between the cities he found Poliska was constant in their lack of interest in the saints. It had been that way for hundreds of years. Anastazja's interest in them was somewhat unusual. She had spoken of a friend that sought out a cathedral in Poliska. Stojan knew of none. The bishop's odd building was the closest he had seen of one. Yet she insisted she had heard of those that made a pilgrimage—somewhere.

This very question he posed to Anastazja.

"I know no one personally who has done this. But I heard told of many people who had family who made the pilgrimage."

Stojan squinted, his hawk-like face looking like he was making out a mouse at a great distance.

"So you know of rumors. Rumors are not proof."

She smiled a large and inviting smile, "Fair enough Stojan. You are an interesting man."

Though his face remained the same he enjoyed her approval. It was pleasant, and almost important to him.

As he turned to leave she asked a final question.

"And the horses?"

The shock shown in his eyes, though he was turned away.

He spoke immediately without turning back.

"They are mine."

"Strange that they were not with you when you arrived."

"These are strange times," was his reply as he walked out. Had he turned he would have seen the grin on her face.

—

That night was filled with thoughts. Stojan considered all that had happened to him. He was not a stranger to a sleepless night and considered it part of his job. This night was no different. It is said that dreams are a way for the saints to visit with questions and provide answers in their own cryptic ways. To Stojan it was a way for his mind to unwind, to display the absurdity of his existence.

This job, and the commensurate payment that came with it was a final turn for him. He would perform the deed, accept the magnanimous payment and then travel far far away.

In a way the bishop had already provided that next step, for he was clearly many hundreds of kilometers from his previous locale. Perhaps the bishop knew of his plans? Perhaps he had decided that this was his actual reward—the instantaneous travel to a new city in which he was unknown. Stojan did not believe in faith, or the saints, yet here he was.

Try as he might he could not remain inconspicuous.

And the would-be thieves? He had not killed them. Their lives meant nothing to him and he should have taken them. Things would be cleaner. No witnesses. But instead he had spared their lives. Though he threatened them they would probably talk, and tell of a mysterious stranger that prevented them from pillaging the blacksmith and his daughter. He was sure they could not identify him, but there would be enough information to generate much interest.

What had he done? What was he doing?

His mind struggled to make sense of some of it—any of it. Yet, nothing did make sense. His actions were not seemingly of his own volition. Before traveling here he would not have hesitated to kill, like he had done with all the others in the past. And he would not remain here. He would complete the job, then failing payment, make his way back to obtain payment and perhaps watch the life drain out of the bishop.

Instead he spared lives—something he hadn't done in years, since he took so many.

His eyes were wide open now. He looked out the window into the clear evening sky. The moon was almost full this night and it shown brightly, a massive white sphere in the sky with a distinct blue halo. A bird flew in front of it now and again. He continued his musings.

He should have been on his way. Regardless of distance he would already be two days closer to his destination. By his reckoning he would still need more than a week by his best estimate to ride back, probably two or three. Or perhaps a month?

And the girl? It was not his concern that she was here, alone. She did not matter.

Yet she did.

Was he still in a fog, or perhaps the fog had been dissipated? He felt different—like a great burden had been lifted. But it hadn't. He was still responsible for the slaughter of over 70 people in one day. He could still see their faces, smell the blood, hear the screams. They were all bad; every one of them. Each and every one of them was responsible for the death of his daughter in one way or another. There were no degrees of guilt; just guilt. And they all paid the ultimate price for their participation. He could not bring her back, but he could make all that were responsible join her.

Instinctively he touched his sword. Even at rest it was by his side. Even at night he was fully clothed, protected.

Another bird flew in front of the moon—this time a bit larger. It was closer now—circling and crisscrossing—almost providing a late night ballet for his viewing pleasure. He watched.

Tomorrow would be the funeral. Many townsfolk, no doubt, would be there. Each was an opportunity to be discovered, every person was a potential conversation filled with lies and deception.

Then it would be over. He'd be on his way. He'd take one horse as his own and the second as a pack animal. It could also be sold if need be. There were two other horses in the barn and tending to them no doubt was when Anastazja had found the others.

He would make his way back to the bishop, reclaim his payment and seek vengeance on the one who had hired him to kill a man that was already dead.

Or he would simply disappear into the countryside, and explore this new land.

Uncertainty?

This was new as well. And it unnerved him.

He continued to stare out the window to the moon, and thought of the old tales of it being so much smaller in the night sky, of not having a blue halo around it. The tales of the moon before the second coming, and the great battle that turned the world upside down.

He thought for many minutes and would have drifted off to sleep had he not been interrupted by a visitor.

THE RAVEN

Nearly silently the largest raven Stojan had ever seen abruptly landed in the window. It was over half a meter tall and its black feathers shown in the moonlight. The plumage was not just black but shown with iridescent greens, blues and purples. It was quite a sight to behold and Stojan did not move, nor did he startle when it arrived.

The raven stared, and took a few steps back and forth on the opening in the barn—not a window proper so there was no sill to rest upon. Nonetheless the raven's claws did a fine job of holding on. It seemed disinterested in the man attempting to sleep, yet showed no desire to leave.

This could very well be a resting place for the great bird, thought Stojan. As long as it didn't make too much noise he would not wave it away. His loft provided an excellent vantage point to watch over and listen. He'd reviewed the house and the exits and found sleeping out here to be an acceptable way to guard things he had no business guarding.

It stopped and stared.

—

The day had arrived.

"You!"

Stojan looked up to see the three men bursting into the large kitchen of the farmhouse. Many townsfolk had turned out for the funeral, as expected of one so well known. The new arrivals pointed to Stojan, making the inconspicuous far less so. They were angry and appeared to be happy they had found him.

He did not wear his sword at the behest of Anastazja so was unarmed.

They ran over to him and pushed through the crowd, drawing their respective weapons. They meant harm of the most lethal kind. As they made their way it seemed the other visitors immediately knew who he was.

Some of the faces were familiar.

They'd found him.

Before the first man reached him Stojan grabbed a large butcher knife and hurled it at him. The knife stopped, in his chest. His momentum kept him moving towards him and he collapsed on the floor, but not before Stojan had done the same with another knife and the second attacker. Reaching down he grabbed the sword from the hand of the man as he fell to his knees and in the same motion swung it around in a large arc—cutting through the throats of two attackers. The man and the woman fell slowly.

It seemed it all was in slow motion, but he was being overwhelmed. He thought of Anastazja and where she was but could not spare the concentration— a fleeting thought only.

More came at him, some dressed for a funeral, some not, and he now had two swords—thanks to the donations of the now-dead. His attackers all came at him with the same single-mindedness—no regard for their lives, and no regard for the solemn event. No respects were paid that day.

He hacked at the next as he kicked the second attacker in the chest, causing her to fly backwards only to be run through by the advancing attacker behind her.

Stepping over bodies he quickly knelt and thrust upwards with both swords lifting a man off the floor and practically into the high ceiling.

Withdrawing the swords quickly they were out of the dead man's body before he started to fall. Stojan continued on his way. Each person attacked with bloodlust and meant for him to die. There was no hesitation.

One after another they fell this day. One after another they came at him. They all met the same swift fate.

Another attempted to attack from behind but he spun and cut him at the torso.

Each swing was at his fastest, each thrust was with all of his strength. Blood flew—painting the walls and everything in the room. It sprayed forth, it spattered and it was everywhere.
He had gone berserk in the room and continued to hack, and to stab, and to slice. One after another they fell that late morning. The only option was to finish them, to finish them all. He wasn't fighting for his life; he was fighting for hers. There was nothing he wouldn't do, no one he wouldn't kill to keep her safe.

At last only two remained. The man and woman team decided to flank him and swiftly he dropped to the floor as he stabbed each one in the lower abdomen. Their sword strikes only half-realized by them.

They fell as he withdrew the blades. An inconceivable amount of people had died that day, far more than should have been able to fill the room.

Stojan stood in the middle of it, breathing heavily. Slowly his wits returned to him. In slow motion he looked around and surveyed the room. Bodies piled up in all manner of obscene gestures, turned this way and that in such manner that only dead, broken bodies can. Swords stuck out here and there—punctuating the grotesque pile.

Then he saw her.

In the corner of the room was Anastazja. She wore a yellow dress and her substantial hair was up in a bun. The dress's pristine yellow was splattered with so much blood as to make it look like a mottled orange at first glance. She looked up in sadness and horror, slowly, surveying her dress, her hands.

Her face continued to tilt upward and she looked at Stojan. Her eyes were big and round, she was in shock and the very pupils implored him. It seemed his heart stopped at that moment. All was frozen, all was a blur—save for the eyes. He was lost in them, his own anger, and the shame. And something else. For an eternity he stared into them. And stared. And stared.

Her eyes were replaced with those of a raven.

———

Stojan looked at it, still on the edge of the window. It stared at hm, intently. Looking about the room and the sky, he breathed deeply and his heart beat rapidly in his chest. The sky was still dark but the moon had moved—the sun would be up soon.

Laying on his back, he pushed up a bit to rest upon his elbows and looked back at the giant bird as it kept its eyes on him.

The images were fading now—the killing, the blood, the bodies. The anger was subsiding—along with the sadness. The image of Anastazja was immutable, and he felt it would never leave him.

He continued to stare back at the bird, and spoke as if it could understand him.

"This has not yet happened." He was asking but also stating.

He continued as there was no reply as expected.

"Will this happen? Is this a portent of things to come, or a fevered dream due to my worries?"

The bird tilted its head slightly, but the eyes never left him.

"This has something to do with you. Are you the harbinger of such death? Have you come to warn me, or to taunt me?"

The raven stared and slowly opened its mouth. Would it speak? Stojan felt anything could happen now.

Alas it did not, but instead shook its head, rustled its feathers and took off.

Stojan moved toward the window and watched it fly.

A FUNERAL MISSED

Stojan did not fall back to sleep. Since he did not believe in portents, he believed this just to be a dream.

He would make it through the funeral, aid Anastazja any way he could, and move on. But first he would go for a ride to clear his mind of dreams and death and ravens.

Choosing the horse that seemed to be the most alert he was out and about in no time. It was a fine horse—dark in color and mild in temperament. It seemed to have both stamina and speed and enjoyed a lighter rider.

He rode at first without direction—the moon still providing some light. The cool breeze blew in his face as he pushed the horse harder and harder. It seemed he was without direction or purpose, but then thought he once again caught the raven in the sky, and in the same direction he'd seen it fly off to. Perhaps he would find its home. Eventually his curiosity got the best of him and he rode in its direction.

That was when he saw them.
It wasn't a nest of ravens, but men—lots of them.

Gathered in a spot ahead was a group of men and horses. It was a camp. With small tents.

He stopped his horse—they had not heard him…yet.

It was clear they'd been there all night, perhaps even before that.

Had the two thieves talked, or was this blacksmith more well known than expected? He noted to ask Anastazja about it when he returned.

The raven was nowhere to be seen, but he was certain it had flown overhead. Was it a pet of one of the men?

It occurred to him that it may be an advance scout, trained to seek out and lead them to their prey. The bird could find the secluded house from above with ease, and even track down the missing horses.

Stojan had assumed that the thieves were a pair, and that one had convinced the other to accompany them—a fluke, and opportunists. Now he wondered if they were scouts for a larger group—sent to follow the bird and confirm the location.

Again he cursed his leniency. Had he adhered to the black and white finality that had become his life he would not be in this situation—and neither would Anastazja.

He had been lucky; there was no stirring, and it appeared that no one kept guard at night. It would be risky to attempt to approach any closer, nor would it be a good idea to take them by surprise. The two thieves were an easy affair. Here, there were too many of them, and his sense was that unlike the apparent thieves these were hired mercenaries.

He returned as quickly and as quietly as his horse allowed, periodically looking up to see if he was being followed by a certain extra large raven.

Upon reaching the barn he dismounted, then moved to the other horse. He looked at the floor of the barn, then to where he had slept.

His face grimaced. His hand became a fist and he shook his head slowly, from side to side.

The anger in him was apparent, and anyone looking upon him would judge him in conflict—almost as if in a conversation. In one fluid motion he unsheathed his sword and stabbed it into the floor. He was on one knee, both hands on the pommel. His head hung low. His eyes were closed.

Not much made sense. The man he was sent to kill was already dead. His deed was done before he did it. He could simply move on.

“Stojan…? You pray?”

It was a gentle voice; inquisitive, quiet and respectful.

It was Anastazja.

He did not look up. She waited patiently.

Again he had been so consumed with emotions that he'd allowed someone to sneak up on him. Again it was the young girl.

He lifted his head, his face shown the sadness. She seemed affected by this and started to speak, to comfort him and apologize for interrupting. He replied.

"We must leave," he said in soft tones unbecoming of him.

As the words sunk in he came up to his full stature, but left the sword in the floor next to him. It wasn't going anywhere.

Moving towards him she asked, "Leave? When? How?"

"Now." He pulled his sword out, with some effort, as it had been stuck with considerable force.

"No. I cannot Stojan. Everyone will be here today—the funeral. It is disrespectful."

He listened, looking at her disheveled hair that looked like it had taken residence upon her head just that morning.

"Stojan what do you mean we must leave? For how long? If you'd like me to go with you on an…"

Why do I do this?

He spoke and cut her off, gently.

"You are in danger. Word has reached those who would harm you. Men gather as we speak to come take this house by force—to pillage it and everything in it."

He walked closer to her.

"You must believe me that you are in danger. We have only minutes to leave."

"My home?"

He nodded.

He moved past her and she followed; her eyes welling up with tears.

They spent the next few minutes gathering supplies and whatever monies she had. Lanterns were lit but only two and they were kept away from the windows—lest any see stirring in the house. As they were about to leave to gather the horses he asked her a question he'd had on his mind since he arrived.

"Anastazja, tell me the truth about your father."

"What do you mean, the truth?"

They both froze in the doorway.

"I see the modest home of a blacksmith—a blacksmith who does not specialize in weapons."

At that he thought he saw the slightest reaction register in her eyes.

"One who simply toils and creates unremarkable items."

"Yes?"

"I see no hoard of wealth, no gems, no jewels, no ancient artifacts."

She is not afraid.

"Yet a group of mercenaries are poised to take your home by force, with no regard for you."

"And?" She asked naively, as if he was stating something obvious, something mundane.

"And?!" This he almost yelled.

"Do you wish to lose your life?!" It was the most emotion he'd shown—or felt—in more than a year.

Before she could answer he continued his reprimand.

"What are you not telling me about your father?"

He wished to ask so much more, to ask if he had made powerful connections, or if he owed a great deal of money, or if he'd made an ill-advised deal with a baron or worse. Or if she was somehow involved. And in a way he was asking her why he was there.

"What do you know that you are not telling me?"

She had no response but instead ran back into the house. He followed. She made her way into an alcove in the kitchen—the pantry.

With her fingers she felt along a pantry wall, and eventually found the seam she was looking for.

With a click the panel slid aside and revealed a thin set of stairs. They both held their lanterns in the opening. The stairs just ended at a landing—perhaps an unfinished second level.

Or a hiding space.

She darted down and brought up a large black wrapping of leather.

Closing the panel she made her way into the kitchen and set the leather down on the table. He set down the other lantern he was holding for her.

Stojan recognized what it must be—swords and other weapons were kept in oiled leather to protect them from the elements, from rust. Much like his sheath.

He looked at her and nodded. Before she could unwrap it he said, "Let us take this with us. We can speak of it later."

It was gathered along with the other belongings and loaded on to the horses.

And that day Stojan and Anastazja left the home of a little known blacksmith to be pillaged by ruthless mercenaries.

No battle would take place; no funeral would be had. Those that did show up would find a house occupied by unseemly men. The lucky ones were turned away.

THE ROAD TO REVELATIONS

With two extra horses in tow—one tied to each rider's horse—and a considerable amount of supplies, the two rode into the early dawn.

The road wound to and fro through the countryside, meandering through the hills and the tall grass. It was a road that had been used to travel between cities. This particular road was chosen so that it took them as far away from the nearest city as possible—in the opposite direction. Very little was discussed about the actual destination or what would occur upon arrival, but instead just a brief hurried discussion on where they did not wish to travel. It was a lush and green land, and their chosen day of travel was supported by a clear sky with just a few small puffs of clouds. The scene was serene and quiet.

For the majority of the morning Stojan remained silent—lost in thought. For the first time he felt both guided and directionless. He was finally making movement towards the bishop, to an answer. But, he now had an unexpected companion. With this he was unsure. He would not allow himself to even consider what was happening. To this he was numb, and would remain so until the journey was over. He experienced a certain freedom unlike he had in a long time. Contrary to the vivid dream no one recognized him and the countryside was new to him. The gentle isolation he felt was renewing.

Anastazja was also quiet. She was absorbing the events of the last few days—so quickly had life changed for her. Her father was gone, and she'd just abandoned her home on the word of a stranger.

She halted her horse.

Stojan tilted his head and stopped his as well—he was riding ahead of her as the pseudo-trail was rather narrow and not wide enough for two to ride abreast. The tree branches would have been unkind to the riders in this tree-rich area of the trail.

She did not have to call out; the sound her horse's hoofs no longer made was enough.

She narrowed her eyes at him. For the first time since meeting him she was angry. She stared at the back of his head—his ever-present hood was up. A light wind blew.

She could not see that he was looking down at his horse's mane, awaiting the inevitable.

"I think it is time that you told me the truth."

The words went through him like the worst of sword pierces. It cut him to the bone and uncovered what was underneath —a black heart that had been sent to kill her father.
He looked around gently. This would be as good as any spot to camp. He wanted to put as much distance between them and the mercenaries, but they were there for the house, not them. At least this was the belief.

He dismounted, pet his horse gently and walked over to hers.

She stared him down and though the words had cut him, the expression did more damage. His lack of expression served to anger her further. So callous was this man.

"We should make day camp here," he said matter-of-factly.

She dismounted, keeping her eyes on him, her gaze unrelenting.

He knew she would wait only so long for an answer—whatever lie he decided to tell. The clock was ticking but he filled the time to set up the camp.

They allowed the horses to graze in the taller grass as they unloaded some of the supplies.

When it looked like he could delay her no longer he finally answered.

With a question.

"Show me what is in the wrap…"

He sighed, and looked at the ground.

"…and I will answer your question."

She removed the wrap from the saddle bag, running her hand across the smooth hairs of the horse in the process. Her face showed momentary joy. The item was large and almost as tall as her. It looked to be of some weight.
At the makeshift campsite among the various items unloaded she placed the large wrap in the grass, dropping something unseen at her side. The black leather glistened in the sun—looking almost like some sort of exotic dessert. Slowly she unwrapped it, loosening the built-in belt it was created with, carefully undoing it so that the contents were kept in the middle—protected from the grass and the ground. At last it unfolded unto Stojan, the forest and the sky to reveal its contents.

Two swords.

She looked upon it with much admiration, though her face was still that of anger.

Standing over it her hair blew gently in the wind.

He looked upon the swords—or perhaps a sword and a large dagger—as the smaller sword was barely large enough to be considered one. They shown in the sun—oily from the wrap. They were unremarkable save for the fact that they were expertly made. Both looked to be crafted with care. Simple straight swords with a crosspiece.

"Do not touch," she said sternly, still staring at the blades.

She reached down and lifted the large dagger which became a sword in her hands, matching her stature perfectly.

She played the tiny sword in her hand, creating circles in the air. Slowly she waved it around, looking at the blade, the hilt, examining it all. Slowly and reverently she did this. These were not the actions of a child playing warrior with their father's sword. She had clearly handled it before, or one like it.

The joy in her face could not be hidden and Stojan noted the ease at which she moved it. Her control and strength were remarkable. Either the sword was exceptionally light or she was far stronger than she looked. She had a confidence about her.

And had been trained. Somewhat.

He looked at her, feeling bittersweet at both her joy and the conversation that was about to be had.

"And the other?" He asked in quiet tones.

Without looking away from her sword she replied, "Mine as well. This one is for now, the other is when I am older. And have grown a bit."

Her father, it seemed, had crafted two swords for his daughter—one to match her stature now, and one to match her stature when she was a full grown woman. Clearly the'd been created with love.

This seemed like a keepsake a blacksmith would create to send his child with out into the world. A superb gift for her adult years, but the smaller sword had him confused. Why create the smaller for a temporary time? Only the excessively rich would do such a thing. They might commission a sword for a spoiled child and pay a heavy fee for it. And that sword would most certainly be ignored, forgotten like any other stimulus provided to the over-stimulated sloth of the rich.

This was not the forgotten commission of the wealthy. Nay, this was finely crafted specifically for Anastazja.

She stopped moving the sword and froze it solidly, only her eyes moved to meet his.

"My father told me that very soon he would retire and would help me train. He was a swordsman in his day before he became a blacksmith. He vowed never to create any more weapons, save for these."

"They are beautiful."

As are you. Thought Stojan.

Her movements were graceful yet strong. The sword was a perfect match and deserved such an owner.

"But now he will not train me. Because he is gone Stojan."

She reached to her side and picked up a length of leather—the item she'd dropped. She placed the sword belt upon her waist while still wielding the sword. This feat did not go unnoticed.

Her eyes moved from her waist to Stojan.

"He is gone, along with my home." It was an exceedingly accusatory tone.

Stojan looked back into her eyes—the way a child might look into a teacher's eyes expecting a reprimand.

"Because you are here. You have come into my life and taken both my father and my home. I have nothing now."

The anger and sadness in her voice was palpable. She appeared to be close to collapsing—both physically and emotionally. The tears in her eyes made them shine all the more in the sunlight. It seemed the birds were unusually silent now.

Dispatching the warrior at his weakest had left devastation in its wake—something he had not considered. Until now. Now all that was left was before him.

He was truly sorry for what happened to her, but his sorrow was absent of any guilt as her father's death was not his doing, unless his mere presence was all that was needed to distract him?

No, that could not be. He was sent to kill him, not to distract him. Surely anyone could have done that, or anything.

He'd been thrust into a reality that was not to his liking. He watched a good man die and leave a child to the world. And now he was cursed in such a way that he would never suspect.

He cared.

His thoughts were shaken abruptly by the coldness of her accusation.

"Tell me now why you are here, and who you really are."

Did she hate him before she even knew the truth?

A twig snapped.

Stojan froze as Anastazja moved her brows together, wondering what trick the tall stranger would produce, what lie he would tell.

Still looking at the girl Stojan's hand moved to his sword and quickly turned to run. He was not running away, but rather, running towards the two figures behind him.

She watched as he cut one down before her as he emerged from behind a tree. Two more sprang up from either side to move in. They had death in their eyes and meant to end Stojan that day.

They'd found them.

Stojan spun around and in the same motion swung his sword at the neck of a man about to strike—his quickness spelling doom for him as it cut into him. He dropped his sword and grabbed his neck and the assassin took advantage of this, deftly cutting him at the legs.

Anastazja watched in silence as Stojan danced with the men—a performance that was once enthralling and horrid.

Two were now down but two more took their place, as one attempted to attack him from behind. They were yelling instructions to each other and one was frustrated that his instructions went unheeded. The man who'd just lost the element of surprise swung at Stojan and caught him about the chest, grazing him as the tall man made motion to move backwards almost as if he was swimming. His chest was no longer in the path of the blade.

Stojan's blade came up to meet his and a distinct metal on metal sound was heard, again and again as more blows were parried. The blades now danced along them.

It was all very intense for her and her senses seemed heightened as she observed. Without realizing it she had slowly walked towards them and was now three meters from her wrap. Realizing this she glanced quickly over at it.

A fifth man was present, and stood near the wrap. He had most certainly been sneaking up on her and would have either done her in or grabbed the sword displayed for all to see.

Had his baser desires not gotten the best of him she'd probably not been alive to witness it.

The man smiled an evil smile as he saw the large sword before them—displayed so beautifully in the sun. It rivaled the most presentable of items shown by those selling goods at a market.

He greedily moved towards it.

Anastazja's eyes met his. He smiled. She did not. They both did not move for seconds, then suddenly he made for the sword.

But now to her he seemed to move in slow motion.

"That..!" She screamed the single word.

She sprang towards him. Recalling the encounter later she would never be able to remember if she ran, or leapt. She would only remember that she crossed the distance between them as quickly as she could.

"...is!"

To him it was a blur. The surprise shown in his face and he raised his blade to protect himself. He needn't have wasted the effort.

She stabbed hard into the man's chest—the small sword doing a surprisingly good job of cutting through the man's hardened leather armor, his flesh and his ribs. His eyes widened as he became aware of what was happening.

The force of her collision knocked him back and down into the grass.

"*...mine.*"

She snarled as she landed upon him—all of her weight behind the thrust. The sword sank deep and was only stopped by the hilt pressing against his armor. Even the ground did not stop the little sword, its sharpness was pristine. She wielded the only sword in the battle that had been sharpened with love, oiled and stored until this moment. It was a virgin this day and had taken its first victim. It would not be its last.

The man exhaled his last breath in a sickly gurgle; his mouth contorting as if to form a word. His eyes would not close that day and would forever show his surprise.

She looked at him, her knees digging into his ribs, her hands upon the hilt, her muscles tense. Perched upon a dead man, holding onto the sword as if it was the mast of a morbid ship.

She was anger on fire, and had the sword not killed him perhaps her eyes would have that day.

She breathed deeply now, catching her breath, still gripping the sword. The reality of what she'd done slowly seeped into her as the rage started to subside into horror.

She blinked and her head turned slowly to the left.

The others were dead and strewn about the area. Stojan stood a few meters away—his sword also piercing a man now down in the lawn, as if he was casually pushing around the grass. He titled his head and looked over at her. Their eyes met. He looked nonplussed, as if he'd just done a job.

The two had fought together.

He turned his body to match his head, and walked slowly to her, keeping his sword down. She noticed the color, and that it dripped.

Now directly in front of her, he looked down at her. She hadn't yet moved. She stayed perched, not knowing what to do—her recent actions were so foreign to her.

Stojan looked down at the blade Anastazja had just protected with deadly force.

He cleaned his sword in the grass, giving her a reprieve from his stare. She was perhaps in shock. He knew she needed to withdraw her sword and would gladly do it for her, but also knew she would not permit him to touch it. So instead he waited and cleaned his sword far more slowly that day. And kept his head down.

After a minute the sound of the sword being removed was heard but he continued to clean his. When he looked up she was gone, leaning against a tree with her head down behind it. No doubt this was her first. The gruesome sights had not affected her as much as did her own hand in the battle.

Her temporary sickness would pass.

While he waited he started to round up the men, dragging them together in the center. Going through their things he collected weapons and monies. The former he cleaned and the latter he deposited into his own bag. He would split this with Anastazja when she was able to talk.

He also collected any supplies and those he moved to the saddle bags. No doubt the horses of these men were a short distance away.

He would seek them out for additional supplies and more identification, but these horses would not travel with them. Instead he'd just set them free.

They were clever trackers and had followed them shortly after they left. Why he did not know.

Anastazja returned from her recuperation by the tree, looking a bit pale but healthy nonetheless. She had cleaned her sword before returning.

Stojan smiled ever so slightly upon seeing her. It was a distinct feeling when she neared. Distinct. Familiar.

She looked back at him apprehensively, but not after first checking that the sword remained in the wrap on the ground. It seemed she was still wary of the man. She looked at her sword once more, and carefully sheathed it—no doubt worried it was not clean enough to be put away.

Kneeling down she wrapped the larger sword back into its protective cocoon, and held it in her arms, against her chest. Holding it, she surveyed the area and was clearly looking for the man she'd just killed. Eventually her eyes fell up on him and the others—in a neat pile created by Stojan.

Slowly she turned and the wrap was placed carefully in the saddle bags. But she did not return immediately. Stojan watched as she just stood there, looking off into the distance, motionless. He knew she wasn't searching for something, but instead was trying to make sense of what was happening. Thirteen or fourteen years old was a bit young to take your first life. As she stared into nothing he in turn stared at her—her hair every so often waved about, like the flame of a distant candle.

He was about to answer her question, but he had even more questions for her now.

He continued to watch her and felt a certain peace watching her from afar. Here he could protect her but his distance would prevent him from hurting her. He wished that their relationship would continue this way.

At last she turned and walked back to join Stojan. When she arrived she stood again silently—looking at the ground, the trees. It seemed she was not going to speak and was in shock. Stojan was glad to have dragged all the bodies together off to the side.

He broke the silence eventually by telling her that he gathered whatever monies they had and would give her half. Then there was more talk about the supplies, riding on ahead for a bit and making another camp. The conversation was decidedly one-sided with the only responses being a distant "Oh" and "uh huh" periodically.

Eventually they made their way to another campsite, and this time Stojan made sure it was off the beaten path much farther than the impromptu stop they'd made previously.

He thought only of Anastazja as he rode. He prepared the camp—wondering where her thoughts were at this time.
As night fell and the two sat staring at a small fire, she eventually spoke.

"I killed him."

Stojan looked at the fire along with Anastazja, thinking it best to keep his eyes from her.

"Yes, you did."

Stojan's tone was comforting but strong. To him it was necessary. She'd done nothing wrong, and had only protected herself.

To his surprise there was nothing more that night. She did not elaborate, or speak of her feelings. She showed little emotion.

They would eventually speak of the event, but not today, or for many days.

To Stojan it was another round of fighting, of killing, of preventing others from doing him harm and taking advantage of him. It was what he had done countless times, and he'd dispatched them with relative ease. His silence had allowed him to consider many things recently, and this was one of them.

However, these were not the hired trackers and killers he'd originally thought; nor were these the men that were nearby plotting to take over the blacksmith house. They were just another band of roving bandits. They'd killed, but they made their livings on preying on the weak, not on a trained killer who'd honed both his skills and his sword on the armor of others.

They were not prepared for such a thing this day. Seeing four horses and only two—with one of them being a child—made for ideal prey that day. Surely these two had fallen on hard times.

They were only right about that.

Stojan stared at the skies as Anastazja stared at the fire. He informed her that he would keep watch and that she should get some sleep. With that she made a bed of the leathers they had with them. He noted she kept the sword wrap close to her. It looked like two slept together instead of one.

With her asleep he continued to ponder—allowing his thoughts to roam in a way he normally would not for freedom of thought sometimes leads to remembering, and experiencing again what one must never experience once.

He poked at the minimal fire.

It became clear to him that as a blacksmith's daughter she and her father had not been lax in her apprenticeship—not as a swordsman, but as a metalsmith. She had been thoroughly involved in the job, and it had built an unusually strong body for someone so young, and relatively petite a frame. That explained with satisfaction to him her ease at welding the weapon. Though it was created to precise sizing for her, it was no magical or exotic weapon. She simply had the natural strength to wield it, and those muscles were tested daily in the forge—lifting and wielding the tools of the trade. No doubt her father had pushed her and taught her as much as she was willing to learn. And knowing Anastazja this short time he knew she eagerly and happily learned.

He was a good man, her father. Stojan thought of that for a moment, feeling like he had been at a crossroads and before he could choose a path the fate of it had befallen him.

What if he had killed the man? Would he be so eager to accompany Anastazja, or would he have simply disappeared into the forest? Or would he have disappeared—reappearing in front of the foul bishop—his deed done?

He wrinkled his brow at the thoughts now assaulting him. He wasn't used to so much musing, so much mindfulness, yet it now came so easily to him.

He could not answer any of the questions he posed to himself that night, but continued asking.

If he hadn't been there would the man have died anyway? If he had killed him would have stayed with Anastazja?

He inhaled deeply.

If he'd killed him and the man's daughter had witnessed it, would he have killed her too?

He stared—hard—at nothing. The thought struck him as any sword blow. Stojan felt as if the thought forced him into a corner and his brain was locked onto the thought. He was someone who was hexed, or drugged. For minutes he froze, unmoving and unthinking except for two conflicting thoughts.

Finally movement. He slowly turned his head over to Anastazja and looked upon her still form. She slept—her breath rising and falling slowly.

The two thoughts in conflict were no more. It was at that moment on a dark and cool night that Stojan hadn't changed, but that he became aware of it.

The fire went out.

He blinked and poured a small amount of water on it, lest the smoke wake his companion and draw more attention than the small fire would.

He slept lightly that night, waking briefly at any sound that was out of place. It was something that was natural for him—this awareness while resting—and he'd gotten quite good at it. It served him well, and now it served them well.

THE BRIDGE

And it was for some time that the two traveled together—each keeping quiet—and sharing a certain mutual solemness.

It seemed to Stojan that Anastazja would not breach the subject of his sudden appearance. It was a fragile wall between them, and he was happy not to disturb that delicate barrier. He respected it but also dreaded the eventuality of moving through it.

His immediate concern was his bearings, and his direction—literally and metaphorically. He still did not know exactly where he was, and for all he could determine he was still in Poliska, but nothing else made sense. The direction they rode was taking them out of the country, eventually. His primary onus was to leave her home behind him, and find the bishop.

What exactly he would do when the bishop learned he had the daughter in tow of the very man he'd been sent to kill was another matter entirely. By the time he reached him perhaps he could resettle Anastazja. Perhaps he'd even share a bit of the massive reward he had been promised.

Blood money.

The thought sickened him. Another dead end.

Though their trail lead fairly straightforward, his thoughts did not. Try as he might every avenue lead to a dead end.

Where was he going exactly? What had he done?

These past few weeks had made him feel… differently. More accurately, they'd simply made him *feel*—something he was no longer capable of.

These thoughts were dangerous—they interrupted the senses, they distracted. And they made him feel confused. This would not serve him nor his young companion. He must make a decision soon.

The decision he found, was made for him.

Stojan looked at the sky—clouds had gathered and for the last hour he had seen slight flickers. There would be rain soon, and the clouds seemed angry; almost impatient to unload their burden. The clouds and Stojan shared that this day.

The trail seemed to take an abrupt shift to the left, and into a more forested area.

He turned to follow but his companion did not. He blinked and looked over to her.

He stopped his horse and said simply, "This way."
She turned her head to her left and rebutted, "No, this way."

He furrowed his brow. "I believe…"

"Why do we need to follow you? How do you know which way is the correct way?" Her voice was loud—perhaps louder than it needed to be, as if she was yelling over nonexistent thunder.

"The trail probably turns for a…"

"Where do we travel to? We've been traveling for many days now." She challenged him and cut him off.

Another flicker of light in the sky—this time a tendril of lighting.

She stopped her horse but would not turn to face him—continuing to yell with turned head—as if the conversation was an inconvenience.

Her recent quietness it seemed was not a contemplation, but rather a smoldering frustration and anger at the situation. And now it showed in the tone of her words.

"I just want to go home."

Stojan paused, but Anastazja seized the opportunity to continue riding ahead where the trail diminished, along with the options.

Not-so-distant thunder erupted in the sky above them.

He followed her. Immediately they saw it, in the clearing.

"See? There was no reason to turn."

The trail ended at a bridge crossing a gorge over a rushing river.

Stojan moved his horses up to where Anastazja stood—at the edge of the bridge.

He looked upon it with much distaste. Two large poles held ropes which extended to the other side of the gorge, at least a hundred meters across. The lower ropes held slats forming a path, the other two were tied periodically to the slats with a rope railing above it. The bridge was wide enough to ride across but looked as if it hadn't been used in some time. Squinting to see better, Stojan noticed that not all of the wooden slats were present, and the bridge dipped a bit more than he would have liked.

"It is not safe."

"Who are you to say what is safe and what is not?"

"Anastazja…"

More flickers in the sky.

"No. Tell me. Who are you that comes to my house and disrupts my life? Haven't I followed you enough? I have no reason to follow you blindly."

She yelled to be heard above the periodic thunder. It seemed the eruptions were every few seconds, with bright strikes in the sky now and then.

"The bridge is unsafe."

"Answer the question."

He paused and noticed that the rushing sound he heard was not from below but to his left, where the trail had turned. He ignored it.

“Nothing? You will not answer and yet you wish me to follow you.”

She motioned her horses forward, slowly.

He dismounted and walked quickly to where she was, which was now onto the bridge proper. Both horses were now past the entrance. She was looking ahead.

“Stop!”

She ignored him and spurred her horse ahead which was having a bit of trouble with its footing. When it was obvious the animal would not continue she dismounted, falling into one of the railing-ropes that had been strung as a support. Had she been more careless she would have fallen to her death below.

Stojan’s eyes widened at the sight and he ran to the entrance, gingerly placing a foot on the first of many slats.

She looked down to the river below, then to him.

“I go my own way.”

Thunder.

The bridge moved with every step she took. Within moments she was already many meters out. Stojan untied her second horse from the first and was able to move it off the bridge. Anastazja’s horse was not so easily coerced. It seemed unable to move at all.

His gaze darted from the horses to the gorge and then to Anastazja.
“I was sent here!” he yelled to her, hoping that would stop her. She did indeed stop.

Turning back to him and holding onto the ropes she yelled back.

“By whom? Who sends you to my father?”

Anastazja’s horse took a few steps forward as the bridge dipped slightly. It was confused and was just looking for safer, more stable footing.

“A bishop.”

"You lie Stojan. What would a bishop want from us? And…" she added "There are no bishops."

She turned as if to continue, then took a few more steps.

"No…" he said too quietly for her to hear, his silent plea did not fall upon her ears as he realized what was about to happen.

He knew if he ran onto the bridge his attempt to stop her would just cause her to run further. He could not physically remove her from the bridge, but with each step she was tempting… He must do something. He continued talking.

"Yes, a bishop. He sent me there—to that very spot."

"For what?"

Behind her a purple strike of lighting appeared, framing her as a silhouette for a brief moment.

She was now backing up, and just running her hand along the rope—feeling her way backwards. It would not be long until she found one of the missing slats.

"To kill a great warrior."

She paused and considered.

"Oh, and you think my father made a weapon for such a warrior?"

"No."

"Then who?"

Her eyes widened as if realizing a horrible fact.

"You killed him!"

"No! I did not!"

"I…"

His eyes welled up, and she stumbled, still moving backwards, creeping along.

Stojan's face felt a gentle mist. They were much too far from the river. It was beginning to rain.

"I was there to…"

"So you were there to kill him!"

"Yes… but…" He had nothing left but honesty, and each word implored her to come back in its own way.

Anastazja recalled the event—so vivid in her mind. Her father calling, the stranger appearing, the blood, the look on her father's face. It was clear that her father had done himself in with his own axe.
"But *what*?" She cried as the wind picked up. She was still creeping backwards, almost autonomously.

"I did not. He cut himself that day."

She frowned in sadness and had trouble speaking, her eyes filled with tears.

"And if he hadn't? You would have cut him down yourself that day?" The last word squeaked out as she cried and closed her eyes tightly. The bridge swung to and fro in the wind and beginning rain.

"Anastazja…"

He moved onto the bridge without thinking, bumping into the horse's saddle bag slightly. It moved, and started walking forward. He stopped, his eyes wider now, his face softened with worry and sadness. So many things were in motion. He looked down at the gorge and saw just how flimsy the bridge was and why the trail no longer came this way, but instead turned.

He had no answer. Surely he would have killed the man? That was his job—the job he had done so efficiently and coldly for the past few years. A version of what he had done some seventy times that day. The day he lost his daughter.

It was progressively windier on the bridge, with each step bringing more rushing of air to match the rushing of water below. He saw the rain fall on her, then him.

"I can only tell you that your father died by his own hand."
She stumbled, her foot finding the missing slat before her eyes had.
She gripped the rope tightly, and attempted to wind her arm around it for stability just as her leg fell through the opening where a slat should be. She was now only waist above the bridge— her legs dangling.

He made motion to run to her, gasping at the sudden change in her height, but immediately froze knowing he'd hasten what was about to happen.

"I had nothing to do with your father's death."

She looked down at the gorge, her eyes wet with tears and rain.

"I care about you, Anastazja… And…"

The brightest yet of the strikes happened in the sky above them, lighting everyone up with a great flash. He could see the pain and suffering on her face in that brief moment. He saw her confusion, her sadness, her loss. She looked so alone—out there on the bridge—with death awaiting her below.

Crack. The thunder came on almost immediately after the flash. At this the horse ran forward.

It all happened at once—the horse running, the bridge finally giving in, the lightning and thunder, and Stojan completing his sentence as a whisper.

"…I love you."

The horse stumbled, its full weight hitting the bridge as all of its legs burst through the holes between the slats. This erupted in a wave which snapped one rope then another—just meters past where Anastazja held on.

She bounced up then down as the bridge was like a wooden sculpture of water.

And then it fell.

The force of the horses's movement carried it forward, and off of the bridge as its bag was caught on the rope and the slats.

Stojan watched in horror as Anastazja moved downward. It looked wrong. He reached his hand out as if he could catch her, some 30 meters away.

The bridge separated and both sides swung to their respective sides. Before he could do anything it was done.

The bridge now dangled after striking the face of the cliff. It twisted and swung slightly in the wind.

But she remained.

Instantly his head darted around, looking for anything that could help but instead he just went on all fours, spun around and began climbing downward as both the wind and rain picked up.

He climbed dutifully with hands and feet, finding purchase as best he could, sometimes grasping, sometimes winding. As quickly as he could he climbed. Approaching the breaking point he saw her—dangling by her arms at the end, with a saddle bag above her.

The lightning flashed, showing her face. She was alive but unconscious, her face wet with rain. Anastazja was oddly posed, with one arm wrapped into the saddlebag straps. As he made movement to untangle her he realized that in her last moments she had tried to save the last vestige of her father—the sword in the wrap.
One movement after another his arms and legs worked together. It seemed he had no thoughts, but was just motion—working quickly, efficiently and without doubt. So determined was he, so focused that he did not recall climbing back up the dangling bridge.

He only remembered the sound of the rain and the lightning, the softness of her body as he effortlessly carried her back up.

He looked upon her in the grass now, and the wrap laying next to her. He gently moved her head to use it as a supporting pillow. She groaned weakly. Clearly she had hit the cliff face hard, and the various heavy slats and rope had not been kind. She was badly hurt. Her hands were bleeding from abrasion, and her leg moved in a way it should not be able to. She barely breathed. He could only imagine what the impact did to the rest of her. He moved her hair gently out of her face as the rain slowed down, showing signs of abruptly ending. It washed some of the blood off of her forehead.

She would not be long for this world, and the one thing that gave Stojan meaning would be taken from him.

Again.

He stood upright, his eyes were fixed upon the sky and then the trail. There were no horses—not that it mattered as they were so far from any city or town.

He ran, towards the trail, into the forest, and drew his sword.

He was not running away from her, but towards *something*. It was maniacal, this desire. His legs carried him onto the trail and he followed it, without destination save for whatever would save Anastazja.
The rain had already stopped or was prevented from reaching him by the canopy of the trees.

He wiped his eyes as he continued his sprint—towards a solution made entirely of faith.

THE MAN AT THE WATERFALL

The trail continued to veer closer to the river.

Stojan ran with sword, contrary to his typical habit, so focused was he. Everyone and everything was the enemy—this included any errant branch that got in his way.

A ray of brightness reached him, only briefly as he ran past the beam. The clouds were breaking up and perhaps there would once again be sunlight that day. The sudden storm was dispersing.

As the trees began to become more sparse the hiss and rush of what only could be a waterfall was heard.

Rounding another bend he saw that the trail became more distinct as it approached. And then he saw it. The great waterfall shown white and misty in the sunlight. It rushed over a great cliff and split a trail in two. It was this waterfall that fed and became the river below. He sheathed his sword and began to run even faster. At this point he could discern that the trail let right up to the waterfall and crossed it at a midpoint, some seventy or more meters up.

As he continued his hurried pace he beheld two things—the trail abruptly ended and at the end of this juncture stood a figure.

Stojan's pace had become a brisk walk now and he made his way towards the figure— the crashing of the water getting louder and louder as he approached. The waterfall was now a wide background and he stood mere meters from the end of the trail and the figure. It looked to him that there once stood a great bridge that completed the path across. It must have been a great sight to behold—this bridge that crossed right in front of the waterfall. It was not too close but close enough for the gentle mist to reach you now and again. And the sound was quite loud, yet soothing.

Every so often the man would look around—as if half expecting someone to push him over the end of the trail—and then return his gaze to the water below.

One of these glances fell upon the tall intruder. Stojan froze, lest he spook him into falling.

“Stop. Stop where you are,” the stranger yelled at Stojan. His voice was filled with sadness, and something else.

“You threaten me?” was his measured response.

“Do not come any closer.”

“Or?”

“Or what?”
“Yes, my question exactly—what is it you will do if I come closer?”

This obviously confused the man at the waterfall. He did not have a response.

Stojan continued his approach.

“Stop.”

“Once again you command me yet offer no reason.”

Stojan continued and stopped just two meters from the man. He was a bit shorter than Stojan, a little stocky and wore many layers, carried bags like those who sold goods at the market or had prepared for a long journey. He wore a very short sword or perhaps a very long dagger. His clothing was of greens and browns and earth tones—deceptively muted for such colorful clothing. They’d clearly been chosen with care. His brown curly hair blew in the breeze.

The man turned his body to face Stojan.

"I don't want you to come any closer... I..."

His eyes found the grass below.

"...I wish to be alone."

"I am in dire need of water... of..." Stojan's words were unconvincing. He knew water would only prolong things for Anastazja. Her wounds were fatal. And this trail had taken him to some sort of viewing ledge, instead of the river below. He could not obtain the water here even if...

"Why are you here?" Stojan asked, after eyeing the man up and down. His defeat was settling in, he knew not what to do. He felt numb. Anastazja was surely already dead, and in his haste he had allowed her to die alone.

"I wish to kill a man," was the quiet response.

"Indeed, then we have something in common," Stojan offered back.

"No, no we do not, I am sure."

Stojan took a step forward, experimentally.

"Tell me: how do you expect to find this man at the end of a cliff? Where is he?" Stojan surveyed the surrounding area.

"Right here." The man's words were said with finality, and shame.

"So you expect to jump? Into the waterfall, and to the rocks below?"

Stojan pointed to the waterfall and to the area far below, speaking loudly.

"Yes."

Stojan walked up to the man, to his horror.

"No! Stop."

He wanted to leap forward and grab the man by his collar.

"Give me your supplies, your clothing, your weapon. Perhaps you have something I can use!" Internally he brightened slightly at the prospect that this man had something that would help. He knew the finality and absurdity of such a thought, yet he permitted it.

His brow furrowed, his eyes wide, the man shook his head.

"No…"

"Surely it makes no difference if you die naked or fully clothed, wealthy or penniless, armed or defenseless?"

The man stared, first at Stojan, then as if he was looking through him. Moments passed, then what seemed like minutes. Stojan grew weary of waiting, and thought of Anastazja. He could take the man, but then risk spooking him into jumping. Then he'd have nothing. His patience was almost gone. His hope was depleted it seemed.

"Tell me this: why do you wish to die?"

The man inhaled deeply, and when he exhaled his breath it seemed a part of his soul came with it.

"Do you know of love?" He asked, rhetorically.

He looked at Stojan, as if accusing him of a crime.

"I have held love, in my heart. I have held it, and caressed it and given it a home—felt its warmth, its tenderness, its fragile yet intense feeling. I have bathed in it, experienced it, at once swam and floundered within it. It surrounded me and was within me. "

The man spoke loudly now to be heard over the rushing of water, as if speaking to an audience.

But his words were intimate.

"I have held it, given it a true home."

The man's words stirred something in Stojan—something up until now he'd put great effort into ignoring. His denial of it held no power over it; quite the opposite, he found.

The man's eyes became fixated on Stojan, they were wide now and filled with sadness, anger, finality. He was examining him as he spoke.

"And do you know what the most deceptive thing of love is?"

There was no answer forthcoming from Stojan, whose thoughts were split between the waterfall, Anastazja and a great distance. Time was lost now. He felt as if he watched a play, put on for his benefit to distract him from the inevitable loss a short distance from where they stood.

"The ease of it."

He spread his hands, as if giving a sermon. His face was vivid with expression as he smiled wildly, almost maniacally.

"The sheer simplicity, ease and nature of it. It exists as a matter of fact, like the sun rising in the morning, or that fire is hot."

He paused, and looked down into the crashing water below.

"Or that something dropped will always fall."

He turned back to Stojan, who remained quiet.

"Yet it is not. You are tricked into believing this—that love will always stay, and remain, and live in your heart. Surely how can something so intense, so correct, that which completes so fully… how can that not be a constant?"

He balled up his fists and tensed up, then pointed an accusatory finger at Stojan, as if he was on trial.

"You will be convinced, beyond even the very shadow of a doubt that this love exists and will continue."

The man took a step back, his words giving him more cause for defeat. He dropped his hands to his sides.

"But it does not. That is the greatest of deceptions."

He looked at Stojan as if for the first time.

"I have held love and given it a place, and will never again. For where it stayed there is now an emptiness, a blackness, a hole, and this hole it seems is not compatible with life."

He shook his head while he spoke.

"The more room you make for this love in your heart, the greater the opening, the crevice, when it leaves. True love becomes a canyon."

Stojan had been listening intently the entire time—his body rigid and unmoving as the man spoke of this infinite sadness. At last he was done. Silence.

Stojan's quiet reply startled the man.

"I need your help."
So unusual was the reply, so askew of the conversation, so unlike what was expected of the stoic figure the words stunned the man.

He shook his head, as if the ward off a hex, or confusion, or too much drink.

"You want *what*? You want my *help*?"

It was a simple question, without any malice.

"Yes." His words were slow, and measured, and imploring. This was not expected. The smaller man was feeling futility, hopelessness. The last thing he expected to feel was useful. Yet this was being dangled in front of him right now by the tall stranger.

He hesitated, as if considering to move forward.

"I have a companion, she is very young, and she has… suffered a…"

He paused for a moment to say the words.

"… a fatal blow. She still lives but I… I came for water or… something… but need much more."

It seemed both men were just as desperate.

His voice became lower and absolute.

"She must not die."

Perhaps it was the intensity with which the stranger said those words. Perhaps it was the gravity felt by them, or the resolution seen in his eyes.

The man at the waterfall—for the first time—took a step forward. His voice changed and he said gently, "Your daughter?"

Stojan found that the lie he was about to tell felt nothing like one.

"Yes."

Had the man detected the tiniest bit of deception he would then leap below, as the talk with Stojan allowed him to recreate his pain and suffering even further, to clarify it and to convince himself that this truly was his last day on Earth.

But he did not. His hopelessness had turned to concern, and it could be seen upon his face.

He looked at Stojan, his face, his body, his stature, the way he held himself.

He walked up to Stojan, placed his hand on his shoulder and said quietly, "Take me to her."

For a brief moment Stojan looked into his eyes, and exchanged sadness, suffering and pain. For a moment he thought the man deceived him and gave him false hope. He did not want this false hope, and he resented the man for it.

With that he turned and ran back into the woods, the smaller man keeping up behind him. They ran for many minutes, silently. Stojan did not look back and once again unsheathed his sword to do away with any errant branches that decided to cross the path of him and the man of the waterfall.

Quickly they came upon the scene and the man's brows drew together when he saw the fragile girl. Almost all of the life had now drained out of her, yet she found the strength to open her eyes at the commotion. She smiled a weak, frightened smile at both men.

The shorter man dropped to his knees in front of her and stared. Tears ran down his face as he looked at the severity of her wounds, then to her eyes half-closing now. She would not be long for this world, it was clear.

He swallowed, and reached into the bag at his side.

He opened the bag, and unfurled a small blanket. Within it were many bottles, flasks, scrolls and containers—all wrapped carefully together. This unraveling would take some doing to put back together. But the man recklessly opened it and some of the containers tumbled off the blanket into the dirt.

In one hand— after much rooting around—he found a flask. Clasping it to his breast he looked upward.

"Forgive me," he said, almost silently. Closing his eyes briefly he seemed to be in a trance. The flask was of glass, wide at the bottom and narrow at the top. Wax had been used to seal the top over an existing cork, and there was a small pull-tie in place. Before Stojan could interject to hurry him along he had already pulled the tie, removed the cork then and was gently supporting Anastazja's head. Which the other hand he lifted the bottle to her lips.

Stojan became concerned at the danger of what was being administered and realized that whatever was being given would not make matters worse.

It was then that he understood why the man had asked for forgiveness as he was clearly administering poison to Anastazja, the girl of golden hair, and eyes that reminded him of the sky. The girl that was at once a stranger and family.

The help he sought had become the expeditious seal of death for her, from one who was about to take his own life. This poison was meant for him, and the waterfall must have been his secondary plan when his cowardice became known to him.

In the blink of an eye Stojan was at once furious, hopeless and frozen with indecision. He wished to strike down this man for killing her, but had he not spared her from suffering—suffering that could be avoided by a death that could not?

She coughed as the liquid had drained.

The man stood up as Stojan's eyes bored holes into his head, his stare was so intense. His hand moved to his sword, slowly, instinctively. He would give this man his wish to die this day. It would be a swift death, with an even swifter strike.

He looked down at her, still now but with grey hair. He looked back at the guilty man that had killed her, or brought her peace or both. Soon he'd kill this man and he would join her. Their eyes met. Both men stood in silence as the taller reached for his blade.

“Stojan?”

It was Anastazja. Her voice was stronger, and she opened her eyes to find him. Again she repeated his name and the other man backed off further.

The tall man, his rage now dissolved at the sound, knelt beside her, dropping his full weight into his knees.

He reached for her hand and found it to be warm.

“Ana?”

The color in her face had returned, but her hair remained the same grey color. Stojan looked back at the man, who seemed to be nodding. He looked back at Anastazja only to find that her hair once again glistened in the partial sunlight, with golds of all hues. He rubbed his eyes and once again held her hand.

“You are … better?” He asked experimentally.

She moved her hands and made movements to get up.

Stojan attempted to comfort her, to guide her to remain prone.

“I feel no pain?” She was confused, and delighted, and it shone on her face. It was as if one had placed a lantern, a beacon upon the grass that day and it rivaled the sun. So bright and full of life was her smile that the two men found rejoice in it.

Stojan smiled, genuinely without governance, perhaps for the very first time in many years.

Anastazja looked over at the man from the waterfall, and Stojan’s eyes moved to follow hers. He was also smiling, and tears were running down his face.

Anastazja made her way to her feet, and stood strongly as Stojan moved to the newcomer. His hand was outstretched and the man slowly, emotionally grasped it in kind.

“Thank you” was all Stojan said to him, but the two words conveyed many. The man looked like he was struggling to find his voice. He wiped the tears from his eyes with his sleeve, looked at Anna and then

Stojan.

The man's voice was creaky as he replied, "No sir, it is I that thank you."

Stojan continued to shake his hand.

"You have given me purpose once again, and allowed me to make a difference."

"I am in your debt," both men said simultaneously.

Stojan's head tilted at what he thought was such an absurd statement—his heart so recently filled with gratitude. His face looked briefly incredulous.

"I am so glad I could help your daughter."

The tall man's eyes went wider and his smile turned serious, as if a secret had been told that day.

It had been.

Anastazja tilted her head but remained silent. She was still smiling. Now even more.

—

It was agreed that the man would join them. He felt that they had given him purpose and would accompany them for as long as they would have him. He explained that his name was Dagmar and he was from the east. The shorter man had much to teach them, he affirmed. He was very wise in the ways of herbs, and potables. Stojan told him that he did not believe in magic, though Dagmar detected something odd with that affirmation.

He also seemed to be a bit of an historian and was not shy to volunteer information—even when not asked.

After much traveling Stojan finally asked him something that had been bothering him.

"Tell me, friend, why did you ask for forgiveness before saving Anastazja?"

It was asked with genuine curiosity and respect and it allowed Dagmar to answer honestly, albeit a bit sheepishly.

"There were three reasons, really." He took a breath as if revealing an intimate secret. After many moments had passed he continued.

"I thought that it would not save her and that I had given you false hope. That caused me great sadness. That once again I had failed."

The two continued to listen.

"I was aware of the side effects."

At this Stojan's left eyebrow began to rise and his face became concerned.

Seeing this Dagmar waved at him, as if to wave away his concerns.

"No no," he said quietly. "All is as it should be." He smiled. Though it was a convincing statement, the position of a certain left eyebrow told Dagmar that more would have to be revealed at a later time.

Stojan thought of Ana's grey hair. Was this the side affect, albeit temporary?

After some quiet Stojan realized the third reason had not been stated so he asked, "And the third?"

Dagmar's pace slowed and his eyes became distant.

"She—your daughter—reminds me of someone very special I knew a long time ago." At that Anastazja smiled.

Stojan nodded and the three continued walking. With his face turned away Dagmar finished almost silently.

"I did not want to lose her twice."

THREE TRAVELERS

With some effort Stojan and his companions had found the three horses that had been spooked.

Fortunately for the travelers they now had one horse each, and Dagmar reluctantly accepted the ride, but absolutely refused to take possession of the horse. This was acceptable since they had not offered.

Making camp nearby the strangers had much conversation.

"To where do you travel, friends?" Dagmar was curious, more curious even than Anastazja at times.

Stojan stared at the fire as his younger companion looked at him for information. When none was forthcoming she reflected the question back on to the asker.

"It seems you have me at a disadvantage—or perhaps advantage—depending on your point of view. I have no destination."

Stojan reflected upon the fact that this man very recently was truly at the end of the road—in more ways than one. He really had no destination, save for the bottom of the river. He smiled inwardly and stole a glance at Anastazja, who didn't notice as she waited intently for elaboration from the newcomer.

Stojan turned his head to him, and in an effort to steer the conversation away from the recent past and towards something that would give

Anastazja something to look forward to he simply said, "Where would you go?"

The two turned to Stojan as he continued.

"Where would you go, if you could? If you had the means to travel; the supplies, the conveyance, the monies?"

Dagmar had been given a new lease on life and the question was like what is asked of a young boy who is only now leaving his home to seek his fortune. It brightened him and gave him pleasant pause.

This was not lost on Anastazja. For Stojan it was simply a means to keep her entertained, and keep Dagmar talking. At least that was his thought, but contrary to his plan he found himself very much interested in the answer as it filled an emptiness he now had. What to do now, and where to go? He wanted to seek out the bishop for his monies, and to punish him for attempting to meddle in the affairs of Anastazja. However, the events that had occurred of late were because of him.

He was comfortable with his young companion. She was, clearly, very important to him. His desire was simply to make her happy and to protect her. The two had a loss that made them compatible. Stojan found he had no desire to wonder how long this would last. That it existed was more than enough for him.

What they did with their time became almost meaningless, that they spent it together was where his heart truly was. With her.

"Amira."

Stojan blinked, coming out of his deep thoughts. He wasn't sure if he missed an entire conversation, or if this had been the first time Dagmar had spoken.

It was the latter.

"Amira?"

"Yes." He answered Anastazja with a great smile.

"Amira! It is a land far away. It is a land with great libraries, and knowledge. It is, some say, the place of the second coming—the original battle of the forces of evil and good."

Anastazja's eyes were wide with excitement.

Dagmar glanced at one, then the other, as if drawing a consensus.

"I have read about it, and the knowledge I have has come from there. To be able to travel there myself would be wonderful."

He paused, looking slightly downcast.

"However, it is far away. In fact one must cross a great sea to go there. And it is not without its dangers."

Stojan, in spite of his aloofness, was genuinely interested.

"And what would you do there?"

"What would I do?" Dagmar looked incredulous. "Why I would explore! I would seek out the libraries. I would seek out the cathedrals, and I would seek the truth."

Stojan, ever stoic, asked, "And what would you do with this truth?"

"What?"

Stojan stared back—waiting for an answer to such a simple question.

"What would you do with this truth? Once you have it in your grasp?"

"I would share it." He smiled.

"I would share it with everyone. Too many things are unknown in this world. Too many secrets, and when there are secrets there are those that would use them to wield power over others."

Anastazja was nodding slightly now. Dagmar had a way with words, or rather a way to convey his emotion through them. What he said seemed sincere, and altruistic.

"Knowledge is power."

"So you wish to go to Amira to become powerful then?"

"What…? Well, no…"

His face changed, from excited to confused, to friendly and back to confused. He looked at the faces of the other two—searching for understanding.

Anastazja laughed; it was a tiny laugh full of life. It lifted the spirits of all three as Dagmar joined in on the laughter.

Stojan smiled.

Still smiling greatly Dagmar exclaimed, "I would wish to go there with you, my friends, and take this knowledge back to Poliska for all to benefit."

Stojan pondered this noble cause, but would say no more on it. Instead he just quietly listened to the conversation between Dagmar and Anastazja. Much was told that night. Anastazja was full of questions, and Dagmar did his best to answer.

It seemed that he was an excellent teacher and had found a very interested pupil. Stojan himself wondered what kind of pupil his young friend would be. He would find out soon enough.

———

The next morning produced a sunny and promising day. Both Stojan and Anastazja were up at dawn—but it seemed Dagmar was a deep sleeper. They let him be.

"So are we going to Amira?" It was what Anastazja said as a *good morning* to Stojan, her excitement still present from the night before.

She seemed to have suffered no ill effects from the fall nor from the cure that had been administered to her. She was in perfect health as far as Stojan could determine. He was still suspicious of such a miraculous potion, but extremely grateful for its application. When he asked Dagmar of its origin the reply had been once again the magical land of Amira. He would not say much more other than to say the container was filled with 'instructions.'

The campsite had been established up the path a bit—away from the bridge. Stojan was happy to put some distance between them and the site of the fall.

His guess was that it was midway between the bridge and the waterfall.

Leaving a groggy, one-eyed Dagmar the two walked together up the path, towards the waterfall.

"Please tell me you want to go, Stojan."

He looked down at her. "I am grateful for Dagmar and for what he did for us." His smile brightened as her eyes met his, filling him with gladness.

"But I am at a crossroads."

"You do no intend to leave…?" She grabbed his hand and he accepted it. Her grasp was tiny, and warm, and strong.

"I am not leaving you…" The words surprised even him. This statement opened up a world of possibilities. Had he committed so fully to her already? Had he gotten his wish—to be far away from his crimes? Why not just accept this life? It seemed he had been given a second chance. Perhaps even a second chance to be a father.

"I am not leaving you, but I am at a crossroads as to where I… we would go."

She squeezed his hand.

The feeling of him being so distant returned. He felt that he left his past behind him. The roar of the waterfall was getting louder as they approached. He enjoyed the feeling of leaving all the bad behind, and this new feeling of… feeling.

They walked quietly, hand in hand, until they reached it. Anastazja was absolutely amazed.

"It is so big! And beautiful!"

Indeed it was. Stojan was seeing it for the first time. To him it had just been a backdrop in a desperate conversation he'd had with Dagmar. Now it was most impressive—the froth and the mist and the water fell from such a great height. Two rivers met here as this waterfall emptied into the river passing below. The white sand-like particles fell in slow motion and surrendered more than crashed below. It was an enchanting spot. How odd that only a day ago it was where a man had tried to take is life, but instead had saved another. To him—this second—it was a very special place.

Anastazja gripped his hand even tighter and just watched. Together they viewed it as if it was a play, and indeed it was but the stage had been set by nature itself and the actor was a river forever falling to earth.

"I'm sorry."

Stojan had apologized softly while still looking at the waterfall.

The waterfall continued its roaring and paid no attention to Stojan.

"I'm sorry for what I have done, and what I had come to do."

Anastazja watched the flow, and listened to Stojan. They were important words, and though Stojan was a strong man it was clear to her that much strength was required to express them.

"But you did not."

"No. I have done nothing. I was witness to your father's passing Ana, and I wanted to help him."

She pulled herself ever so slightly towards him, standing shoulder to shoulder—or rather—shoulder to head.

"I would have helped him but there was nothing I could do."

His words were slow, as he relived it.

"Then I saw you. I did not expect you."

His voice choked up as he continued.

"I am so sorry for your loss, Anastazja. I am sorry that your father is no longer with you. But, I am grateful that I am able to be here with you now."

She experienced the warmth of his rough hand as she felt a tear announce itself.

"He was a good man to raise such a daughter as you. You are an eager learner, and Anastazja?"

She looked up at him as he looked down at her.

“You are strong. You have a strength about you that I am sure he knew, and was very proud of.”

He looked away again, back to the waterfall. She continued her gaze, however.

“I tell you that I was sent to kill him, but I did not. I will do everything I can to honor him.”

Those words said that day told Anastazja many things; however curiosity remained.

“Why were you sent? Who is it that would want my father to die? And where did you come from?”

He looked at her and now it was her turn not to look back. Perhaps she feared the answers to the questions, perhaps she was just lost in the waterfall.

“A man who calls himself a bishop found me, and offered a great deal of monies to kill your father. He seemed to fear him. In fact it seemed that he would pay almost anything to prevent his downfall, and this downfall was at the hands of your father. Or at least, it was foretold.”

“Portents? Of the future?”

“It would seem.”

“Do you believe in them?”

“I…”

“Who told him of this portent? Were you privy to such a thing?”

“No. It was a foul place, and the bishop was none the cleaner. His seemed an evil, anxious man in league with something… unidentified.”

“Do not go back!”

“I have no reason, but to thank him.”

“Stojan!”

Anastazja was shocked.

“He led me to you.”

Once again he looked upon her, watching the shock drain into relief, then sadness, then happiness.

She hugged him, this tall man of dubious origins, who made her feel safe.

“Truly I have no reason to return.” His barely perceptible words were muffled by the awkward clearing of the newcomers throat.

“Hello!”

Dagmar stood behind them. How long this had been going on was in question, and so was Dagmar’s intentions at that moment.

He smiled a large smile and took off an unusually shaped hat, waving it about as if to dust if off. It was unlike a helmet or a skull cap. It did not seem to serve a purpose other than to be decorative. It looked flimsy and almost appeared to be an accoutrement of formal garb for a lady, except that it was rather drab in color. The head covering was a cylinder with an almost flat top. The brim was wide and rigid, and there was a band of leather where they met, like a miniature belt. Along the cylinder were small rivet holes. As absurd as it looked he somehow found a way to make it work, and it looked natural on the smaller man. Somehow the majority of his unkempt hair stayed within the hat, with a manageable portion spilling forth underneath.

Stojan tilted his head, as the two disconnected.

“I took the liberty of riding ahead a bit, having never been this way. The forest clears as the path continues to follow the river.”

He looked excited as if he had stated a solution to a problem.

Stojan merely raised an eyebrow.

“All rivers empty into the sea.”

“Of course.”

Anastazja looked confused at this proclamation from Stojan, but then realized it was in jest. They both waited.

“The sea! We can follow the river eventually to the sea. And from there we can reach it. We can go.”

“Go where?”

“Amira!”

TWO TEACHERS

“How long have you been standing there?”

Stojan’s voice was less friendly than Dagmar would have preferred.

“I… I only recently arrived.” Dagmar smiled.

Stojan was unconvinced. The three looked at each other as the waterfall majestically fell.

“A bishop sent you, you say?”

Anastazja clicked her tongue in amusement. Stojan was not so inclined.

“Let us go back to the camp.” Leading the way Anastazja and Dagmar exchanged glances. She examined his hat when Dagmar wasn’t looking, which was most of the time. He seemed to be looking around at his surroundings constantly.

They walked back in silence, following the tall man until they reached the camp. The breach in privacy had upset him, though this particular quietness was difficult to discern from his normal stoicism.

Upon reaching the camp Dagmar plopped down, while Ana tended to her horse—always petting or brushing it when she had a free moment.

“Tell me Dagmar. This potion of yours, how do you come by such a powerful formula?”

Dagmar sat upright.

“And why are you not using such a thing to treat the ill?”

He stroked his chin.

Anastazja noted the man looked cornered. Surely they had all shared something just a day or so ago? Stojan’s behavior seemed odd.

“Would not someone of your skill be a precious commodity to those of royalty throughout the land?”

“It was all I had.”

He blurted his response out quickly, trying to curtail the inquisition. It worked. Temporarily.

Anastazja looked shocked. Stojan just continued to stand, and wait. Certainly there was more to this answer.

“Can you…”

“No.”

He stood up, almost defiantly, embarrassed. He removed his hat, and ran his hands through his great head of curly brown hair.

“No…” His eyes elongated as he pulled at his scalp, pushing it backwards in frustration. Making a moaning noise with half-formed syllables he continued.

“No… I cannot make more.”

He paced. Anastazja looked at Stojan, who appeared to be almost enjoying things. He had a strange way with asking questions, as if he always knew the answer before he asked.

“That was all I had. It was not something I created. It was…”

He stopped pacing.

“…something I was given.”

Stojan looked pleased, but still waited for more.

"And where did you come upon this special potion?"

"The contact is no more. She is no longer someone I have relations with."

He looked truly sad at this, so sad Anastazja wanted to run to him and give comfort. Her desire was to stop Stojan from further inquiry. Surely he'd said enough, and the concoction was in the right place at the right time. She owed her life to both Dagmar and the formula. She felt protective now.

"What of the origin, Stojan?" Her voice was defiant as she interjected.

She felt herself becoming angry, a bit more than she expected. Her voice was louder now and she found herself turned towards Stojan and confronting him, to the defense of the man who'd saved her.

"Why do you question him?! He who has saved my life. I owe my life to not only you but to him."

Dagmar stood, unmoving, his mouth open. Whatever the answer was it caused him pain to recall it. And something else. His eyes darted back and forth between the two.

She took a deep breath, and looked Stojan in the eyes, who seemed smugly pleased with himself.

"What difference does it make? Why?"

Dagmar looked uncomfortable, to say the least.

"That is why."

Stojan turned his eyes from Dagmar to Anastazja: the girl of promising skill with the blade, of the late Leonard, trained as a blacksmith's apprentice.

The girl of eyes of blue and hair of crimson.

Dagmar swallowed.

Stojan folded his arms, now looking back at Dagmar, who now took on the persona of someone who was caught.

Red handed.

Anastazja's anger turned to confusion. It wasn't the only thing that had turned suddenly.

"What are you looking at?" She was now confused and annoyed at both.

Stojan's eyes were not quite focused on hers. She tilted her head up, as if some sort of bird had alighted upon it.

Instead she saw her own hair. It was no longer golden blonde. She grabbed a handful from the side—from her shoulder—and pulled it in front of her face. Incredulous, she yelled, "*What?!*"

Dagmar looked down at the grass, finding respite between the blades.

She looked at a satisfied Stojan, and then stared at Dagmar. She would wait all day for him to look at her, if necessary.

He did finally look up. Her hair was of fire, but also of gold. The red was slowly fading away back to the golden blonde.

"When did you notice?" It was Dagmar, still looking at the ground.

Anastazja looked at Stojan for an answer. He walked over to her, placing a hand on her shoulder, then her hair. He looked fascinated by it.

"I noticed the moment you applied your serum, as did you. But then recently I've noticed changes that come and go."

Dagmar looked up, finally.

"There is a pattern," said Stojan, and he looked into Ana's eyes.

"Forgive me. I knew that you would defend our friend Dagmar, but I had to know."

"Know what?"

"That your hair changes color with your emotions."

It was Dagmar that finished.

"So you knew? You knew of this? This is a side effect that you waved off?"

Stojan waited for an answer. His expression seemed of slight amusement. Ana was not so amused.

"I suspected, as the formula is not quite for her. I knew there might be a … difference. When I saw her hair change color that day."

"What day?!" Ana burst in.

He turned to her. "The day you fell, Ana."

She looked back at Stojan, who had taken a step back, arms folded once again. He seemed unconcerned.

"That is the only side effect, that I am sure of. You have been healed of your wounds. I promise."

Stojan smiled at the girl with golden hair.

"I am eternally grateful to you, Dagmar, as I have said." He nodded and looked upon Ana while speaking, as if to reaffirm his gratitude.

Dagmar chose not to speak further, looking very embarrassed—almost ashamed. He needn't be—thought Stojan—because he would have happily accepted Ana as the girl with purple skin.

Ana, however, had many questions on this. After the initial shock wore off she was quite excited to possess the only hair that could change color on demand. That day she had mostly red highlights that quickly faded. One of the many questions she bombarded Dagmar with was what other colors the hair would turn, if any, if it would ever all turn, and how easily she could control it.

Stojan saw this bombardment as a sort of punishment for this minor side effect of Dagmar's work. It amused him far more than it should have—watching the little girl so excitedly ask questions about a product with no instructions. As it turned out, that was exactly what the problem was caused by.

Instructions.

Dagmar would not elaborate other than to say that this is what the bottle was filled with.

“Instructions? How can a bottle be filled with instructions?” Ana struggled to understand, but instead had to focus on her other questions, as Dagmar could not sufficiently elaborate on the answer.

It seemed that he himself only understood so much of it.

Stojan was cautious to accept any other concoctions from the would-be alchemist. The same would go for Ana, if he had anything to do with it.

He most certainly did.

—

Without a true direction the three decided to ride along the river as far as it would take them.

After a short while they fell into a rhythm—riding for some of the day, hunting and then teaching Ana what they could.

Stojan was determined to help her conquer her fear of the blade, created by the event of her lucky blow with the bandit. As it turned out the blow was not so lucky. Her skill was impressive, helped along greatly by her unusual strength due to working so hard with her father.

This training would not have been possible without the kindness of her father, who crafted her a blade that was a perfect fit for her size. Stojan was able to teach her the same way he would teach an adult. There was no training sword made of wood, no inferences to a time in which she would have a true weapon. And, she had already fought.

Her respect for Stojan grew as he patiently and tirelessly taught her. He too gained from this as it served as a way for him to dispense with restless energy, and he felt quite useful teaching her a skill that until now had been bound somewhat by guilt.

Due to the affects of the potion, he had an indicator of just how determined—and angry—she felt while training. He found that this was an ideal tool, a visual representation of something that would be almost impossible to determine. An indicator such as this sped up her training dramatically, and showed him just when she was in control, and instead controlled by rage.

No other fighter—to his knowledge—was as in touch with such thing. She was able to channel anger into skill, rage into strength, and will into focus. Instead of separating mood from skill she had combined them through his expert training and the built-in indicator she now possessed.

What started out as a way to appease her questions and honor her father became a daily routine that brought them closer. She tirelessly pursued her skill. And he tirelessly taught her.

Dagmar often watched with fascination as the two fought and trained in a field, or among the brush, or between the trees. It seemed that battle was to be taught anywhere and everywhere. The ballet of the two was a sight to behold and Dagmar knew that only a father and daughter could train so closely. The clanking, the running, the sounds of bodies clashing together was often poignantly accented by laughter.

Watching them sometimes made him muse about family, and what he lost—the possibilities, the events. He tried not to dwell but could not help it. Though he had been given a second chance he still missed what had not yet happened, and would never now. But there was no happiness in this, and instead he focused on what he now had. And he too was able to teach Ana.

Other times, especially at night, were filled with lessons with Dagmar, who was more than eager to teach her about history, the ancient times, and this magical land of Amira.

Stojan sometimes found himself sitting-in listening quietly, but this took the form of him sharpening his blade nearby, or being lost in thought. Much of it sounded like nonsense, and he was half-convinced that Dagmar was making it up as he went along. He'd make an excellent salesman, he thought.

Stojan too would learn, if only through osmosis.
And thus it was that Ana was slowly trained, matter-of-factly, by the deadliest assassin in all of Poliska while being educated by the preeminent historian of Amira.

"What do you know of bishops?"

It was an innocent question—but one that seemed to come from nowhere. Ana's history lessons were frequent, but she seemed to have a particular curiosity on this subject.

Always the willing teacher, Dagmar happily complied. He looked around a bit, as the two sat in the shade provided by the large tree they'd found.

Excursions to identify flora sometimes turned into walking history lessons. This day was no different.

"I know enough to know that they no longer really exist."

She tilted her head and brushed her hair out of her eyes.

"As I have said the old religion of Poliska was one of priests and bishops, and this was of a time before the second coming."

"Yes."

"In the aftermath much was lost as those left tried to make sense of things. This occurred at a time when the intricacies of what was built clashed with society."

He continued when he saw that he confused her.

"Technology."
"Yes, you have mentioned this. You said that your potion was composed of this technology."

"Yes, it is part of the old ways. Really everything is, but those at the time chose to separate technology from other things, not understanding that in a way everything we create is technology."

Seeing that he was making progress he dodged a branch and continued.

"Your sword is as much technology as was the potion, or the way a blacksmith works. Some things contain more, some are quite concentrated. In the old days they made great progress."

"But what does this have to do with bishops?"

Dagmar's insights and wisdom were extensive, but so were his tangents, Anastazja found. She'd learned how to sometimes manage his teachings to gain the most knowledge on the subject at hand.

"Oh yes, well at the time some of this technology was at odds with the teaching of the bishops you see. It seemed to some that the ways of the bishops were at odds with the ways of technology. But really they were not. They were just describing the same thing."

He nodded and smiled at this.

"The problems arose when some of the bishops and the lesser bishops decided to gain power with this, to ignore what technology taught them."

"Power?"

"Yes, you have been listening. Like everything, the demise of mankind has been about power and those that seek it. For whatever reason. When one considers the good first then one does not encounter this conflict."

Anastazja looked slightly different but was still listening.

"So what I know of these bishops is that when the great battle took place their place in history ended. They lost their power along with so many that lost their lives. When the sweep occurred there was little left for them."

"The sweep?"

"Oh I may have called it something else. It is when the churches fell and along with the statues."

"Statues?"

This seemed to be one of the times Stojan had warned her about—Dagmar's skill for making things up as he went along, to please the listener and keep them enthralled.

He stopped, and leaned on a tree.

"Yes. The Saints. After the great battle they were found to dwell within the cathedrals. The places that caused them to gather was found to be their homes, as was often believed. However, when the survivors feared the evil had won they manifested themselves within the statues.

"For a very long time it was common practice to sculpt and create the likenesses of men and women—some great leaders, other very important icons in religion. These were made of stone and even sometimes metal. They lasted for millennia, though some showed signs of aging—like missing limbs, etc. But these were very common. In fact there wasn't a

city you could visit that did not have a statue."
"The sweep was…?"

"The sweep was the time that men and women rose up to destroy what they could. Though they could not destroy them, they could limit their appearance. Meaning, they could not destroy the saints that had come to Earth, but they could destroy their vessels and their homes."

Anastazja leaned as well.

"They destroyed all of the statues in Poliska, as we assume was done throughout the rest of the world. And most of the cathedrals were destroyed in the battle, those that remained were forgotten or avoided."

"I have never seen a cathedral. I have seen a picture of one."

"And no statues. I do not think a statue has been seen for hundreds of years, possibly an entire millennium—since the sweep."

Dagmar proclaimed this last point as if to prove all of his previous conversation.

"Perhaps there are some left. But…"

"But then that would mean… Wait, tell me of the saints again?"

Ana had now lost her ability to steer Dagmar and once again was lost in his lore. She would sort it out later, and repeat some of it to Stojan, who had a way with separating what he thought was fact from fiction. She had not quite had her question answered. Now she had more.

"Why do you ask about bishops, my dear?"

Ana once again looked distant, and found something interesting within the tree bark.

"I do not wish to betray Stojan. But he told me once that he had worked for one."

Dagmar seemed very impressed.

"Stojan worked for a bishop? Pfft. Perhaps a man that calls himself a bishop. It is a label he has taken to impress or confuse others."

Like 'Alchemist,' thought Ana, though she was much too polite to vocalize this. Her thought amused her, and she suppressed a giggle. It occurred to her that Dagmar was indeed right, and that many gave themselves labels to impress. Stojan himself was someone she thought was very skilled with the sword, seemed to know battle, the intricacies of melee, strategy, and an infinite confidence in tactics, yet he had no label for himself. Perhaps these labels were given to oneself when trying to enhance confidence?

Or obscure a lack thereof.

It did make her think about her own label for herself. She had often aspired to be a blacksmith like her father, and knew she would be the greatest in the city, even moving to a larger shop within the city. At the same time her growing desire to eventually use the blades her father had created for her was at odds with this.

So what was she then? A blacksmith apprentice with an affinity for the blade? Could she have two labels?

"Anastazja?"

It was Dagmar, he looked serious, but also concerned. She had been lost in thought.

He touched her arm.

"He's not your father, is he?"

She looked into his eyes, her expression was difficult to read, as if she had two answers in conflict.

She chose neither.

"I think we should return."

With that they did indeed make their way back to their current resting place, mostly in silence.

Thoughts of bishops were forgotten easily, and both were lost in thoughts for completely different reasons.

To Ana her small comfortable world of the farmhouse and forge was suddenly much larger. There was a part of her that was still numb from her father's passing. Her own near-death experience had shown her Stojan's heart, and she knew it to be pure; but she still did not know him. Their travels seemed unending, and in these weeks she had gained much in the way of skills and knowledge. She was eternally grateful for that, but felt that being a nomad was not her path. This conflict kept her quiet for now.

Dagmar continued to muse on the two strangers he now traveled with. He was convinced now that they were not father and daughter. He saw love between them, but there was more to this. Perhaps Ana was discovered by Stojan? An uncle perhaps? He did not believe anything nefarious was afoot, but not knowing drove him a bit mad. He regretted asking Ana and should have asked Stojan.

Ana was less likely to kill him though.

———

That night after her lesson in history, Anastazja asked a question out loud that she'd asked in her head many times.

"When will we stop traveling?"

The two men looked at each other, then to her.

"We have been traveling for many weeks as far as I reckon. Will we settle in a town?"

That generated thoughts of being the town's blacksmith, and of Ana working hard by the forge. Since both men were slow to respond, Ana continued.

"The sights I have seen are amazing. But have we not run far enough?"

Dagmar's eyebrows showed his reaction to this, while Stojan was unreadable. She continued.

"Yes, I know that we run." She looked back and forth. "But, I do not know what we run from?"

She put her hands on her hips. "Or is it that we run *to* something?"

"There is a city up ahead."

It was Stojan, and said with some trepidation, as if revealing a poorly-kept secret.

“We can go there?!” Her excitement was genuine.

Dagmar just seemed to be watching, as if in the audience in a play. His face showing his mild amusement.

Stojan looked at Anastazja and nodded, slowly.

Dagmar thought it looked like a father who finally agreed to allow his child to ride a horse for the first time—knowing it is dangerous but a step that must be taken. He didn’t remember ever hearing the big man sigh, but that day it seemed he did.

They had been on the road for some time, and avoiding the cities had suited Dagmar nicely.

“We can leave for it tomorrow.”

Dagmar’s amusement abruptly faded into concern, but he said no more.

THE CITY

"Stojan, how do you know of this city?"

The next morning revealed a beautiful sunrise. Their camp site was a short distance form the river that they continued to follow. Both men thought it best as it provided water, food and a place to clean up. It meandered somewhat but lately it kept a fairly straight course.

Dagmar had unrolled a scroll of his own—apparently a crude map. The brownish paper had iconic scribbles for mountains, cities, forests and the names of a handful of cities. Rivers were also drawn upon it. He viewed it, squinted and looked up at Stojan through his curly locks.
The two were alone together as Ana was taking a morning walk to the river, so excited was she to finally end her nomadic existence.

Stojan became introspective as he answered. The pause was unusual, even for him.

"I have only recently gotten my bearings. Following the river has helped me to determine where we are. The fact that it now straightens itself out tells me we are near a city I am aware of."

Dagmar, squinting again, looked down at his map. Stojan's vagueness did not help.

"Stojan…"

Dagmar stood up, allowing the scroll to retract without regard.

"I have something to tell you."

It was like talking to a brick wall, thought Dagmar. He never knew if the conversation would anger Stojan, or make him completely disinterested. Before he could muster the courage to speak the brick wall had interjected.

"You seem nervous about entering the city."

Dagmar just listened as Stojan expanded. This was much easier than trying to make his point.

"I am not for exploring this city myself. I would much prefer to continue to travel. In fact I would much rather travel far far from here."

Perhaps I will not have to explain.

"But…" Dagmar felt the conversation turn.

"Ana has been on the road for a long time. She is young, and misses her home."

Stojan softened, as he always did when speaking to or about Anastazja.

"Well, why did you leave it?" Dagmar almost grabbed his mouth, but the words had escaped.

Stojan raised an eyebrow. "I will tell you." Dagmar was pleased that there was no sword involved in the explanation. Though he had no personal experience, he always detected something in Stojan that made him feel that expressing himself with his sword was always an option. Stojan did value life, but sometimes it seemed that value was strictly limited to himself and Anastazja.

Stojan looked around as if to verify the absence of said girl.

"We were run out due to bandits. The home was lost and as many supplies as we could take were brought with us."

Dagmar imagined a battle in which there were many deaths, none of them being the man standing before him. He did not believe that bandits would ever be that foolish, regardless of their number.

"Tis true."

The soft voice startled Dagmar, and a look of something unidentifiable crossed Stojan's face.

Sometimes Anastazja moved like a gentle breeze, silently and without warning. It was most surprising and impressive. It was also annoying. Stojan's training was only making it worse.

Ana stood with the men, near Dagmar, having just appeared from behind a tree. She had taken a different path back to the camp, as was taught by Stojan. She was an excellent pupil.

"We were run out and had but moments to gather what we could."

"Well then…" Dagmar smiled a large, uncomfortable smile, looking like he was about to sell an unsuspecting passerby an ointment, or salve.

"It is good the city is near us. Yes, yes. Very good. I am so very sorry that you have lost your home."

Though Stojan was quite pleased with his enthusiasm, he did not understand the sudden change. After all, it looked as if Dagmar was about to also voice his concerns. His unconvincing smile contained fear.

"I think we are far enough."

Stojan's voice was emotionless.

"We have come a long way and traveled for many many weeks. I think we have traveled long enough and the time has come to look for a city in which to dwell."

Ana brightened, Dagmar did not.

"And we have had a most unusually long summer to benefit us."

Ana shook her head slightly—clearly disagreeing with the statement. It seemed to her that the length of summer was exactly as expected.

With that the three made haste to pack for the trip, two poor liars and a girl.

—

In their travels Ana had only encountered a few animals—deer, squirrels and the like. For the most part, larger animals had not concerned them, or concerned themselves with them. Stojan had taught Ana a respect for them, and to her surprise Dagmar had confirmed that most predators were afraid of the humans that walked on two thin legs. Ana's respect for these larger animals grew, but so did her curiosity. One such day found Ana testing both her curiosity and skill, its sight was not reported because it had been done in secrecy and discovered by accident.

An increasingly troubled Dagmar took a much needed walk. Though confident with his weapon —and various other items he carried with him —he was not foolish. He had taught Ana on more than one occasion to understand the animals, and how most paid little attention to those that appeared to belong. The lumbering hunters would alert and scare animals at a great distance, but if one was nonchalant one could approach quite closely.

"How close?" she asked with much interest—her blue eyes lighting up.

His answer seemed to disappoint her.

He remembered the lessons fondly, and it had given him much purpose in the recent weeks. Her desire to learn was motivating, but it was the way she trusted and believed in him as a scholar that truly created within him a desire to be better—to teach her as much as he could. Even his knowledge of Amira.

Lost in thought, walking slowly, he looked to see that he'd wandered much farther than expected and found himself crowning a small hill. As he made way to come down the other side he beheld a beautiful sight that cheered his mood.

It was a field of giant yellow flowers. The flowers were of considerable size and height—almost comically so. Dagmar had never beheld such a thing, but had read about them. They were flowers that grew to two or even three meters in height, and they were known to follow the sun during the day. Thousands of them stood that day, in an impossibly large field. Yellows of all kinds filled the eyes with beauty.

Indeed the entire field all seemed to be saluting the sun and where it shown in the afternoon sky.

He walked slowly, descending into the mini-valley drinking it all in, and from his elevated vantage point that was when he saw them. Two figures were in the field of sunflowers, and from his unique perspective he could make them out—dark against the background of ever-flowing yellow.

It was Anastazja, and she was standing near a large animal. He froze, becoming instantly concerned. The animal was easily twice the mass of the little girl. And, it wasn't alone. Off to the side there were a group of them, and this one had ventured forth. They were deer, about six of them.

She stood still yet moved with the flowers; as if she was one of them. She swayed ever so slightly in the breeze and had she not been so darkly dressed he would have missed her entirely.

She was moving towards the lone straggler. At least he assumed that was the case, as he didn't see any movement, but she seemed to be closer to it than she was when he last noticed them.
Reaching into his bag he pulled out a short tube. It was made of a black substance that resembled a sort of brushed leather and was rough to the touch. Turning a dial and pulling at it he moved it to his right eye.

It was a device he came into possession of, just like the substance that brought the three of them together. It too brought with it much joy and fear—the latter being something he would forget from time to time.

He watched with much greater clarity now—as if he was only one third the distance to her—as she approached the deer.

He could see the look on her face and it was one of concentration and delight. This serene mischievousness made him smile widely in spite of himself, as her expression was contagious.

Approaching at the wrong time could result in the animal rearing up and attacking. Hooves could do considerable damage, despite how gentle the beasts appeared. And that was without the inclusion of antlers. He quickly panned to see if he could find the presence of said antlers on the other animals, but could not determine that conclusively. He panned back lest he miss something.

She moved closer to the deer and was only a meter or so away now. As much as he tried he couldn't make out individual movements—her body just seemed to flow towards it. She must have been downwind from it, because it was completely unaware of her presence. Was this a game she played when she went for her walks, or had he caught her at her first attempt?

And then it happened.

She reached out with her hand and ever so lightly tapped the back end of the animal. It moved but was not startled, as it was brushing away an insect or a branch. Her face lit up and she withdrew—slowly and happily—making her way back away from the animals. As she moved away from it, her speed increased exponentially.

Dagmar was grateful for the unique vantage point the slight hill had provided. This seemed like a recurring event that he was glad he had beheld. Anastazja displayed much joy when she did this and it was obvious now that this time was not the first.

He did not speak of this to her, or Stojan. Instead it was a part of her he had been privy to and was happier for it.

It added to his sadness the next day when they would have to part company.

—

"I am sorry."

It was Dagmar, and they'd only been riding a short distance. The morning had seen them eat, pack up and leave at first light.

"For what are you..?" Ana replied after it was obvious he wasn't going to continue.

"Hold."

It was Stojan this time, and the loudness of his voice startled both.

"We are surrounded."
His companions scanned the area—they were on a road flanked by very tall grass—so movement was hard to discern. But it was there—at least twelve, perhaps more. Dark, large figures were moving in on them.

To Ana it looked like the deer she was so fond of playing games with, but darker, and bulkier. And with heads that hunched down into the grass as they ran.

Wolves.

“They approach from all sides,” Dagmar said to no-one as his head rotated back and forth, holding onto the reigns for support.

Ana too scanned the area. The road was a distinct path through the field of tall grass, and only some of the figures were visible. They winked in and out based on the movement of the grass. Fortunately they happened to be at a higher point than those approaching them—not ideal for the would-be attackers.

“Wolves do not attack in this manner.”

Dagmar’s confusion was heard in his words.

“Agreed. This smells of something unnatural.” Stojan looked over to Anastazja to reinforce the magnitude of the words. She looked back with quiet conviction. It occurred to her just then that wolves might also stalk the same deer she did—but with much different intentions.

It was then that the horses also detected something awry, perhaps they picked up the scent, or it was the unnerved nature of their riders.

Stojan patted his horse’s mane, in an effort to stabilize the beast.

“Do we… dismount? What is the proper…?”

Dagmar was clearly confused.

“Shall we not ride…?”

They were now on the trail ahead, and behind them. The animals were truly closing in on them, as if they’d been dropped out of the sky in an almost perfect circle, with the three travelers in the very center.

“What do we do?” Dagmar was frightened, and asked no one in particular. Ana was oddly quiet and simply pet her horse.

“I have a feeling *that* will be answered soon enough.” Stojan spoke slowly and confidently about something he knew nothing about. There was a certain finality about it, as if this would provide some sort of relief. He looked over at Ana almost apologetically.

The horses all fused closer together, as if on cue.

Anastazja looked over to Dagmar, as if to implore him to find some magic within his bag.

He looked frightened—far more than his companions, but alas did not bring forth any sort of magic that would dispel the beasts.

"This is my fault—I have brought this upon you."

Stojan turned, with a look of incredulity on his face—a considerable amount of emotion that neither of his companions had really witnessed before.

It was Dagmar, and he was apologizing.

Dagmar looked at Ana, then Stojan.

"They have found me."

Stojan all but rolled his eyes—with an odd look of relief.

"No Dagmar, they have come for me—strange things are afoot and I find my presence here is the cause."

"You? What could you possibly cause with your mere presence?" Dagmar looked back and forth from Ana to Stojan, searching for an answer. Anastazja seemed just as confused, but remained quiet.

The beasts continued to close in, and Dagmar could see one now up ahead on the trail, forming part of the almost perfect circle. No doubt one existed directly behind him judging by the look on Stojan's face. They were closer now, perhaps some 30 meters away, and moving dramatically slow—prolonging the inevitable.

Ana's eyes moved back and forth between the two men, who seemed to be having a contest of who was at fault for the sudden appearance of the wolves. It made no sense to Ana.

Dagmar was almost annoyed. "They have come for me, to take back what I have stolen, to retrieve what I can no longer return." He looked at Ana, sheepishly.

Stojan scanned the area, slowly, intently. Dagmar watched as he rotated in his saddle, determined to survey the entire field it seemed. He squinted. This went on for a long minute.

"Here."

Stojan looked at Dagmar briefly, catching him only with the corner of his eye. He was holding something out towards Stojan. It was dark and cylindrical in appearance. Since their horses were huddled together he could easily lean and reach the offered item.

With some apprehension he did.

"Place it on your right eye, close your left and look through it. Point it at what you need to see and it will become closer."

Stojan did as was suggested, tilting his head back as if looking at a bright light and pulled the item away.

"Turn the ring at the end until the view is clear."

Stojan dropped the reign and did just that. Dagmar thought he saw him smile. He scanned the area, pulling the tube from his eye multiple times, as if in disbelief. Ana watched with fascination.

The black tube was thrown back to Dagmar, who caught it with both hands—a horrified look on his eyes—as if a fine glass heirloom had just been tossed his way nonchalantly.

It had been.

"They do surround us, but there is a fork in the road ahead."

Dagmar shook his head and took a breath, "We will never reach it. These beasts are clearly not of sound mind and…"

Then they heard it—a distant sound, like something miniature was saying "aww aww" and "oww oww." It sounded both distant and near, and seemed to come from everywhere.

Ana looked up to see the source of the sound, and the two men joined her.

It was a bird of great size flying in a circle. The black thing continued the slow circle, soaring and flapping only when necessary, perhaps only 20 meters above them.

Afraid that he'd taken his eyes off the wolves too long, Dagmar panicked and looked back, then fumbled with the device as he placed it to his eye. Ana's gaze alternated between the spectacle in the sky, Dagmar and the wolves. She had much to look at.

Stojan seemed the least surprised of them.

"They… they become confused," Dagmar said, keeping the device on his face. He rotated, and focused mainly on the animals in the road.

The bird gargled, as if to communicate something new.

Ana looked up again at the new sound. It seemed the bird was capable of all sorts of calls.

"What does it want Stojan?" Ana stared at the tall man who looked more serene than he should.

"They are frightened," Dagmar said to no-one, continuing to scan the area.

Stojan took a breath, and with authority announced, "We are given an opportunity." He turned his head to Ana and winked.

"We must not squander it. Come, let us ride forward." With that he spurred his horse slowly onward making sure his companions followed suit. Ana was next with Dagmar bringing up the rear—awkwardly holding the reigns and the device to his eye. Stojan looked forward—much like the bird above—as Dagmar continued his circles.

"They are breaking ranks, and are disoriented. Some are walking away, while other look around for a leader."

Then he said something that caused Ana much concern.

"They are wild again."

As they continued to ride out of the once-closing circle of wolves they could see a fork in the road. It seemed the beasts had descended upon them just short of this. Whether it was intentional or random was unknown. Though the circumstance seemed so, their behavior was not—they were controlled by something. Or, thought Dagmar, they *were*.

Continuing to ride forward as quickly and quietly as possible was their only concern.

The bird continued to circle and seemed to follow along with them—always keeping just above the three. Every so often it would produce the gurgling sound. To Ana it almost seemed like it cheered them on.

At the fork they could see that the grass was not as high, so more was visible than before—including straggling wolves, the fork itself and the hill top ahead. One road had a group of three wolves, standing, looking lost; the other was open.

"Which way Stojan?" asked Dagmar. "What did your map say?"

Stojan shook his head and took the fork sans animals.

"It seems the wolves have decided for us, as my map showed no fork."

With this the three travelers made their way down the road, leaving a large group of wolves confused and pensive. Much vying for control would be had that day as the wolves had been pulled together from three separate packs.

The bird continued to circle and follow for quite some time, until they were able to see their new destination. It never did land, but instead just flew away with a few "aww aww's" as it left them.

With considerable effort Anastazja kept the multitude of questions only within her head. For now.

She was ecstatic to be finding a city, and possibly settling down again. Though too many things were unknown she realized that the nomadic life was wearing on her.

Dagmar seemed lost in thought, and indeed he was. He thought much about what he wanted to reveal to his companions, and their recent encounter. His desire to take his own life had been reversed, as he was now afraid to lose it. There was some humor to be had in this, he mused. Still wanting to avoid any encounters, he had only been prepared for those that walked on two legs and carried a weapon of metal. Those that walked on four whose weapons consisted of teeth and claws had not been considered. A coordinated attack on him and those he traveled with gave him grave concern.

I am placing them in grave danger, he thought to himself. *The longer I stay with them, the more likely I bring death upon them.*

Though Stojan was clearly a fine warrior—the best he'd ever seen—it was still not his destiny to be brought down by those that pursued Dagmar.

And Anastazja; she seemed so out of place. The girl had no home, yet adjusted so well to being on the road, on the run. But from what, or to what?

The more time he spent with them, the less he understood them. He almost snorted out loud at the absurdity; yet it was true. Dagmar considered himself to be a learned man who pursued knowledge and the truth above all else. This pursuit had lead him to pain and suffering but also to great and wondrous things. It seemed that wonder had found him, and rescued him from death.

Perhaps this *was* his path? But again, why place these good people in harm's way due to him?

Stojan remained quiet, and continued the lead. He was pleased that Ana seemed to just be absorbing the events. His appreciation for her outlook grew every day. Though he did not quite trust Dagmar it seemed a prudent thing for him to continue with them. What the future held was uncertain. To Stojan they were traveling in two directions at once, and he could not quite understand why he felt this way.

But feel this way he did.

The return of the raven gave him pause, but brought some clarity, for till now he had not been certain of its reality. It was easy to believe that the initial appearance was just part of a waking dream, so odd had it been. But, two appearances solidified his belief in the real—the here and now. Yes it was indeed real, and both times it chose to be of service.

His involvement in the supernatural was like losing one's foothold on a steep roof; if you did not find purchase you would just continue to fall… and fall.

What awaited him on the ground he did not know. And, he was ever curious of this bishop. Had he not met Ana he would be well on his way to seek him out for payment. Instead the man had delivered him to something that gave him meaning again—it was a gift of immeasurable wealth beyond anything he could have hoped for. Stojan was sure this bishop was of a singularly-minded evil, yet the end result was decidedly positive. This he found quite confusing. And he had not yet found purchase, so he continued to slide. It seemed his bargain marked the beginning of this slope for him.

All three travelers fell into their respective silence for a surprisingly long time. They had much to think about.

BUDZISZYN

Stojan's quiet contemplation was all but shattered by the appearance of a simple sign. One word brought back intense memories—anger, hate, guilt. It reminded him that he had relaxed his grip on things, that he was not as in control as he thought, and that danger was ever present. And perhaps it was something worse than danger: exposure.

The sign they approached was of unremarkable workmanship—made of wood and stood about two meters tall. It was far wider than it was tall, and the sign itself was just a strip, barely tall enough to contain the word displayed in white on blue painted board.

"Budziszyn."

Ana's reaction was one of hope, as she was finally making her way into a town of some size. She visibly brightened but her enthusiasm was singular; her companions seemed to be affected in a much different fashion.
Looking at Dagmar she read the sign out loud.

"I have never been there, Dagmar. Have you?"

Smiling slightly, and after a short pause he responded.

"No, no. I have not. I think it must be a city of respectable size."

But Stojan was now in a different time; reliving events. The sign to him marked an event of his past that he had left behind three years ago. He had been on the run all these years. Confusingly he had been brought full circle to where it began. When he left he stayed far from the Vistula river, as his thinking was that they would track him easily that way. Instead he made his way southwest towards the smaller cities and tributaries. It had been an excellent strategy; it was far easier to track a man in a straight line than it was to fan outward where options multiplied. Hiding and moving among the smaller towns had been taxing, but it had worked.

Clearly the bishop had used unusual ways to find him. He reckoned that he'd rode straight for no more than two days to reach the bishop, based on what his men had revealed. And that meant the bishop was still far to the south west.

Ana's house was apparently much closer to the river, and much father north than he suspected. He had been transported over a hundred kilometers, perhaps two.

Following the river, it was inevitable that they would run into Budziszyn. Eventually. With the recent events Stojan was sure he had weeks to plan something.

But what? What would he plan? He could not cause Anastazja to live the life of a nomad forever while he ran from the results of so many deaths. He was a wanted man—a dangerous criminal who lived day to day without any regard for another save for his next meal and to be left alone.

The jobs he did take were out of necessity and he hated those who would hire him as much as those that died as the result of it.

There was no other plan. Until now.

He closed his eyes. Or perhaps they were already closed?

If they were this close it was surprising they hadn't yet run into anyone that knew of him, and his deed. And Ana was not even aware of the city. She had not heard the phrase coined to describe Stojan.

'The Butcher of Budziszyn.'

"Stojan!"

Ana's face was full of surprise and humor; she had never seen Stojan so lost in thought.

"Surely a sign does not cause so much meditation?"

He looked at her smiling face and could not help to smile a little. It was a stark, pleasing contrast to the darkness into which he had just immersed himself.

Stojan had a flashback to the time just before the attack at her farmhouse. His feeling at the time was to weather the event, and if he was discovered he would simply leave.

The vision, presumably from the raven, had proved otherwise. And yet he felt, once again, that this would be the course of action.

From the direction of the sign came a man on horseback. The sight snapped Stojan into the here and now. He was riding slowly, and did not seem to be riding to engage them but rather to simply travel outward. There was still some distance between the city and the sign, as they were at a crossroads. No doubt one of many travelers they would see going in and out from the city on this early morning.

"Excuse me?"

The older man spoke as he approached them. His demeanor was neutral but not unfriendly. He rode a large horse burdened with large saddle bags.

"Yes?" said Dagmar in response.

"Coming or going?"

"What?"

"Are you coming or going?"

Stojan's lips started to form a challenge but Dagmar was too fast for him.

"We are coming—to the city… What..?"

"Unfortunate."

Stojan's eyes widened slightly as his grip intensified. The slightest word out of place confirmed what was inevitable. Would it start before they even entered the city proper?

“Oh why is that?” asked Dagmar in a friendly quip.

“Looking for a little companionship is all. Perhaps more.”

A still-smiling Ana traded glances with Dagmar while Stojan kept quiet, thinking it would make him less recognizable.

“Companionship? To accompany you?”

“Yes. But I would not want to inconvenience your family. I would not be averse to the protection a group brings while traveling between the cities.”

He smiled for the first time.

“And it is nice to have someone to talk to.”

Ana and Stojan both looked conflicted, for entirely different reasons. In fact their reasons were exactly opposite.

Dagmar—enjoying his ability to speak freely and uninterrupted—continued to take the lead.

“To where do you travel, friend?”

“To the port.”

Dagmar’s face looked like he had bobbed for apples one too many times and come up with the one rotten one.

Seeing the look the stranger explained.

“Well, call it what you will. It is my destination.”

It was Stojan’s turn to look confused. It seemed a mention of a port made Dagmar uncomfortable. Stojan made a note to ask him about this later that day.

“I… well. Oh. Is the cove so nearby?”

The stranger panned through the faces of the other three, with a smile of inquiry. He seemed surprised they did not know of it.

"Well of course. Yes. It is close by. We are almost the northernmost city. It is but two day's ride from here."

At that moment a large group approached them. In concert they pulled their horses to the side to make way. The group—much to Stojan's relief—was simply passing by and going north.

Stojan watched them carefully, keeping his head down. They seemed to be uninterested in the group, save for one or two glancing at the merchant, or Dagmar, or Ana's hair. To them he was apparently invisible. He nodded at no one in particular—a goodbye to the disinterested. Watching them go he assessed them as hands for hire in some capacity. He knew enough about concealing both arms and armor to know that these men were probably doing just that. It was not uncommon, but he noted it nonetheless.

The conversation continued without his participation.

"Are there any other cities near here, perhaps a day's ride or less?"

Dagmar's question did not go well with Ana. Her face showed protest at the mere thought of avoiding the city when they were so close.

"You are not from here—from the south, downriver? No matter, yes there are a few villages."

Stojan had known the answer, as the zigzag southwest route of small villages was exactly the path he'd taken a few years prior. This would not do either, as the townsfolk would be just as aware of him as the people of Budziszyn. Surely they had been thoroughly questioned about his presence, and no doubt much searching had taken place. Though three years or so had passed it would still be fresh in their minds.

His options were decreasing and it seemed the walls of inevitability were closing in on him. A feeling of futility came upon him. He truly had no options, save for one. And this one option would certainly upset Ana. And from the looks of things Dagmar was none too keen to opt for this as well. Stojan at last spoke.

"We were headed to a city for supplies, but the choice of city was not of concern, just that it would refresh us."

Ana tilted her head, as if weighing the statement for truth.

"And we are in dire need of refreshment," Dagmar countered.

"What do you offer..? For this companionship and protection?"

Stojan and Dagmar were clearly bargaining for both options. Ana thought it a masterful ploy.

"Offer?"

The stranger looked at Dagmar for the first time it seemed. Was it recognition, or something else. Regardless it seemed his demeanor changed considerably, for the better.

"Forgive me. I am Oliwier. I have stopped you fine people and not even introduced myself."

Ana smiled at the pleasantry, so enjoying the interaction with another at last.

"I am Ana!" she exclaimed proudly, not being able to bow she just nodded her head.

Both Dagmar and Stojan took a breath, their mouths moving in slow motion.

"And this is Stojan, and Dagmar!"

The man's eyes smiled, then his mouth.

He but glanced at Stojan but focused mainly on Dagmar.

"Well! A pleasure! Such a polite young lady having the luxury of the protection of two fine men indeed."

Ana looked proud at the recognition, and the ability to take the lead in the conversation. She quite enjoyed the interaction with the stranger, and now felt that her foray into the city was less important. It was just the interaction that she craved—wherever that occurred.

"And I have not answered your question. I would not normally do this, but since you are clearly respectful men I would make it worth your while. A bright young child is not the result of a duo of ne'er-do-wells, so I feel I can trust you."

Ana beamed.

Stojan, ever suspicious, spoke up.
"Well, it is really up to Ana."

"Yes, let's!" Her response almost cut off Stojan's response, so quick was she.

Stojan had gambled, he'd won, and Dagmar had lost.

"Indeed. Thank you, young Ana." He nodded his head to her and smiled.

"I offer to pay for any refreshments needed, as well as a handsome sum for the pleasure of your fine company. To the … cove we go then, fellows… and lady."

With that the three became four, a murderer avoided recognition, a thief delivered himself into the jaws of retribution and a girl started an adventure that would last years.

A NEW STUDENT

The road to the cove had been uneventful, though it contained far more conversation than Stojan would have preferred. Ana was more than willing to volunteer almost any information, but was respectful of her relationship with both Stojan and Dagmar. The latter seemed to be of more interest to Oliwier.

His questions seemed general enough. Stojan felt there was more to this stranger than was revealed, but surprisingly it did not seem that he recognized Stojan's appearance or name. Much energy was focused on trying to determine the desires and knowledge of the man, and in the end Stojan truly believed he had no clue he was in the presence of the assassin.

Dagmar—in spite of his obvious discomfort—spoke at length on his travels, his findings and his abilities.

The stranger was absolutely fascinated with Dagmar's knowledge of the arts, and their night camp between cities consisted of a history lesson—not just for Ana, but for both. He had two eager pupils that night.

"Tell me more of Amira."

Dagmar continued and expanded for his newest pupil, hesitantly at first and then gladly. It was a symbiotic relationship and Oliwier digested as much as he was given.

Even Ana did not realize Dagmar could talk so much.

"The world was indeed turned upside down. There was much turmoil, and the earth itself split. There was upheaval in the truest sense of the word—the very land was torn apart. New rivers were formed; old ones changed their course and some ceased to exist at all."

The stranger continued to listen, munching on some jerky he took from his bag.

"The world as we knew it was no more, and sadly many were gone. Along with them went much knowledge and next to the loss of life perhaps that is the greatest loss."

"What do you mean the world was turned upside down?"

The stranger had asked a question Ana had wanted to for some time. The answer seemed implied but she did not quite understand. She assumed it was a subtlety lost upon her.

"Oh, let me show you."

Dagmar brightened, ran to his bag and rummaged for a while. Ana watched the stranger who showed much interested in what he was about to produce. Or perhaps it was the bag itself he was interested in?

Dagmar returned with a small disk. This he thrust forward, near the fire so the stranger could see it with more light.

"A compass."

"Yes!" said Dagmar excitedly, complimenting his student on his relatively mundane knowledge. Ana knew what a compass was, and wondered why this was such a miracle.

"Look at the needle."

After much jostling the red portion needle came to point at a place slightly to the right of the 'S.'

"And?"

The stranger was just as underwhelmed as Ana.

"And? That is not where it is supposed to point. In fact..."

"It is not pointing to the S. It is pointing to the N. The red is decorative."

"No no! The red, or black on some, was the true indicator."

The stranger scratched his head.

"You are saying it is backwards?"

He did not seem genuinely confused. Perhaps he was patronizing his teacher, as not to discourage him? It seemed that Ana watched both with interest.

"Yes! *Magnetism*. It is a thing of the Earth. And at the time of the second coming it did flip. Completely."

Both Ana and the stranger sat up straight upon hearing this.

"It is thought that perhaps this was the very thing that caused them to come."

Them, thought Ana. It seemed her teacher reserved only the most interesting of history lessons for others.

When Oliwier looked doubtful Dagmar rushed to continue.

"But there is uncertainty, and we do not know if one caused the other, or if it is just another thing that befell the old world. So much happened at once."

Oliwier shook his head as Dagmar withdrew the compass from his face. Ana outstretched her own hand and Dagmar complied. She looked it over closely and smiled, acting like she'd been given a gift. It was a fragile thing and the needle balanced ever so gently upon its rest. She watched it and listened.

"You know much of history, friend Dagmar. You have even taught me a thing or three. Not only do you afford me protection…"

He glanced quickly over at Stojan, who sat quietly.

"…but also companionship and now lessons in history of the old world."

This was of course exactly what Dagmar wanted to hear and much to the chagrin of the others this served to fuel his desire to talk.
"After a time those that constructed compasses just made them with the needle pointed in the wrong direction because they misunderstood which way the main arrow was supposed to point."

Ana looked at Stojan, whose eyes spoke of not wanting to be part of the conversation.

"Tell me Dagmar. You spoke of Amira and their magic…"

"Tec."

"Yes, yes. Do you know much of it? Is it real?"

At this he became very excited.

"Hold. Have you *been* to Amira?!" He had become ecstatic at the prospect.

Ana watched as the briefest of suspicions passed over Dagmar's face only to be replaced with a look of humility.

"Sadly, no. I have yet to travel there."

"Yet? Your ambitions are large! How would you even accomplish such a thing? What would you do there? Where would you go? What would you seek out?"

Ana was certain she saw Stojan roll his eyes, though she knew he would never admit such a thing. The well-to-do merchant seemed like the type that would fund Dagmar and his exploits. Perhaps when the four became three they would instead become two and Dagmar would go off to Amira. Stojan mused about this for a while as the two continued their chatter. How he would get there was another story. He half-listened to the answers that night, thinking most of them—like most of what the self-proclaimed alchemist said—were embellishment. As long as no planning was made at this time he was content to accompany the merchant and Ana to the destination. It was two more days of thinking, and it allowed him to consider the options.

And anything was better than returning to Budziszyn.

SOME QUESTIONS FROM OLIWIER

"Tell me of them."

A new day had arrived and as usual Ana and Stojan had gone off a bit to train. Since the group had more than enough time—thanks to the luxury of a camp between travel—they thought it prudent to take the time to continue their routine.

Dagmar and the visitor were alone and chatted over the morning coffee — a treat introduced to Dagmar by the merchant.

"They are my friends."

Dagmar smiled and composed his words; searching the face of the stranger for any indication as to the reason for his inquiry.

"They are very close—father and daughter. She is a bright girl and always willing to learn. I am very impressed by not only her physical skill but her desire to be a good pupil."

He looked Oliwier in the eyes.

"As are you."

Dagmar smiled his most charming smile, in an attempt to dissuade the stranger from any further questions—questions he did not want to answer since he himself did not know them.

It worked, and it seemed the question was just in passing.

As usual the merchant had an infinite amount of questions about history, Amira and Dagmar's travels—the latter Dagmar found he gave all too freely.

Sometimes he wondered if this man had even better skills of persuasion than he did. If so they were impressively subtle.

—

"What do you think of our new companion?"

Stojan rarely engaged in idle chat while training with Ana, but lately her skill had increased to the level that he hardly had to advise adjustments. This made for some silent times and it seemed that he now filled the silence with questions best posed when they were alone.

She parried his blade easily, and slid it down, stepping to the right with her body. Stojan turned to strike, but did not—seeing her anticipation.

"Excellent."
Ana smiled slightly at the compliment, but concentrated and answered.

"He is interesting, Stojan. He is very interested in Dagmar and cares not for us."

The two backed away from each other, with Stojan suddenly raising his blade to attack. Ana did not move.

"I think I prefer it. I am glad for Dagmar to have another pupil to teach. And I am glad that his pupil seems too eager to listen."

Stojan continued the lesson and moved into standard exercises he used as a base for the training. Not too long ago they represented a challenge to the young girl.

Stojan sheathed his sword—a bit early for the exercise. Were they over already? He walked slowly up to Ana, who kept her blade out.

He smiled, looking quite satisfied.

"It seems that you are much harder to mislead than Dagmar."

Looking both confused and proud she asked, “What do you mean?”

“You kept your blade out.”

“Yes.”

“Did you not think we were done?”

“I was unsure.”

“And in being unsure you thought best to err on the side of being armed and not dropping your guard.”

“Yes?”

He smiled.

“Dagmar drops his guard too easily. He gives up too much. And a sword is only one way to attack, to invade.”

She sheathed her weapon and Stojan immediately grabbed her as if he meant to throw her to the ground. She thought this was the trick, and that she’d failed.

Instead, he hugged her.

She did not smile, but her eyes did as they looked up at his chin.

THE COVE

Stojan considered the distance to the cove in question. Though it was relatively close to the city they had avoided, he hoped there was little interest in him since he'd originally traveled the opposite direction. He was still on alert and was ready at any time to abandon the journey and keep himself and Ana out of harm's way. It was much less effort to avoid a place like that than the city that had made him famous. Recent interactions with strangers and passersby showed there was so far a complete lack of awareness of him. Of the three he was the least interesting to those who would look upon them.

Though he appreciated Dagmar's history lessons and presumably useful knowledge, he was not above parting ways with him if the situation should demand it.

Ana's safety—and his continued anonymity—was tantamount.

What he knew of the cove from years ago was that it was a small city that opened up into a bay.
If what Dagmar had said was to be believed, there were once many vessels that left the cove. It had been a port of call and great sailing vessels came and went daily. People were able to travel for days in the ships that were not made of wood but of metal. Yet they floated. According to Dagmar the old world had been filled with such vehicles. Conveyance was to be had of all types, and what would be considered a caravan now was merely a personal conveyance for the average inhabitant of the old world.

This was still easier to believe than the machines that painted lines in the sky. Hundreds if not thousands every day would be seen.

Stojan much preferred a sky filled with clouds, rather than lines.

Considering that his initial route had been to the southwest, perhaps this new direction would offer less of a chance to be discovered. His map, like most, was fairly crude. He knew the sea was to the north, but what else was beyond was in question. And the mythical land of Amira was out there, but he knew not which direction.

Dagmar and their new companion covered much ground when they spoke. Just last night he'd explained in detail why the maps were so crude.

"Most maps were inaccurate because the very lands had changed shape. Some borders were no longer valid. Whole countries fell. And not many maps were written down, but instead recorded in a special fashion that was easily lost."

Dagmar's methods of communication were dramatic.

Stojan thought about the conversation and where he was in the world, in many ways.

Everything he cared about was lost just a few years ago, and he found himself confusingly caring again. Everything he cared about now traveled with him. Direction was meaningless. Home was wherever they were at the moment.

The road to the cove was uneventful, and their speed was lackadaisical. This slow pace was enjoyed by all but Stojan, who was used to traveling as fast as possible when he had a destination. He'd had ample time to ride and think, and having a purpose served him well. A goal hardened his will. His group was doing the opposite, and this seemed to be at the behest of their employer. He would periodically stop and look at flowers, or ask a question of Dagmar, or proclaim he or his horse was tired.

It gave Ana a chance to run in a field, but having no such desire to run or participate in the exhausting talks Stojan was left to muse, to consider and to observe. It was his observations that were starting to unnerve him.

Oliwier watched Anastazja dismount and run into the surrounding field. They were among particularly high grass. Stojan had protested that the location was not ideal to stop but the merchant had joked that there was nothing that would suddenly jump out and that the road was quite visible.

"She… runs off?"

He asked Dagmar and Stojan, looking concerned and almost irritated.

Ana's direction was perpendicular to the road and in seconds she was gone, consumed by the high grass.

"Errr…"

Clearly unnerved he searched the faces of both men, who seemed nonplussed. Seeing that he was making no progress, his face and conversation changed course abruptly. With a big smile he turned to Dagmar.

"I must say, friend Dagmar, your knowledge is as complete as one could imagine. I'd say I have gotten quite a bargain in enlisting your help."

"Tis nothing but the accumulation from many years. I cannot help but seek it out."

"I understand you, some interests become desire; desires become quests and quests become obsessions."

This accurate statement affected Dagmar visibly. He felt a bit exposed now, and the stranger had picked up on something very deep. It was true that he was obsessed with the old world, and Amira. An obsession was a proper description as his judgement had been clouded by this pursuit.

The stranger winked.

"We all have likes and dislikes, interests and obsessions."

His charming smile put Dagmar at ease, externally. Internally he still felt like he had revealed too much about his personality. It had been an exhausting two days.

In a short while Ana appeared as abruptly as she had left, smiled at Stojan and mounted her horse.

The rest of the journey saw a much quieter student and pupil. The majority of the conversation was had by Stojan and Ana, who rode behind the two men as they made their way two-by-two.

"I am not sure if your daily hike is advised while we travel."

Ana's eyebrows raised slightly as Stojan continued.

"It is one thing to walk when we are at camp and have surveyed the environment. It is another thing to do so as we travel."

She nodded slightly, her expression uncharacteristically unreadable.

"We have not surveyed the surrounding area and we have encountered much…"

He struggled with his next word; something he rarely did. She let him pause then answered for him.

"I understand."

Her response was solemn but Stojan thought he detected something other than disappointment. After all it was just a day or so until they were back to establishing a camp, or even staying in a city for a bit.

But she was clearly excited, and keeping a secret. It looked as if she would reveal it at any time, but her eyes darted forward to the men in front of them. Apparently it was only for Stojan.

He'd ask her in due time.

——

The cove was unremarkable save for one thing.

The water.

Of the four travelers Anastazja was the only one who had never seen a lake—inland or otherwise. What she was seeing this day was the edge of an ocean, or was it a sea? There was much confusion from Dagmar's description. Though he affirmed again and again that he'd never seen this cove, his learnings had taught him all about it and the sea.

He explained with enthusiasm that a great sea existed there, and that it opened into the ocean—the very ocean that separated Poliska from

Amira. He could not quite explain the difference between an 'ocean' and a 'sea' except that the sea was a smaller version of the former. And, with all the changes in the landscape he was not sure of just what was out there.

"No one is, really," was his response.

To Ana it was the most amazing thing she had ever seen. The color was that of the sky, but deeper blues with more depth. And, it did something the sky did not; it sparkled. Their vantage point as they approached was from a higher land so much to her enjoyment it revealed a massive amount of water—going on as far as the eye could see. Even Stojan was impressed and looked hard at it.

"I want to go!"

Stojan smiled at her request and nodded—he would happily comply later once all was settled. Perhaps a tour of the shore would brighten the spirit further. He did not know if Ana could swim. He would have to keep an eye on her near the water.
"We arrive" was all the merchant said. Rather than looking relieved at the end of a journey he looked troubled. Perhaps he was considering the business he'd have to take care of.

Indeed he was.

Stojan was not sure what he was enjoying more—the vivid scenery of the sea or the expression on Anastazja's face.

The cove was a collection of buildings along a path that lead to the shore in a winding fashion. Much like a frontier town it looked recently established. The path eventually lead to the water and then wound back —like a great snake that desires to visit the water but then decides it is best to stay dry.

The majority of the buildings were small and one story with the only exception being one with much overgrowth at the edge of the shore.

The group rode in with no welcome, no gates and no ceremony. It was a very open area and understandably relatively deserted. Other than scenery and some fishing, a cove like this was for the most part a dead end.

After all, sea travel was very limited. To the north it just became colder and colder, according to Dagmar.

“Please, let us retire and rest.”

Oliwier pointed with his thick fingers to a building almost right next to the large building. Between them was what looked like an abandoned smaller building.

“There I can provide compensation as promised.”

The four rode to the destination down the path. People milled about, with most looking like hired hands. It seemed the those that lived here did so because the job provided lodging. There were fishermen but their scarcity meant the food they caught was minimal and not meant for trade. Others seemed to be workers of some sort, though Ana could not determine what they did exactly. None seemed particularly friendly and everyone had somewhere to go. It was a skeleton crew of people, and none looked happy.

Tying the horses the four entered the building in question. Though unremarkable on the outside, the inside had qualities like an Inn, though it only had but a few tables. No doubt the building had been taken over and repurposed—something that was not uncommon.

“Please please sit.”

The group complied and much waving was done to bring over drinks and food, this was gladly accepted by the group. For Ana it seemed like the first time she’d had home cooked food in ages.

Stojan was surprisingly good at cooking on the road, and Dagmar’s input had helped as he was also an above par cook in his own right. Still, this was a meal that she could sit down for—on an actual bench—and eat. She didn’t have to kill it first. She enjoyed the luxury while she pondered the thoughts she kept to herself for some time now.

“So what will you do?” Their host tapped Dagmar’s sleeve with his balled up fist, wet with the gravies of their meal.

“Perhaps you should stay here, for the night and decide in the morning? I would include lodgings as part of payment.”

He smiled at Dagmar, as Ana shook her head ever so slightly at Stojan, doing so in such a way that neither Dagmar nor the merchant noticed.

Stojan was enjoying her new found silent communication. What had spurred it on was something he had yet to discover.

"I think we will have to move on."

Stojan seemed to answer for the three of them and Dagmar did not disagree.

Oliwier was crestfallen, however.

"No? Not just one night? Rest for you, your horses. Ana—"

He gestured towards her.

"You can spend more time at the water, even a swim?"

He smiled his charming smile once again. The more his charm increased the less Stojan trusted him.

"What about you Dagmar? If your companions cannot stay perhaps you can."

He nudged his sleeve again with his fat fist.

"There is still so much to learn from you."

Stojan had said his peace and regardless of what was offered he and Ana would leave. Because of this, he was only peripherally involved in the conversation, leaving more focus for other things.
This focus lead him to notice Ana behaving rather nervously, and looking over her shoulder. To her credit it was subtle, but Stojan saw it as an alarm of sorts.

Something was wrong.

Stojan stood up.

Ana stood up.

Oliwier seemed unaffected and did not even look up, but instead said, "Friends, sit down."

Dagmar looked at Stojan, then Ana, then the four men blocking the door. He watched as Ana nodded to Stojan.

“What? What is happening?” Dagmar asked no one and everyone all at once.

The merchant continued to talk, not looking up, but instead still looking over at Dagmar, who sat next to him. He had a habit of looking at Dagmar’s chest, or arm, or side, but never his eyes.

“I said sit down!”

His voice was raised, but not by much, as if he was trying to keep it down a bit.

Neither Ana nor Stojan complied as Dagmar himself sat up, ready to stand at any moment. The merchant’s balled fist turned into a grip as he grabbed Dagmar’s sleeve with his fat thumb and index finger, still not looking Dagmar in the eyes. His demeanor had intensified and he seemed almost drunk.

“Tell me, friend Dagmar… tell me more about Amira.”

Stojan and Ana exchanged glances.

“How was it again you know so much about it?”

He smiled a pained look.

“Tell me more of… the turmoil, how things changed, so many many years again?”

It was a taunt.

“Sit… *DOWN.*”

His eyes finally looked up at Stojan—the eyes of someone completely different than the merchant. These were the eyes of a corrupt man, a man who was tired, and frustrated.

“No one is leaving. You are greatly outnumbered.”

Stojan seemed to be calmed by that statement, while Ana remained alert.

“Tell me Dagmar. Tell me about Amira.”

He said each word slowly, independently as if they just happened to be next to each other, forming a sentence.

Stojan noted he was carrying two conversations; one with he and Ana, and one with Dagmar. His eyes were mostly closed.

"Well, I…" Dagmar stumbled for words, looking trapped, and afraid.

"What did it look like, Dagmar?" He still gripped his sleeve, and it was now soaked with the food and gravy of the meal, his grasp relentless. "What did it *look* like?"

With this he looked into Dagmar's eyes for the first time. He looked deeply, searching.

All four eyes went wide.

"You saw it didn't you? Yes…"

His eyes widened even further.

"So it is you."

Dagmar looked down at his sleeve, the grip even tighter now, his arm was pinched and it was now painful as the man continued to tighten.

"I wasn't sure. Even when the girl said your name."

He looked at his arm, again.

"Why did you think you could do this, Dagmar? Why did you think you could steal from not only me, but *them*?"

Dagmar could not hide the terror in his face—most of the color having drained from it.

Suddenly a hand was placed upon the merchant's shoulder.

"If your men exit immediately they will be allowed to keep their lives."

Completely unaffected by the threat, the merchant continued speaking.

"Tell your hired sword to take his hand from me and he and his daughter might be allowed to leave."

"You don't know who I am?"

Stojan was genuinely surprised.

The fat merchant took a loud breath.

"I do not care who you are. You are surrounded, and have found yourself in the midst of something not of your concern. I don't fault you for your association. Your employer is staying with me."

He turned his head to Stojan, but did not look into his eyes, instead looking at the hand on his shoulder.

"Take your hand off of me, and I will tell my men to allow you and your daughter to leave."

Ana watched, and was confused by the surprise in Stojan's face. He was not afraid, he had no fear, but he was genuinely surprised at something—almost disappointed. His brows were together slightly. She was however, starting to feel angry. Dagmar was being treated like a criminal, and her first foray into a city of some kind was met with this mistreatment.

Stojan did take his hand off of the merchant and away from the three to confront the four men at the door.

Walking directly up to them he looked each in the eye. His sword was sheathed and his demeanor was not aggressive, yet the men were affected by his visitation.

One of the men started to open his mouth, and then closed it.

It was not Stojan's stance or what he said. Instead it was the absolute calm with which he walked up to them, and looked each and every one of them in the face. He looked into their eyes carefully, each and every one of them.

He was looking for something and did not find it.

It unnerved them—this tall man clearly trained as a mercenary himself—moving in such an unorthodox manner, the way he reviewed them as if he was their leader. The way he searched their faces for… something. This man had no fear whatsoever. It was most unexpected.

Was it some sort of intimidation tactic? The result was four men frozen in place, with one of their captures walking freely about as if it was his room. So certain and confident was he in his movements—it was beyond confidence. It was a nonchalantness that was unnerving. Their concern was the man with their leader. They knew a little of him, what he had done and what they were to do to retrieve him. This other man was unknown. He appeared to be a mercenary himself, but traveled with his daughter who was similarly dressed, complete with a miniature sword. Perhaps royalty? One of the men raised his eyebrows, intimidated at the thought.

At that point Stojan could have easily just exited the building. Or sat down. Or ordered a drink—had the only bartender not swiftly run out the door when the men arrived.

Ana's head was swimming with confusion as she watched.

Stojan walked back to Ana at the table, and all eyes were upon him—even the merchant. He sat down and shook his head.
"So curious."

The merchant released his grip slowly from Dagmar, as he looked over at his men. More than one of them shrugged—an action that detracted from their threatening presentation.

He looked back at Stojan, and squinted.

"You and your daughter are free to go."

Stojan sat up from his casual relaxed stance.

"Well, yes, of course we are."

The merchant's brows started to come together.

"Once we receive payment as promised of course."

Dagmar realized that Stojan's smile was more threatening than his usual stoic expression, and couldn't help feeling grateful for currently being in his good graces. He looked over at the merchant for a reaction.

"You push your luck, and the saints are in the details friend."

Ana looked at the men, their sheathed weapons, their stances. It was just as Stojan had described in the past. Though they had tried to look menacing she knew it would take too much time to draw their swords. The close grouping would make it difficult for them to swing their swords properly. She imagined a battle in the room, and was quite excited at her own imagination. She pictured some of the men threatening her, and her drawing her sword. She even imagined defending Stojan from the merchant's attack. The thought of Stojan being hurt by the brutes made her tense up slightly.

"On second thought, you are right. We will leave."

With that he rose, and tapping Dagmar on the shoulder said, "I'm sure you are in good hands, Dagmar, perhaps we will meet again."

Ana looked mildly shocked as her eyes met with Dagmar's. Only one man stood in front of the door and this was due to his slow nature, not his desire to challenge them. As they walked up to him, he looked down at Ana. She looked back, ready to do battle if necessary.

His eyes fell upon her hair.

"How did you do that…?"

Instead of moving he dumbly stood there looking confused and fascinated.

The other men turned.

The delicate blonde colors—ambers, golds and the like—looked like they had been dipped in bright red ink.

"It wasn't…"

"What? How?"

Each man quietly exclaimed their own confusion.

"Hold on…"

It was the merchant, seeing the spectacle from his table.

"Come back… Stop…"

It was too late. Stojan, having been in the doorway, already had his sword out and under the chin of the man that was partially blocking the door. It was certain he also felt a sharp pain in his side. He had him from behind.

Ana now had her sword out and stood with her back to the pair, surveying the other three men.

It looked like they now had a hostage too.

The merchant's eyes went wide. They darted from the scene to Dagmar, who looked even more cornered than before, his curly hair in his eyes now.

"This is not good. Oh Dagmar."

"Release him!"

It was Ana. She yelled to the merchant.

"Oh Dagmar." He repeated and shook his head, a wild recognition in his eyes. Satisfaction, then disappointment.

"You used it. And you used it on a child. That was dangerous."

He closed his eyes, still shaking his head.

"This will not bode well for you. You can not return it now, can you?"

He looked at Ana, sword still outstretched, anger still in her eyes.

"Under what circumstances did you do this? This is so unlike you, so I have heard."

The other three men had their hands on their respective grips, but did not draw their weapons.

Ana and Stojan remained in place, with their captor standing now on his tip-toes to release some of the pressure under his chin. It did not work.

Dagmar looked at Ana and she shifted her eyes slightly to his. With that Dagmar's head tilted and he smiled a sad smile, his memory filled with the events of the day of the bridge.

With his head still facing Ana, his eyes panned to focus on the merchant, eyebrows forming a slight tent. For the first time he looked defiant.

"I did what was needed, and what was right."

The merchant narrowed his eyes.

"For once. It cannot be undone. And you have nothing to retrieve now so you…"

"Oh but we do."

Stojan rotated to point his captor at an angle, allowing him not to be taken from behind. Clearly he'd heard the additional men approaching.

There were many.

The merchant motioned to one of the three men, who came to his table.

"Make sure we take their saddle bags with us. We can sort through it all on the way," he seemed to say to all of his men at once.

Stojan's dagger seemed to bite a little harder in the man's side and he yelped a confirmation.

The merchant finally stood up, as his henchman put a hand on Dagmar's shoulder, saying, "Don't move."

"You are completely surrounded. Eh, this is not going to happen. The whole city works for me. Put your weapon away and let him go."

Stojan's hostage looked unconvinced of the stated outcome.

The merchant continued, speaking in even tones.

"As I said you press your luck. You can kill him but we will still take you."

Ana glanced back at Stojan momentarily and seeing the look on his face immediately turned back, and for a second she closed her eyes. She knew what was to happen.

The yell the man made as Stojan simultaneously slit his throat and stabbed his innards was quiet and unassuming, but it was a signal for Ana to attack.

The man was tossed aside as Stojan handled the men blocking the exit, accumulating outside.

Ana—sword already out—jumped and lunged at the closest man. His sword still in the scabbard he instinctively blocked with his forearm. His clothing was not sufficient to stop the unusually strong blow, which partially severed his forearm.

As the body segment swung sickeningly her follow-through and spin had taken him under the chin and she split his jaw in two.

He slowly reached for his face as he collapsed—shock and disbelief racking his entire body.

The other man near her had his sword barely out as some of his attention had been on the unexpected dismemberment. She looked him in the eyes and ran him through the chest. Both his hands went for her sword, gripping the sharp surface in an instinctive move to stop it.

She let go of it and shoved him to the ground, her palms striking him in the chest, on either side of the hilt protruding from it.

Stojan was busy slicing, parrying and chopping. He made much use of the bottleneck the large doorway presented. The same method worked for each who pushed their way in, one after another.

The merchant had backed away a bit, and he pointed wildly at the henchmen holding Dagmar in place, shaking his slightly curled index finger. Dagmar looked at him and then his captor and launched unceremoniously forward, crashing through chairs to rest under a table temporarily. Like a giant frog he leapt, skittering like a frightened animal.

The merchant screamed "Uggh!" as the henchmen went after Dagmar.

Having pulled her sword from the man she'd dispatched, Anastazja swung at the henchman, who angrily parried the attack. His arm moved back, almost causing his own sword to touch his face.

The fierceness of the attack and strength behind him was not expected from one so young. Though she was of above average height for her age she was still just a child.

Again she attacked, in a combination of moves. This one was clearly trained, and knew not only skill but strategy.

He swung and she cut him in the stomach, his hardened leather only partially blocking the deep cut.

He backed away a step or so, dropped his sword and put his palms up. It clanged onto the floor—mere inches from the crouching Dagmar.

"I yield! I yield."

Thoughts of cowardice and chiding took a secondary position to thoughts of staying alive. His attacker's hair was now all bright red, her blue eyes were fiery with the passion of battle. He looked at her incredulously, shaking his head slightly. She was like an animal, but a skilled, controlled, highly trained animal. And her hair was bewildering.

Relatively new, he knew nothing of what went on at the cove, save for the fact that the men were paid well and sworn to secrecy—a position he had not yet earned in the ranks.

She outstretched her sword and yelled "get up!"

Dagmar was already crawling out from under the table, leaving the relative safety.

He looked over at the merchant in the corner of the room and drew his own sword. It was almost the same size as Ana's. The heavy man put up his hands instinctively and did not move, valuing the distance between him and the attackers. He looked upon Ana's hair with fascination and appreciation.

Bodies had piled up in the doorway and that caused Stojan to back up a bit, allowing the attackers even more opportunity to expose themselves upon entry.

In a short time they no longer entered, but accumulated outside.

Sensing that he had a bit more time now, he looked back at Ana for the first time—his quick glance catching both the captured man and those she had dispatched.

"I will kill you all."

This he said to the doorway, not loud enough for the potential attackers to hear.

It wasn't a threat, it was a promise and a prediction. He knew what he was about to do, and not since his dream had he fought so many.

And this was the second battle he'd waged with Ana. Their daily challenges and constant training had produced an excellent outcome.

His only concern was if she was ready for an actual fight again, or if she had only just increased her skill without the heart for an actual battle. After all, she was so young. It did not seem right to him for someone so young to take a life. But that paled in comparison to that life being Ana's. With that in mind he had so effectively, tirelessly and thoroughly trained her. Ana's desire to learn, and his enjoyment for teaching her had made it almost effortless.
"Sit down," Ana said to the man she kept at bay. Both he and Dagmar complied, simultaneously. The man wasn't the only one intimidated.

Dagmar's eyes went from Stojan to the merchant, who still stood with his hands up.

"What now, Stojan?"

Ana yelled, awaiting instructions. Her blade dripped and it bothered her. She was getting used to the sights of battle, but the fluids and parts of others on her blade was something she could not stand, or stomach.

Stojan backed up further, slowly. His head whipped around to the merchant, then to Ana, then to the men still gathering at the door but not entering.

"Oliwier!"

One man experimentally yelled into the inn, seeing Stojan retreat.

Stojan's head whipping back again he yelled to Dagmar, "Bring him to Ana and do not get yourself captured again."

Dagmar drew his blade again and corralled the heavier man over to where Ana held the man at bay. He searched his trousers and his belt and brought up a small dagger.

The merchant walked slowly and looked at her hair the entire way.

“Remarkable. Saints be praised,” he said under his breath.

Dagmar wrinkled his nose, having heard the words.

Stojan backed all the way in and came to join Ana, Dagmar and the would be captor. The merchant and his men were now outnumbered.

The men outside remained.

“Oliwier! Do you yet live?”

Stojan shook his head at the merchant, and placed his long index finger upon his lips.

They were far enough away from the door that the existing men could not see in properly—their eyes being adjusted to the bright sunlight outside and not the darker area within.

“How many are out there? I will know if you lie to me.”

The merchant thought for a moment and said, “As many as 50 more men.”

He thought of adding a comment about his captors not being able to make it out alive, but thought better of it. If he was going to survive it would be because of his prudence, not lack thereof.

Stojan appeared to accept this answer as the truth.

“How do we leave here when there is only one exit?”

Ana’s question made both Dagmar and the merchant trade a fleeting glance.

“Speak!”

Stojan yelled at both men at once.

A MOST PECULIAR STORAGE

"I… there is a back door to the inn."

"Why have they not tried to take us that way then?"

"Because it is… unknown. A secret entrance."

Stojan looked at the man, with very little patience left. His frightened henchman looked at him with some confusion as well.

"You misunderstand my question. I mean to ask about a road out of town. You have but one entrance, and it is visible for a great distance. Surely you know this and use it to your advantage?"

He shifted his weight, and it almost looked to Dagmar that he was going to strike the merchant if the answer was not to his liking.

"You and your men can see someone coming. They saw all of us coming. They knew of the visit before we were even here."

Ana nodded, then chimed in.

"Because we were followed."

The merchant looked at her with surprise.

"How can… how did you know that?"

"I saw them."

"Your time alone, eh?"

"Yes."

Stojan looked at her, realizing this was the secret she held. It would not have done much good knowing they were followed, as he had his suspicions about the little man from the beginning. His only frustration was being cornered like this.

The small cove had a very defensible entrance, and no one was going to approach from the water save for the small fishing boats that went out a short distance and returned. Stojan had an idea.

"The shore—the fishing boats…"

"Yes?"

"Is there an island nearby, another cove perhaps, and entrance to a river other than the Vistula?"

Dagmar seemed to clam up and the Merchant quickly shook his head.

"No, no. If you are thinking of escaping by boat that will not work."

He glanced at Dagmar who looked at the floor.

"There is no island or landing nearby. If you try to escape by boat you will be tracked and eventually come back to land. That or be swallowed by the sea. It is quite large."

The merchant had been unusually helpful, but perhaps was attempting to instill a sense of futility, causing Stojan to surrender.

"Then that is that."

Stojan thought about reinforcements, the food they had within, and word spreading to nearby Budziszyn about his location. Soon they would come for him. The butcher had at last made a mistake and was now cornered.

And Ana would be free to flounder on her own.

Assuming they were not all killed first.

Still, boarding a small fishing boat had promise. If they could make it out some distance—disappear on the horizon, then double back to find the inlet for a river, or even somehow make it back to shore undetected.

They would not have their horses. The fishing boats looked small, with only room for the three of them and not much more.

Stojan looked at Ana—her hair almost completely back to the natural blonde coloration. He had failed her.

"There is another way," said a quiet voice.
It was Dagmar, looking at the floor.

"If we can make it to the large building undetected."

The merchant started to protest but Ana's blade swung near his face immediately silenced him.

"What good would that do?" asked Stojan.

"There is a place to hide—an underground shelter."

"You can't begin to under…"

Again Ana's blade shook and silenced the protest of the merchant. It dripped.

He looked tired and defeated.

"A hiding place? What then?" asked Stojan.

"Yes, a place of hiding, armored to the above ground, known only to me…" replied Dagmar.

He looked at the merchant.

"And Oliwier."

Dagmar immediately shook his head.

"No no, Stojan. We do not know each other. I have… been here before."

“Without his knowledge?”

Stojan pointed his sword at the merchant—who was unusually quiet now —looking for confirmation.

“He seemed to know you though.”

“*Of* me.”

Stojan looked at Ana, then to the merchant. He pointed towards the back of the building.

“The men will eventually become brave enough and enter again. You. You say that no one knows of this entrance?”

“Only me,” replied the merchant.

Stojan grabbed the merchant by the shoulder and sheathed his sword. In its place he held his dagger and placed it into the man’s side, motivating him to move quickly.

“Go, show us, quickly.”

He eyed the man that had surrendered, who still stood among them.

“You value your life?”

The man nodded quickly, brightening slightly to what was to come.

“If you do then you will stay here as long as you can. When the others eventually enter you will do your best to convince them we are in there.”

Ana looked at Stojan—surprised at his trust and generosity. Still, the man had been the only one to surrender, and looked like the work he signed up for was not to his liking.

The merchant pointed to what was probably a kitchen.

“You will tell them we just moved to that room and will kill him so they should be very careful.”

The frightened man nodded vigorously.

He looked hard at the man, as if to transfer his threat to him.

Pushing the merchant in the general direction of the back of the makeshift inn, he glanced back one more time at the doorway.

The merchant was pushed and eventually did the leading. They did go to the kitchen, and then to a pantry stocked with foodstuff. At the very back was a thin door that was pushed out of place. It reminded Stojan very much of the one in Ana's pantry. Perhaps this was a common place for secret entrances and the like.

Just before they exited Stojan violently withheld the man, placing a brake upon his body so he could go no further. He stopped and yelped slightly.

"I warn you: not a sound. I will run you through the very instant you make a sound above your fat, heavy breathing. And no tricks. Do not drop anything, or kick something or…"

"Yes. I understand. That is… painful."

They peered out slowly. The alleyway was cramped and dark and smelled of garbage.

The four were able to make their way out, with Dagmar doing his best to seal the door from the outside, lest they discover the means of escape all too quickly.

Stojan froze, and so did the others.

They could hear the men talking. There was some sort of argument going on at the front of the building. It would be only a minute until they braved the entrance.

They continued, and winding around the back of a building, they slowly slinked into position on the far side of the large structure.

Entering an oddly shaped door they walked in.

It was an indoor pool of some kind. Dagmar closed the door behind him and very little light entered.

Though it was dark Ana could tell from the echoes of their steps that it was a very large hollow building. They walked towards the great rectangular pool, towards the top of a tower—jutting forth from the side of it.

Ana squinted and marveled at both the size and perfection of it. It was truly a rectangle, almost perfect in shape. And it was as if carved from one giant block of stone. In fact it looked like the entire foundation of the building was smooth stone and this had been perfectly excavated from it.

The tower coming from the side was dark, and looked like it was made of metal.

There were rungs on it, to aide in climbing.

Just then she was afraid.

“We are not descending into water?!” Though she whispered, the question was obviously filled with concern.

“Can we not just hide in here? There’s no reason to go into the pool.”

As they walked up to it she could see in the semi-darkness that the water moved, slowly. It lapped gently back and forth, as if the pool was connected to the lake outside of the building.

The pool clearly ended before the building did, so it made no sense.

Dagmar whispered back, while looking at the merchant.

“The safe area is below. Do not worry no water will get in. We will be safe in there. We will be completely dry.”

“But why is it in the pool? Is food stored in there?”

From what Dagmar had been teaching her Ana thought perhaps the coolness of the water—in combination with metal—would keep food cooler and preserve it far longer than a pantry. She seemed satisfied with the thought.

“Yes. There is food in there.”

Again he looked at the merchant when he spoke.

While the others stopped at the edge of the pool Dagmar walked onto what looked like an attached pier.

A small protrusion had a rounded door on one side. Instead of a doorknob or rung, it had a large ring in the center.

He was able to grab a great ring and turn it. He grunted, and eventually the door swung open, like the cover of a trap door. But this was rounded on the top and bottom, made entirely of metal, and looked very heavy—almost too heavy for Dagmar.

Stojan watched with interest, and Dagmar wasted no time descending and disappearing down the stairs.

Stojan prodded the merchant to go next, knowing that Dagmar waited below. Then Ana and finally he descended. Looking down, then out again, he descended the stairs as well. They made a distinct metallic clink sound when his feet hit each stair. The steps were not whole but had slats in them.

The smell was unlike anything he'd ever experienced—so devoid of life. It was like an old crate had been opened up after many years of storage, though it was not musty here.

When he came to the bottom of the stairs Dagmar ran past him back up the stairs. Confused, Stojan started to ask why he'd run back, only to see that he was sealing the door, tightly.

To his surprise he could still see in the cramped room.

Rectangles hung from the ceiling on the sides of the room, and looked as if they were covered in a soft material. Some of the material had holes and a spongy substance of yellow color was within.

He now smelled other foreign scents. Some were slightly foul, others were unnatural or that of a pungent flower or mushroom patch.

The barely visible light came from candles on the ceiling, wrapped in metal rings.

The candles did not flicker.

Ana was fascinated.

All eyes were on the interior. The cramped space went on farther to another rounded door that was swung open outward to another room.

"Come, let us sit down and rest."

Dagmar lead the way, with Stojan once again holding the merchant. He was wary of him escaping, even with a great iron door in his way.

Everything was made of metal and more than once Ana almost knocked her head into a protrusion. Though she found the storage area quite impressive, the close, unfriendly quarters made her uncomfortable.

They passed through another room, then another, with all of them being lit by the flicker-free candles.

Stojan wondered how long it would be until they required fresh air as the door seal seemed exceptionally tight. Though it was dank in the rooms, it was not oppressively so.

"Here, we can sit."

The room they were now in housed four tables and benches. Again, everything was made of metal—not one thing seemed to be made of wood. Everything was of a silver sheen or darker color, but all was of metal. Every so often Stojan saw a sign, but the letters seemed to be jumbled up, and some were just unrecognizable.

This was more than storage.

They sat at the benches, and Dagmar seemed to visibly relax. He got up and walked to a cabinet, removing an item to bring to the table.

It was a bottle of wine.

He smiled. Stojan did not.

"This is not a time to celebrate."

The merchant reached slowly for it saying, "Oh let me…"

He bumped it, hard, throwing it into Dagmar's lap, but not before he was able to bolt from the room into an as yet unexplored area.

Stojan looked at Dagmar, as if to question him on whether they should even be concerned.

Dagmar shook his head and picked up the bottle.

"There is but one exit."

Then his eyes went wide.

"That I know of."

Stojan's face showed his resentment and he almost hit his head standing quickly.

Then they heard it.

It was a sound that shook the whole building, and it was unlike anything they'd ever heard. It resonated.

"We quake."

Ana held onto the table, which seemed to be fastened tightly to the floor, like everything else.

Stojan looked at Dagmar, who now seemed to realize what was happening.

The group ran into the next chamber, ever careful not to hit their heads—especially the tallest of them.

What they saw astounded them.

A room of lights. The walls had protrusions and chairs. And the walls glittered—as if hundreds of fireflies had alighted and were all communicating with each other feverishly. The lights were of many colors and the sight made Ana gasp.

In the center of the room near a wall was the merchant. He had a look on his face that was both satisfied and challenging.

The room continued to quake.

"The walls hum… Stojan?"

Ana was at once amazed and confused. Stojan saw that there was not another exit, so he stood his ground patiently, waiting for Dagmar to explain. The merchant wasn't going anywhere.

"What did you do?"

He asked the merchant.

“It is done, and cannot be undone.”

“What… what is this?”

“It is more than storage Dagmar.”

Stojan was unaffected, and watched the lights. Some had a certain pattern to them, and he was absentmindedly trying to figure out which lights turned on when. It reminded him of the display of candles the bishop had a few months back. Perhaps this was also some sort of prayer area as well.

Stojan was more interested in what this dead end of the storage area was than what the merchant had done. It seemed that Dagmar was very concerned about something.

Then it felt as if the building had shifted. It lurched and Stojan had to take a step back. The humming continued and he thought he heard the sounds of birds coming from the dead end room—not exactly tweets, but something like it. Some were deeper sounds.

“I told you I cannot undo it. You will have to wait.”

The merchant and Dagmar were still arguing, with the latter looking more and more concerned.

“What has happened? Are we in danger?”

The merchant smiled wryly.

“Let us just say that you will want to make yourselves at home here. You will want to rest. I will have no plans of escaping. Let me warn you not to try to open any door for a while.”

Stojan looked at Dagmar, then the merchant as he finished.

“That would be a very bad idea.”

He smiled as Dagmar looked over at Stojan, who opened his mouth to speak.

“A trap.”

The shorter man nodded, his body lit up with the numerous flickering lights in the dim room.

"Yes. Our roles are reversed now."

"What is all this, Dagmar?"

Ana sounded frightened and spoke at last.

Oliwier—looking smug now—turned to her.

"I will give you a tour, all of you. Relax. Please."

He spread his hands.

Stojan stepped out of the room, and walked all the way back to the entrance of the storage area.

As he approached the stairs he noticed another door closed at the bottom. It had been previously open. Next to it on the wall was a lantern, round in shape with thin rings around it. It glowed a menacing red and lit up much of the hallway.

"I would not touch that!"

It was the merchant, yelling down the hallway, his voice was almost swallowed up by the chambers.

The three arrived and the merchant in very serious tones addressed Stojan.

"We are under the water now—under the very sea. If you open that door and then the next we will be flooded with seawater and then drown. No, we are no longer in the dock."

Stojan listened and as much as he wanted this to be a lie it seemed the merchant was speaking the truth.

"We travel by a means quite common in the old world."

"Travel?" Ana said quietly to herself.

"And we will reach our destination in about six days."

"Six days? Destination? You mean we are moving within the sea? And we will do so for a week? How will we breathe? What will we eat and where will we relieve ourselves?”

“It is an underwater ship,” Dagmar said with fascination.

“Then who steers this ship?” Stojan’s new questions surfaced as fast as the old ones were answered.

“No one. It steers itself. It is all I know of it. And again, it cannot be stopped.”

The merchant turned to Dagmar.

“It is an automatic machine—a means of conveyance. It steers itself quite safely, as far as I know. There is nothing to do but wait until it reaches its destination.”

Dagmar said nothing, a look of awe coming over him. Stojan did not share his wonder and asked, “And what is this destination?”

Without taking his eyes off of Dagmar he answered Stojan quite triumphantly.

“Amira.”

A NEW JOURNEY

When it became clear that indeed it would not only be a bad but deadly idea to attempt to open the sealed doors, Stojan became calm, as did the others. They were truly moving at a very rapid pace, twisting and turning, presumably—all done automatically by the metal vessel. The merchant seemed very willing to explain as much as he knew, which was actually very little. All he seemed to know was that the vehicle was from the old world, had a means to power it that he did not understand, and had been adjusted in such a way that he could press a few controls to send it on its journey. It traveled that way—to and fro—from Poliska to Amira.

The merchant had been present on but a few journeys, and had become quite frightened on his first journey. Six days was a very long time to be trapped in a metal can the size of a house, under the water so far down as to cause instant death to anyone who exited it.

On one journey he thought he had run out of air. On another he yearned to see the sky and wondered what time of day it was. He was alone and he feared losing his mind.

Once he had an urge to try some of the controls in the room with the lights, but thought better of it as he had been explicitly warned. All he was to do was set the controls in the way he was shown after making sure the vehicle was sealed in the proper manner.

The next few days the group ate food that was stored in a kitchen pantry—most of it was quite tasty but some was unfamiliar.

Ana found the lavatories to be what she liked the most. They were simple and like everything else, made of metal. Though the seat was cold she was happy to oblige and all she had to do was turn one knob, then another.

It was all very civilized and quite the contrast to her nomadic ways of late.

Though Stojan's lessons with her were all but impossible due to the close quarters, Dagmar's lessons continued, with two additional pupils.

The merchant admitted that he had played somewhat ignorant to coerce Dagmar into revealing as much as he could to him. However, Dagmar did indeed have some knowledge that was valuable, and the merchant listened along with Ana. Stojan had a way of looking disinterested while listening intently.

When Stojan became restless on the second day the merchant revealed a special pole that descended from the ceiling. It had a rectangular soft area, with a window on it. Two handles snapped down and allowed him to rotate it about.

When Stojan pressed his head to it—which he was only willing to do with others in the room, lest it be a trick—he was able to see dimly lit water.

The merchant explained that they were too deep in the sea, but that on the last day they could look into it again and actually see the surface.

Time was an issue for Stojan, and the others. Without the setting and rising of the sun they were becoming disoriented and irritable. There were no windows.

Much theory and conjecture was had about the conveyance, between Dagmar and the merchant.

Ana listened in on the conversation, and thought that their guesses were wildly wrong, an assumption based entirely on her own assumptions and guesses.

The merchant would speak very little about his involvement in the travel, and the machine. Stojan had little need for this information so he did not push this, or threaten him much, save for a daily reminder that he would kill him at the very first sign of treachery.

"Because, if this is truly as automatic as you say, you add no value and I can kill you at any time."

Having seen the damage wrought by Stojan, the merchant was happy to appear as compliant as possible.

The merchant apparently was in the employ of another merchant with vast connections in Amira. And he in turn worked for someone whose control was over an expanse of land almost the size of Poliska itself.

"Oh Amira is very big. Poliska would fit inside it many times over."
Even Dagmar did not believe such a thing. And the more he listened to the merchant, the less he believed any of his own knowledge—or his understanding of same.

Reading and regurgitating his knowledge gave him comfort, and some esteem. But this merchant had actually been to Amira, and now he was to do the same within a conveyance that was actually from the old world —a device that was far more complex than anything he had ever encountered. He found that it frightened him. The mixture that had saved young Ana was created by the same people that created the great metal conveyance that was now bringing them to Amira; and to Dagmar Amira was the old world itself. More than just another land, it was what represented the old ways. It was a land that was perhaps trapped in time.

A device such as the one he and his friends were unwitting passengers of would not have survived for even one hundred years, let alone ten times that amount.

Ana was quick to explain how even the strongest steels break down in the rain. Although her father once had a bit of the lighter metal to work with, she thought it not strong enough to create a vehicle that spent its entire life in the water.

But those thoughts and resulting arguments between her, Dagmar and even the merchant were moot, as here they were indeed being conveyed under the water.

Devices of the old world had been kept in a way that was… unnatural. Many items—even whole buildings—supposedly had been kept by the saints.

As part of his learnings, Dagmar had come to say a number of phrases from the old world.

"Saints preserve us," he'd said more than once in front of the merchant.

"Indeed" was always the answer.

He now knew the origin of this prayer, and the reason for the odd look each time he had used it.

It was not a prayer to save someone's life, or even keep them safe. It was an echo of an earlier time in which the people pleaded for the saints to protect and keep them from joining the masses that perished. Alas this effect was only enjoyed by the objects of inanimate nature; those that were alive could only live out their lives normally. That is, those that hadn't perished in the quakes, the chaos, the famine, the rise of disease and damage caused by the destruction of a world that was far more connected than it wanted to admit.

But the very energies that radiated from the visitors was enough to halt the aging process, the decay, and the passing of years for items of their choosing.

Some said it was simply the proximity. As time went on this belief spread and more and more migrated to the locations of the saints. These locations became the very centers of these new cities, but in some cases they already were.

Ana was unsure if the talk between Dagmar and the merchant was simply a challenge to see who could invent the most absurd of stories. While Dagmar now spoke in a challenging manner with his information, the merchant spoke matter-of-factly. She still preferred Dagmar's demeanor, as the merchant seemed to be attempting to scare them. Each story was more intense and each had a more and more horrific element to it.

She did not enjoy these talks and by the last day felt she had left the stable land of Poliska for the frighteningly volatile world of Amira.

All thoughts of it being a magical place in which wonders never ceased were replaced with a harsh reality of the unknown.

And the saints lived there.

The odd mix of tension and relaxed attitudes continued.

Stojan mused about what exactly would happen when they would arrive. In a way it seemed advantageous—they were going far farther away from Budziszyn than he ever dreamed. The bishop's dealings had sent him hundreds of kilometers but that did not compare to how far he traveled now.

Perhaps this was the ultimate goal; and the actual promise of the bishop —his deliverance far far away. He just needed it to make sense.

Acceptance of this fact would make for a less stressful existence.

Ana seemed to soak up the experience, as she did most things. She only needed to socialize with others, and it would help if they all weren't trying to kill her.

"Tell me, merchant…"

Stojan sat down at what had become the dinner table for them, the lighting in the room being set for evening.

He looked down at his food, then the merchant.

"We are at an impasse. Though we are the captives of your conveyance, you in turn are ours. You have not made any attempts to overtake us, or summon any ancient magic that would help you."

Oliwier smiled and listened respectfully—he was at his happiest when he was eating.

"Once we arrive, what is there to stop us from killing you, or continuing to use you as a hostage to obtain our freedom?"

"Mmm…"

He chewed and then answered calmly.

"Stojan I have no intentions of holding you or your daughter. What you did to the men in Poliska was unfortunate, but you were defending yourselves."

Stojan raised his eyebrows at this change of attitude.

"I like you, as it turns out. In fact I find that you and your daughter are highly skilled. The truth is that what Dagmar did cannot be undone. Bringing her before my lord would only prove that the item no longer exists. It is Dagmar that I must contain, so that… justice can be served."

Stojan listened but did not eat, having done so with Ana previously.

"My thoughts are of allowing you to leave."

"Allowing me to leave?"

"Yes yes, I do mean you and your daughter of course of course."

"So we are your prisoners in your mind?"

"When we arrive everyone there will be of my ilk and not yours. You trespass with our property."

Stojan thought best to let him continue.

"However, I do understand that you could indeed use me as a sort of hostage—to make your way out of the conveyance, then onward. But you would be out of place and not understand the perils."

"I have overcome and outrun perils before."

"Yes, you have been on the run for some time. Oh, do not look at me that way. I do not know of your history, and contrary to your incredulity I know of no Stojan, nor am I aware of any hired sword with such expertise and disregard for life."

Stojan seemed to accept this as it continued to confirm his odd experience in the matter.

"Especially one that travels with his young daughter."

He looked over his shoulder to see if Ana was near—no doubt she was in the rooms they had made their camps for the journey.

"So I make you this proposal: you do not interfere with my relationship with Dagmar and I will allow you to go freely on one condition."

"You already stated a condition, therefore there are two."

"So be it, I stand corrected."

Stojan smiled slightly, willing to at least listen.

"And you and your daughter perform a job for me."

Seeing the interest on Stojan's face he continued with much vigor.

"Yes. If you agree to perform this job for me, you will not only be left alone but I may be able to intercede on the ultimate fate of your friend Dagmar."

Stojan could not hide his interest.

"The alternative is rather messy, is it not? At best you kill me, exit the conveyance and come upon forces that immediately identify you as an interloper. Even if you make it past them you will be hunted—far more enthusiastically than you imagine you are now, in a land many times the size of Poliska..."

His eyes widened and he nodded knowingly, trying to drive the point home.

"With elements more amazing and horrible than you can imagine. Things you have never experienced."

I have already experienced the touch of the saints, mused Stojan, but thought it best not to reveal his hand. Let the fat man continue to think of him as a hired sword and nothing more. The plan seemed to have the best chance of Ana's safety.

"And placing a sharp dagger into your sizable abdomen with the command of just reversing our course, or..."

"No, it does not work that way. Once we arrive they will expect the container to open, and reveal what is inside. Many will be there. It is quite a spectacle to have this conveyance arrive. I think you already suspect that, which is why I am still alive and enjoying a meal with you."

Stojan tilted his head.

"And what of Dagmar?"

"He will have to answer for his theft; but again he is a valuable and knowledgeable man. Much of his knowledge is quite detailed, albeit some of it ludicrously inaccurate. Still he is an asset that would be ever more valuable should you complete the task."
Stojan took a deep breath to speak.

"...and before you threaten me with an instant death at your hands know that your daughter will be safe with you. No one—especially me—will try to harm her. That is not my bargain with you. She is just part of your package, Stojan. And I accept that, as I accept the extreme consequences for challenging that."

The merchant's demeanor was serious, and sincere. His charm was apparent and in spite of what Stojan initially considered it was indeed the best course of action. Better to have a plan of action with a native than wander aimlessly in a land of supposed dangers.

"I accept this bargain."

"Stojan!"

It was Ana, her presence had been undetected.

"What bargain do you make?"

He turned to her and motioned her to sit. She refused but still stood, looking upset.

The merchant smiled experimentally—he knew his charm would only make matters worse, as Stojan's daughter was the most wary of him. The decision had been made by her father. Now all she had to do was allow it to happen.

With less than a day to go many conversations were had between Stojan and Ana. In the end she did indeed agree.

The most difficult conversation was when he found her crying in her room. He would have walked passed her door had he not noticed her hair. For the first time it was a different color other than the natural amber, or the fiery red.

It was black. Or rather, it was a mixture of the blonde and black. It fascinated him and he entered. She did not turn around, so immersed in her feelings was she.

Sitting down on the floor next to her he just remained still, and silent.

Eventually she looked upon him with large eyes—filled with tears. She had been crying for some time. Her face was framed by the black-and-blonde hair now.

“It is gone…” She wept more and closed her eyes, causing two big tears to run down her reddened cheeks.

“What is gone…?”

“I cannot believe it has taken me this long to even think of it. I am ashamed. What will I do?”

Stojan being a bit confused racked his brain thinking what she could mean and thought of it immediately.

“Your sword.”

“Yes…”

She opened her eyes and looked at him, and it caused a stirring that made him want to do anything for her, to ease the pain she had, to comfort her that moment.

Instead he continued to listen.

“We left it—I left it. I know that we could not have gone back. I should have taken it with me into the inn. It all happened so quickly. Then I was worried about this… these rooms… this thing we are inside of.”

She looked around at the ceiling, the walls.

“Now I will not have a sword when I am older, or if I do it will not be the one my father made for me. It is such a loss to me. These are the only things I truly treasure.”

She looked over at her smaller sword in scabbard, leaning against a wall.

He put his arm around her shoulder, and experimentally pulled her towards him. She placed her head on his chest. Already the black in her hair was dissipating.

“It is a loss. Your father was a great craftsman, there is no doubt.”

He moved back in such a way that made her pull back and look up at him.
“He made three very special things.”

Confused and tired from crying, she squeaked out quietly, “Three?”

He just smiled and pulled her back to him.

The conversation with Dagmar had gone quite differently. Stojan had simply told Dagmar that he and Ana would be traveling without him.

"What have you agreed to?! We have the advantage and you just hand me over? I am aware of Amira and can be a guide!"

Dagmar was not keen on the plan, however. Stojan had held firm on his decision, and explained that this was indeed the best of all options.

"And you have the means to turn us around? To convey us back to Poliska? To overcome what awaits us? You can produce a map of a land many times the size of Poliska? You possess a weapon of magical nature that can defeat those who oppose us?"

"No," was the answer to each and every challenge.

"But I do not wish to die, Stojan."

Stojan's response was the first time that he had ever spoken to Dagmar without his stoic demeanor.

"Dagmar. I am in your debt. But I feel that death does not await you and this bargain is truly the best way to insure that. We will come for you. You undervalue yourself. Remember that."

Dagmar was left quiet and speechless after the exchange, and for the rest of the time kept quietly to himself. Every so often the merchant thought he caught Dagmar eyeing him up from the corner of his eye—no doubt assessing his sincerity from afar.

He did, and he was.

ARRIVAL TO A NEW LAND

Dagmar continued to watch the merchant, but did not converse with him. Stojan in his opinion was distrustful of everyone, except for Ana. And yet he believed that this was the best plan of action.

Since their containment some days ago, Dagmar had watched the merchant. He had yet to try to escape, to affect controls, to somehow send a message. His actions were indeed in line with what he had told them—that the conveyance would automatically bring them to Amira.

Dagmar was attempting to make peace with the fact that he was to be handed over to those from which he had stolen. It was a moment of weakness and desperation that caused the action on his part, and that had lead to the day at the waterfall.

He was perversely excited about what would happen next, and he realized that his fear of death had been affected by the day at the waterfall.

His willingness to take his own life made that same desire of others less frightening. At the same time it made the action on his part that much more shameful.

It seemed that when one considered taking one's own life, when others attempt to do the same it puts everything in prospective.

Neither is a good idea.

His life was his to take, or rather, to keep and value.

Watching Ana and Stojan made him value not only his life but theirs. And his contribution had been the wisest decision he'd ever made. It was in a sense an accomplishment that he was proud of that far exceeded any understanding of anything else from the old world. It was something he had *done*.

She was whole again, and the miraculous formulation had done exactly what it was supposed to—with the fascinating side effect.

Stojan's words fell upon him hard, and he believed in them. He did not know why, and he experienced something he had never had in his life. He had faith in Stojan.

The future was uncertain, but he would experience Amira, at the hand of his captor. Perhaps there would be mercy, perhaps not.

But, it comforted him that Stojan and Ana would be on their own terms.

———

The torches built into the walls had once again changed colors, and according to the merchant they could look into the tiny window in the pole that protruded from the ceiling. This they did and took turns. One by one they were shocked at what they saw, and more than one of them gasped and yelled.

Seeing the sun for the first time in almost a week was enough to greatly cheer up both Ana and Stojan, let alone the other amazing sights they beheld.

When one placed their forehead against the surface, it kept all of the surrounding light out, and one could focus on the vision before them.

It was as if one became a bird soaring just a meter above the water, flying effortlessly toward land. Grabbing the handles on each side one could rotate the pole, and thus the view as well.

Waves flowed and the water was dark blue. It was a sunny day and ahead was green—the greens of trees.

And something else— a sandy beach.

The merchant looked again, having been the first to view it and now the last. He pushed the handles into the pole and the pole into the ceiling.

He turned to the other three, and spoke solemnly.

"Please, as we agreed, allow me to exit first, then Dagmar, then the two of you. I will speak to those that will receive us, and you will be free to go."

He gestured to Anastazja and Stojan.

Dagmar looked solemn but resolved. He had intentionally kept quiet and did not ask any questions. He'd had enough of talk and wanted it just to be over.

Unlike Ana, Stojan had used the viewing pole for something other than sights; he attempted to assess what awaited them—the size of the group, their armaments, the structures and vantage points. He tried to make the most of the limited time he viewed the area, without appearing too suspicious.

He was able to make out a part of individuals gathering nearby, next to a tower structure. There may have been buildings behind it, but he could not tell as the window for viewing was quite tight and focused. A section of the sand had been manicured into a square, not unlike the hidden building they had left just days ago. Presumably they would drive there.

It was all still so very hard to believe, that a great metal container moved not on top of the sea, but within it. And somehow they did not run out of air. And the speed at which they moved was that of a galloping horse, and that it still took them more than five days to reach Amira. The merchant had explained that he did not believe they moved in a straight line, but that it wound a bit before entering an even larger ocean. They were to disembark upon the shore that was closest to Poliska.

Stojan had done his best to obtain as much information about the shore as possible, but that was minimal. A mist obscured much of what he saw of the land, turning colors into grey and making most objects dream-like.

However, he had a substantial conversation with the merchant regarding his bargain and quest he was to embark upon. This he insisted and would not cease his urgings until the merchant had divulged as much as possible. It was clear that the merchant was enlisting them for this quest clandestinely; he did not wish anyone to know about it, including Dagmar. The latter was, according to him, that if Dagmar didn't know about it he could not speak of it. It was a safety measure according to him. Stojan accepted this with the other information.

He had committed.

AN AGREEMENT

True to his word the merchant unlocked the bottom door, made his way up the stairs and unlocked the top. When they all emerged, one by one they stepped onto the platform of the ship, and then onto the awaiting dock. Like the pool it seemed to be made of a smooth rock.

The men and women standing there were dressed strangely.

The four travelers blinked and squinted—their eyes slowly becoming accustomed to the natural light on the partly cloudy day.

It was cool and a breeze blew, which smelled of a tangy saltiness. It was a smell similar to the cove in Poliska, but with much more intensity, in Ana's opinion.

Stojan counted eight men and two women, all clad not in armor, but in a sort of colorful shiny garb, like very long winter coats. They all looked rugged and had lined faces, with most of them having sandy hair. Three of them wore hats with a brim made of the same material as their coats.

One of the two women walked up to the group, and this caused Ana to press closer to Stojan. Dagmar remained as inconspicuous as possible, which was to say, not at all.

"Oliver. What news have you brought of Pola?"

Dagmar nodded to Stojan. Previously he had attempted to explain to him that the language of Amira was different but not different than that of

Poliska.

"They speak the same language, but there is some diversity caused by our long separation," he'd said.

"Before the second coming most of the world spoke the language of Amira, though those in Poliska also spoke our native tongue."

Since Dagmar could not demonstrate this discrepancy, due to the fact that he'd never really heard or spoken any other language, his description fell upon deaf ears.

But now Stojan was hearing the difference for himself.

The concept of an accent was now starting to make sense to him. It was a way for words to be spoken in an incorrect manner, but still close enough to the proper way as to make sense. He found it both interesting and annoying. His annoyance only added to the stress he felt at the moment, for at any second the merchant could renege on the agreement, and he would have to act. In his mind he had already killed him for it.

The group eyed the visitors with amazement. They seemed particularly interested in Stojan, his exceptionally tall thin frame and hawk-like features made him an interesting visage that day.

They looked at him, and Ana, and Dagmar.

Wasting no time the merchant yelled to them, touching Dagmar on his shoulder.

"This is Dagmar. Please take him. He is a willing prisoner of mine. Do him no harm but do not allow him to leave."

Two of the men walked over to retrieve him.

"And these are my friends—passengers that have paid handsomely for the trip. They will receive refreshments and then are moving on."

The woman who was obviously the leader furrowed her brows, and looked suspiciously at the merchant, but in the end seemed to accept his introduction.

Two men went into the craft.

Stojan nodded but did not smile. Ana looked on expressionlessly at first.

With that they walked further off of the extended platform and dock, and into an awaiting building. Ana looked around and almost became dizzy —her head circling around to contain all of the sights.

She was amazed by the tall painted tower—now very clear to her. It was many stories tall and painted in red and white. It was the most decorated building she'd ever seen; like something from a great party. At the top was a glass structure. She marveled at it, much to the delight of most of the group as they seemed to enjoy the reaction.
Passengers were not a common occurrence.

Everything seemed to go rather smoothly, and was as explained by the merchant. His efforts and charm were in full display, and Stojan knew that the merchant's concern was on his and Ana's freedom.

To the merchant it seemed this quest was very important—even more so than Dagmar.

It explained why Stojan had trusted him. The merchant was sincere—sincerely greedy.

The building was unremarkable on the inside save for the astounding windows—they were not framed in huge boards, but instead in very thin slats. And they were huge—taller than Stojan, and thin. Ana could not help but walk up to one and press her hand upon it. It was cold to the touch and ever so clear.

Though her house had windows the glass was much more thick and was not as easy to see through, being a bit tinted.

The windows were easily three meters tall and two meters wide. And there were at least eight of them each separated by a thin strip of wood.

How none of them had become cracked or broken by an errant stone amazed her. There weren't even any scratches.

The interior was similar in that it seemed pristine. Table and chairs abounded, but the chairs gave her pause. They were made of a very thin metal, as if bars of silver had been shaped into ovals and then combined with unseen rivets. Her eye as a blacksmith apprentice gave her much fascination. The seat and backing were made of what looked like a thin, brightly-painted wood. Experimentally she grabbed one of the chairs and pulled it and was amazed by its lightness.

She wanted to sit but not remove her belt, so decided on just standing and moving the chair about.

The view out the windows was amazing. The sea went on as far as she could see, and like the area they left days ago it went on to meet the horizon. The ceiling was at least two stories tall, with no arches to support it. From the ceiling hung great blades, painted white. They did not spin and were not low enough to pose a danger at this time.

As she watched the infinite ocean she could hear soft arguing from another room—it was the merchant and a woman's voice.

She heard very little other than "You return with no goods?"

This apparently was answered satisfactorily and the arguing quieted down into a conversation that could no longer be heard.

One of the men walked up to where they stood—being polite enough to wait for her amazement to subside—and asked them to come with him.

He led them to another room, similar to the great hall they were in. The walls were perfectly straight and smooth, again with no support beams in sight, even in the corners. The walls were painted a neutral grey-blue, and upon the ceiling was attached a pattern of criss cross rectangles—white in color with thin strips between them. A few of the rectangles were semi-transparent and apparently were skylights as some of the sunlight shone through them—albeit in little intense strips—as if the skylights had no windows but just cracks in the ceiling. She wondered if water ever got in through the cracks.

Stojan was none too keen about being placed into a room with only one exit.

Shortly thereafter the merchant appeared, and spoke to Stojan.

"As promised I have supplies but alas have no horses for you, so the first portion your journey will have to be on foot."

Stojan wrinkled his nose at this.

"It will be good to use our legs again," he said to Ana.

"Here."

With that the merchant handed what looked like a scroll to Stojan.

"The supplies are outside."

A NEW QUEST

What seemed like the beginning of captivity became the start of a new quest. Ana was understandably confused, having not been privy to the long discussions between the two men.

What she did notice was the look of uneasiness on the face of the merchant. To her it looked like someone who was getting away with something through theft or deceit. His mannerisms were hurried and he moved quickly, especially for the normally slow-moving stocky man she'd had to be trapped with for five days or more.

She couldn't wait for her to be alone with Stojan to finally reveal what they had agreed to, as her imagination was none too kind about it.

Looking over his shoulder yet again, Oliwier hurriedly said to Stojan, "There there, you should have everything. Again I am sorry about a lack of horse, but just outside of the port there are stables, and you may be able to buy horses there."

Again he looked back, then glanced quickly at Anastazja, then her hair.

"As we discussed, the more stealth employed the better for you both. Go now."

He turned and walked quickly back into the building.

Stojan looked down and noticed they were standing on an area that was black like rich earth, but was hard. Yellow lines had been painted on the ground, and looked as fresh as if they were just applied a week previous.

They were spaced apart equally, as if someone had placed a very large box and drawn a perimeter around it and then moved it to the next line.

It looked like it was part of a ceremony of some kind.

He walked away from the building to the road. It too looked like it was made of compacted earth.

To Ana it looked like tar that had been pressed perfectly to make a smooth surface and as she walked on it she almost bounded, trying to see how flexible it was. It was much harder than she thought.

Stojan was almost running and Ana struggled to keep up, having to break into a gait now and then to compensate.

She turned back to look at their place of arrival. From this distance she could see the small rectangular building with a roof that was flat. The windows facing the water could still be seen as they reflected their environment—the sky, the water.

Behind it now could be seen another building, this one tall and with a dome.

The sight made her slow down as she admired the amazing shape. It was a stark contrast to the other building. While the square one was mostly featureless save for the great windows, this building was taller and looked to be of construction she was used to. This building was of stone construction and the dome that topped it was of a copper color, though she did not believe it could be made entirely of metal.

Just then she remembered she had just traveled under the water for a week in a vessel constructed exactly that way—entirely of metal.

She turned back to find she had lost some ground with Stojan, and ran to catch up.

After a time she noticed the road deteriorated into broken patches and then finally dissolved into a path of ground, stones and grass—the kind of path she had been used to. Why the people who created the road only established it for some few blocks made no sense to her.

It was as if they were meticulous about maintaining it and then gradually forgot about it the farther they traveled from the odd square building. Perhaps they ran out of the tar-like substance?

It—like so many things in the last months—made no sense. Or perhaps it made a sense in the way that Dagmar would have understood it.

Her thoughts of him made her concerned. What would come of him?

"Stojan what did Dagmar do? What crime did he commit?"

She asked while struggling to keep up.
He looked at her and realized then just how much longer his legs were than hers, and slowed down a bit.

Without looking at her he responded.

"Dagmar is a good man, but his zealousness towards the old world was his undoing."

She continued to look at Stojan as they slowed a bit, and listened for more.

"I think his desire for knowledge and truth caused him to do the obvious but not honorable. He stole something to examine and to experiment with. But fortunately for him those who would prosecute him value his skills—even more than he does."

"So you do not believe harm will come to him?"

"No."

He looked at her and slowed to a casual walk.

"I believe that in the end he will redeem himself with them. And that we may be reunited with him, if that is our destiny."

She tilted her head slightly.

"You believe in destiny?"

"Ana I believe in only what I can see and what can be explained. But that has been greatly expanded of late. You and I have seen many things that cannot be explained, or whose explanation defies our understandings of the world."

She nodded, and then stopped.

"I don't know what that means."

He stopped in the middle of the road, and looked into her eyes. His own had a twinkle.

"Neither do I."

She smiled as they continued walking at a fast but tolerable pace.

Taking deep breaths she took in the landscape. Trees and grass looked familiar yet this was a different land, separated by a great sea. They had traveled at the rate of the fastest galloping horse—constantly—for some five days.

They walked for some time and she said very little outwardly, but her thoughts were quite active that day. Though she had ample time to think inside the conveyance, this seemed like the first time she was able to truly breathe and think. Thoughts turned to wondering about the animals nearby and her favorite pastime.

She worried about Dagmar but what was ahead of her filled her with wonder, and for the first time in many days she was alone again with Stojan. His company made her feel safe, and protected, and much more it seemed.

The path was now thinner than before and they were surrounded by trees, shrubs and taller grass. No one passed them coming or going. Judging by the sun it was mid day and the sunlight was warm and welcoming. The merchant had told them that Amira was so large and expansive that it experienced a difference in weather from winter to fall to spring to summer—all in the same day. South would give them a very hot summer with many more months of heat. And it never snowed. North would give them very long and cold winters.

In Poliska Ana enjoyed the four seasons and the changes they brought. Here in the nearby vicinity the weather would be similar.

"Stojan, just how far do we travel?"

He looked around and after a short time found a secluded area off the road. A downed tree made for an acceptable resting spot. Only then did he answer.

Handing her food from his pack he spoke.

"My instructions are to travel to the next city and obtain horses on the way. Ultimately we are to retrieve an item and return it to the merchant."

"Return?"

She was clearly surprised.

He smiled. "Yes, we are to return with the item. It is at that time that I think we could once again be reunited with friend Dagmar, should we decide that is best for us."

Best for us?

"Can you tell me more of this item? Or your instructions?"

He hesitated a bit, chewed, drank some water and then continued.

"Understand that I do not fully trust this merchant. It is only recently that I did not wish to kill him. But I now understand his motivation and in understanding this I understand him."

"Oh, what is his motivation…?"

"Greed," said Stojan.

"Greed?" asked Anastazja simultaneously.

They both nodded.

"Ahh."

"And what is this item that he lusts for?"

"It is simply a book. One of many books that exist in the land of Amira, apparently. We are to find it, retrieve it in good condition and bring it to the merchant. I found this to be an acceptable task with less risk than remaining with the… *unknown* element of the merchant's employer."

"Oh Stojan, you agreed to a quest?!"

She was clearly excited.

He exhaled and closed his eyes, knowing what he was about to experience.

"I believe that is.."

"We are on a quest in Amira?!"

"…an accurate…"

"Oh Stojan! This is wonderful! How are we so lucky?!"

He gave up and decided not to finish his response. Instead he just bathed in her excitement, and stared.

Her hair was no longer amber, but instead the fiery red he had seen in the past. This time however it had lines of lesser reds, and had more definition than the pure deep crimson he remembered from the very first sight of it.

She spun around, a great smile upon her face.

It was a work of art, and was already subsiding, fading back to her original natural colors.

He just shook his head, closed his eyes and smiled ever so slightly. Her enthusiasm was healing for him, and he drew not only strength but rejuvenation from it.

He also knew it potentially could be their undoing. The merchant had cautioned him to make sure none saw what they saw. Demotivating a girl of this age to be less enthusiastic was not of his liking.

He had already advised and even trained her to keep her emotions in check, but found that this very energy was what made her a formidable fighter. Controlling her excitement and focusing it was what had made her strike a single deadly blow in her first confrontation. He knew this was what made her an exceptional combatant.

That, and intense training by the deadliest man in Poliska.

But outside of battle he did not wish to quell this excitement. Ana had been through so much since his arrival, and whatever he did for her was not to suppress her enjoyment of life. So he was in a difficult position—a position he would not reveal to her.

“Yes. We have a long way to go. Perhaps I should have asked you, dear Ana, but it seems you would have agreed.”

She smiled further and responded with a healthy nod of her head.

“Oh I do!”

Stojan revealed little of their new quest except for vague generalities. He was busy working out the specifics in his mind. Managing her excitement as well as his instructions, and keeping the general populace from seeing her hair occupied almost all of his thoughts.

Almost. He still had a nagging feeling that something was not as it seemed but he knew not what.

HORSES AND TRAINING

In no time they had found the stables mentioned by the merchant, and they were part of a small town not too far from the cove.

They found the people there to wary and tight-knit, and relatively poor. It seemed that none of the amazing things from their landing spot reached them. Stojan found it odd that they seemed so isolated and different. Their housing was like that of a frontier town and had almost never encountered the like in Poliska. The sights here seemed to be in contrast.

Eventually he was able to find the stable master, and with the coins provided by the merchant he procured two horses.

Anastazja was thrilled to once again have a horse, and hand off her sizable pack to the saddle bags that easily took the burden.

Stojan noticed the sad, distant look in her eyes but said nothing. He knew she thought of the sword that was now lost. He was humble enough to not think past a month or so, but if he was allowed to be with her and see her to adulthood he would do his utmost to making sure she had a sword that deserved her fine skills.

Stojan had instructions to ask for a specific man and mention the merchant, but not speak to anyone else. It was understandable that anyone would be suspicious of those that came from the cove as like its twin was mostly a dead end. Anyone who approached from that road was a visitor from far far away, and therefore involved in something very difficult to explain.

"Those coins were different."

They were both on horseback and making their way to the next city proper.

Ana commented on the monies Stojan had used to pay for the horses. Though they had a considerable amount of money with them, he chose to use the minimal coins provided by the merchant.

"Our money is no good here."

"How can money be no good, Stojan?" She asked politely, clearly enjoying being back in the saddle again.

"We are in an entirely different land, and its governance is also different. Our monies were made in Poliska, and recognized for their value. Here things are different."

He seemed to be repeating the words he was told, and didn't understand things clearly himself.

"Gold is gold, silver is silver… and the coins you used were neither. Do they value something other than that?"

"I was given specific coins for the stable-master. He values them not for their content but for their history. I was also given coins similar to what we are used to—gold, silver and copper."

"So strange."

She looked at the horizon, and the trees. Some of the leaves were starting to turn and the landscape was a great forest, with rolling, gentle hills. It reminder her a bit of Poliska but the mountains she was used to seeing were not there.

"Dagmar mentioned that there are great mountains here, do you think we will see them?"

"I do not think we will be traveling that far in our task."

"Quest," she corrected.

“Fall it seems is finally here, though I am told the seasons may be different here.”

Ana again thought Stojan’s perception of the length of summer was perplexing. To her it seemed to last just as long as it was supposed to.

He guided them off the path a bit, to a field of shorter grass. The location was at the top of one of the shorter hills—giving them a good vantage point.

He stopped, tied his horse to a tree and motioned for her to do the same.

She dismounted and gave him a curious look, peering around for some sort of clue. She missed the fields of flowers at home. Here the grasses were shorter and sprinkled with tiny vivid blue and violet flowers.

“You did not think you could escape your training that easily?”

She brightened and backed up, then ran into the field.

He walked to follow her.

With all the turmoil Stojan knew that this strange act was something that grounded her. It was an odd familiarity; the training and fighting. To her, and him now, it was part of being home.

“Perhaps you have become stiff, being contained for a week?”

“No.”

He almost laughed, her answer was serious and she did not joke while they trained. His minor test was a success.

That afternoon they sparred for some time, and he found her to sorely need it, as it both lifted her spirit and grounded her.

Afterwards she asked a question rather firmly.

“Stojan I think you should tell me as much as you can of our quest.”

“Oh?”

“Yes, it makes no sense for me to be ill-informed. I should know as much as you do. This can only hurt us if I am to be ignorant.”

"That is a fair statement."

"Then tell me please. Tell me more."

Swords sheathed and thirsts quenched they returned to their horses and the ride.

"I do not know the lay of the land and do not have a map. Our first destination is to find a man that provides a map to us. This will give us the direction we need to proceed."

Ana was thrilled that Stojan agreed so easily to explain, so kept quiet as to motivate him to continue.

"There we can seek lodging for the night. We will then proceed to a large city. You see, we have to travel from city to city to reach our destination. The plan is to travel, stay for the night, refresh and continue. You may find it a bit repetitive after a while and think less of your quest than you do now."

She looked at him with doubt.

"It is mostly travel to a far away destination, and then return to the merchant. It is fortunate that we retrieve what should be a small concealable item."

"Ah!" She laughed.

"You mean to take the fun out of it! I see your ploy Stojan."

She smiled at him.

He had indeed tried to minimize the excitement of the trip, and with that any dangers. She was already on to his attempt at misdirection.

"I just mean to prepare you for the tedium of travel."

She remained smiling, her head filled with all the possible wonders.

Stojan's head was filled with similar imaginings, but with the addition of the dangers that awaited.

"This book—are we purchasing it?"

"No. We are to locate it and it is ours for the finding."

"Indeed? Is it in one of the great libraries? Is that why you hide it from me? Are we to travel to one of the Amiran libraries that Dagmar spoke of?"

"I do not know if those exist, I know only of this, our supposed destination."

She thought for a moment.

"Stojan, if Amira possesses the means of conveyance such as what we experienced, why does the merchant need two strangers on horseback to retrieve it? Can he not just send away for it, or have some similar conveyance retrieve it?"

"All excellent questions to which I know not the answers. I am as new to this land as you, and was not the recipient of the history lessons as you were."

"You were present for most of them!"

"I was not listening."

Some times Anastazja was unsure if Stojan joked. This was one of those times.

"Well, it will be a wondrous thing if we do travel to the libraries… but the books are not for the taking. Dagmar says that the books in Amira are greatly prized and… hidden from the saints."

"Why would a book need to be hidden from those that are all knowing?"

"Because they are not!"

It was her turn to be the teacher. Like most of Poliska, Stojan had a healthy understanding of the world, and nature. He counted on the way things worked, and that knowledge did not contain the mythical belief in the old world and the saints.

He was starting to understand that Poliska was truly unique—a uniqueness that he now wished for. This land was different.

Until he had met the bishop his world worked a certain, dependable, explainable way. But as it seems in much the way he strived to protect Anastazja from the dangers of the world, so did Poliska protect him.

Even as a murderer on the run.

THE FIRST STATUE

The road was unusual in that climbed some very short hills, maintained the height and then came back as quickly as they'd cropped up. And, these small but steep hills popped up from time to time, as if the very road had attempted to reach the sky and then lost interest. It was like riding on the back of a giant snake.

It some areas the dirt gave way to an almost slippery rock. Stojan thought that he would not want to use this road to run from a threat, especially in the rain. Try as they might they could not ascertain the purpose of such a road. For the most part they enjoyed the ups and downs that day.

As they traveled it was more and more common place to encounter others who did the same. Commerce and travel in general was something they saw on the road many times a day, with others not giving them much notice. They nodded their respects and continued. Some would pinch their foreheads as they passed, and this was understood as a sign of acknowledgment though the meaning was lost on them. It wasn't until they encountered a man with a wide-rimmed hat—similar to what Dagmar favored—that they understood it. Those with hats were grabbing the brim, and pulling it down ever so slightly as a salute. Apparently those without hats did the same to their invisible headwear. It wasn't long until Stojan was doing the same with his thin skullcap, though he simply touched the forehead with his fingers. He found it exhausting but encouraging—as long as they were greeted in a friendly manner they could continue on their trip unmolested.

Their most interesting passer-by was a small older man atop a horse-like creature. Stojan had seen such creatures here and there in cities, and understood them to be good work animals, albeit at one third the size of the horses. This one looked like cross between a horse and one of these donkeys, being a bit larger but still retaining the larger ears.

He was right.

The man was quite thin and sinewy and his hair went every which way—the stark white being quite noticeable from afar. He hunched a bit on his animal as if he was galloping, or ready to speed away at any moment. However, this was just his preferred posture and it looked very uncomfortable to Ana.

The sizable saddle bags were all but empty as they flapped in the breeze.

Whether the man was undernourished or just small in stature was not apparent. He did not greet them and despite Stojan's excellent use of the common greeting he just stared and then looked away as he passed.

Stojan looked over at Ana and she shrugged.
As sun down was approaching they both hoped the clouds that were forming meant to keep their rain for some time—at least until they reached their destination.

According to the map the library was located inside a small town just ahead. Every so often houses could be seen and these looked out of place among the farmland, as if a great hand had come, picked up a house and placed it in the middle of a field.

As Stojan would learn later the opposite was actually true.

"There does not seem to be much to this town."

Ana could smell the brown grass as they rode by—many many kilometers were covered by it, and it waved in the breeze. She wanted to jump off of her horse and run into it, without destination or care. She would ask Stojan if she could do this on the way out of town, perhaps tomorrow. For now though she was perplexed that she did not quite recognize it. Farming was a part of most people's lives in Poliska—as it seemed to be here—and even more so for her and her father. But try as she might she could not quite place the color or the smell of this particular crop. Amira was filled with beautiful sights as well as unidentifiable scents, and anything was better than the metal prison she had been in for so long. She appreciated her freedom and was once again reminded of it, thankfully.

“Is there a center to this city, Stojan?”

She asked this while tipping her head upward—continuing to sample the air.

“It seems quite scattered. My hope is a place to stay after our visit. But we can make do if no such place exists. I have never visited a library of books before, and certainly not one in Amira.”

“I do not know what to expect either…”

She finished his thought for him, then expressed her concern for something new.

“I am worried about the old man we saw.”

“Oh?”

“He rides so slowly out of the city and we are approaching sundown. He did not look to be loaded with supplies.”

“I think we will see him again, soon.”

“You do? So I should not worry?”

“No. Worry not for him.”

The road continued to wind here and there but kept mostly on a straight path. There seemed to be no end in sight of the fields, though the houses became more numerous and densely packed. Eventually the fields did end and they seemed to be approaching the town proper.

It was his turn to change the subject.

“Ana, when we were approaching the cove you had a secret. Was the secret that you knew we were being followed?”

Taken off guard and slightly embarrassed she answered.

“Yes. When I went for my walk I watched the men on their horses. They were following us and had paused to talk. Soon after I started watching them they rode again. They were making sure they kept their distance from us."

Stojan just looked forward but continued to listen.

"As not to be discovered."

"Yet they were."

"Yes."

"Why did you not tell us about these men?"

"I was afraid of the conversation being discovered. We were never alone."

Stojan digested this as he rode, never looking at her. But then, in the same tone as before he continued.

"Ana…"

"Yes Stojan?"

"You did nothing but watch them?"

It was her turn to pause, and blush slightly.

"I did more."

"What did you do then?"

"I wanted to see if I could touch the horse of the last rider."

"And did you?"

"Yes."

"Did they notice?"

"No."

The resulting silence made her squirm a bit. She was not sure what to make of it. He expressed no anger or disappointment; he made no reprimand. Stojan just continued to look forward and ride, and she couldn’t tell if he was smiling or not.

She would just have to assume.

THE GREAT LIBRARY OF AMIRA

Though there was no sign in the outskirts to warn them they did approach a small city. This one looked like it had been established for some time and they rode in looking forward to their first real meal in Amira.

There was a part of them that was always challenging what they saw; comparing it to that of their homeland—the people, the language, the land, and now it would be the food.

There was one difference, and it was what greeted them upon entering the city proper. It was not a guard, or a gate. It was something that Anastazja had never seen in her life, and Stojan had only seen the back of, once.

A statue.

It stood on a pedestal that was within a walled fountain, though no water spouted from it. Instead it looked like a moat that was home to a few ducks. Birds also gathered around it enjoying the water now and then.

Ana marveled at it as they rode by. It was twice the size of the tallest person she'd ever seen, and made of some sort of green-grey rock. It was clearly a man in robes with a sword at his side, and it was carved to perfection, save for a chunk missing near the base. Ana could not take her eyes off of it, and half-expected the man's eyes to turn back to watch her. For a moment it frightened her. Stojan just glanced and kept his eyes forward. She clearly had questions now and it looked as though her head turned halfway around tracking it as they continued.

Looking like any smaller city in Poliska—save for the statue that greeted them—they identified an inn eventually. Stojan mentally checked the bag at his side so as to use the proper Amiran monies.

Every so often they drew extended looks from the citizens, and he assumed it was due their appearance. Though their clothing was similar, he was after all considerably taller. And, exceptional color change not withstanding, her natural hair color was quite a bit more vibrant than the mostly browns he saw in the population. Some of the people were of much darker skin tone too.

Stables were found before an inn, so Stojan and Ana's horses were deposited there for feed and keeping. They walked on foot and took most of their possessions with them—something Ana encouraged them to do ever since the cove.

The two travelers made their way through the small city. Stojan's habit of seemingly always looking forward amazed Ana. She sometimes thought it made no sense that someone who was apparently always prepared for battle be so oblivious to everything around him save for the narrow band in front of him.

Stojan's head was so immobile it reminded Ana of a horse with blinders on.

She looked around the city and took in the sights, the smells and the people. It was a busy little city with all manner of citizens and craftsmen. Surely they would find this librarian here, among so many.

"We are being followed."

Ana's head sung around to look up at the source of the voice—her smile instantly draining away.

"What."

Stojan said nothing else and continued to walk, and look forward. Anastazja traded glances with various people going about their business.

When the tall man did not elaborate Anastazja pressed.

"What do you mean we are… by whom?"

Stojan spoke in even, unnerving calmness.

"He lurks off to the right, and moves between the kiosks. A small boy."

"A small boy?"

"Do not look. Remain calm. I have been watching him since we arrived, and he us."

Ana did not doubt the big man, but could not remember a minute in which Stojan had looked anywhere but straight ahead. She did not look around herself much lest she be reprimanded.

"Let us find some refreshment from travel. There." He pointed to a nearby inn and turned to make his way. She continued to flank him and shrugged.

As she entered she sat down at the nearest table and once again her face showed surprise. Stojan was gone.

Ordering some food and drink she decided she would also order for her missing partner. The food and drink came and so did Stojan, with and additional person in tow.

It was a small, sandy-haired boy, no older than nine.

He was wide eyed and looked recently frightened—no doubt by whatever interaction he had with Stojan.

The two sat down.

The big man took bread and handed it to the boy, then immediately took a drink.

"This is David. He has something to share with us."

The two travelers ate and watched the boy devour the bread. The inn keeper's helper smiled as he brought forth two cylinders of metal, and immediately shook some on the food—simple spices and apparently the custom of those serving food—to sprinkle a little and then offer more to the patrons.

Anastazja brightened and reached her hand out, to which he complied and handed it to her. She shook it on her food as well—the black flakes landing on the bread and other nibbles.

Stojan reached out his hand towards Anastazja, as if asking her to both stop and hand him the cylinder. He looked forward as he ate.

"You're looking for a library, aren't you?"

Anastazja nodded but Stojan did not, as he was now sprinkling some of the flakes on his food.

"I know where it is."

"We seek a great library and a library master," Anastazja said in comforting tones, explaining the unexplainable to the boy who was probably confused. She seemed so much older than the boy now.

"Do you know of someone like that? Perhaps your father works for him?"

Stojan ate without expression, showing no interest in the conversation. He placed his half-eaten bowl of stew in front of the boy, who immediately dipped his bread into it. Anastazja continued to explain but had yet to eat.

"No," the boy said with a mouth full of food.

"No?" Anastazja looked down at her food—she was starving and it smelled inviting.

"No." He continued eating happily. She looked at Stojan for clarification but none was forthcoming, he just continued to eat his bread and drink.

"Many people come to seek out the library."

Stojan continued, as if translating the thoughts of the hungry lad.

"None have found it because they were here for the wrong reason. None come for the right reason."

He stopped an as if on cue, without looking up the boy finished, "To put an end to the saints."

Anastazja, her mouth finally full of food, stopped chewing.

She smiled, tasting her food for the first time. It was meat familiar to her, but a bit sweeter and with more spice. The salt and pepper made everything taste better, but she found both made her very thirsty.

After they had finished eating in relative silence, it was explained that once cornered the young man had revealed much.

He was only to follow them—at the behest of his uncle—and report back. The description of them had come from him earlier and this sort of thing had happened before.

Others who sought the library were followed and watched. Young David was very good at eavesdropping and as a child it made him inconspicuous. At worst he was thought to have bad manners and was a nosy urchin in search of food.

He had never been recognized for what he was—a spy for his uncle.

Stojan had told him that he would simply like him to join them for a meal—an offer that made young David quite excited. He had never gotten more than a copper or a piece of bread. This was an entire meal and he was a guest at their table.

Though he was sure his uncle would be upset with him, he hadn't revealed much—except for the one thing his uncle was looking for.

"None of them will ever see the library! Feh. I doubt most can even read, let alone understand what treasures are here!"

His uncle would rant while David helped him with cleaning and upkeep.

"No one? Why?"

"Because they all come for the wrong reason—to pillage it, to take the books and to sell them as trinkets, as oddities. It's doubtful anyone truly wants their knowledge. And if someone does it's for the wrong reason."

Eventually after hearing many permutations of the same rant, David had worked up the courage to ask.

"Well uncle, what *is* the right reason?"

"To get rid of the saints forever!"

This David did communicate to Stojan, partially because he carried the secret with him for too long, but mostly because he was absolutely terrified of Stojan at the time.

This information was happily accepted.

Anastazja shook her head.

"But…"

That was all she was willing to say, lest she ruin any workings Stojan had already started.

David was to report back to his uncle, who would inevitably complain and then tell him to ignore them. This is what had happened so far, without fail.

In this case he would do the same, but they would follow him from afar. That way if his uncle still did not receive them through David, they could introduce themselves directly.

Not too keen on it, the now-full boy complied.

It was a good walk and not at all in the location expected. Anastazja pictured it on top of a hill, overlooking the rest of the city—a great palace of sorts.

Instead it was quite different.

As they approached a particular avenue the travelers broke off and waited while they watched the boy.

He entered a small house in an area of town that was opposite of the welcoming fields. This area looked like very few buildings had been built there recently, and that the town just diminished and was engulfed by the surrounding nature. Trees, overgrowth and grass all intermingled with the few buildings here. It looked like the kind of place that the homeless would seek out and squat upon. One would also be equally likely to find wild animals had taken residence there.

The house looked like it had been built into—or just collapsed into— a nearby hill, as if it was happy for the support.

Anastazja half expected that the hill itself was a a secret lair of the library master, and that he would emerge from the top to yell at them.

After a while the little boy did emerge, and walked in their direction, glancing quickly and shaking his head. He looked a bit fearful, but Stojan appreciated him keeping his word. He knew this to mean that they would not voluntarily be received.

"What now Stojan? He is in there. Do we just knock on the door?"

"I think we should wait a bit. I have no desire to peer into his home, and the sun sets shortly."

"Then…"

She stopped, and smiled. She no longer worried about the old man that left the city on their way in, for before her he stood. He exited his house experimentally, and peered around—a sour look on his face.

He yelled at no one in particular.

"I know you're out there! You found me!"

He continued to peer around, placing his hands on his forehead as if to help him see.

"David is always hungry and his stomach wins every time!"

He yelled in the opposite direction. His back was to them.

"Show yourselves!"

Stojan nodded at a smiling Ana and with that they left the protection of their darkened corner.

They walked towards the man and as he swung his head around demonstrably he saw them.

"Aha!"

He folded his arms upon his chest and tapped his foot.

"Let's go then."

They picked up the pace and Ana looked around, concerned that the man that was so clandestine simply yelled on the street with no regard for being discovered.

As they approached he went back into his tiny leaning house mostly covered with vines.

They followed through the creaking door.

The house was lit with lanterns that flickered, and Ana could smell the remnants of some kind of cooking. It seemed that everything smelled good to her since they'd arrived.

Modestly furnished and cramped, the house looked infrequently used.

He went to the door and applied a large bar to lock it. Ana thought the bar was far sturdier than the door itself.

"Sit down then."

Stojan noticed his hunch continued whether he was on a horse or not.

"No then?"

Barely allowing enough time to comply, the man had decided they were not. He was eternally grumpy. Up close Ana noticed his hair was quite thick and wiry, and all white.

"So you want to see the library?"

"No."

"No?"

Ana and the man said in unison.

"We have come for a book, that is all. We do not wish to invade your great library, or your home."

It was said sincerely and matter-of-factly, the way Stojan often communicated. It still surprised Ana. She would be crestfallen to not see the library of Amira and all its wonders, but every sight was new and Stojan seemed to know best.

She watched the man as he considered this, and noticed indentations in his nose next to his eyes. It was a minor thing but still looked out of place, like he pinched it often.

He looked back at her, as if seeing her for the first time.

"Oh, you are a beautiful girl, aren't you?"

Stojan pushed forward.

"We are here to retrieve the book, and pay you appropriately for it."

"Appropriately." He said the word with disdain.

"I'm sure, young man, that whoever sent you has no idea what the books are worth. Because if he did he wouldn't pay me with money. He wouldn't buy the book at all."

The cryptic comment was lost on both, and Stojan continued his attempt to make the purchase.

"I have only brought money, and instructions."

"No you haven't. You brought something else."

The man glanced at Anastazja then back at Stojan. He looked at them with a hint of approval, their faces, the swords at their sides.

Anastazja was lost in the conversation—it was at this point baffling how the man spoke.

"Right!"

She turned behind her, as if he had answered someone's question.

He once again glanced at the locked door and then turned his back to them, exiting though a tiny archway in his tiny house.

They followed him after glancing at each other.

There was no secret entrance, no pantry sliding door.

Instead he just opened a flimsy wooden door, that revealed another door. This one was made mostly of glass, with a tiny metal frame. The metal was that of the ship they had traveled in—silver and brushed. There was no knob but instead a bar that ran across the middle from left to right. It avoided the glass and jutted out slightly to span the width, returning to be connected on the other side.

There did appear to be a key lock of sorts and a tiny piece of metal she took to be a lock. There was a tiny painting on the glass itself, no larger than her hand. She could not make out the words overlaid upon it, but it looked intricate.

He pushed the bar and the door silently swung open. Reaching back he grabbed a lantern and motioned Stojan to do the same.

The three entered the doorway into an entryway. The old man turned back to close the wooden door, then came back to the glass one. It was obvious he took this precaution often.

The giant hill the little house rested against was in actuality the library they sought it seemed.

Ana thought the interior was quite similar to the building at the cove at which they'd arrived, and thought briefly of missing Dagmar.

She was cheered they were so close to their goal. Perhaps in mere days they would be back and reunited with him. But then what?

They walked up to a wall of large glass doors—similar to the windows at the cove. These windows went from ceiling to floor and were out of place. The old man walked up to them and awkwardly using his hand he slid one, then another of the giant windows apart. They slid begrudgingly as if he was doing it wrong.

They opened enough to let all three in and Ana touched the edge that had previously been closed. It was rubbery in texture.

The interior was dark and the lanterns did a poor job of lighting it. Fortunately the man had hung many lanterns from various places near the entryway. In some places they hung from ropes that were attached to the second floor ceiling, and they hung just above her head.

He went to light a number of them with his own torch and in no time they could see things clearly.

It was like nothing Ana had ever seen before. To the left was a counter top made of an unknown material, blueish in color, with sharp ridges. It was high—too high to use to eat off of unless you were supposed to stand.

Behind it was more space, and a doorway.

To her right she saw them. Not one, not hundreds, but probably thousands.

Books.

They did not lay in a pile, or open on tables, but instead they had been placed on shelves so that only their spines were shown.

Her jaw dropped slightly as her eyes lit up to take it all in.

Stojan surveyed the area and then looked up to see the extra log ropes that were used to attach the lanterns to the second story ceiling. His eyes followed the stairs and he was sure he saw similar shelves upstairs.

"There are so many…"

The old man just watched her, and Stojan. He eyed them as carefully as they eyed the bookshelves.

After a minute of silence Stojan spoke without turning to face him.

"Why do you study us so?"

The man pulled his head back, while the rest of him stayed hunched.

"I mean to determine your true intent, swordsman. You are curious, both of you."

He looked from the amazed Anastazja to the stoic Stojan.

"Many have come to seek a book from me, but none came for the right reason."

"And what is that reason, keeper of the library?"

Stojan asked a question to which he already knew the answer.

The man said nothing but continued to stare. When Stojan turned to him he spoke, as if unwilling to answer the side of his face. He looked into his eyes.

"We live in ignorance. What we know now is a fraction of what we once knew. Those that seek to be free of this ignorance that has been forced upon us—those I am willing to teach, to entertain."

"You consider us ignorant?"

"Very much so. Even I am ignorant, but I learn, each and every day. In fact young David knows more than anyone in this city with what he has been taught by me. And that is only because I talk to myself when I read."

"Read?" asked Ana as she continued to pan around, now discovering the upstairs from her position—a position into which she was still frozen.

He glanced at her, almost annoyed.

"Yes, read. The books. As many as I can before I die. And then before that pass on the knowledge of this library to another. And one day we will no longer need to conceal it."

"For what reason do you conceal it now?"

"Them."

Stojan waited for more.

"And the ignorant people of Amira. They would see this only as a place to pillage. Each book is worth a sizable amount you see. Even the esoteric ones, even those would fetch a price for their uniqueness. But even if I was pillaged and the books scattered that would be quickly contained."

"By them."

"Exactly."

The look on Stojan's face demonstrated that he did not clearly know who 'them' was, but he assumed.

"You doubt me. That is understandable. I think I know who sent you."

“Oh?”

“Yes, a merchant, no doubt. I have been watching and waiting. I have learned much.”

“How long have you been the keeper of the great library.”

He smiled.

“Follow me.”

Stojan and Anastazja followed the man as he walked to one of the shelves and ran his finger over the spines of various books. Each spine contain the title of the book, and more words, and letters. Up close Anastazja could smell them. It was an unusual smell and it gave her great promise.

“You both can read I assume?”

“Of course,” said Stojan.

“Somewhat,” said Anastazja.

“You don’t teach your daughter to read!?”

He elbowed Stojan hard.

Anastazja realized that had been the first time she had seen him struck while his sword was sheathed.

Stojan looked down at the man who continued searching the books.

“She is a fast learner. I am sure her reading skills will grow with her other skills.”

She smiled at him, feeling a little embarrassed at her apparent lack of skill.

Not much reading was done in Poliska other than some rudimentary teachings in school. She half attended her small school as she spent so much time in apprenticeship with her father. Truth be told she had grown bored with the teachings and the limited books, as she had read them quickly. There was little else to read, even after asking her teacher and her father. Most books available were very thin, and written in parchment. It was not uncommon for a class to work out of a single book. She'd been taught basic math, reading fundamentals and a limited history. None of that included the fantastical lessons that Dagmar tried to impress upon her.

Ana continued to be amazed. There were so many books here that she didn't think she could ever read them in a lifetime. The old man walked through shelves of books—not just shelves along walls but freestanding in the middle of the room. He chose a book seemingly at random and upon withdrawing it he stopped.

"Here." He handed the book to Stojan, after flipping to a page near the center of the book. It was a thick book, yet so small. The books Anastazja were used to were so large out of necessity—they maintained their fortitude and were much easier to write for the scribes.

Stojan grabbed the book and looked down at it. He looked, and looked, and wrinkled his nose.

"Well? What does it say?"

"The words are small. I cannot read this."

He handed it back to the librarian as Ana watched with fascination.

"They *are* small, and so very perfect."

He looked at her, hesitated, patted his shirt as if looking for something, and then decided against some unseen action. With a look of minor disgust he spoke to Stojan.
"The people of Amira are ignorant. And it is our duty to make sure our children have more than us. Some day we can break free of this ignorance and Amira will in turn be free. Knowledge is power."

"We are not."

"You are not what, ignorant?" The little man looked up at Stojan with contempt.

Stojan looked irritated.

"We are not from Amira."

Anastazja withheld her shock. She had learned with Stojan not to reveal much to strangers.

The little man looked at both with awe.

"You're not? Wait. Wait."

He walked away, to a nearby table. Like the building that had received them the chairs were made of a very thin material, with molded metal bars. They were very light. He pulled one out and sat down, suddenly looking both tired and cheerful. The three books were placed onto the table.

"Where are you from then?"

Stojan looked at Ana.

"We are from Poliska. We…"

"Pol… Poliska!!"

The man shouted and cut him off.

"You can understand me—what I am saying?!"

"Yes of course," said Ana. "Some of the words are hard to understand, some are said incorrectly, but we have figured most of it out. We were forewarned of this. Our… friend taught us of 'accents' and the like."

"Accents. Amazing."

The man spoke and looked down at the table. Ana saw that letters had been carved into it near the corner.

"I would have expected so much to change. Amira has been cut off from the rest of the world for so long. There is trade and people come and go, and the universal language of the old world but… Amazing. You came all the way from… Wait."

He put his hand on Stojan's sleeve.

"You came all this way in search of a book? Just one? And you have no desire or instructions to see the library?"

"That was the way I interpreted the instructions."

“How… how did you get here? Wait.”

“Our instructions were to retrieve a book, make proper payment and bring it to a merchant. He and his people hold our friend at a cove.”

The man waved his finger.

“A cove…”

“Yes.”

“A sailing ship. A trader like from the ancient times.”

“No.”

It was Ana this time.

“No. It was a metal containment. A conveyance that traveled under the waves.”

“You are from Pol…iska. The sweep. That means…”

The old man looked amazed, and then made for an awful change. The awe and amazement was replaced with fear and panic.

“Oh no. David.”

He said it softly as if he had just lost the boy. As far as he knew he had.

“What? He is… safe.”

Stojan’s last word had to be yelled, as the man shot up from the table towards the stairs. He ran up them as fast as he could, bumping into more than one of the lanterns on the way up. They swung to and fro and spun, casting an eerie light upon the interior, as if the library was on fire.

Ana looked at Stojan and stood up, but not before scooping up the book.

Stojan moved to the stairs and was about to yell.

Ana remained at the table, not sure what to do. She clutched the book to her chest.

“Oh no. You must go! We must go!”

Stojan stopped halfway up the stairs. He could see the library master at a window looking outward. The upstairs seemed to have windows too, but they were covered—presumably in dirt and overgrowth. Only one had a panel of wood on it, and he peered through it. He looked at Stojan and angrily yelled.

"Go! I said go! Out the back. You will find it. Go now if you value your lives!"

Stojan turned and leapt down the stairs. Ana was already moving towards the back but knew not where to go.

Stojan was next to her in seconds and together they eventually found a door. This was offset into the wall, had been painted grey and a wide flat bar jutted from the center.

A large red square with writing on it was on one side.

Stojan pushed hard on it, not knowing what to do and was rewarded with it swinging open.

Running down the stairs he stopped halfway to watch Stojan and Anastazja leave him, and heard the men enter the main doors.

There were at least seven of them, all carrying lanterns and torches.

They entered the building, saw the torches swinging to and fro and their eyes fell upon the librarian. He stood his ground and kept looking up at the second level, in an attempt to convince the men he was not alone up there.

He stood and waited for the inevitable.

That night Stojan and Anastazja would escape into the night, relying on their stealth—both innate and learned. Moving in the shadow of darkness they would go on to steal horses—being confident that their own horses were under scrutiny. Against their better judgement they would ride into the blanket of night, out the back end of the city.

A great fire would be reported to have blazed that night—a fire that burned into the morning, as if fueled by a great amount of tinder. Some would say that it was a hill that burned and not a house. Others would say that they remembered a house on the hill.

What remained was unrecognizable.

A SHORT REST–AND A GUEST

Barely able to see his face, Ana sat under a tree and rested. No fire was lit and they were both very tired. Stojan had insisted they ride for some time, and they looked back many times to make sure they were not followed. When Stojan was finally satisfied only then did he allow them to rest. The moon was only a sliver and it hung in the sky above them.

She sat and thought, and looked at Stojan.

"We were not even given the chance to tell him which book you came to fetch."

"Ana that does not matter. The book was a ruse."

"What do you mean?"

"We were followed."

"Yes, we were but..?"

"That was our purpose—to be followed. The merchant used us because he knew we would be trusted. He knew I would find a way to infiltrate the library and speak with the library master. They followed us. They followed us very very carefully, unless they sent word and already had men here. The latter is more likely."

"Oh Stojan. What of the library… and David?"

"I know not. I am beginning to form an opinion on what is happening, but only the barest of understanding."

Though he could barely see her in the darkness, he thought her eyes sparkled much, and that was due to tears she was holding back.

It upset him to see her affected like this. She was at an age in which she took in the world at face value.

Them. Stojan thought about the word, and what was behind it. He struggled to remember what Dagmar had said about the old world, and the turmoil, and the true nature of what had become of Poliska, and Amira.

He still hated the bishop, but now he was starting to hate something else. Them. If it was what he imagined then he truly had no control of his own actions, and he had stumbled into something dark—a darkness that he thought he could hide from Ana.

Little was lost since they kept so much of their belongings with them. In addition, Stojan and Anastazja now carried all that was left of the great library of Amira, as far as Stojan mused. Unless there was indeed a book the merchant desired? He was uncertain.

Anastazja promised herself that she would teach herself to read them, somehow.
"I will light a small fire and keep watch."

Ana nodded and made a place to lie down for the night near the fire. She accepted Stojan's proclamation without question—so exhausted was she from the day's turn of events. She looked up at the sky and surveyed it; the stars looked the same as far as she could tell. Ana watched and took it all in. She thought about the library, and being on the run from the merchant and his men. The events all played through her mind as she started to doze off. Just before finally closing her eyes she thought she saw a tiny shooting star, it twinkled with red and blue as it moved lazily across the sky.

Stojan sat and watched her. He too was tired but he was happy to be alive and aware. The spot they'd chosen was advantageous and should be easy enough to defend. No one would sneak up on them that night.

Thoughts of Dagmar and what he'd told them about Amira entered his head. He attempted to reconcile what he'd been told. Perhaps he would try to explain it to Ana as a way to clarify for both of them.

It was fantastical and it gave him pause to fill her head with fairytale, but the more they experienced together, the more the mundane was left behind. The way the world worked was far different than he ever imagined.

Even his days of being on the run in Poliska were still simple and predictable—as distasteful and dark as they were.

That night he looked around for a raven, and as the sun came up he caught up on some sleep—without dreams.

Anastazja watched him for a time and then ate. She stretched and took a short walk—never more than a few meters from Stojan. He had picked a fine place in the darkness to his credit; they would see their intruders for quite some distance.

With that thought she sat back down, and although she wanted to take a walk she decided instead to fish out the book from the saddle bags.

The partly cloudy day provided ample light to see the pages and words.

She ran her hand over the book—the cover was protected by an overlay of very thin paper covered in a clear protective shell, as if someone had painted it with a coat of colorless varnish. The paper moved like paper, but kept the shape of the cover. She pulled it to her nose and smelled it. It was a dry, satisfying smell.

To her amazement she found she could read the cover and it made her look up immediately to Stojan to share. She smiled as he slept peacefully.

Gingerly opening the book she moved the cover, then the first page, then the next. Some of the words and symbols did not make sense, but the vast majority of the words did.

The book the librarian had chosen at random to test Stojan's reading skills was not a workbook, or a memoir. Until recently she thought all books were history books, but Dagmar had corrected that thinking and enlightened her to all the wondrous flavors to be had. Not all books were created as a recorded history. Some were not even manuals for understanding a complex subject.

Some were simply written for entertainment, as an expression of hopes and dreams. These were written purely for enjoyment.
The book she held before her was clearly one of those.

That morning she spent reading, and although some of the concepts and words were difficult to understand, she felt at one with the writer of this book.

Time was lost as she read, and Ana found herself having to exert much effort to close the book and return it to the saddle bag. For a few minutes she considered keeping the book on her person, but realized it was not something Stojan would have wanted.

"You are awake."

Stojan stood up, dusting himself off.

"Yes."

"You only slept a short time…"

"We have precious time to rest, and those who might yet still follow us will be likely to travel at first light. So should we."

He was focused on their purpose, but could not help notice Ana's mood. It made him smile inside that she was resilient and seemed so happy.

"Is there time for a walk? Or training?"

He blinked, having just woken up minutes before.

"A short walk, perhaps. Go, but not far." He looked at her sword belt and nodded. He needn't have said *And take your sword.* She, like him, was always armed. It was something he did being constantly on the run, and she quickly adapted to this as the norm.

Without a word she left, to go explore and walk into the fields as the sun was just climbing the sky that cloudless day.

He made haste to eat and drink and refresh to prepare for more travel, watching her disappear into a nearby field. At that moment he questioned the decision to allow her to go. Time was of the essence and to allow her to be separated from him seemed suddenly foolish.

And yet he did. It seemed the most solid of things in his life were assumptions and beliefs. His relationship with her was one they both readily accepted. Of that he was certain, and yet the simple things in life that he'd always known as fact were what he now questioned.

He shook his head and almost laughed at the absurdity.

Upside down. Wasn't that what Dagmar had said? That the world was turned upside down long long ago.

Indeed it was, even from his perspective.

Her walk made him anxious, and he focused on his task at hand, and what they were to do next. What he did, what he planned, and what he shared with her were sometimes three very distinct things.

In a short while Ana did return, and this relaxed him visibly. She seemed to notice and smiled greatly, feeling welcomed and missed. It seemed sometimes to her that this man reserved all of his emotion for her alone.

"Are you ready? Have you eaten?"

It was unusual for Stojan to ask two questions at the same time—she sensed his anxiety and assured him the answer was yes to both.
They mounted and rode quickly in the same direction they'd gone. Stojan explained that from their vantage he'd watched the road and none had passed by. Therefore it was less likely that word had been sent ahead.

He picked up the pace so Ana kept relatively quiet—enjoying the weather and the scenery. The fields and rolling hills were full of browns and greens. Autumn was slowly seeping in and so were the richer colors it presented.

Soon they approached a crossroads and had passed more than one traveler. Again Stojan slightly tilted his head and pinched near his forehead.

Stojan stopped his horse and without looking at Anastazja asked, "Which way Ana?"

When she hesitated for some time he added, "To which direction are those that follow us least likely to go?"

“To the left.” She picked it purely at random it seemed.

He pulled his horse to the leftmost path and rode at a slower pace.

“Oh Stojan did you see? There are deer here like in Poliska, but they are different.”

“Oh? Tell me about them.”

“These deer and brown, and almost gold—they are not the red deer we are used to. And their tails are white. So pretty are they.”

“Do their deer also have great antlers? Sharp, dangerous antlers?”

She smiled at his attempt to warn her not to play her game with animals she did not understand. She played back.

“Oh yes Stojan, great antlers.” She moved her hands as far apart as they would go. He glanced quickly and looked back in front of them. Satisfied his message was received he said nothing more.

The next town was larger than the last, but still rather small. Just as the previous town, this one featured a statue near the gate to welcome visitors.

It seemed that statues were the norm in Amira, and were considered part of every day life. Again they received their fair share of stares, and this made Ana uneasy. They were here to purchase supplies but not to seek lodging; Stojan considered it too dangerous. When this caution would be eventually lifted he would not say.

“What do they want from us, Stojan?”

Unlike the last city visit they stayed on their horses. There would be no storage at the stables this day.

“I am unsure. We did what the merchant needed to do—we lead them to the library. I assume he retrieved whatever they needed.”

She looked at him, hoping for an absolute answer.

“But we were privy to the conveyance, we know of the merchant, and the cove, and the library. Our knowledge is dangerous to them—even though we are but bystanders.”

"What good is our word? What difference would that make?"

"Perhaps the librarian was right in his warning: knowledge is power."

"So they mean to catch us…? And then what? To send us back from where we came from? That would not be such a bad thing."

"I do not think it is that easy. And Ana, I do not think free passage back to Poliska is all our fate would be—should we allow them to capture us."

Again Ana thought about being forever on the run from those that would do her harm. It seemed that she was destined to never be at peace but instead to look over her shoulder as a nomad. With this she became sad, and silent.

Stojan stopped his horse. After a few steps Ana did the same—she was lost in thought.

Startled, she looked at him.

"Up ahead."

The town bustled with people coming and going; purchasing goods and selling same. No one stood in the front of the road to confront them. She looked again.

Some of those visiting the merchants stood very still, and they were rather large. These men were not laborers, or merchants but mercenaries of some kind. One was almost as tall as Stojan and twice as thick. There were at least seven of them, and they stood out clearly now.

"Follow me."

He turned around and rode quickly and she followed closely behind him. Barely exiting the city they saw even more men coming from the road, from the same direction they'd just been before entering the town.

Neither direction was an option.

They traded glances. Stojan looked around before he could say a word Ana was already in a light gallop perpendicular to the road.

He followed as they rode through the nearby field—being careful to doge any obstacles. An errant step into a rabbit hole would mean a broken ankle for their horse, and immediate capture. This meant they could not push their horses much.

A tree sprung up here and there and slowly but surely a sparse forest was making itself known.

The men followed them into the field and were not as careful; some were closing the distance. Their gap was still considerable but at this pace the men would catch up in only minutes.

"They mean to catch us, surely."

Ana yelled as she held on tightly.

Stojan focused, splitting his attention between Ana, the trees, the men and the ground. It seemed that Ana did the same.

That was when Ana saw the man. It was just a face. He stood so still next to a tree as to almost be one with it. She rode passed him and as if in slow motion they looked at each other. His face was lined and his eyes were intense. His skin was the color of oak, and his hair was jet black and even longer than hers. His clothing was a colorful blur save for the hat he wore—it was like nothing she had every seen. In his hand was a staff and it was kept at his side; a modest thing made of a thin branch no doubt, decorated with various baubles.

In those mere seconds Ana felt a great wisdom from the eyes; even more so that the librarian or Dagmar. He did not judge, and showed no emotion. This was someone who had seen much and spoke very little; a man that was respected by others and a teacher.

And that day he looked upon Anastazja with much interest, as if he expected her to be there that very moment.

She swung her head to Stojan, expecting that he too had witnessed him. She looked back again and he was gone. She looked at the ground and focused on not running into a tree.

Stojan was focused on where they were going, and those they attempted to outrun.

She gripped the reigns even tighter and focused—the image of the man still fresh in her mind. She went over it, overlaying it on the ever-changing scene in front of her. He was an old man, but his eyes were bright with intelligence. She wanted to ask Stojan about him, or ask where they would go, or if he thought they could truly lose the men in the sparse but increasingly dense forest.

After what seemed like an eternity Stojan looked at her and started to slow down. They continued at the slower, safer pace for a bit.

"Unless this is a trap it seems we may have lost them."

"Did you see him?!"

"No, I have not seen them for some time. In fact I lost sight of them just as the trees became more abundant."

No, him, not them, thought Ana. She decided not to pursue it.

"Stojan I do not wish to run forever."

Though he heard her he had no words of comfort, no words of encouragement, or even explanation. He did not wish to lie to her that day. She deserved the truth, and she already knew it.

Eventually they did stop, and rest. Stojan thought that in mere minutes he would be confronted by their pursuers.

"I'm tired of running."

Again Stojan had nothing to say, but acknowledged her words.

When it seemed that no one would arrive to challenge them, he eventually spoke.

"It seems that we cannot venture into a city—at least one that is nearby. We are wanted by the merchant's men, and most certainly by those that employ him."

Long forgotten was Stojan's concern with being hunted for his crimes, as that was replaced by an entirely new set of transgressions, and Anastazja was a willing participant. She too was wanted.

Perhaps they wished to reclaim what was theirs in the form of the recipient. Would they be able to separate the formula from the girl, and would she then revert to…

He squinted his eyes.

No. What was done was done. It could not be undone.

Though he was unsure exactly why they wanted them, he was not at a loss for possibilities. They were numerous. Perhaps it was all of the reasons combined.

He had been quite naive to think they were actually being let go—to wander Amira unmolested. No, they were prisoners as surely as bars were in front of them.

However, their prison, it seemed, was thirty times the size of Poliska.

Those that could control a great machine of the old world, that controlled what seemed to be the only route of commerce between two great nations, and those that had access to the tec of the old world would not run out of resources.

If they truly wanted to find them they eventually would.

The question was not if, but when.

Stojan was at his wit's end.

The next few days they kept to the forest, attempting to move in the direction between the two cities. Their supplies would last them for a week or more, as long as they could find water. It rained the next day which allowed them to collect some water to drink to further extend their stay.

After what seemed like a week they fell back into the comfort of their normal routine—Ana was allowed to walk, she and Stojan trained and they would proceed after and farther into the sometimes-sparse and sometimes not-so-sparse forest.

Ana told Stojan of the face of the man she had seen, but he had no knowledge and had never heard of such a people. He had no explanation and neither did she.

The two were becoming accustomed to being alone and existed as travelers who did not seek a destination, but instead avoided an end to their travels.

The land was kind to them, though fall had truly made its voice known. Soon winter would arrive—as far as they knew—and they were ill-prepared for this. Perhaps by then they would have migrated far enough and would be able to enter a city undetected. With Amira's great size surely they would eventually be free of the merchant and the men who sought them out.

But there were so many unknowns to Amira and their guide was detained —or worse.

Dagmar had mentioned that seasons in Amira were similar to Poliska, but that because Amira was so vast the seasons differed throughout. In some territories it did not snow at all and in others it was much colder for most of the year. Here it seemed they would experience a change of season in line with Poliska—Stojan's odd experience not withstanding. He was sure that the summer had wound on far longer than ever—by at least a month. He had no explanation of this and all things considered it was one of the least fantastic things he had experienced in recent time. Of this he was absolutely wrong.

His concern now was winter. In Poliska he knew of places to stay and ways to make it through the cold. It had not been easy, but for the three years of being on the run he made it through them. Here things might be different. One advantage of being captured it seemed was a warm place to stay.

With no signs of being followed this deep into the sparse forest Ana was once again allowed to take her walks.

That was when she saw the young man.

Near a tree both a horse and a boy rested. The young man was not much older than Anastazja, and sat under a tree holding his side.

She put her hand on her hilt and watched him. He seemed to be exhausted and in pain. The horse had no saddle bags nor did it have a saddle. In fact there were no accoutrements present. He himself seemed to travel lightly, with no sword or other weapon present, save for a thin stick next to him.

"Hello!"

He yelled out in a friendly, cheerful manner. She was almost certain he hadn't seen her yet his yelling started seconds after she looked upon him.

“Hello? Is someone there?”

Again, friendly tones.

Looking around her she decided to approach, knowing that Stojan would not approve.

He brightened at first sight of her—not once but twice—as if he was seeing someone familiar and then seeing someone for the first time.

She thought him handsome, with dark features like those she’d seen in towns here. Unlike Poliska the population so far of Amira were a bit darker in skin tone, with features that varied considerably; some were of very dark skin with tight, curly hair while others were blonde like her. It seemed to run the gamut and it was as if many races of humans intermingled in Amira, blending their heritage and peoples together while periodically growing apart.

But most did not have the features of the boy.

She approached with caution and could not help but smile.

“Hello there!”

His cheerfulness was infectious, despite his apparent condition.

“Hello?”

Experimentally she conversed, while continuing to look over her shoulder.

She had no trust for this young man yet.

“Hello! I am surprised to see anyone else so far off the road.”

She nodded and came closer.

“What has happened to you?”

He looked embarrassed.

“I took a fall from my horse…”

“You ride without saddle.”

"Yes, well I…"

"I used to ride that way."

"You did?"

His concentration wavered as he spoke to her, and though his demeanor always remained friendly he seemed to have something on his mind. Her answers engaged and confused him.

"Yes. It is not completely practical some times but my horse preferred it, and was happier when we rode together."

He eyed her up and down, focusing on her sword, then her hair, then he looked her in the eyes again.

"Are you injured?"

He pressed his hand tighter into his side.

"Yes. I think so, but I am sure I will be fine. I hit the ground hard. I suppose that is the only option."

She smiled at his attempt at humor and came closer. She was only two meters away now.

The horse was thin but not malnourished. It looked very content and seemed to like her as well.

"Do you live nearby? Is there a city nearby? Are we near a road?"

She realized that in their movements and constant daily migration going deeper into the forest may actually have brought them to another city.

"No. I am very far. I was on a trip. I wanted to be alone in the forest, to enjoy the colors of the leaves, to…"

"You have little supplies. And you travel alone. That is not wise."

Her words came easily and she felt Stojan's wisdom, as if he spoke through her.

It made her mentally roll her eyes. But she was right.

"Yes. I may have left hastily."

"How far are you from your city."

"I… perhaps three days' hard ride."

"Three days! You are this far by yourself!"

Though the boy was a year or two older she felt like an older sibling reprimanding a younger brother for his carelessness.

The pain showed in his face again.

"I will be fine. I just need some rest," he said unconvincingly.

She shook her head.

"I think not. You will need help. Who knows that you are out this far?"

She tried to reason a way for him to be helped without having to bring him to Stojan, but she was unsuccessful. She knew it was the only thing to do. It was the right thing to do.

"I will be back."

With that she ran away, quickly disappearing into the sparse woods and grass. In no time she had returned to the temporary camp.

"Stojan."

"What has happened Ana?"

It was clear to him she had something to explain.

"I met a boy. In the woods. He is injured and travels with…"

Stojan's eyebrow had a mind of its own.

"…little supplies."

He allowed her to continue and did not interrupt.

"He needs our help."

After some discussion in which Ana felt Stojan said far less than expected, it was agreed that she would bring him back. Stojan's unvoiced concern was the protection of the camp, the wellbeing of Ana and the possibility of a trap. She could have easily been followed and this potential ruse may have been placed here for just that purpose. If that was the case then there was nothing to defend. So he decided to allow her to go, and then follow, which he did.

The boy was brought back to the camp—on foot with horse in tow. Stojan followed undetected, and then circled back to appear as if he'd never left. This task was made easy by the slowness of their approach. He watched them interact with fascination, and realized this was the first time he had seen Ana interact with someone her own age. She seemed a little taken with the boy, but still retained a healthy sense of suspicion.

At last they joined Stojan at the camp, and he did his best to appear as if he'd never left.

"Hello!"

Again the boy was cheerful, though his face looked pained. He walked slowly and the horse followed. Stojan was impressed by the obedience.

"And who have you brought Anastazja?"

Introductions were made with the boy embarrassingly admitting he had not given Ana his name until now.

According to him, he was Fox, like the animal. Though he did not explicitly state it, Stojan surmised that he'd taken the horse to ride on his own against his parents' wishes—so rebellious were children of his age that something like this was all but expected.

He counted himself lucky that Ana was so focused, but she had yet to really enter those years with him.

It was decided that his injury was an internal bruising of both his abdomen and his ego, and all three agreed he was in no immediate danger. A full recovery was expected.

They chatted about the land and he as polite a guest as they were hosts.

He shared information on the land, the animals and what to expect. According to him his father was a farmer a few days ride from where they squatted. His family kept to themselves mostly and tried to avoid the local cities, as they found them to be distasteful. Much turmoil was expected there.

Stojan was starting to form a picture of Amira, and it was a stark contrast to Poliska in unexpected ways.

For some reason Poliska was a very stable civilization, with little variance from city to city. If one was blindfolded and plopped into a random city there they would be hard pressed to figure in which they were.

Amira was quite different as the level of sophistication and development varied wildly. In some cities advanced methods of doing things were employed; in others they matched what Stojan expected in Poliska, as if a number of peoples had come together—each offering a different solution to problems. It made no sense as to why eventually all these differences wouldn't just even out, like they did in Poliska.

It wasn't related to the richness of the occupants of the city, as some poorer cities had advancements that would be worth a fortune. It just seemed… random. That was, until the boy explained further.

"The Saints."

"What about them?"

"They influence. The more their influence is felt the more the old world is present—or at least pieces of it."

That of course told Stojan nothing, and sounded remarkably like the vague teachings that Dagmar favored—speaking in wonders and miracles of modernization, of machinery and of sciences, but with no real tangible facts or examples. Because of this Stojan focused mostly on scrutiny of his story.

If they were going to be ambushed it was not going to happen yet.

And it was agreed that he would stay with them through the night. Stojan's reasoning was that if his injuries were going to take turn for the worst they would probably do so that night.

His presence made no difference in the nightly watch, which was taken by Stojan. This was fortunate since it gave no opening for any deception on the boy's part. No, he would sleep through the night or his abdomen would be the least of his worries.

Sleep he did. He did not attempt to make a break, or pillage them, or slit their throats in the night. No newcomers came and captured them. No great nets were thrown and they made it through the night unmolested.

Stojan enjoyed Anastazja's delight at interacting with the boy, but worried about her attachment to him.

They had many things in common it seemed—both enjoyed their alone time in the forest and both were foolish in that respect.

The boy also rode his horse without any saddle, ties, bits or bridle. He guessed that this was simply a lie and that the boy had left in so much haste as to not prepare correctly.

The impetuousness of youth knew no boundaries.

They would eventually send him on his way, as their general direction was in that of the farm, and then the next city.

The former seemed a much safer place to stay.

"Perhaps you can stay on the farm with my family for a bit?"

Ana lit up at the suggestion—a small farm reminded her of her own home so far away, and she liked Fox.

Stojan was less enthusiastic but saw it as the only option. He would even be willing to commit to labor in exchange for lodging. After all they had no real destination other than eventually making it back to where they assumed Dagmar was held.

If he still lived.

Despite holding the currency of two different peoples the most valuable thing he carried was patience.

If they were not welcome at this farm they would have to make a stealthy entrance into the next city. Stojan was no stranger to this way of living, and loathed it. The three years since his daughter's death moved in a way that was unremarkable, and as if he was in a fog. Hate propelled him forward and gave him purpose, and he was seemingly locked in a cycle of obtaining supplies, seeking out a meager existence, and being hired from time to time to maintain his supply of currency.

That all changed the day he met Anastazja.

Now he lived in a vivid world of wonders and colors and new experiences. He was once again on the run, but now he was not just responsible for himself. The center of his new world was not Poliska, or Amira, or a bishop. It was the young girl he now considered his own daughter—a tremendous gift that came with tremendous responsibility, one that he freely accepted without question.

They made slow strides toward the boy's family farm. He seemed very bright to Stojan and despite outward appearances to the contrary, was definitely withholding much information. What information he could have about a family farm that was worth withholding was anyone's guess.

In only a day he was much better and able to ride. This greatly increased their progress. His requests to join Anastazja for her wilderness walks were denied—a fact that both surprised and pleased Stojan. Her decisions lately seemed very mature, and he was quite convinced that she'd learned much, but worried that it was at the loss of some of her childhood.

Both forays by herself produced no new news of a nearby city, or of an animal she hadn't yet discovered, and Stojan always honored her silence. As long as she promised to take the utmost care her privacy in the matter was her reward.

The second day the two did continue their practice in the field, and Fox promised not to follow or watch them.

The trio made their way deeper into the sparse forest and sometimes field. A creek was easy to cross as it lazily attempted to thwart their progress; the half-meter wide stream was no match for them.

In a dense area their guide just stopped.

A NEW PEOPLE

"Forgive me."

Stojan was immediately alerted, but Ana seemed to think it was in jest.

Fox turned to them, being flanked on either side and giving each an apologetic glance.

"Fox is aptly named. He is indeed sly, but like all of us he is loathe to lie."

It was a deeper, older voice and it came from in front of them.

Stojan looked around and sighed, preparing for what was to come next. The inevitable had arrived, and they'd been delivered into the waiting hands of their pursuers, or to those who would hand them over for a hefty reward no doubt.

Ana's demeanor did not change, save for a look of recognition.

"The man… in the woods," she barely whispered. She smiled.

Sheepishly Fox dismounted his horse and kept his hand on its back.

He turned to his partners as they entered the small clearing. They were indeed surrounded, not by men on horseback, but by men and women who seemed curious, quiet and even calm. It felt as if they were invading their land. Perhaps they were already on the farm.

The man who had spoken walked forward and placed a gentle hand on the boy's shoulder.

"Well done, Fox. Thank you."

Stojan's hand was on his belt but he made no further gesture of attack. Ana seemed content and seemed to understand more than she was letting on.

The man who had spoken was just as Ana had described him—a face that was deeply lined, a complexion that showed considerable wear, piercing eyes that seemed full of wisdom. He was grandfatherly with a sharpness to him, and his nose was similar to Stojan's in that it gave his face a bird-like appearance. His clothing was thin and layered, and made of cloths and skins. Around his neck was a great necklace, and he held a staff that was adorned. Unlike the bishop's staff, this one looked like the tree that donated it would readily accept it back. It was not proud, but seemed to contain the same quiet wisdom as its owner. Atop his head was a head dress made of feathers.

Stojan thought he heard a distant, familiar bird call.

"Please. We welcome you now and promise no harm will come to you."

Stojan made no objection—in fact he made no response at all and his silence made Ana give him a sideways glance. He did not return it. She knew he was always thinking and planning, and if he had nothing to say he simply did not speak. It made her appreciate his words all the more. She thought surely he would object, and felt a certain acceptance.

It seemed Stojan trusted these people, even though he was clearly lied to.

The man gestured to Ana and Stojan to dismount. After a pause they did indeed and the entire group proceeded on foot.

The landscape continued to be a tradeoff between trees and vegetation, but now included large rocks that jutted from the ground.

In no time they found themselves upon a path that had been worn, and though there was no clearing, houses and smoke were seen. The house construction varied, and they came to learn this was entirely due to each having a different function. Some houses looked similar to what Ana had grown up in—created of wood with a roof, albeit a bit wider and more squat. Others looked like large cones that seemed to be spun from a great spider.

Others were nothing more than an entrance built into a hill.

There was an organization to the arrangement as they walked—all the while looking like it was part of the surrounding landscape, as if they had chosen locations and even colors to match what nature had already provided.

Ana felt a peace come over her that was similar to what her walks invoked.

The smells of wood, spices and even meats filled their nostrils and it made Stojan's mouth water.

People were scarce but more and more were encountered as they walked—men, women, children all dressed similarly and all with darker features.

Seeing an entire village of people who were so different yet the same was fascinating.

Ana could not read the expression on Stojan's face. Passersby did not look at him with fear, but instead looked upon both he and Ana as if they were royalty. Perhaps they were an oddity, but there was something more to the looks. Each nodded then looked at the ground. Children waved excitedly with the level of energy being entirely connected to their youth.

A few boys similar in age to Fox stared, and Ana thought she saw one being elbowed by another.

The horses were attended to at a large post.

"You are hungry."

It wasn't a question.

They sat around a large circular table that was constructed under a canopy. It looked well-used and Stojan guessed it was in the center of town. It was not, as unbeknownst to him the village was considerably larger than it appeared.

They all sat down, including Fox. At the table were at least twelve others, men and women—mostly of Stojan's age and older. In fact, all were easily older than Stojan and for the first time he seemed young to Ana.

Food was immediately brought out.

Ana and Stojan noticed that the people of Amira had very limited meats to draw from. They ate mostly pig, cow and chicken. In Poliska most every animal was served depending on abundance and time of year. She enjoyed squirrel, duck, deer with her favorite being rabbit. The recipe for her father's dish being sadly lost with her home. Her promise to herself was to recreate it some day.

These people were unlike the Amirans they'd encountered so far in that they did indeed serve many animals at once, and the dishes were also rich in vegetables both raw and cooked. A wide variety was presented to them that day, and they were both given the option of not just water, but alcohol and tea. Stojan and Ana both opted for tea and found it to be delightful, with the addition of honey.

She found their food to be not just delicious but reinvigorating, and it served to recharge both her body and spirit. People who could cook and serve food with such care and love were decidedly not their enemies.

In fact she thought she would volunteer to be imprisoned if these were the meals she'd have to look forward to.

"I am Stanley Two Rivers. You have met Joshua Foxtail Two Rivers, my son."

The boy smiled a friendly but serious smile.

"We again apologize for being deceitful to you. Deceit is not our way but was required. Fox—like his namesake—is quite sly. But he also is honorable and truthful."

Ana nodded and dug into her food, recognizing the meats for what she had been missing for so long.

"We welcome to our table Watchful Raven and She Who Touches Deer."

Ana and Stojan stopped eating and froze. Stojan squinted his eyes at the leader and a distant look came over him. Ana's reaction was quite different in that she glanced at Stojan, and then the rest of the faces. She felt her face warm as the embarrassment seeped in. Seeing only happiness and hospitality on the faces of those that welcomed them, her blush quickly faded.

Neither voiced their questions or concerns, as the food continued to beckon to them, and questions were only half formed.

At first Anastazja thought Stojan had told them of her game, but then realized that they had been watching them for perhaps weeks.

Stojan's look was due to their choice of bird. It reminded him of the encounter with the raven some many months back in Poliska. He would learn that the raven was a very important bird in their society, and that it represented those that had passed and had come back to watch over loved ones. His bird-like features reminded them of a raven, or the mannerisms of said bird.

Stojan ate and drank and listened. He realized just how tired he was—not just physically, but in spirit. The food was hot, and spiced and cooked in a most delightful manner. Much work had gone into it and he felt he was being treated as a visiting dignitary. He ate, drank and listened and both his body and spirit wanted nothing more than to do exactly what he was doing that very moment. It was water to a parched man, or a comfortable bed to one who was suffering from insomnia. He felt almost drugged and mused that this was the most at peace he had been in a very long time. He looked over at Ana who smiled broadly at him—her look of worry vanishing when she saw him so happy.

His unusual silence had her worried, but she quickly realized he was simply content.

No one else at the table introduced themselves.

"We know that you have been traveling for some time, and have been pursued relentlessly. We are a careful people. You will not be found here."

At last Stojan spoke.

"Why do you welcome us so? Your food, and hospitality knows no equal in my recent memory. We are grateful for this, but confused."

Before Ana could speak Stojan added, "For once I am happy to be confused."

That day Stojan and Ana were treated to good food and a discussion with the people of the unnamed town.

They explained that they were unlike the other people of Amira in that they kept to themselves. The old ways were extremely important to them and that adherence had given them a resilience the others had not experienced. Where there was inconsistency and instability there was consistency and safety.

"But the old ways… of the old world?"

"No, I speak of the *old* ways—ways that came far before the old world. Ways that were old when before the demons descended."

After a while it was decided that Stojan and Ana would stay and they agreed to stay through the winter, something that made Ana ecstatic and removed a burden from his shoulders.

He felt most indebted to these people, and could not find a reason not to trust them. Their initial apologies for lying were heartfelt and sincere—it clearly bothered them to trick Ana and Stojan. The pair's kindness and acceptance of Fox was a test, it was explained that first day.

Ana and Stojan slept well that night, and for the first time since meeting Ana, Stojan did not need to stay awake during the night to watch over her.

They were given quarters with separate rooms. It was not unusual for families here to all share one sleeping room together, and then mingle with the rest of the town for such things as eating and working. The concept of a house with kitchen and kitchen table was not found here—eating was always a ceremony and a celebration, and sometimes done with complete strangers.

Subsequent meals always found someone at the meal first thanking the Earth itself for the abundance.

Ana's questioning of this brought about a most unusual conversation.

"You thank the Saints for your meal?"

"No, we do not."

"You do not believe in the Saints?"

"Oh, we believe in them. They exist, much like a chicken or a rock exists."

"But you do not pray to them—to preserve and protect you?"

"No. As they do neither for us. They are interlopers and provide nothing."

As days turned to weeks Ana learned further about this particular peoples' beliefs. Instead of Dagmar giving a history lesson Ana was introduced to a woman who identified as one of the village shamans. She was versed in history, in medicine and other things that were not quite easy to define. She seemed to be a spiritual leader of sorts but would draw a distinct line for Ana that she was simply a guide, and it gave her no power to provide this guidance. Instead she was simply humbly passing on knowledge. Any who did something to the contrary were not to be trusted.

"Power corrupts" she was told more than once.

Both Stojan and Ana were eager to help and participate in the village. They were put to work and treated with respect. Children often came to them to look at them, and sometimes touch them. The latter appeared to make Stojan quite uncomfortable, unless Ana was not there to see it.

Weekly meetings with the elder that had initially greeted them were full of open discussions about Amira and the ways of these people. They were both told that since they agreed to stay they would be made as part of the village and would both be given a name. This name would come to them based on their actions and interaction with the peoples there, and might be different than the ones they were greeted with. Ana was delighted to hear that she would be given a name that only she, Stojan and the villagers knew. It made her feel like she was part of a very extended family. When her anxiousness was shown, she was told that it would happen one day when the time was right.

Stojan found that these people revered almost everything. They thought nothing of apologizing or thanking a large rock for allowing them to move it, or being thankful to an animal for giving up its meat. The trees were thanked for giving up their wood.

"You worship the Earth?"

Stojan asked simply one day, meaning no disrespect.

“No.”

“But you thank it, revere it.”

“Yes, of course. We appreciate everything Mother Earth gives us, provides to us. We are part of it as well.

“But we do not worship it. We worship nothing.”

Stojan thought of the stark contrast of this attitude when compared to the people of Amira he had encountered. They clearly worshipped the Saints and everything related to them. Yet here there was never a mention of Saints, nor were there any statues to be seen. These people did not work in anything as permanent as stone or metal.

“There is a difference between reverence and worship, friend Stojan. Worship gives power over things, by taking it away from those that offer it.”

Stojan thought for some time on this.

A fall day found Anastazja going for a long walk by herself. She had learned of many animals from the teachers and Fox himself, who still asked from time to time to accompany her. The answer was always the same, however.

This day she chose a different direction and found an amazing yet sad sight. It was a field—huge in size and filled with her favorite flower. But, unlike they did in high summer they no longer tracked the sun. Instead each and every one of the sunflowers held their heads low—drying out before winter. She walked slowly into the field, deeper and deeper into the mass of flowers. Three deer stood ahead. This day she did not play her game and just decided to watch them from afar, standing still.

That same day was deemed proper that a party of villagers lead by an elder would start their collections of sunflower heads, as was the common practice of most in Amira and Poliska. Both peoples collected the seeds for their nutritional value to both people and animals alike. As with most undertakings an elder was there to officially start the process, thanking the Earth for what it was providing. A short ceremony was performed.

It was then that they saw her from the vantage point.

Standing out in the field, brazenly apparent was Anastazja. Unlike the faded plants she surrounded herself with, she was still as bright and colorful as high summer. He hair reflected the sunlight in most pleasant and colorful ways, the ambers and golds all scintillating in the sunlight.

The elder smiled and said to the others, “We now know her name.”

The winter was similar to a the winters of Poliska, and Ana embraced the warm clothing provided by a people that seemed to tirelessly explain anything she was willing to ask. Her appearance changed a bit too as she favored some of the wraps of the people. They complimented her for her choices.

“What do you think they want from us, Anastazja?”

Stojan’s question was simple, but seemed two months late.

“To give us care, to provide a haven for two travelers?”

She was not convinced of her own answer. So much enjoyment was had being part of a community that she really did not question it.

“There is more. I do feel it.”

When she started to protest he continued.

“No, it is not deception. I can tell you we are among good people. We are fortunate to be with them. I feel they are not representative of Amira, however.”

“Agreed, but what do you suggest Stojan?”

“I suggest nothing, I just voice a question. I feel we are being prepared for something. Of what I cannot answer.”

Stojan’s perception was seldom wrong, but Ana simply wanted to relax and not examine things further.

Through the winter the people they stayed with worked tirelessly to maintain the village. Much emphasis was placed on security, planning and making sure the people were well cared for.

The stability of the village mirrored that which both Ana and Stojan were used to in Poliska.

For the first time in years for Stojan it seemed that time itself slowed down. He and Anastazja became an integral part of the society. It seemed to provide everything he was looking for—protection and anonymity from those who would do him and Ana harm, a purpose and even something that felt like an extended family. What he would do in the spring time he did not yet know. Could he stay with them indefinitely? Would this be something Ana would want?

The darkest, coldest part of winter turned out to be the brightest and most celebrated. As they were forced to stay indoors and warm, much celebration of life took place including an exchanging of gifts. When it was their time, a group would make a quest to find the largest evergreen. Pedestals made of snowballs were fashioned and atop each a candle was lit. These were built in a great circle and those in each group took turns passing a gift to one another. Ana received a number of necklaces and hair-ties—most with a yellow flower theme. To Stojan she gave a bracelet she had worked on for some time. Stojan gave Ana a gold necklace he had apparently carried with him but until now had never talked about or produced.

"No matter if we stay here forever or leave in spring I want to do this with you every winter Stojan."

Ana hugged Stojan tightly under the great tree, whispering that in his ear.

As spring approached they heralded visitors from far away. Just how far was not determined as these people did not measure in kilometers but instead used terms that were more general. It seemed that exact measurements were not important except for the preparation of medicine and cooking, especially baking.

When they explained to Stojan that the visitors were from 'a part of the village far away' it was lost on him. He was finally able to ascertain some distance when he asked how long it took them to get there.

"They do not travel from one village to another, but instead just from one part to another. When you travel from one tree to another you remain in the forest."

"And how long will it take them to reach our tree?" Stojan asked with some humor.

"At their hurried pace they will hope to make it here in two weeks, but three weeks is not unexpected."

Stojan's horses had been ridden hard in previous years. He knew that spending eight hours in the saddle was not a comfortable affair, but was the easiest way to cover a great distance and not overwork the horse.

At that rate—even with terrain—he could easily cross Poliska in two weeks. Amira was truly vast then, and the remote village—regardless of it being in the same metaphorical forest—must also be a great distance away.

When the visitors did arrive as with all things they were met with much gratitude, appreciation and ceremony.

The elder that spoke with Stojan frequently presented ideas that seemed absurd or hard to imagine. His way of explaining was gentle and poetic, so even when comprehension was not had the concepts stayed with him.

Today he demonstrated one such concept to Stojan. They stood at a small anthill and he pointed at it. Ana was out for her walk and Stojan was happy to converse with the elder.

"This anthill you see—how big is it?"

"I cannot see under the ground. I would think it contains many ants and may span many meters."

Without saying a word he walked in a random direction. For some time they walked without speaking as the elder looked at the ground. Finally they stopped near a tree and he stood, looking down quietly.

Stojan looked as well.

It was another anthill.

"Tell me of this one."

Stojan looked at him, then essentially repeated what he'd said before.

"This looks like the other hill. I would say a meter or two, perhaps three."

The Elder looked intently at the ants as they went about their business.

"It is the same anthill."

Stojan knew that they'd walked far—perhaps a kilometer. He would never imagine that a colony of ants was larger than a few meters deep. How the elder knew he did not ask, but he believed him nonetheless that day.

———

As Harvest Moon turned to Hunter's Moon, leaves continued to fall and the land was lit up with gorgeous colors of yellows, oranges, reds and purples. Even the browns were vivid to those that looked upon it.

It was at this time that Ana was most excited to walk.

She was cautioned by those of the village who knew of her walks to be careful. Though their warnings were well felt, she would not alter her course or exploration because of them.

This day seemed particularly colorful and she was lost in the palettes that nature played with. Vivid orange and red leaves formed a skirt around one tree, while another waved yellow-red leaves in the wind in an attempt to draw attention to itself.

The trees and the forest floor were covered in colors that would soon all turn to drab brown, but not before they delighted the eyes and spirit.

The vivid landscape caused Ana to be less aware of time and more aware of her surroundings. In fact the colors had such impact on her that she decided she would not play her game this day, but continue walking. Perhaps today would be different and she would stay out so long that the sun would set upon her return.

The air and the crunch of some of the leaves brought back memories of her father. Not only did she ponder his last day, but the days previous and his teaching with metal working. She slowed and almost stopped at one point—so lost in thought was she. It was a very different walk and she was starting to struggle with emotions she hadn't dealt with previously. They were so strong now, and superseded any logical thoughts of returning. She was intoxicated by the feelings—the sadness, the want and need and desire. It was all awash and filled her senses. She looked at her sword, played it in her hand, and sheathed it. She looked down at her hands—they looked larger, and less like those of a child. Even though only a year or so had passed she felt she had grown. She missed her father dearly, and yet had been fortunate to meet his replacement. She'd taken to him and he to her so naturally. The past year played through her mind as she stared—the colors blurring in place of the memories before her.

Her alone time that day was well used.

But it was watching her. And it was hungry, and had mouths to feed.

Taken off guard it came at her, hunched down towards the ground.

It was big—easily three times her weight—and its eyes looked at her and meant her to die that day.

It ran at her and covered the ground in no time. But instead of running at her it was running at something else. For a split second she thought she'd intervened in an attack on a deer, and was already reprimanding herself for dropping her guard.

Her first and only time of losing her concentration on a walk and she was potentially to lose her life.

But it was not a deer but instead something much taller and it had yelled to get the attention of the animal.

It was Stojan and his sword was out, ready to take the weight of the animal upon him. Even at his height the animal was still more massive and if it jumped on him he would surely be mauled. Even a properly placed sword strike would not be enough to stop it. He glanced at Ana and their eyes met for the briefest of moments. He was off to the side and behind her, and his actions were clearly to sacrifice himself.

Her eyes went from Stojan to the wolf. Filled with emotion about her father and Stojan she took a breath and the wolf's progress was in slow motion. Its coat waved in the rushing air as its paws took the ground heavily. The teeth were massive and exposed. It looked hungry and insane.

The teachers of the village had told her that the wolves feared those that walked on two legs, though due to her size they may think it proper to think her a young straggler from her pack.

In seconds it would reach Stojan and she would lose her father again, and it was probably due to her walk that day for she did not return in a reasonable time.

Her thoughts were singular.

She was in the air, her sword out. She leapt silently and her arc crossed the path of the great grey animal. Its head turned slightly in an attempt to track her as she cut deeply across its neck and head from the air.

The head turned now, farther than it should have been able to as it stumbled into the ground and leaves—paws digging in as if the brain no longer controlled it.

Landing just to the side of it on one knee, she leapt up again with an upswing of her sword, again cutting at the head that was sickeningly turned to her. He legs left the ground and her upper swing was only partial as she held it in place, still pointed downward. The sword point served as an additional leg with her other two landing onto the bulk of the animal. She pierced it deeply and held a crouched position.

Her fiery red hair blew in the wind, looking very much like it belonged with the autumn leaves that day.

The animal was dead, its head lay at a position perpendicular to its body, pointed to where she once stood—while the rest of it pointed to where it was once going.

She slowly opened her eyes—still gripping tightly to the sword hilt. Looking around she saw not just Stojan, but others. On the other side of her was a group from the village, and it included both the elder and his son. All of the group stared, and Fox looked at her with awe—his mouth open in amazement.

The only person who seemed unfazed by the sight was the visiting elder.

Stojan sheathed his sword as she withdrew hers—cleaning it on the leaves and the fur of the animal.

The group from the village gathered with her and Stojan. The two backed away from the animal as the group surrounded it.

Encircling it, they all joined hands and soft murmurs were heard from them.

To Ana it looked like a funeral of sorts.

Stojan put his hand on her shoulder.

"When you did not return I became worried and decided to seek you out."

He looked almost apologetic, but also upset.

"I was lost—not in the woods, but my own thoughts I think."

"Much has happened to you Ana."

He watched as her hair slowly turned from red to the natural ambers, golds and yellows it was previously.

Today is my birthday, she thought but did not say as if to explain the depth of her distraction. It had been on her mind for some time, and since the passing of time was more general here she did not celebrate it. But she did think of it—and the fact that her father was not there to watch her grow up.

Before he could react they were joined by the group, each member looking at her hair.

She slowly sheathed her sword and looked back at them, feeling self-conscious about it.

The local elder moved into her space and placed a hand on both her and Stojan's shoulders.

"I am glad you are alright."

He spoke to both at the same time.

"They normally do not attack, though he may have thought someone smaller was easier prey. Some become rabid and do not use better judgement. He chose his target poorly today."

He smiled and looked from Stojan to Ana, and then withdrew his hands.

Ana thought about what she had done. Animals were revered and appreciated with the people they were a part of now. Lives were not taken arbitrarily, and they understood that all things wished to live and to care for themselves—to defend their land and their kin.

They were not upset with Ana, she found.

They made their way back to the village and the visiting elder spoke now and then. Stanley's own son stole as many glances at her as he could, undetected. He was mostly unsuccessful and his failures made her smile each time she caught him.

With his arms in the air the visiting elder's voice resonated.

"Mother Earth has provided a beautiful landscape for us. She is most kind to us. And she has also brought us clarity this day. We have much as always to be thankful for."

Stojan listened and walked, and looked at Ana with both frustration and appreciation. She was young and growing. Her emotions were becoming a new thing to deal with—like a stray animal that appeared now and then. Their training had always focused on her feelings, and her hair had acted as a gauge, thus she knew far better how to handle these new rising emotions. It did not, however, make them simply go away.

The walk was long and beautiful, and the talk centered around nature, the activities of wolves, and the harvest. The two elders did most of the talking and periodically asked questions of the group, but Stojan and Ana were left to their own thoughts.

No talk was made about the morality of what was done. It was simply accepted.

Fox was to be dispatched with others to retrieve some of the coat of the wolf once they returned to the village.

Stojan's head was swimming with thoughts.

—

The visitors from afar were announced to the village and a banquet was held. The twelve visitors were composed of a group led by the elder of the village along with others who served various roles. One of those roles was the navigator. Passing down information via non-written means was the preferred method, and due to this, a village member was specifically trained and experienced in travel. He was more than a guide, but also a walking map. This also happened to be his name.

They brought news in general to the people, and this was quickly disseminated through their very efficient means of word-of-mouth. However, Stojan found that they brought two kinds of news—the general news that was fit for the public, and other news that reached only those in a leadership role.

It was not that they kept the truth from their citizens but rather that decisions had to be made before the announcement was as well.

The elder from the visiting group showed much interest in meeting Stojan, and he was invited to a private meal with them. Ana was not asked to attend and it seemed there were only adults at the table this time.

“We are honored to meet with you, Watchful Raven.”

Stojan had grown accustomed to this name, but found that Ana still referred to him by ‘Stojan.’

“We ask that you participate in a naming ceremony.”

Stojan had been privy to two naming ceremonies since settling in, and knew that eventually he and Ana would receive their names officially. It was a simple, pleasant affair.

He raised his tea to them and spoke.

“I would be honored to attend.”

The visiting elder looked at his local counterpart. He had more to say, but instead the visiting shaman spoke.

“We request that you perform the rite of vision as well.”

Stojan said nothing, having just readily agreed to one ceremony he was immediately asked to perform another. Perhaps if he just waited, he thought, they would exhaust all of their requests and he could answer all of them at once.

He sat in silence.

“The rite of vision should not be taken lightly. It is uncomfortable at first but can reveal much.”

Stojan considered this and remained quiet. He had not been privy to any medicine ceremonies as they were always done in private.

The locals as well as the visitors all looked surprised at this statement. It seemed the visiting shaman spoke out of turn, and without agreement from the others. A possible breach of protocol.

The local elder spoke.

"I feel that Watchful Raven should participate in the naming ceremony with his daughter. It is only right as they arrived together and he is her father."

Stojan never felt the urge to correct that misstatement.

"With this we agree. But the rite is also called for. He has much to learn, inwardly."

"His inward wisdom is his to choose, not ours."

"But something has changed, Stanley Two Rivers."

All eyes were upon the visiting shaman.

"What has changed? Do you now speak of Watchful Raven, or his daughter?"

"We speak of the one to be named Sunflower."

"We have witnessed the miracle of her changes, of her skill as a warrior."

"The changes you speak of have not yet been discussed with her father."

The local elder looked at Stojan with empathy.

"Yes. It changes things. We have discussed it, and will discuss it openly with you. But we feel that the naming ceremony should not yet take place. Yet."

"Of what significance is that?"

The local elder was visibly confused, but still remained calm.

"We feel that the naming ceremony should be done with us, in the red lands."

Stojan was beginning to feel protective of Anastazja. To have those tribal leaders discuss her in this way made him feel detached.

“Both should come with us.”

Stanley Two Rivers raised his eyebrows at this.

“I respect the decisions made by the council, but both Stojan and Anastazja have been accepted into our community. They were our guests and now family. It is right that they be named here, regardless of any travel.”

It was the first time Stojan had heard his actual name in months, save for Ana’s use of it. And she had been referred to as She Who Touches Deer equally as long.

His detachment changed to curiosity and acceptance.

“They should be named by their family.”

The visiting elder looked at the others, then Stojan. He squinted slightly, bit his lip and slowly nodded, as if working out a problem in his mind.

“Yes. We agree to this. We will stay for the naming ceremony, and then take them back to the red lands, if they will agree to travel.”

The local elder looked at Stojan.

“It is your decision. You do not need to answer now. Our brothers from the west will leave us in a few days, and at that time you and She Who Touches Deer can decide.”

Stojan nodded.

THE NAMING OF STOJAN AND ANASTAZJA

As with the other naming ceremonies, a small group participated as an inner circle with the rest of the village participating peripherally.

The naming was to take place at sundown with a celebration to follow.

Stojan was first and was presented to the group, wearing only white tunic and matching pants. He was told the white symbolized a new beginning for him—something that inclusion in the tribe had already solidified for him, for his past seemed to be left far behind.

In the center of the group was a blazing bonfire and he stood close enough to feel the heat. It smelled not just of wood and embers but of herbs and plants that had been added.

The local elder walked to him in the circle along with his son. The older man approached and shook his hand.

He smiled. Stojan remained ever stoic.

"Stojan, you have been brought to us by nature. Our paths have crossed and we have welcomed you into our community."

Still holding his hand he raised it above their heads and turned to the crowd.

"You have passed the first test of trust, and you chose to do the right thing in helping Fox."

He nodded to the young boy, who stood next to him, shirtless.

Their hands were lowered and he released their connection.

"You have been made part of our village, and one step remains—that you take the name we give you as your true name. We honor your given name while also giving you this new name that represents unity with us. We shall call you this from now on and never speak it aloud outside of our tribe."

He spoke to Stojan and periodically turned to the crowd as well—choosing his words carefully and making sure they could all hear him.

"You have been a protector and watcher. You are skilled with your weapon and have taught us much. Your gaze is relentless and you tower above us."

He placed a necklace upon him—made of black and white beads. At the center hung a small black shape.

"Our people believe that our loved ones who pass sometimes visit and watch over us as the raven."

Stojan swallowed.

"Therefore we give you the name Watchful Raven and ask that you watch over us as you have watched over your daughter."

Stojan looked at the elder—not sure what else to do. The elder was given his staff, while his son darted into the crowd to retrieve a small bag.

The elder turned to the crowd, and asked a question loudly and sternly in a voice that was challenging.

"Is there one present that disputes this true name? Speak now or in your silence agree with this forever!"

He looked over the crowd, and they fell to an absolute silence. All that could be heard was the crackling of the fire. He turned back to Stojan.

"Stojan, do you now accept your new, true name and continue to be part of our tribe?"

"I do," Stojan said, his words deep.

"Then tell us all your name this day!"

The elder raised his staff while Fox tossed the bag into the fire, simultaneous with his proclamation.

"I am Watchful Raven."

The fire erupted with flames of green and blue behind him.

Those gathered around said in unison, "Watchful Raven!"

There was then much clapping, chanting and cheer.

Stojan looked for Ana but could not find her.

He was hugged by the elder and motioned to step into the circle gathered there.

That was when he saw Ana. She was in white, like him, but instead of pants she wore a skirt of white. She too was barefoot.

The elder smiled at her, and Fox stayed where he stood.

The elder took her hand, with the same strength and vigor as he had done with Stojan.

"Anastazja. You too have passed the test of trust, when you also welcomed him when he was hurt. You welcomed him into your tribe and today we welcome you into ours."

She smiled at Fox, but remained serious. The fire behind her was back to the normal yellow and orange flames, and she could feel the considerable heat.

"You have shown us your prowess. We gave you the name of She Who Touches Deer because of your stealth and your harmony with the animals of Mother Earth."

She listened, slightly confused, as this was a slightly different ceremony as Stojan's.

"Among our people there are some that receive two true names. And almost none that receive three. Today we choose a second true name for you."

Her eyes found Stojan, and he looked proud—far more than she'd ever seen. The elder placed upon her a necklace with a medallion that was rather large. Then, he placed a thin scarf around her neck. Though it was not wide it was thick with fur. The portion around her neck was like a collar and made from one kind of fur, while the length that flowed down her chest was made from another. Later she would recognize the collar as deer and the lapel lengths as wolf.

"You have proven to be a warrior, and demonstrated stealth. Because of your harmony, we award you a second true name today. Anastazja, She Who Touches Deer, we give you the name of The Sunflower."

Her eyes lit up as she looked from the elder to Stojan and back again. Again the elder was handed his staff, but this time Fox did not leave, for he already had a bag in his hand.

Again he turned to the crowd and asked them sternly, almost challengingly a question. He seemed to ask more forcefully than he had with Stojan.

"Is there one present that disputes this true name?"

He slowly scanned the crowd with his staff, surveying them with scrutiny.

"Speak now or in your silence agree with this forever!"

Ana could hear and feel the fire behind her. As the staff was slowly panned around the semi-circle she looked into the eyes of those present. They were all so quiet, and solemn. She saw her friends and those she'd grown close to.

Then she heard him speak, in deep challenging tones.

"I do."

The barest of gasps could be heard throughout the crowd—not because of the volume, but because of the sheer number of people inhaling. Something nearly unheard of was happening.

To make matters worse it was the person who objected.

It was the visiting shaman.

The elder next to Ana looked at her, and she saw protectiveness in his eyes—a grandfatherly caring and something more.

He yelled out to the shaman.

"Speak now then and tell us why you object!"

"I ask that I join you, Stanley Two Rivers."

Again the crowd expressed their surprise at this unprecedented action.

The elder raised his staff in the air.

"You may join us now, Benjamin Clever Owl."

The visiting shaman took steps towards Ana and the elder.

Eyeing him as he approached, the elder treated him with respect while still showing his apprehension at his interruption.

He bowed his head to both Ana and the elder, then spoke.

"It is with respect for our people, the village, our family, you Stanley Two Rivers and you Anastazja, She Who Touches Deer that I challenge your name today."

He spoke to the crowd and the two who stood in front of the fire.

"I have witnessed an event that has caused clarity. My visitation here was fated, and the outcome foretold."

At the last word the crowd showed considerable interest.

"For what I have seen has demonstrated the prophecy."

Ana looked at Stojan, as if to ask for help. He remained in the crowd, watching intently—his all-white clothing and stature making him stand out. It was the most alert he'd been without feeling the need to enter combat. She looked scared, but he had seen her frightened in far worse company.

"I believe that the name we give today is accurate, but that it is not her true name."

The elder looked at the shaman, and then the crowd.

"What name do you believe to be the true name of Anastazja She Who Touches Deer?"

The shaman looked at Ana with something she'd never seen. Was it fear, was it awe, was it reverence? She could not tell that day, but his gaze caused her to feel concern.

He raised his own staff to the crowd, then looked over them, seeing their pensive faces.

"I believe that She Who Touches Deer is well deserved. I believe that she is indeed The Sunflower of our tribe."

Ana caught the face of her group of friends and they smiled wide at that.

"I proclaim that the true name of she who stands before us is Autumn Wind."

At this Anastazja was pleasantly surprised, as if one was offered a bitter medicine only to find it is quite sweet and pleasant. She tilted her head slightly as the concern in her face drained away. She looked at Stojan, and thought she saw him wink.

This proclamation had the same effect on most of the crowd, who seemed to accept this name as readily as they accepted what was previously offered.

However, the effect on the elder standing next to her was profound.

He looked at her as if someone else was standing in her place. He slowly turned to the shaman, then looked out into the crowd as if to search for the entirety of the visiting group. He searched for the visiting elder. Ana watched as he did indeed find him. The man in the crowd nodded slowly —almost gravely—with much confidence.

The elder turned to the shaman, then Anastazja. He looked as if in disbelief.

An eternity passed as the fire crackled away, ignoring the proceedings before it.

The elder seemed to struggle for words, as if asked to make a monumental decision on the spot. To Ana it was a name—in addition to the one given by her mother and father. Though it had meaning among her new family it seemed that it did not change her.

She Who Touches Deer described the game she liked to play. *The Sunflower* seemed to only be about her appearance. But, *Autumn Wind* was quite beautiful. It made her feel pretty to think about it, and it seemed to be a combination of things. It was a grown-up name that felt right regardless of how old she was, or would be.

The shaman spoke to the elder in quiet tones—whispering in his ear. The elder did the same in turn to him.

Ana looked over to Fox who seemed as uninformed as her that day.

The elder then turned to Anastazja, who felt both exposed and important.

"She Who Touches Deer, Sunflower of our tribe, do you now accept your true name of Autumn Wind and continue to be part of our tribe?"

"I do," Anastazja said without hesitation, her words light but strong.

"Then tell us all your name this day!"

The elder raised his staff while Fox tossed the bag into the fire, as he had done before.

"I am Autumn Wind!"

The fire erupted with flames of orange and red behind her.

The group yelled in unison, "Autumn Wind! We welcome Autumn Wind!"

Both the elder and the visiting shaman hugged her and shook her hand. With that the group ran up to her, and engulfed Stojan, embracing them, congratulating them, welcoming them as if they'd just arrived.

Fox, though he stood next to her, waited patiently and gave her a tight embrace, his eyes focused on Stojan as he did.

The big man smiled.

That night there was much merriment, and Anastazja was congratulated personally by the visiting elder. He took her aside and talked with her.

“You please me by accepting your true name. Thank you.”

Ana smiled.

“I like it. I think it is beautiful.”

His mouth turned to an upside down smile as he thought about her response. He looked up as he tilted his head. It seemed he hadn’t even considered that. He then hugged her.

“Indeed.”

At that moment Stojan arrived, saw her eyes and smiled. The elder released her in time for her to give Stojan a tight embrace. That night they truly felt like a family, like they belonged.

—

Oh Stojan. What do you think?”

Stojan sat and watched the festivities continue. The fire was small now and the hour was late. Many had congratulated them, and Anastazja had made numerous friends since their arrival. This fact pleased Stojan for as traveling with him provided numerous unusual experiences, none of those were what he thought a girl growing up should be exposed to.

Here her friends allowed her to experience what a young girl should be surrounded with. When he was slow to reply she continued.

“Of the naming?”

“It is very fitting, Ana.” He smiled at the ironic use of neither of her new names. To him she would always be Ana—a name he’d used ever since the bridge.

“We have been fortunate, and I am very thankful for our travels.”

She looked at him, expecting more.

“We have been asked to travel again.”

His statement was heavy and sat in the air between them. Her feelings on the matter were mixed.

“I am excited to travel, but…”

He waited patiently as she sat down next to him.

“We have made friends. I am happy here.”

He nodded politely, even sitting he was much taller than her. Her face lost some of the happiness, and was slowly replaced with worry as she continued.

“I’m afraid… to lose them. To… lose our place here.”

He put an arm around her shoulder just as a villager approached, tapping them both as she passed by. It was apparently a form of validation, allowing the giver to make it known without interrupting their space.

Ana looked up and smiled, then looked back at Stojan.

“I feel like we are family *here* Stojan.”

“I agree.”

“Do you want to leave? To go with the elder? Do you know why they want us to travel?”

“Yes?”

She looked at him surprised.

“Yes?”

Again, she looked surprised.

“No.”

“Stojan—you joke about this?”

“I merely answer the questions in the order they were asked.”

Her face brightened as she understood, mentally going over her questions and matching up the answers.

“So you wish to travel but do not know why they ask us to do so?”

“That is correct. I feel that they have a good reason. They have been kind and welcoming, and this is an honor, I think.”

She looked into his eyes.

“One that we should not disregard.”

The two stared at the fire, watching the blurs of shadows that represented those dancing and celebrating. They sat for many minutes, enjoying each other’s company, the sight of the fire, the smells of the burning herbs and the cool night air.

Much was contemplated.

—

The next morning Ana continued the conversation with Stojan.

“I wish to walk again today, Stojan.”

“There is no reason why you cannot.”

He was confused by her question, it seemed.

“But the wolf? Are you not concerned by danger?”

“Ana I am always concerned for your safety, regardless of how much I have taught you or how proficient you have become. I will be concerned as long as I live.”

She stared.

“Each and every time you go I warn you to be careful and to remember what I have taught you. Every time you have left you have remembered —save for one. And it seems that one time it was fated that I was there, along with a large group of warriors.”

She dusted off her outfit and strapped her sword belt to herself.

“It would seem the odds are in your favor. Go and return to me so that I may warn you again tomorrow.”

She smiled, firming up the belt.

"Do not rob me of that pleasure tomorrow."

With that she left, and decided to walk closer to the village in a different area.

On the way she passed the shaman from the previous night. It seemed to her she was fated to run into him, and that their business was not finished.

He smiled ever so slightly.

She nodded her head to him and he waved for her to approach him, which she immediately did.

"Good morning to you, Autumn Wind."

She smiled and almost laughed. She had simply forgotten about the naming, or at least her new name. For weeks she had thought about *Sunflower*, as the murmurs in town, and of her friends was that this was to be her name. Not so for the one she abruptly received the night before.

"Good morning to you, elder."

Seeing her smile he brightened.

"Am I the first to call you thusly?"

Though she was a bit intimidated by the man she laughed lightly and said simply, "Yes. You are."

This seemed to delight the man further.

"I have a question for you but I do not mean to invade, may I ask it?"

"Of course."

"When you walk, what is it you do? Not with your body, but with your mind?"

"I suppose I do nothing."

"Nothing?"

She felt he was leading her.

"No. I do nothing with my mind. I think that is why I enjoy it so."

"Thank you, Autumn Wind. I have enjoyed this conversation. Be safe."

Clearly the conversation was over. She shrugged slightly and continued on her way.

That day she did indeed think of nothing as she walked, and the nothing gave her clarity. In fact she then realized exactly what the confusing conversation was about. It was the nothing that allowed her to think about everything.

He had planted a seed which helped her understand herself, and why she had allowed the wolf to take her by surprise. He had removed any doubt she had lingering in her mind by reminding her what she did while she walked—which was nothing, and everything.

She returned from the walk unscathed and sought out one called Watchful Raven.

"I would like to go."

The look in her eyes told Stojan that she had made up her mind. He would not tell her that day that he had spent most of the time she was gone worrying about her, but instead just replied.

"Just like that?"

"Yes."

"I am in agreement, Autumn Wind."

She smiled. It did not sound right coming from him and she wrinkled her nose slightly, then thought better of it.

"I will still call you Ana."

"Yes please, and I will still call you Stojan."

"Then we are in agreement on everything."

LEAVING FOR TRAVEL

Before leaving, the pair were asked to meet with the local elders. This did not seem unusual because Stojan and Anastazja had sat down with them on more than one occasion. As the only outsiders so far welcomed into the tribe it was the norm.

They were told that they would be gone for a long time. It would in fact take more than a few months to reach their first destination. Once there they were to meet with the rest of the tribal leaders that had been left behind by the ones that visited.

Their group consisted of the group that had been sent previously, minus one person. Apparently it was tradition to have one person stay in the village that was visited. This was done as a learning experience, but also so that they did not grow apart from each other.

"We will always continue to mix."

Stojan made conversation on the way to the outskirts of the city—a concept that was difficult to solidify as the village had no real border.

"Won't we encounter those of Amira that live in cities?"

Their guide shook his head.

"No, we will travel mostly off road in the lands we occupy. We will have to use their roads from time to time, and in those cases we will be cautious."

"Have you encountered many Amirans?"

"In our recent history we have kept to ourselves. In the old days, yes."

The guide went on to explain what Anastazja had already been taught—that in the old days of upheaval the people withdrew to these lands, leaving the turmoil and the struggles to others.

It seemed that while things were in great flux the people just continued to grow and stabilize. In this they had much in common with Poliska, albeit for a very different reason.

When asked what people he was referring to he just continued to say 'The People.' This was their name for themselves, Stojan finally realized. The people of Amira were referred to as 'Amirans' but the people of Poliska knew of no others, really, and referred to themselves this way as well—simply as 'the people.'

The guide explained that there was a name for their people, and in the past they had been separated into many different tribes from all over Amira. As time went on the largest tribe absorbed the others, and they became one great nation together.

It was a nation inside of a nation.

Fox rode next to Ana on his own horse, and neither opted for bareback. Saddles were mandatory despite the minor protests of the boy. Ana kept hers to herself.

Stojan rode in front with some of the others and in Anastazja's opinion was quite chatty.

She wore a thin tunic of whites and browns with a vest of darker brown over that. On her legs were thin leggings also of white with some reds intertwined. Upon examination of the pants worn by Stojan in the ceremony, she sought out her friends and strove to duplicate them in her size, but ended up with pants that were thinner and tighter. This she wore experimentally for their first leg of her journey, but was advised that she find something 'a bit warmer' for the rest of the journey. Having her legs restricted never went well.

They rode for some time in the woods, then the wilderness. The navigator of the group paid very careful attention to paths that Ana could see and paths that she could not.

Much care and effort was used to stay within the boundaries of their land and not cross onto the roads used by the Amiran people. For many days they rode, resting when necessary and stopping in nearby villages.

To Stojan and Ana it seemed sometimes that one minute they were riding in a field and the next minute they were suddenly in the midst of a village. There was no warning and they were sure that had they been by themselves they would have just passed them by. Or perhaps the villagers would have allowed them to pass by.

Thus they continued to trek onward. More than once Anastazja was allowed to pursue a walk, with the only requirement being that she could not go in the direction of a nearby road, for it was thought that the Amirans might be more dangerous than the animals she'd uncover.

While she was gone one day Stojan decided to discuss it further.

"You believe the Amirans to be dangerous?"

"Watchful Raven, you do not?"

It was the visiting elder that answered his question with a question—something he himself had a habit of doing.

"From what we encountered they can, but I do not see them as different from those in Poliska."

"Really?"

Stojan collected his thoughts for a moment.

"We have encountered mercenaries in the employ of a ruthless merchant, and others with similar intent. In Poliska I have encountered a man who considers himself to be a bishop, with only evil intensions. And I have encountered others in the past that were blinded by greed. By the same token I have also encountered those townsfolk here that seem to be good people, like we know of back home."

The elder nodded.

"We have also encountered an old man that wanted to share knowledge, and hoped one day that the saints were dealt with properly. And back in Poliska we encountered a man that changed from selfish to unselfish before my eyes."

"You refer to this Dagmar Autumn Wind has mentioned."

"Yes. So you see that people are good and bad—wherever you go."

The elder thought for a moment and turned serious.

"Do you believe the same for all peoples of this earth?"

Without hesitation Stojan answered.

"Yes."

"Does this consideration also apply to those we call the Saints?"

Surprised at this turn, Stojan did not answer immediately.

"I do not know much about the Saints."

"But please, go on."

"I don't know."

"Honest."

Stojan, out of answers, turned the question back onto the asker.

"What do you think of them? I have only seen those who have been directed by them to perform selfish acts."

He spread his hands and spoke to Stojan.

"We only know of who we have seen, but like all things there is more to the unseen than to the seen. With the Saints there is much to the unseen—too much. We are in the dark. This is also why your rite of vision is important—because it may also reveal something to us about the Saints."

Stojan had considered the rite of vision for some time. He was told that he may see things that would bring clarity, but also things that would bring sadness.

At this time Ana had returned so they did not talk again about this until they eventually arrived.

As they traveled the weather became warmer and warmer. The guide explained that in the direction they traveled they would eventually reach a place that winter would never touch. Then they would reach the red lands— a place that was even warmer.

Word spread of the visiting caravan from village to village, and in some cases their reputations preceded them—specifically the presence of Ana and Stojan. Though in the past an Amiran or two had been welcomed into the tribe, Ana and Stojan were the first not of Amira to be allowed to do so. They were foreigners twice over.

No opportunity to learn or explain was squandered. On the way they were treated to items prepared in villages that had food stuffs—animals, plants, flowers—that only were found there. They drew from these local anomalies and prepared treats and items for the travel. All villages seemed to want to contribute something to them.

"It is good luck to provide a gift for our travels. You honor them when you accept."

Stojan considered this statement.

"It seems a lot of commotion for two travelers, and if you do this for all that travel then…"

"Then we would not need any commerce caravans."

"Yes exactly."

The guide smiled.

"Though it is tradition to give a loved one a small gift when traveling, you are being offered gifts for a different reason."

Stojan waited for the answer, something Ana would not do. She waited patiently with Stojan for the answer—her interest piqued.

"It is because you are on a quest."

Stojan looked at Ana and suppressed the desire to shake his head at her. He knew she would be excited to hear of this. And to be told that they were officially on a quest would forever delight her.

"We are?!"

The guide turned to Ana.

"Yes of course. We are on a quest to visit the red lands so that Watchful Raven can join in the Way of Clarity."

Ana looked at Stojan with much glee, as one does when seeing someone about to do something exciting.

Stojan did not share in the excitement, for he knew there was more to this quest than a vision of some kind. And he had his share of visions. Perhaps this would be his last, and explain to him what was happening around him. If not then at least it provided them with travel together among a great and kind peoples.

His skepticism was only outdone by his bizarre experiences.

Ana enjoyed the travel and especially remembered the kind faces of people who stopped and said hello to her group. The children and younger girls especially made an impact on her and it was as if these people knew how little family she'd experienced and were making sure that she knew she was loved, and valued.

She questioned sometimes whether she was deserving of such love, such kindness and adoration. She hadn't done anything to earn it, she thought. This was not voiced to Stojan for she knew he would give her a talking to about the subject that would last entirely too long, even though she would thoroughly enjoy it.

Anastazja's days were filled with new faces, new foods and new things to learn. The time was enjoyable but also went fast and she watched the seasons change around her. Much to her delight the weather remained warm. Unlike Poliska the area they now traveled in did not experience the seasons properly, but instead had a summer that was very hot, a fall that was very long, and a winter that was practically nonexistent.

As part of their off-road travel they ventured deep into the mountains. Ana's first exposure to this was at night just before falling asleep.

After a foggy day or two of travel they'd settled down for the night. As the fog parted and stars became visible Ana noticed some were missing. Her assumption was that a great black cloud masked some of the sky—above the horizon. Try as she might she could not see the outline of the cloud and thought it an approaching storm front.

The next morning in place of the missing stars was the reason for their masking.

A mountain.

"It is where we go for the next many days."

She pointed and questioned.

"There? We go up there?"

"Yes, we travel through the mountains. It is the only way to the land we need to visit, and the best way to avoid the many Amiran towns nearby.

Anastazja knew the importance of the avoidance, as she'd seen two scuffles between her group and the Amiran mercenaries who seemed to litter the roads. The second scuffle was something they watched from on high. Travel between cities was clearly a very treacherous affair, and done with much peril.

She watched many die in these road conflicts, and wanted very much to help.

Unfortunately their progress and stealth required that they remain out of any conflict, so she was helpless to do anything.

"It is really like this all over Amira?"

She had a partial answer due to her continued learning among the tribe, but wanted a clear answer now.

"From what we experience the Amirans fight often."

"Yes but why?"

This probing intrigued Stojan.

The elder added his wisdom on the matter.

"It is because so much is in flux, and it is the same reason your Poliska was much more peaceful—the lack of flux."

Stojan thought the statement absurd, but only from personal experience. It was indeed more peaceful in Poliska.

"The machines of the past—the things brought to life by the Saints—they offer power and change. This change is random throughout Amira, and many always clamor to embrace and control it. But they cannot. It is a constant struggle. It has brought gifts to some and horrible death to others. It is many things to some, but it is one thing to all."

"And what is that?"

"Disruptive."

This needed further explanation and it showed in Ana's features.

"It disrupts the very nature of civilized people. If they cannot move forward together then they will always be at odds. And if they cannot control the reason for the disruption then they are forever pawns. The wolf that attacked you, dear Autumn Wind—it acted out of turn as it was rabid. It had a sickness about it that affected the mind. The Saints affect men and women in the same way—they bring about a rabidness that they do not understand."

With all Ana had learned about the Saints it was that one word that affected her most. *Sickness*.

She thought about these Saints and even though they still did not seem real she now felt afraid.

"We will never see one will we? We will never get close enough to them will we?"

The elder looked at Stojan, as if assuring him that Ana's question would be answered with comfort—she was visibly upset now.

"You have been given much to think about. Know that we have remained peaceful all of these years. When we reach the red lands we will talk more of this."

He looked at Stojan again, and then finished.

"You are safe."

Ana was not convinced. Stojan even less so.

—

Higher and higher they climbed for more than four days. Ana found her breathing was difficult after a while and it was explained that she simply had less air to breathe.

The landing they stayed on for the night had clearly been used before. Not only were dried foods tightly packed away but also all assortments of minimal supplies were kept there. Any traveler staying here on that mountain pass would be refreshed.

Their guide explained that part of the responsibilities of the nearby village young people was to periodically restock these caches and assess whether they had been discovered by animals, for once they were discovered they made a poor choice for storage.

That next morning just before leaving the guide allowed them to survey the land below. The view was breathtaking, and seemed to be something that few had ever experienced. Ana stared as her gaze slowly swept across the vista—her entire view encompassing hundreds and hundreds of kilometers. It seemed like a view that would make an eagle jealous and something she would remember forever. Tall grasses looked like lightly painted canvas; tall trees seemed as moss; large lakes looked like bright blue puddles and lesser hills were minor bumps in the ground. Everything took on a different perspective and significance.

Stojan saw the land as a living map, and took in as much as he could to remember for later. Small puffs of clouds rubbed against a nearby mountain in a lame attempt to make headway. The mountain always won.

Just before they were to leave their guide looked at them, and then surveyed the land.

"Ants."

Stojan and Ana looked again, thinking they'd missed something.

"We are the people of the ants, for our hill spans all that you see. And all that you do not. It is our village."

Ana smiled at what she thought was poetry.

Stojan smiled for a different reason.

The trek down the mountain path took longer than the journey up due to the fact that the trail wound down a bit more. It made for less taxing travel and was appreciated by all, as it seemed the sky was greedy and withheld its air more than the trees did.

Anastazja did not dare take walks, for fear of tumbling down the mountainside, and thought of what walks would be like in the red lands.

According to their guide it would be some time before they reached them. The travel and narrow paths sometimes isolated Ana, and in place of conversation with Stojan—or private meditative walks—her mind wandered while on horseback. She would thus be lost in thought for hours.

Unlike the people of Poliska—or presumably Amira—the people Ana and Stojan had found themselves with did not celebrate a yearly birthday. Instead, they celebrated a coming of age and then something they called Prime. Other than that they did not talk much about a yearly recounting.

They did maintain a calendar but their reckoning of time was much more broad and even lax than she was used to.

When she brought this up with her various teachers they commented that there had been a time when time ruled all.

"The people of the Old World knew the passing of each and every moment, and tracked it constantly. Everything they surrounded themselves with reminded them of these moments. In this obsession they missed much."

When Ana wanted to know more her teacher had taken her to a field of small flowers.

"Each time you breathe I want you to look closely at a flower. Move from one to the next to the next."

Ana did this, moving her face from one flower to the next to the next, until she finally felt a tap on her shoulder. She turned around and her eyes were tired from the exercise.

"What did you see?"

"I saw a flower of course, then another, then another!"

She was frustrated with the pointless exercise. Surely doing this with two or three flowers would have proved whatever point she was trying to make, but the teacher had her do this for some time.

"That's not what I saw."

"Well, what did you see?"

The teacher then turned Ana slowly, grabbing her by her shoulders, then pulling her closely.

It was a field of flowers they looked upon.

"While you saw a flower, I saw a meadow. Those that choose to focus on each and every flower will never see the meadow, just as those that focus on each and every moment will never see their lives."

Ana looked upon it and nodded.

"It is up to you which moments you choose. Do not choose them all."

With that lesson Anastazja truly understood that her memories were made up of what she chose to remember—to experience and to focus on. In her mind every day could be her birthday, just as every day could be the day of her father's death.

It had been a profound lesson and why she had forgotten about her birthday entirely.

But today she was reminded of it, with the change of seasons, and her growth. Though it had been only two years or so she had grown much. And her small sword was almost no longer a fit for her. At some point she would have to replace it.

She thought about her prospects for some time, and only because of the lesson in the field did she not dwell on it too long.

THE LIBRARY OF THE PEOPLE

"We will make a detour." Their guide had spoken this unprompted. He had a habit of announcing changes to their journey seemingly out of nowhere, and not in response to any particular conversation.

More and more of the landscape changed. Greens gave way to browns, grass gave way to gravel and trees gave way to shrubs. It was decided that the group would now split up, with only the guide, Stojan and Anastazja taking a slight detour and the rest heading to the village.

The others bid farewell and safe travels, and explained that they would see them at the end of the day.

Their path took them down hills and passes made mostly of rock, and Ana was now starting to see why the lands were named so—as some browns actually approached various shades of red. Hidden in so many outcroppings and hills and jutted rock was a platform of sorts.

As they approached it Stojan mused that it looked like a foundation was made at some point but a building never built.

He soon found he was wrong, partially.

Planted in the semi smooth rock platform was a number of small triangular monuments. Each one was small pyramid of stone, with surfaces that looked smooth.

In the very center was a larger pyramid, all of some sort of reflective obsidian.

The guide walked up to it after dismounting and rubbed his hands gently along the surface, and then looked at his palms, then the sky. It was a cloudless day and still quite warm. When he seemed happy with the position of the sun he spoke again.

"We will visit the library."

Ana brightened. "There is another library in Amira? We have visited the great library but we feel it has come under the control of those who sought us out."

"Or worse," added Stojan.

He turned to them and spoke gravely. "There were many libraries in Amira—some great and some small. The library you visited is probably one of hundreds, even thousands that littered the entire land."

"Thousands? I cannot imagine!"

Ana experienced both disbelief and excitement. She wanted it to be true.

"It was a common thing for every city to have at least one. That was before the world was turned upside down. Much was lost, and that included the libraries. So much knowledge perished with the people, as knowledge is not only stored in books."

He mounted his horse again and they made their way down the great uneven stone with the flat top. Where the great thing met the earth he circled here and there, and in what looked like a small cave he stopped. Motioning to dismount the horses he himself did so and entered the cave. It reminded Ana of the tiny cave they stayed in on top of the mountain and expected the same amount of room. Truly it was just large enough to house a few people.

The guide removed from his pack a small dark square. Dusting off a location on the wall he squinted and pressed the square against it. He moved his head to the rock and listened.

He waited.

"Tell me more of this time in history, I wish to understand."

Ana asked politely, and was frustrated by hearing only a part of the story —out of order. She wanted to know how things happened as they happened and did not want to squander the opportunity of learning. The guide turned to them, as if waiting for something to happen. Perhaps this was a rest and the darkened area provided respite from both the bright sun and the heat.

"When they came much was in flux. The barrier that protects our world from damage itself was in flux. Your friend is right in that our ways of navigation were turned upside down. But that is not what is meant by that."

He thought for a moment, trying to put a thousand years of history into a paragraph.

"The people at the time were a people of great accomplishments, of conveyance, of communication. Much of the world was unified by this, but not in spirit. They could talk, but they could not understand what was in their hearts."

"But you said the language of Amira was the language of the world, and that is why we understand you."

"Yes. The words were understood, but not the meanings, the experiences. The world was growing apart when they came. Men and women lost empathy for one another. It is not like our nation.

"And that was when they came—through a doorway that had been opened. We do not know if the doorway caused the turmoil, or if the turmoil opened the door. They descended upon us. At first there was only one. But then they others came."

"People? Travelers?"

"They were not people. They had no form. They were called Angels, then Saints. We call them demons, but we know that they are a people from a place we cannot go."

"But they can go here?"

"No, they could not, at first. But then they found the soft places."

Stojan and Ana traded glances.

"Places made soft, and accepting—by the belief of their people. In those places of worship a warm place had been made for them. They found they could occupy these places."

"The church?"

"Yes, Stojan, the church—as it is known now. Or at least in Poliska."

"I do not understand," said Ana.

"Where people came to worship, a soft place was made that allowed them to thrive. The more belief that had been expended in the same place, the more a welcoming environment had been created. Like a home prepared for a visitor, or a well-worn path. Soon more and more came and learned to occupy these places of worship. They tricked the believers into thinking they were a part of their religion."

Stojan could not believe his ears but listened intently.

"They used their faith against them."

"Surely they caught on."

"No. Because they *wanted* to believe. And this desire was used as a weapon to control. The more they wanted it to be true the more the interlopers were more than happy to oblige."

"But surely not everyone."

"No, there were those that would not take their deception so easily, and there were those that simply had no faith. But whatever faith was had was quickly adjusted to fit the actions of the visitors. For that is the nature of faith—it adjusts to what already is, and to anything that proves it to be true. And this was during a time of disruption. The Earth experienced great changes—immense storms, quakes and upheavals. The maps no longer applied, for the very borders and shores were twisted. Flooding brought water to deserts and new mountains arose where there were none. Other mountains sunk back into the Earth. One thousand times one thousand times one thousand perished. Many times over."

Stojan's disbelief was rivaled only by his interest.

"Those that survived were only a fraction of what once was. After a while the visitors stopped coming. It is not known why. Some said the door closed. Perhaps there were only a few."

"Why do we not know of this? And why did it not affect Poliska?"

"Poliska was special."

He smiled, as if about to tell the only positive portion of his story.

"The people of Poliska were deeply faithful, but their faith was very specific, and a leader of their faith learned one of the secrets of the Saints and used it against them. Opposing forces joined together as they now had a common enemy and goal. Both the faithful and the faithless despised those that would use faith against them."

"What did they do?"

Ana was enthralled.

"They made the places of worship no longer soft. And, they did this in a way that was efficient and effective."

"They destroyed the statues," said Stojan.

"How did you…?" Ana was taken aback.

"Because dear Ana, there are no statues in Poliska. There have been none for hundreds of years. The nursery rhymes are not there to lull you to sleep; they are there to remind us of why we are free."

"How did you know this?" Their storyteller was now interested in Stojan's response.

"Because I saw the last statue in Poliska. And, it is why I am here now."

He would say no more about that. After an uncomfortable silence the guide continued.

"The upheaval affected Poliska as well, and their peoples were equally diminished—despite their great sweep. But Amira is not Poliska. The interlopers took up residence, and each over time became a saint."

A great click was heard from within the wall.

"Our great nation reveres all, but worships none. We have no soft places for the saints to dwell within. And we build no statues."

Just then some dust started to fall from near the top of the great wall. A distinct frame could be seen as the dead end turned into a doorway. A block of granite swung in as easily as if it was made of wood, but very slowly.

"How do you know so much of this history? This is even more than the elders have revealed." Stojan asked him after a few moments. He did not answer but continued with his task.

Their guide walked in once the door was open wide enough and he was followed by his companions.

Anastazja immediately smelled the stone and an earthiness unexpected.

A dim greenish light came from within. It wasn't Amiran magic or tec—it was something much more common, but just as impressive. Mushrooms.

Carefully planted and presumably cultivated were thousands of mushrooms, but these glowed dimly in rows that lined the great entryway and the walls. They were planted in tiny decorative overhangs at just the right heights to provide the room with a pleasant light.

It was an impressive room and Ana took in the area—bathed in the gentle bluish-green light.

As large as the room was it was at last disappointing for it was just a single room.

And it was apparently empty.

Still remaining silent, their guide moved over to the door and pushed it closed again—it swung effortlessly and happily obeyed. Within seconds she heard a large snapping sound—as if two great rocks were slapped against each other.

The door was now closed and she felt almost trapped.

Their guide turned to them as if waiting for them to speak.

"Your underground hall is impressive—it seems like an impenetrable room yet there is no treasure. Though there is much space for it."

Stojan meant no disrespect and was merely stating his observation.

The guide smiled at Ana.

"You are correct that treasure is here, Watchful Raven. But not here."

Anastazja folded her arms. It was warmer in the room than outside. The closed space reminded her of the great conveyance, and she hoped they would be on their way soon. The cryptic comment fell on deaf ears.

He walked to the opposite wall. In the dim light she could see many symbols. Carved into the stone were tiny outline pictures. Some she recognized as birds, others as rope, still others and parts of the body. They were all intricate.

He ran his fingers over some of them, as if he was reading with his fingers. Perhaps in the dim light he needed to feel the pictures as much as see them.

That was when Anastazja heard the distinct sound of stone being pulled against stone, and some of the symbols became a door as they slid away to the left.

The guide cupped his hand under one of the nearby mushroom planters and pushed up. A section moved upward. He handed this square to Ana, and then one to Stojan. He took one for himself as well.

Stairs.

"Blow on them, but not too hard."

He blew on his own torch and to Ana's delight the mushroom glowed many times brighter than it had before.

She and Stojan did as told.

They entered the stairs slowly and carefully, as both Ana and Stojan expected them to be slippery. Surely there was much fungus growing in the dark here with the mushrooms—making for surface that was dangerous to walk down.

The stairs were quite the opposite, and care had been taken to make them gritty and easy to navigate safely.

Holding her small mushroom torch she followed him downward—her smile lit up with blue-green.

At least two floors down they walked until the stairs opened into a short landing. Again the guide ran his hands over symbols, and again this door slid aside.

"We are here to make a deposit… and one withdrawal."

He walked through the door and the sounds of his voice and footsteps were absorbed immediately.

Ana and Stojan followed into the darkness. Though she could not see it, it seemed the room had no ceiling. Were they outside? Ana wasn't sure, but felt she could breathe easier.

"It is still light out."

When Stojan said this he gave the guide a most peculiar look.

To the side of the door was a great metal crank. Next to it was a release latch. He pressed it so that it allowed the crank to turn. This it did, slowly. The wall it jutted from seemed like it did not stand entirely straight, but rather had the slightest of slopes, as if falling inward.

Ana's attention was taken away from the sight because the lighting started to change—as if the sun was rising.

She looked behind her to the room, and up. And up.

The guide closed the door quietly behind them.

They were not in a cave, or a room, or even outside.

They stood at the entrance of a hall and it was the largest room Ana had ever seen. Though it had four walls it did not have a ceiling, as all four walls met at the top—almost coming to a point. This was were the light was coming from.

Slowly moving down from the ceiling was a great sphere. It sparkled and looked to be made of glass. Perspective played tricks with her eyes and she struggled to ascertain the size of this great ball. The farther it moved down from its perch inside the great point, the brighter it and the room became. Light poured down from the opening onto the ball and was absorbed, reflected and cast throughout the room. In no time the entire hall took on a bright and cheery look as if the sun itself had come down to nest within the building.

Ana stole a quick glance at Stojan, expecting him to stoically glance back at her. He did not. Instead he seemed transfixed and in awe—an awe she had rarely seen from him. He thought the orb to be quite beautiful and stared at it as she started to scan the room.

Though they had gone down three levels of stairs, the entrance to the hall was not at ground level; it was at least three more floors up. In front of them were additional stairs leading down to the actual floor.

From here Ana could see what she thought was a walkway, but later realized it was an entire loft structure built around the walls. Instead of being a thin catwalk allowing only one person to pass, it was wide enough for her farmhouse to rest comfortably upon it. The magnitude of such a room was difficult to grasp. Upon the walkway were shelves filled with thin boxes of all colors.

The ball continued to fill the room with the white light, giving warm definition to everything.

In seconds the ball stopped and the crank behind them made a satisfying click.

"This is why," the guide said, answering a question from minutes ago.

"I thought your people had an oral tradition."

Stojan did not follow but asked the guide as he scanned the great hall below.

The guide scanned the basin of the hall, then looked at Ana instead of Stojan.

"Our oral tradition is so that we can never lose our information, but we also collect knowledge. Some of our ancestors were the keepers of the flame, and in the same sense we are keepers of the flame of knowledge."

Ana smiled but was confused by the exchange. She turned her head back down to look at what they both stared at. They started to slowly proceed down the stairs and her face changed. Her smile of amusement slowly turned to an awe that was equal to Stojan's.

Racks and rows upon rows of shelves—so tiny from afar—lined the edges of the walls. This was repeated three times on three separate lofts.

The pyramidal structure contained treasure indeed.

Books.

The library that they had visited long ago could fit on any one of the lofts, and still leave room for a group to pass it by. This hall contained the one hundred times what that library did, perhaps even one thousand.

"Welcome to the Great Library of The Navajo."

Entering the landing of the base floor Ana could see that structures were built upon the shelves, and that each shelf was over two stories tall. The structures were made of metal and had their own railing and stairs.

The two visitors looked up at the massive walls, the lofts and the ball that hung in the center lighting the room generously.

Their guide took them to a great square table in the center of the room. Nothing was out of place and the table was of a beautiful stone, and had a sheen upon it. Everything was surprisingly free of dust, unlike the small library they had seen in the farming town.

Chairs made of a varnished wood were arranged around the table. Ana counted at least 40 and when she was done she saw that the guide had taken seven books from his pack and placed them on the table. They looked so tiny in comparison to the table as a whole.

The guide took his pack and placed it on the floor.

He smiled at Ana and Stojan.

"I will be returning these books to their shelves, to where they belong. Feel free to look around, but first…"

He walked towards a smaller shelving structure. It stood by itself near one side of the table.

On it were twelve books and each one was massive.

"The catalog."

Ana tilted her head to read what was written on the spines. With some difficulty she could make out some of the words.

"Each book represents a section of the library. To find a book you simply look here, should you desire to find one."

Ana was overwhelmed while Stojan watched intently, remaining true to his new name.

The guide disappeared to return the books, and in minutes was running all over the great hall. It looked like an exhausting process and she thought she heard him talking to himself. He was. Stojan smiled.

Though intrigued, Ana was fearful of damaging the great book, but paged through it. It was hand written. Each chapter told of a special kind of book while each line showed a name and where the book was stored.

She read through it sounding out the words as best she could.

As she did she glanced at her own pack.

When the guide eventually returned he smiled.

Stojan looked at Ana, then the guide.

"You can tell him."

Confused, the guide looked at Ana, who appeared to be slightly embarrassed but full of excitement. Finally she spoke.

"I have my own book."

"You do?"

She reached into her pack and brought out the book that had been her private treasure for so long—a book she had read one hundred times or more in the last year or so.

The guide smiled a great smile. Stojan watched as she paged through the well-worn pages. She'd taken such great care with it but it still showed signs of use.

"May I?"

The guide inquired respectfully as he reached out his hand.

She complied proudly. He accepted it and looked it over—in ways that seemed unusual to her.

He smiled at her, as if he were a cat that swallowed a canary. She explained the origin of the book and how it had been chosen by the library master just before they left. She did not know if it was a gift but was happy to have it—even if she had stolen it.

"We have a tradition here. We borrow books and then return them. There are always some books on loan to various villages. However there is one thing we also do."

He looked over her book and moved to the great catalog, paging through it carefully.

"We do not have this book. Therefore you are welcome to lend it to us."

Surprised, Ana listened.

"And in its place borrow another."

She looked at the great book in front of her, then back to the guide and then eventually Stojan.

"You were looking intently though the catalog, have you decided on your withdrawal?"

Shocked, Ana tapped her chest.

"Me? You mean to allow me to… Oh, I could not!"

"It is done with the utmost care and trust, just like your book will be treated in your absence. "

He looked at Stojan as if to get confirmation. He nodded.

Flabbergasted, she looked at the book, turned a page and stopped. She was overwhelmed and confused.

"It would take me forever to choose a book here."

The guide smiled knowingly.

"If I may?" He reached out his hand to Ana while looking at Stojan.

"Please."

Stojan motioned with his hand for them to go, and then gratefully sat in the chair. He paged through the great book before him and relaxed.

Hand-in-hand the guide walked Ana around the lower level and Stojan could hear the animated chatter.

After some discussion and covering what seemed like vast distance the pair ascended some stairs to a loft.

He stopped them in front of a section of shelves that were the width of at least five horses, head to tail.

"Here we are. It is what you said you liked, and also where your book will go."

She looked at the intimidating wall as he placed her book on a shelf. For a second she felt the loss of saying goodbye to it.

"I will return to your father to talk. Please, do not be afraid. Take one that speaks to you for whatever reason. It will be your book to have as long as you like. One day you can return it, but only when you are ready for another."

Intrepidly she agreed. So engrossed was she that she didn't watch him go.

After an hour or more had passed the guide got up.

"We will run out of light soon. I am sorry that I must hurry her along. I did wish to give her as much time as she needed. It is a monumental task to choose only one, I suppose."

Stojan's surprisingly large smile startled him, but not as much as the sudden presence of one called Autumn Wind.

"OH! I see you've chosen."
Looking embarrassed Ana simply said "yes."

She clutched the book to her chest.

Neither he nor Stojan asked what she had chosen, but would eventually have to mark the book to show it was gone now. The guide had explained to Stojan that with so many choices he had asked Ana what kind of book she would like to have.

Her response was simply "poetry."

At long last the three made their way up the stairs. Stojan was asked to turn the great crank—which took many minutes to accomplish but due to the inner works of the gears was quite easy to accomplish. The sphere was returned to its place, the room once again dark was exited. Ana could not help but stare as this happened.

―――

As the sun was setting the three were able to find the village.

Unlike the others this was not shrouded in a protective forest, but instead was located on various structures of rock—each one of varying heights. To Stojan it looked as if great rocks the size of buildings were tossed into a great basin, then were smoothed and polished.

The guide explained that water once flowed here and had relentlessly shaped the rocks into something smooth and rounded. The water had also flowed underground, and this was where they now traveled.

The village they now entered was not above ground, but rather, below it.

THE VILLAGE OF ANTS

Villagers milled about in the sun, tending to various things. Ana recognized that they were drying foods, using mortar and pestle to reduce herbs and things to powders, and in general making use of the dry hot air.

The rocks and landscape all looked the same to Ana, but she quickly started to recognize which holes were actually entrances.

A massive entrance was found and even the horses were led in.

Ana pet hers, already enjoying the cooler air.

They were treated with the same warmth they'd come to expect at each and every village, but Ana of late noticed distinct differences in the people.

With the more barren surroundings and warmer climate, clothing and food were much different from the very first village she and Stojan had been guests in.

The heat of the sun was used to their advantage, and round flatbreads were the norm for meals.

The animals of this area were also the most distinct from those in Poliska. Though many animals were familiar, the lands they were now in were home to lizards and insects she had never seen before. Some of these lizards grew quite large and unfortunately for her so did the insects.

The one called scorpion appeared to be very menacing. She was told they weren't bad eating though.

Ana was not sure if this was said in jest or not. She had no desire to find out.

Stojan as always absorbed what was happening around him in his usual stoic manner, but seemed even more quiet than usual. His thoughts were ever-present and Ana wished to explain to him the teachings of moments, and suggest that it was time for him to go on walks by himself.

But she did not, as she was also busy enjoying everything she saw and experienced.

This land had fewer and fewer plants, and more and more reds, oranges and yellows. The plants that were found here were of a very unusual nature. Instead of leaves they had spines.

Unlike the other villages they were not met immediately by a welcome group. Both Stojan and Anastazja found this to be odd, but felt welcome nonetheless for it.

The sun would be setting shortly and there was an increased level of activity among the people here. It was explained that the temperature varied greatly between night and day, so many precautions and advantages were taken in respect to such a thing.

It made Stojan once again think of the ants, and how these people were like them. Nowhere else in the entire nation was seen such a clear comparison than with this village on the edge of the red lands.

They entered the tunnel system and were told they would eventually reach a room they could rest in.

The walls were lit with candles and torches of various sizes, and produced very little smoke or odor. The reddish rock of the tunnel looked smooth and rounded as if it had been carved by tools that were dull but persistent. Stojan had to duck to make his way through one tunnel entrance.

Ana abruptly stopped and their guide turned around to see her looking more than concerned.

"How far will we go?"

"Go? Into the tunnels? Not too much father but it is rather extensive."

Still she remained unmoving.

"I do not wish to go any further."

"It is not that much farther."

Villagers brushed past them and some smiled. Some were intrigued by the conversation that was being had in the middle of the tunnel. This stopped the progress of a few travelers within the tunnel and it caused the group to move to the side, then back again, then to the other side. It was not a proper place to stop and have a meeting.

The guide looked at Stojan, but his face was unemotional—no help would be had from him in convincing Anastazja.

Finally an expression of understanding came over him and he smiled.

"Ah. Yes, you feel uncomfortable?"

Ana did not reply.

"I understand, you feel enclosed. Do not worry, the tunnels are safe. We have lived in them for over a century I think."

Again he smiled at Stojan, then Ana, but no progress was made. She was uncharacteristically quiet.

"We… must not stand here. We impede the progress of the night shift."

Seeing that Ana only wanted to move in the opposite direction, he walked behind her. She turned immediately.

"Follow me then."

Ana and Stojan followed closely behind and could not see the pained look on their guide's face.

He said nothing and eventually brought them to the tunnel entrance.

"I will return as soon as possible."

He turned and left, clearly not enjoying the turn of events and even his diplomacy was tested by Ana's refusal to go any further.

"I do not like it either."

Stojan's words were welcome to Ana, but she continued to stare at the people milling about, the wondrous structures of rock, and the darkening sky.

"I cannot."

Stojan stared along with her, and didn't press the subject. He had not seen Ana so troubled and adamant. Of this she was certain—she would not spend the night in the cave tunnels. Stojan was the only one who noticed the slight change in hair color that night.

After some discussion the elder who had traveled with them came to visit, and prepared a place for them to sleep outside. To their surprise the entire village did not retreat into the caves at night but rather kept a number of people outside, to keep watch, to patrol and to regard the night sky.

This village was unlike the others and seemed more prepared for attacks, even though they seemed to possess the most defensible of positions.

Rather than sleep the pair of visitors sat with some of those spending most of the night outside and chatted.

Ana found the people to be friendly but reserved as if they had gone through a recent trauma. She did not pry and felt comfortable making light conversation. She marveled at the night sky which somehow seemed larger than her past viewings of it, and mentioned this to the girl she now spoke with.

"Big sky."

"The sky does seem bigger, yes."

"Big sky. That is what we call it."

Ana for once appreciated the short answers of the conversation and was feeling a bit better about the situation. She drank in the openness of the sky, and did not care whether she had done something insulting to their hospitality. She was not going to voluntarily seal herself up again. After all, she had done that for a week, and didn't realize the impact it had on her until just now.

Unlike the people of the other villages these people did not run up to the new visitors. Their reputation had not preceded them or these people simply did not care. Either way she was glad for the relief. Staring at the stars she then realized just how exhausted she was from travel and the constant interaction with the people around her.

If it were up to her—she mused—she would find a nice quiet place to hibernate for a long long time.

Just not in a deep cave.

Stojan also seemed to enjoy the night sky and the open air. Perhaps he too was affected by the time spent in the conveyance, or he also just simply did not like deep caves.

That night they did sleep, and the elder they had traveled with did do his best to make them comfortable. They found the accommodations outside perfectly comfortable and to their liking.

—

They were greeted by a stunning sunrise and both were up to watch it. The stars and darkness fought a valiant battle but the light of the sun eventually won—washing the sky in reds, oranges and even pinks. The latter was something she noticed quite frequently around the red lands.

“My apologies.”

It was a new voice. Tired, quiet and feminine.

Leading a group of four was a woman would walked into the area not from the caves but from the outside. She wore an outfit made of thin cloths, some skins and around her neck was a scarf of animal scales. Her hair was long and dark as the night, with filaments of white throughout.

She wore a vest of animal scales adorned with various badges. Her face was slim and long like Stojan’s and she was relatively tall.

Stojan and Ana stood to greet her.

She reached out her hand to Stojan, then Ana.

"I am regretful that I was not here to receive you yesterday. My party and I were out on an important task."

Her voice was strong and that of a leader.

"I am Talana Ant Warrior. I welcome you to our village."

Her grip was strong with Ana and she looked deeply into their eyes when she greeted them. She said their names and had a peculiar look cross her eyes when she said Ana's new name. She explained that she was both the leading elder and the shaman for her people, as the elder had recently passed.

Ana wasn't sure if that meant naturally or not. She did not ask.

"I see you have decided to enjoy the night sky with my people. I will come to have a meal with you shortly if you will allow it."

"Yes."

Stojan and Ana had replied in unison.

The tall man stretched while Ana surveyed the area—planning her next walk. She dreaded any talks about staying in the cave and had already heard the conversations in her mind. They all ended with 'no.'

In a short time the elder had returned from the caves with two others—one of them being Fox.

He greeted Stojan and then Ana and Ana found herself smiling a bit more than normal. She was embarrassed that she had actually forgotten about their young companion and thought that he was returning. Regardless she was glad to see him and noticed his attire had changed to that of these people—with furs and skins replaced a bit with scales and the like.

He seemed nervous around their new leader and glanced in her direction often. Fox unrolled a large blanket and placed it upon the ground. The three sat down, and Fox exited—still smiling at Ana.

With her came another woman with food who began to lay it out before them, with bowls and cups. The beverage that was served was cold, and the flat bread was warm, and filled with all manner of thinly sliced greens. She wasn't told what meat she consumed but she happily accepted it. There was a spice to this and she appreciated it.

"I am told you are here for the vision way."

Stojan looked confused.

"I agreed to perform the rite of vision, but I do not know what that is."

"They are one in the same, Watchful Raven. We have a different name for things than our brothers and sisters do in the northeast—among the trees."

Stojan nodded his understanding.

"Do not take this lightly, however. The vision way is not a way that is comfortable, especially for someone who has never performed it."

"I understand."

"Do you?"

Ana looked at her in surprise. Her tone was challenging. It seemed that shamans from all villages spoke freely and had no use for protocol. This tone did not sit well with Ana.

Stojan just looked on, waiting for more. This silence pleased the shaman and she continued.

"Do you understand what you are about to take part in? Tell me what you know, Watchful Raven."

"I just did."

When this was not enough he commented further.

"I have told you all I know, which is what I was told, which is that it is a rite that may give me clarity."

"It involves a drug."

"Oh?"

"Yes. You will take a concoction that I will create for you. It will make you very sick, and at that time you will expel any bad energies within so that you may see clearly—perhaps for the first time."

Stojan's eyes narrowed slightly. Ana did not like the conversation or this shaman, she found.

"I *have* seen clearly. It will not be for the first time."

The shaman glanced at Ana, then back to Stojan. She seemed unconvinced.

"Perhaps your clarity was only brief. This will be something different."

"I do not believe in energies good or bad. Things are what they are."

"I have much to learn about you. I have only been told a few things."

She scraped the last bit of food stuff from her bowl and ate it.

"In learning more about us will you still concoct something for me to drink?"

"You speak your mind, Stojan Watchful Raven. I like that about you and I like that in you."

Stojan was unfazed by this compliment and remained skeptical.

Ana was content that the conversation had not turned to her and realized she would be more than happy if it remained that way. For too long she was at the center of attention.

The shaman smiled and while her eyes stayed towards Stojan, her face moved to Ana in an unnerving way.

"Tell me about your father."

Ana froze. The ambiguity of the statement confused her. Did they know? What did she mean?

The shaman's eyes caught up with her face and now also looked upon Anastazja.

She felt as if a great light were pointed to her—so focused was the shaman. Her blues eyes looked back at their brown counterparts.

"What would you like to know?"

The shaman smiled.

"What do you think of him performing the way?"

Ana exhaled. This shaman knew something more than she was telling.

"He is a strong man and I have always known his decisions to be sound."

The statement sounded solid to Ana, but not so to the others.

"How long have you traveled together?"

Again Ana felt exposed in a way she could not yet define. In all the time she had spent with these people she had never encountered such scrutiny.

"I think it has been over two years that we have traveled among your people."

Ana swallowed hard, and looked down at her drink.

"And before that?"

"Yes, we traveled before that."

Ana was too busy looking at the inquisitor to notice Stojan and the prideful look on his face.

Stojan was unmoved. He had seen Ana and a wolf; he had trained her with the sword; and she applied that same training to the tongue it seemed. It was the first sign that the shaman was frustrated—ever so slightly.

"You approve of his decision to perform the way?"

Ana looked at Stojan for the first time and with a look of pride said a resounding "Yes."

"Good. We will begin tomorrow."

With that abrupt announcement she stood up. Stojan and Ana did the same, not knowing what to expect next.

"Will you walk with me?"

The question was posed to Anastazja.

She simply nodded and followed.

Ana longed for the time at the village in the trees—in which she and Stojan were treated gently—the place that gave her her new name.

Then it hit Anastazja like an errant sword blow: the shaman had yet to call her by name—any name.

Talana walked with her out into the open land, passing by many villagers who milled about; those beginning to move things into the sun for drying, those assembling parties for patrols, and all manner of outside business.

"I have been told that you like to go for walks."

"Yes I do!"

"You have a good understanding of what it is to clear your mind. I know this to be true just by speaking with you. You have also been taught well."

"Yes."

"Do you also think yourself to be a truthful person."

"Yes."

Ana was ready for the inevitable, as she looked at the rocks, the ground, the sky.

"I believe that as well."

There was, strangely, no more said on that.

Instead they just walked in silence, making their way around the area. It was thus for more than an hour.

Ana thought she was being tested, or that the many questions would soon start. They did not. She let her mind go and just continued to walk with the strange woman who clearly did not trust her, regardless of what she said.

To Ana's surprise she did not leave her out in the wilderness to find her way back. She did not challenge her to some sort of battle. Nor did she ask any more prying questions about Stojan, and whether he was her real father or not.

Instead she just walked, and looked at the lands, and sometimes to Ana, and smiled.

She seemed to enjoy the walk as much as Ana enjoyed hers.

When they returned many villagers looked upon them as they arrived. They seemed expectant, though no one spoke to them.

"Thank you for the walk."

Again she did not address Ana by name.

Ana did not reply other than to give a tight-lipped smile.

Her task now would be to find Stojan, and then perhaps take a proper walk without anyone mucking it up.

The thought made her smile a genuine smile, which was very fortunate for the young man who was watching her.

Fox and Ana chatted for some time outside as thoughts of finding Stojan were put on hold for a bit.

"Watchful Raven."

It was Talana, and it made Stojan turn from his chat with the visiting elder and visiting shaman. He drew to his full height and said nothing.

"I will have my concoction ready for you in a few hours. I ask only that you do not drink any alcohol today. We will proceed as the sun sets."

Stojan simply nodded, but thought it odd that she would warn him about alcohol. Surely he would not have any mid-day merriment today.

When she left, the visiting elder smiled while the shaman did not. He chose to speak first in her immediate absence.

“She is suspicious of you, and your daughter.”

“That is understandable.”

“It is? You are too generous, Watchful Raven.”

“I too would be suspicious if foreigners came to my land, especially if it was hidden and guarded from the outside world.”

“Indeed you are wise.”

The shaman spoke without irony and seemed genuine.

“I simply state the obvious. I know this to be obvious to her. There are a great many things she is not telling me.”

The elder looked impressed at the assessment.

“You know this?”

“Certainly. It gives me far less to worry about then.”

“The vision way is difficult. And it is not the discomfort but rather the acceptance of what you see, feel and hear.”

“I am as ready as I can be for such a thing that I have never done.”

That day Stojan ventured outside, and after spending much time watching a boy and a girl stand entirely too close to each other, he approached Ana—after Fox had departed.

“Did you enjoy your walk?”

“Yes.”

“But you say no more of it, eh?”

“I felt it was an intrusion and thought she wanted to talk—to continue her irritating questions.”

Stojan was surprised at the annoyance Ana displayed.

“And?”

"She did not!"

He just smiled and stared off into the distance, admiring the otherworldly look of the giant stone curves that surrounded them.

"Are you afraid?"

"No. It is a ritual. And…"

He noticed she was closer now, and holding his hand. She was stealthy not just in combat.

"…I know whatever path it sends me on with be one that includes you."

She squeezed his hand and pulled herself closer to him. Her eyes found the same spot in the infinite in which he looked upon and said nothing more.

STOJAN'S VISION

The shaman, the visiting shaman and the visiting elder all came to collect Stojan. The found him shortly after he parted with Ana and had been walking about the outer rim of the village.

The visiting shaman held a very large wrapped rectangle. A thin skin was wound around it but he could still see the general shape.

"It is time."

Stojan nodded to the one named Ant Warrior. They all stood and waited.

"Where will this occur?"

"Wherever you are."

"I am here."

"Then let us begin."

Stojan learned later that the spot was truly up to the one who chose to be part of the way. And in this case it mattered not to him. A growing part of him wanted it to be over as soon as possible.

The wrap of the rectangle was unwound and laid down on the hard ground. A number of skins of wines were laid down—and one ceramic flask. Though it looked nothing like the one used by Dagmar he still drew a comparison to them. Both were seemingly magic potions.

The object at the center of the wrap was a colorful painting—made of intricacies Stojan had never seen before. Objects and animals were depicted in a very squarish style not true to life but very stylized.

The painting looked grainy and he was not sure if it was something that had been made with strings, or delicately laid bits of rock.

It was placed in the middle of the blanket and left little room for anyone to sit down—except along the edges.

"Remove your outer-wear, your weapon and anything else that hinders you."

He did indeed take off most items and was left barefoot with only a light shirt and pants. The heat of the desert was dying down with the sunlight.

Night would once again win the battle.

"Sit… and drink."

The dark-haired woman motioned for him to sit—directly on the painting. He followed her direction with some trepidation. He sat on the painting, and was handed the drink. He knew not to smell it, as he had been forewarned by the visiting elder. Information was minimal as they were careful not affect the outcome or seed his expectations. At least this is what they told him.

He removed the loose cover, and drank the liquid. Its taste was not entirely unpleasant and Stojan considered that he had imbibed and eaten worse. This liquid was very grainy, and a bit chalky. He detected many herbs that he did not recognize, and the entirety of the carafe went down his throat quickly.

Taking the bottle back, the shaman looked at the sky, and then him. Stojan was bathed in the orange-red light of sundown and his face took on a glow to them because of it.

He looked back at them, swallowing a few times to make the remnants of the taste go away. It did not work. He eyed up the water-skins also on the blanket.

She shook her head. "These are not for you, friend Stojan."

He was taken aback, not having heard his real name for some time, save for Ana.

"You visit from a far away land and have come to us. I ask now that the bad energies and spirits who haunt you be dispelled. Be gone so that Stojan may think about what has happened, and what is to come."

She stared at him and all he could do was stare back. Shortly after he felt a sickness come upon his stomach, and he meant to empty it.

"Stand! Stand now and take my hand."

This he did and she walked him a short distance away until he could no longer walk. He stopped and emptied the contents of his stomach. Again and again he did this until there was no more. Even then he still felt the urge to vomit and gave in to it, only heaving with nothing to show for it.

She held his hand the entire time, and when he was done she wiped his mouth with a cloth.

They walked back slowly to the painting and the steps became shorter and shorter. The more he walked the less land he covered. Seventy pairs of tiny red eyes watched as they left the area. The sun was already down now and the stars looked brighter than ever; lighting up the blackness as if a great brush had been pulled across it in one great stroke. After what seemed like an hour he was back at the painting. He tried to sit but instead he did not feel the ground. Down and down he fell, through and into the painting. The sensation of falling was intense and real. He looked up and saw the tiny square and stars above him as he plunged deeper and deeper into the darkness—until the painting opening was the only dim star in the sky. It was the only one and he was surrounded by complete blackness.

The was an eerily familiar feel to the blackness and disorientation, and he recalled his first encounter with Anastazja's father. This felt like the fog, but different.

There he stood, in a familiar room. The mist continued so that he could only make out what was near him.

The man smiled and handed him a large bag. It was heavy and made all manner of metal-on-metal sounds. Clearly it was filled with coins and jewels. Stojan looked at the bishop and down at the floor. There was a well. The bishop motioned for him to enter it. Confused, Stojan just stood there and before he could do anything he felt the hard push from a hand to his back. He plunged into the well and on the way in craned his neck to try to see who had done it. All he saw was white. And a smile.

Down and down he fell into the vertical tunnel—finally landing in a great splash at the bottom. The water rushed up the sides from his weight and volume entering the small space. The water ran down the sides and as it did it took with it the tunnel itself.

He instinctively grabbed onto something for support.

He was back in the forest in Poliska. He watched the farm once again, but this time he only saw Ana, and she was much younger—perhaps eleven. She played and scampered in the yard—running around with much energy. Her hair was in short pigtails and she looked like she had not a care—so happy was she.

Then another girl entered the yard of the same age. Her hair was brown, and long. She too giggled and played, as if they were friends.

Stojan recognized her just then, and his stomach sank, and pulled, and moved, as if he were doing summersaults. It was her. Her features were the same. She looked so happy.

It was his daughter.

He watched intently and smiled. He peered out from the tree and enjoyed them both.

They laughed and played together; sometimes holding hands, and sometimes playing by themselves in the bright sunlight.

He felt a hand on his shoulder, and almost jumped as he turned to see what it was attached to. The massive man before him was the big man he had watched die almost thee years ago.

"Thank you."

The man smiled warmly, looking into Stojan's eyes.

Stojan stared at him, then glanced back at the yard. His daughter was gone and only Ana remained, but now she had a shovel, and was crying. She slowly dug a hole all by herself and paused to wipe the tears from her eyes. He wanted to run out to her, and glanced back at the man next to him. He was alone.

Glancing back to the yard Ana was gone now, and so was the yard. He heard his breathing echo and once again was at the bottom of the well. He did not sink but instead floated. The water was rising slowly and he noticed regular markings in some white paint, or perhaps it had been scratched into the surface by someone before him.

Slowly he floated up with the water level—looking up he could not see the top of the well.

The regular markings seemed to go all the way to the top.

He spun around to see if there was anything to hold onto but the walls were gone. He stood on his feet but could feel water. It was raining. Lightning flashed over and over again in an ever-increasing warning. Recognizing the bridge, he made his way to it. Preparing himself for what was to come he came to the edge. There was no river but instead a great field of yellow, and it cast a light upwards immediately quelling the rain, the lightning and the clouds themselves.

Though it was quite expansive and distant he was able to see everything clearly, as if it was directly in front of his eyes. He was able to make out the yellow as individual flowers. Every petal revealed themselves to him in perfect detail. The field was filled with beautiful healthy sunflowers and in the center stood Anastazja.

She walked ever so slowly forward and reached out to touch something. It was a sculpture of a deer. Now seeing more of the area at once he saw that she was surrounded by many many deer, but all were the sickly white and not the rich browns and reds he expected.

They were all statues—yet she still daintily and carefully crept up on them.

She finally reached one, and touched it upon its tail. The color from her hand ran and seeped outward to the tail, then the rest of the deer.

Startled now and fully aware, it scattered away, leaping over some of the other frozen animals.

Again water threatened to fill his lungs as he was surrounded by dim light. Asserting his balance he once again began floating upward, and passed a marking or two.

He tried to make sense of the markings and thought he recognized it as numbers, but before he could read further he was on a trail.

He hiked alone and came upon a pass. When he rounded the corner he saw a mountain in the distance. This was not snow-capped and did not jut into the sky like a sharp knife. Instead this was squat, and brownish and almost rounded. The lighting was as twilight and he struggled to see. He looked down. The path he was on was not made of gravel, or grass, but instead of small rectangles with a seam in the middle.

Books. Hundreds of books lined the path that led all the way to the mountain.

He felt heat.

Turning around he saw a statue of a man holding a torch. Though he was made of marble the torch was not.

Stojan looked down and saw that the area directly behind him had been lit on fire.

He looked at the statue; it did not move but instead had a sly look upon its face. The torch continued to burn as Stojan turned around just in time to see the path erupt in flames like a fuse. The fire ran the length of it as it accelerated. Faster and faster it moved until it reached the mountain base.

That was when he realized what it was made of.

The mountain caught fire and flames spread in such a fashion as not to even resemble fire, but instead something alive.

He blinked and watched it rain ash, and bits of pages. The entire landscape was of white, and ash, and flame and bits of paper making their way downward. A great darkness was cast upon the land.

Barely able to breathe now he tried to hold his breath and closed his eyes, only to open them in the well.

Upwardly he moved again, and thought he could see a tiny pinpoint of light at the top.

The white markings went up as far as he could see with one exception—one of the markings was in red.

He resolved himself to this upward movement and watched the markers pass by.

It seemed the more he accepted the movement the less the well disappeared.

He closed his eyes momentarily and when he opened them he was in a great cathedral. Massive pillars stood around the inside perimeter. Each was as thick as a horse and three stories tall. Long chairs were set in rows and at the front was a stage.

Light shown through the windows and every color of the rainbow was represented in the glass. Thousands of small tiles had been assembled to produce scenes of those with swords, those sad and suffering and those performing various tasks. The people wore unusual clothing—coats of white that went from neck to floor. Great devices as large as a house were depicted, with many many cables of metal twisted into them.

The windows had impossible detail.

He walked through the building, looking from one window to the next as he slowly progressed. His footsteps echoed.

The windows told a story, but of what he did not know. Just before he reached the front stage area he looked at a window. This one had a white oval and the people all shielded their eyes as beams of light emanated from it.

They were all happy and amazed at the sight, as if they welcomed it.

Stojan looked around to see if he was alone. He was.

Glancing back to the stage he noticed the windows had all changed. Instead of the scenes of people in unfamiliar clothing, of great devices and activities surrounding them, they were all replaced with the same scene.

Each window now showed bodies strewn about, great fissures in the Earth, a horizon that was clouded with red and black and lightning that emanated from the sky.

The building was now filled with a reddish light due to the windows and it took on an eerie appearance.

At the front on the stage was a great disk of stone—perfectly smooth and circular.

Then he heard it.

Echoing in the great hall was the call of a bird he'd heard before. He needn't have recalled it as it landed on the large stone disk.

Standing in the center it cawed at him three times.

He recognized it as the great raven from the barn in Anastazja's home and it was as large as he remembered.

It squawked at him again as if in warning. The reddish light of the room grew darker and it made him want to make haste to the door. When the feeling overwhelmed him he turned and ran.

His progress was slow and the windows loomed and cast their light on him showing all manner of suffering and death and change.

His hand reaching for the door found that his hand was in a barrel. He pulled it out and instead of a door handle came an apple. His fingers dug into it so determined was he to pull the handle that had been there moments before.

He looked at it and it was not heathy. The flesh was instead dried and pulled and of mottled colors—not unlike an old man's skin. Repelled he dropped it into the barrel with the rest of the apples and quickly the rot spread to the others.

He went to wipe his hand on the barrel but instead found the door handle again.

Reaching the door he gave it a great heave and it scraped his hand as the door pulls would not move.

He pulled with all his might and there was no movement or progress.

Quickly turning back to the front as if to see if the bird would render assistance he no longer saw it but in its place was a great scale made of gold. It was beautiful in craftsmanship and immense—filling the entire stage area. The lighting was again pleasant.

He ran back to it and this time drew his sword.

Indeed it was a great set of scales. On each side was a golden disk and they were connected to a length of golden rod by three chains each. The rod moved slowly back and forth as the dishes moved slightly up and down—teetering back and forth in opposition.

He skid to a stop in front of it.

One the edge of each sat a girl; they both looked unharmed and happy. Their legs hung off the side and swung lazily back and forth. He recognized them.

From behind the scale came the bishop.

He carried his staff and the end was on fire—like a massive torch.

He glanced at Stojan and then moved the head of the staff underneath one of the dishes. The ground below burst into flames.

Stojan's eyes widened. The bonfire would easily engulf the disk and the heat would be deadly.

He blinked and the bishop was already under the other dish, lighting it as the other.

Again the flames erupted and again the fire was not close enough to heat the dish too much.

He wanted to run and act but could not move, instead he looked up at the ceiling and saw the stars. The windows, walls, ceiling and entire building was gone now and instead the scales stood by themselves outside in the night. The only light seen was the flames underneath. Both dishes remained equal.

The flames grew higher now and even at this point of equilibrium the dishes would heat up and the girls would suffer.

They no longer smiled but looked sad and pained, but yet did not exit. They still swung their legs in a disturbing fashion while their faces became contorted. He could see that the metal dish they sat upon was burning them.

The bishop now looked at Stojan and stood in the center—in front of the scale.

The smile on his face contorted into shock as a white sword erupted from his chest.

It was withdrawn and behind him stood one of the statues. His body slumped to the floor. It then walked up into the dish with Anastazja and the heavier dish moved down while the one with his daughter moved upward.

Stojan was filled with the most horrible of feelings as he watched the disk go farther and farther into the flames.

Again the sound of the great raven was heard and it landed on the dish with his daughter.

The rising sun was casting additional light on the scene now—adding some reds and oranges.

He thought he saw the dishes stop.

Stojan could not longer feel the heat of the flames, and blinked.

The scales were gone, and replaced with the visiting elder, shaman and resident shaman.

He blinked again.

He was sitting in the middle of the blanket, but not on the painting. Instead, shards and pieces of it were strewn about the area surrounding the blanket. His hands were rough and looked like they had been cut recently—dried blood was on them.

The shaman of the village known as Ant Warrior looked tired and now held his hand.

"Welcome back."

Her face was bathed in morning sunlight.

Stojan took a deep breath.

He looked at her, then the others.

They watched him—waiting for a response. For a long time he stared at them, collecting his thoughts. Finally he spoke in a tone most unexpected as he looked into their eyes with much resolve.

“You will not subject Ana to this.”

So taken aback was the visiting shaman that he gasped. The elder closed his eyes tightly, and the woman that held his hand squeezed it.

She grabbed both of his hands, pulled him upward and hugged him—tightly.

The elder opened his eyes to see Stojan’s tired but slightly surprised expression. The visiting shaman smiled a smile of wonder.

She whispered in his ear while still embracing. It was a gentle voice—filled with a warmth he had not heard from her.

“We will not, friend Stojan.”

They pulled away from each other and she looked at the others.

“I am convinced.”

“You have not yet heard him tell of his vision.”

“I think he just did. We will speak with him but not now. Now…”

She looked at Stojan.

“…he must rest. And tell his daughter that he is well, for I am sure she worries.”

They walked to the village in the rising sun. The blanket was collected but the destroyed painting was not.

Stojan was given water as they made their way in silence. The visiting elder and shaman fell back slightly and whispered to each other the entire way. There was much to discuss.

Back at the village one of the first to receive them was Ana. Again she had stayed outside and looked as tired as Stojan.

The shaman tensed up, taken off-guard by the rapid pace of Anastazja. She ran at them with a rate that looked ferocious.

In barely enough time she stopped and hugged Stojan tightly—ignoring the others.

They watched her grip him and saw considerable strength. The leader could see Stojan's face—it was filled with relief and happiness and some sort of mirth. He clearly found her exceptional embrace to be both inviting and slightly painful.

She walked along side him and barely regarded the others.

—

That day Stojan would sleep soundly into and through the night. He slept deeply after eating a considerable meal alone with Ana.

She slept soundly herself that night outside while he slept within the tunnels.

The next day he was called upon to speak with the three who had been with him the night of his vision.

The demeanor of the leader had changed.

"What has changed now, Ant Warrior?"

Stojan was the first to speak in their meeting.

"To what do you refer?"

"Though I have yet to tell you what I saw there is a distinct change. Why?"

The leader explained that Stojan's time was quite tumultuous. Many who go through the vision way sleep soundly or see the visions while remaining awake. Stojan however had sat and then became quite animated, resulting in the destruction of the painting. This in and of itself was a sign of something grand.

"Your vision way was not a request for you."

The visiting shaman nodded, looking vindicated.

"I was hesitant for this. Many things have been explained to me about you and your daughter."

Stojan looked at the faces he sat with.

"We do not take things lightly in the red lands. Unlike our brothers and sisters we are exposed to the folly and violence of the Amirans. Only recently had we truly learned to avoid them properly."

"We believe that all that one can know is already present. I was told that the beginnings of something was upon us."

The shaman known as Clever Owl again nodded.

"But you cannot simply name a thing to make it real. If you name a rock a cloud it does not then float upward."

She narrowed her eyes at her counterpart, almost scolding him.

"I believed this was done—so anxious are we to have resolution."

Stojan then went on to explain his visions as best as he could, remembering not just scenes but also what he felt—as this was equally important, according to the elders. Though he was honest, he chose to describe much less than they expected. He withheld some of the visage because to reveal all made him feel exposed.

When he finished she thanked him and then continued.

"I now know this to be true."

Confused, Stojan inquired.

"What?"

"The prophecy."

"Which? I know of no prophecy. Nothing was shared with me."

The other shaman spoke.

"Our prophecy states that one will come to eventually free us, and the Amirans."

She raised her hand to quell the speech of the other shaman.

"Your daughter was given the name of the one who would free us."

Stojan looked at the three of them, thinking they were joking.

"I believed this name was given in the same manner one tries to make a rock a cloud, as I said. It does not work."

Stojan nodded.

"However, your experiences and your vision have shown me that she is indeed here with us, and we are grateful. You are not mentioned, however."

Stojan smiled.

"Of course not."

Stojan was quiet as they all exchanged glances. They looked certain yet confused.

"I accept that your daughter is the Autumn Wind."

"Your people have already named her thus. Her name to you changes nothing for me, nor does it change who she is."

Each looked as if they wanted to speak.

She took a deep breath, collecting her thoughts and distilling what she was about to say.

"You are at a crossroads. We feel you are at the end of your journey."

Stojan smiled.

"We would prefer to stay where there are no caves then."

"You do not understand. The red marking on the well signifies an end."

"Or it is another bit of nonsense created by my mind in response to your potent elixir."

"You must search your thoughts, and your heart."

All eyes were intensely upon him, and the warmth of Talana was contrasted by the concern and almost anger of Clever Owl. The visiting elder just watched expressionlessly.

Stojan drew his brows together. The discussion was not to his liking.

"Then we will leave you."

"What? No!"

It was the visiting shaman.

The elder spoke for the first time.

"Though we speak of responsibility and prophecies, none of this can happen without free will. It is your free will that has set things in motion, and will fulfill whatever is to happen. The choices must be yours and not ours."

The female looked on with some scrutiny as the other shaman looked angry.

"You are free to go of course."

"No…"

The shaman spoke quietly, as if trying to stop the inevitable. Alas he could not.

Stojan was filled with a purpose, but unlike those that surrounded him it was to be as far away as possible from the people; to be where he could protect and survive with Ana.

Stojan stood up and as respectfully as he could he thanked those around him and stated in no uncertain terms that they were leaving.

LEAVING THE TOWN

"Today?!"

Stojan answered Ana's incredulous question.

"Yes. As soon as we are packed."

"Stojan? What has happened? Was it the vision? Are we to continue the quest? Oh what is the quest then?"

Stojan began packing things with Ana, bringing items outside to her makeshift sleeping area.

"Our quest is to be far away from here."

Ana was ecstatic. She would no longer be exposed to the caves and feel awkward, and they would continue their quest. Perhaps they would be allowed to explore Amira. There were now infinite possibilities.

Seeing the relief on her face, Stojan chose not to take any away.

Before they left that morning they spoke with the guide who volunteered as much information as possible about the surrounding area. He tried to tell them of nearby cities, of landmarks and of Amirans.

The local shaman also spoke with them.

"I bid you farewell, Stojan and Anastazja—those we have named

Watchful Raven and Autumn Wind."

She hugged both Ana and Stojan and her embrace was sincere and warm.

As she pulled away from Stojan her eyes held tears, and it was the most emotion Ana had seen the shaman demonstrate. It seemed she was about to cry for Stojan.

The visiting shaman did not say goodbye, but the visiting elder stopped them just before leaving.

"I wish you both well in your journeys. You have enriched my life and I am better for knowing you."

He shook Ana's hand and then while shaking Stojan's pulled him towards him.

"You are a good man, Stojan. We sit with those who go through the way not just to protect them, but to listen, for those who have visions speak."

He stopped shaking his hand but held it tightly.

"You spoke much and I learned of your past."

Stojan looked into his eyes, trying to determine his motives that day. He spoke quietly.

"You are a good father. To both of your daughters."

With that they disengaged.

The boy named Fox ran to Anastazja.

They hugged for some time, and he also had words that were unheard by anyone other than the listener.

Stojan raised an eyebrow, then continued packing his saddlebags.

They were allowed to take a pair of horses with them, and directed to both the safest place to make camp and the nearest Amiran city.

They rode off into the growing heat and the pair of travelers were filled with trepidation, excitement, relief and curiosity.

Not until they were some many kilometers away did Stojan realize just how long it had been since he and Ana had ridden together—alone.

Ana turned and smiled to him.

"Will you ever tell me of your visions Stojan?

"Stojan."

"Yes?"

"I called you Stojan."

"Yes you did, Ana."

"Does that mean we do not have to use our other names again? I have so many now."

She laughed, and Stojan smiled back.

"I believe those were only for the tribe. And you are always Anastazja to me."

Ana smiled but decided not to voice her thoughts.

They made their way through valleys of rocks, and marveled at the plants they had learned to be 'cacti.'

Lizards scurried now and then in the sun, and Ana watched it all from under her wide-brimmed hat.

"Where will we go first Stojan?"

He stopped his horse under the shade of an outcropping, she followed and did the same.

"I think we should stop to rest here, and give the horses shade first."

Indeed she was quite thirsty.

Once resting and refreshing themselves Ana decided it was time for all manner of questions.

Stojan did his best to answer those regarding where they would go, what was best for them and his visions.

The latter was provided minimally, much to the dismay of Ana.

“Suffice it to say that my mind showed me all manner of things I have experienced, and some I haven’t.”

“A prediction of the future?”

“Doubtful, no more than dreams are.”

“And what of our quest?”

“I think our quest is to find the path to where we belong. As long as we are together I care not what form that takes.”

“Nor I Stojan. But can we rejoin the people of the trees again? Can we ever go back to Poliska?”

Before he could answer she continued.

“I did so enjoy the first village. The people there were so friendly, and I made many friends.”

Stojan smiled, enjoying his time with her and her expressions.

“Then perhaps that should be our first quest—to find the people of the trees again.”

She brightened.

“Can we just move though the villages on the way there?”

“Eventually, but I think we may need to take a road here and there. And we are far from the next village, should we even be able to find it.”

That day they found an area they thought would make a safe place to stay for the night.

Though there were yet no trees to conceal them, the landscape and rocks made for suitable protection.

Ana did not yet feel like walking, and started to think it was connected to her proximity to fields and trees and the like. The open landscape would not do.

"The supplies we have with us will last for a few days, but we must find water. I think it is time to revisit the people of Amira."

According to everything told to them by the guide, the nearest city would be just a day's ride to the north. Stojan thought that after almost three years, and after spanning a distance greater than crossing all of Poliska many times over he felt they would be safe.

And there would be no more talk of quests, prophesies or visions.

Indeed they did find a road that would lead them to a city. Their very first encounter with people of the cities was uneventful. The men on horseback were dressed similarly to both Stojan and Ana—leather vests and coats, some tassels and even wide brimmed hats were worn. Their attire did not draw much attention, though Ana's vest made of scales was shiny in the sunlight. It looked unusual, but not out of place.

"Can we not just move along the land—as we did in Poliska?"

Ana had become nervous seeing a number of other travelers, and was starting to hear the warnings of the elders in her ears. Stojan answered.

"The lands here between cities are barren, and unlike our journey here we no longer have a guide. Going into the city is full of uncertainty, but going into the barren lands between them is certain death. A wrong turn and we are lost without water with no true map."

She listened but was unconvinced.

"The city will provide supplies, nothing more. Then we will move on to the next. Once the lands become more habitable we can just travel between them. And if we encounter a village we can refresh there."

Stojan knew that the villages would be hard to find, as they had moved between them only due to their astute guide.

Again Stojan enjoyed the private conversation with Ana while they pursued an obvious and attainable goal. It made for much chatting and it seemed the two had many things to catch up on.

At a rest stop, Stojan broke a fairly long silence with a question that had been on his mind.

“Did you celebrate your birthday with your father?”

When Stojan asked about her father, it never sounded quite right to her ears; she loved her father dearly, but she felt at times that Stojan was also her father. She did not have two words to represent the same concept so instead she just accepted the word. But it did not stop her from feeling slightly odd.

“I did! We used to go into town and pick something out, but then he would always have something else wrapped for me.”

Stojan smiled.

“I am sorry that you no longer have those things, Ana. I am sure they meant much to you.”

“Oh but I do, I have at least one of my gifts.”

She patted her sword with a bittersweet look. He knew she missed the other but was grateful for it.

“For your birthday?”

“Yes, for my thirteenth, that same year.”

Stojan thought for a moment, not wanting to end on a poor note.

“Do you think you will want to celebrate your birthday again? We are free to do that now, Sunflower.”

She laughed at the name.

“Well we do not have to!”

“There is not much we have to do Ana, but there is much we should do. I feel it is important and want to celebrate them with you. Though I am not sure what you would like as a token.”

“Perhaps in a year I would want a new sword.”

Stojan could not help but chuckle out loud as he shook his head. She had very simple wants, and they were in line with his it seemed.

“You laugh…? Stojan!”

"I am delighted Ana. Really. I find your tastes to be in line with my wants, but…"

He smiled wider, clearly enjoying her response.

"…are you sure there isn't something else you may want? A trinket, a token, some sort of clothing?"

"Mmmmm…"

She thought and hummed at the same time.

Stojan's amusement turned to embarrassment, and it caught Ana off guard. She had never seen him embarrassed.

"What is it?"

"I do not know how old you are."

"Ha!"

She laughed and looked proud.

"That's easy. The people reckoned time on the old calendar, but on our calendar it tells me my age."

"What do you mean?"

"I was born in 1200 in the year of All Saints."

He waited.

"So… this year I will be 17 years old."

Stojan was quiet, concentrating, and overly serious. She thought surely he was about to play a joke.

Then he smiled, as if finally catching the punch line to a joke.

"Oh, dear Ana. I think you are confused by our time with the people and their calendar."

He smiled but she thought she saw pain behind his eyes.

“Stojan. No, I am not. What is it?”

She put her hand on his arm. He looked uncomfortable, as if on the edge of some emotion.

“You are… No no. You are 17.” He nodded.

“But that means your are born 17 years ago, which is… *1207*.”

Before she could speak he spoke again.

“We have been with the people of these lands—the Navajo, the people who are like ants—for three years.”

She did not know him to stutter so and her face showed the concern. He seemed confused, as if under the influence of something.

She shook her head as if to clear her mind, and then spoke with confidence.

“Stojan. I know in which year I was born. We marked the calendar at the house each spring. You cannot tell me I am wrong.”

If he was joking it was no longer funny to her.

He made no response. His eyes showed only that his thoughts raced, but without resolution. He knew she was not mistaken about the year of her birth. There was no inconsistency in all of Poliska for the marking of the year. And from what he had seen it looked like the people of Amira also used the same calendar of All Saints.

Yet he was at an impasse.

“Stojan, please. What is wrong. What vexes you?”

He looked back at her—eyes still distant.

“I believe what you have told me. It was 1221 when I found you, and it is now 1224. But, whatever the year it is not 1217. Dear Ana, I know this cannot be the year, because it is the year my daughter died.”

She held tightly to his hand, and softly wept, for she could see the pain and sadness it caused him.

TRUE INTENTIONS

"What does it say, Stojan?"

Ana was interested in his map, but judging by Stojan's disappointed looks it was not extensive.

"This is not a map as such we would obtain from the great library. This is a simple note provided by Clever Owl."

"Well what does it say… or show?"

"It shows that we are on the right path and a small outpost should be up ahead."

Stojan examined the tiny scroll. It showed a simple line drawing with just a few notations. It had led them directly to the outpost.

He regretted not simply following the river, but was told that it became rather steep and treacherous. It was not like in Poliska where that policy would always provide fresh water and food. Here rivers went down embankments or even disappeared underground. Or so he was told.

"Anything else?"

"Yes. That we should have been given a larger map."

Ana was amused at Stojan's attempt at a joke. She liked it.

It was mid-day as they progressed on the road. Their direction was taking them back in the direction they'd come from, but only in broad strokes. Stojan was happy they were encountering more and more green and scrubs and grass—it meant they were going in the right direction and into climate that could support the pair of nomads.

Then he heard a wondrous sound. Looking to Ana he knew that she already heard it.

It was a loud sound, a metallic sound—musical in nature but it just repeated the same two notes.

It was a gong, or a bell, and it sounded very large.

Rounding the hill they saw it.

The outpost represented by a simple 'x' on their map at the very top was instead a cathedral.

Ana was in awe from not just the sound but the sight.

"It calls to me. It is so beautiful—this sound."

"I agree."

Stojan and Ana rode down the path, with the former bearing most of the burden of apprehension. It seemed that the building stood alone—not as part of city, but as a solitary structure all by itself. The bell continued to ring—one tone and then the other. It was a slow sound that gathered the attention of the listener.

Slowly they rode down the winding path and as they did they found the welcoming tone was contrasted by the lack of any other sounds. No wind blew, no gravel moved, no birds called out above.

They approached the building and were able to see more of it now. It was a grey brick building of three stories or more.

"It is a beautiful outpost Stojan."

"It is not an outpost Ana. It is a cathedral."

She was stunned.

"Or at least a church. I have seen one like it before, but not as grand or complete."

Stojan thought and remembered that he had seen two like it; the second being in his vision. This was eerily similar, and he did not like the familiarity.

The bell continued to ring.

"I see no one around."

"It seems we are the only ones here."

They continued down the path towards the sound of the bell and the sight of the building. A physical structure she could enter and peruse was inviting to Ana. She was not sure if they would have sleeping quarters, or if Stojan would be open to such an idea. She thought not. The sound stopped.

"I wonder who moves it… or who stopped it…"

Ana was looking up.

"It is wrong that we see no one. This is not right."

"I see someone!"

Stojan turned.

One lone rider came towards them at a high speed. Stojan glanced at Ana and was ready to draw his sword.

The rider was slight of build and dressed as the people they'd just left. Ana recognized him and brightened, but noticed the grave look upon his face.

It was Fox, and he looked both glad and disappointed to see her.

"Fox! What are you doing here? Did you follow us? Why are you here?"

He was clearly tired, and looked both upset and exhausted—as if he had been running from something terrible.

"I have come to…"

He looked up at the cathedral, and appeared as mesmerized by the sight as Ana was by the sound.

Ana looked back, half-expecting a great bird to swoop down—based on the look on his face.

He blinked to regain his concentration and continued.

"I tried to follow you—your path. It is not…"

Clearly flustered and with much to say, he breathed heavily.

"There is too much to tell."

"What is it."

It was Stojan, and he was quite annoyed and it showed by the loudness of his voice.

"You are in danger, Watchful Raven and… especially…"

He looked at Ana with much concern, but did not say her name.

"The elder is dead. Poisoned."

Stojan looked back at the cathedral, expecting that someone would burst forth. Ana's face showed shock.

"I came as quickly as I learned… or figured. It is not certain but I think you are in danger."

"What is it Fox, tell us in simple terms."

"You have been misled by Clever Owl. He is in league with something sinister. I think he poisoned the elder he traveled with. I think he means you harm. I think he means for you to die."

His last words were said to Anastazja.

She looked at him as his face changed. He looked down at his stomach; curiously, then pain showed on his face. A moment later she heard a loud popping noise from behind him. Glancing between his contorted face and the source of the sound she saw a group of men on horseback. Smoke emanated from a long tube that was pointed towards them. He was still some distance from them.

Fox was now holding his stomach and looking down with a look of pain —his shirt showed a bright red color that was spreading.

Again she felt part of her saddle suddenly change, as if it had been cut or punctured. Again she heard the popping sound.

Stojan looked at her and yelled.

“Move.”

She and Stojan rode as Fox attempted to spur his horse, but did so weakly as if only making the motions.

The two on horseback split up and both rode around the cathedral at a rapid pace.

Eventually meeting behind the building they stopped as Stojan yelled an answer to her unasked question.

“It is a weapon of some kind.”

“Oh Stojan is he dead?”

“I know not if he is. The weapon has a range and speed I’ve never seen. They will be upon us soon.

Behind the cathedral was what looked like a small abandoned trading town. Buildings were small and did not look permanent, but stood strongly in defiance of their shoddy workmanship.

Men and women were exiting the buildings and coming towards them. At least two of them had bows and said weapons were trained on them.

Stojan thought quickly.

They both drew their swords. Ana had never fought on horseback and had only been trained by Stojan on various maneuvers—consisting mostly of relieving certain trees of their fruits.

“We are surrounded. And what of Fox?”

Ana was reserved, but obviously frightened from the wound Fox received. A weapon that could give that kind of wound at that distance was frightening.

The group continued to approach—now with others. They poured out of the small buildings and joined the group, almost mindlessly.

"They point their bows at us, but I see no other weapons."

Stojan was frustrated at the situation. They found themselves in a precarious position, and without any means for retreat. They'd clearly been led into a trap and they followed the instructions perfectly. They could make a break for it but at this range they may end up with an arrow in their horse or their persons. If one of the group carried a weapon like what was used on Fox they'd have little chance of escaping.

"If they meant to kill us they would have."

Ana nodded, tendrils of red showing themselves in her hair.

"How many are there?"

"There may be more in the buildings and…"

"Oh why won't they leave us alone?!"

Ana interrupted Stojan's carefully-measured tones with her frustration. His frustration was in himself for finding themselves surrounded with no escape, and matters were made worse now by the appearance of the group from the front of the building.

But no Fox.

"We just let them take us?!"

Ana yelled in frustration.

"Yes. Let us see what they want."

"They mean to kill us!"

Stojan's calm mixed with Ana's frustration.

The people continued to walk closer and now just a few meters away some looked at Ana and her hair with something unexpected.

Fear.

Tendrils had spread and turned to mostly red now, and the slight breeze blew strands across her face. Her gaze was set now and she meant to do harm to those who meant to do the same to her.

"Come down from your horses."

A man walked to the front of the group and commanded them thus.

"And if we do not you will kill us?"

Stojan asked matter-of-factly.

Like you have done to Fox, thought Ana, her face like stone.

"We will only kill you if we have to."

It was clear to them that this was not quite the truth. Ana wondered if the projectile that killed Fox was meant for her and the operator simply missed them. Surely an Amiran killing one of the people would be cause for quite a conflict. She would certainly see this so. Wouldn't they? She had yet to see Fox or his horse.

She held her sword close, and continued to look down on the people before her—literally and metaphorically.

Stojan glanced at the four newcomers and saw the weapon with the long snout. It was not pointed at them, but instead sticking out of the saddle bag. Perhaps it took a long time to load or could not be done so from horseback, so the rider had sheathed it.

Stojan calmly started to dismount, still holding his sword in one hand.

He looked at Ana, then the leader, then those with bows. Slowly he moved. It was a feat of dexterity to dismount while holding a sword but both he and Ana were able to do it, at Stojan's insistance; partly due to his undying desire to train her as much as possible, and partly due to him starting to run out of things to teach her. This made him glad.

As he swung a leg over Ana was loosening her own bindings and legs from her stirrups. Ana's feet were pulled upward and her legs compressed. Her torso started to move ever so slightly, as if feeling the saddle with her backside. An onlooker might say it looked a bit like the dance a cat performs, before it pounces.

As he swung his leg over many things happened simultaneously.

The leader began to yell, "Drop your…"

Stojan's leg swung all the way over.

Stojan said to Ana quietly, "Jump down, Anastazja."

The leader was met with a rather long sword on the top of his unarmored head as Stojan's sword was swung as part of his dismount in a great arc —the dismount and force of his landing carrying additional force.

And Ana left her horse.

It was not a dismount. Those who witnessed it saw it as more of a controlled fall in which she left her horse and was suddenly above them. A leap would have taken too much time and would have allowed them to release their arrows. They did indeed do this, but for other reasons.

Ana, like Stojan, landed upon her enemies with a sword blow that started on her horse and ended with it slicing through part of a body. In her case her shorter sword sliced at an arm holding the arrow back in the woman's bow. Her eyes went wide when she saw what was about to happen and released the arrow to defend herself. It seemed that though her bow was an excellent ranged weapon, it left the wielder defenseless for close, unexpected combat. The arrow was let loose as her other arm was raised in a defensive posture. This arrow would land a mere meter from her that day and was soon joined by her right forearm. Stumbling backward the now one-armed woman took an arrow in the back that was let loose by the man behind her, fear showing in his eyes by what had just happened. His desire to shoot had outpaced his desire to aim properly.

Ana's eyes quickly moved to him as she spun her body to the counter-clockwise, allowing herself to clear the stumbling form of the woman she'd just injured. Her sword continued its path as she swung it in a loop to catch the man behind her. He only looked at her hair as she took out his throat—blood flying against the others grouped in unfortunately close quarters.

He dropped his bow and grabbed his throat as he headed for the ground.

He knew he'd be dead in moments as the blood spewed from between his fingers.

Stojan had already moved on to the man behind the third bow-wielder. He was the only man whose sword was out and ready, and he swung it at Stojan as his face was sprayed with blood by the man grasping his throat.

Ana's strokes were quick, and tight; punctuated with acrobatic spins while Stojan's were long swings and thrusts with his sword that was a miniature version him—tall and thin. His reach thus was greater than any who opposed him in the group as he mowed men and women down. Neither he nor Ana traded glances as they worked their way through the group. Stojan's face remained stoic as one working a craft while Ana's was of pure passion and anger. Her red hair moved with her as if trying to catch up to the blurry movements. The group was taken off guard by the methodical tall man and the smaller girl who dodged and parried and spun—finding purchase with her sword in flesh and in necks and between bones.

Stojan operated in silence as a direct contrast to the gasps and shouts of pain, along with Ana's periodic heavy exhales from exertions. Some would say she growled. Those that did were probably dead now.

Two ran from the scene—a man and woman—as the last was cut down.

This gave Ana an opportunity to look behind her to see the four that approached them. Only seconds had passed and the wielder of the weapon was dismounting with only sword, leaving it still stuck in the bag holster.

No one else pointed a bow at them, but instead just ran into the fray.

Ana watched the couple run and stumble and then she turned to face the new four adversaries.

Stojan walked slowly to the one that approached him, and this calm walk unnerved him so that he held his sword up and backed away slowly.

Ana just froze and raised her sword at an angle in front of her, her hand held low near her stomach. It was a defensive, almost casual stance. She looked at her sword tip with a head tilted slightly down. Her eyes moved from it to the one who approached her as she stared at him through her crimson hair.

He saw her eyes behind the hair, and her motionless body.

He surprised himself at how taken aback he was by it all. It was not like fighting others. This was a young girl whose hair had magically transformed as an embodiment of anger. And she moved fast; with tight, powerful movements with exquisite control.

She was a stark contrast of beautiful form and deadly movements.

And she just stood in front of him.

His weapon would not fire again but he knew not why. His master had explained only how to use it, and given minimal instructions otherwise. It was a deadly thing that could kill at a great distance—far more than a bow with needing very little arc to compensate. But he was helpless to use it now, and had missed on his first and second shots. He thought for sure that at this moment he heard another one of the weapons fire, but he wasn't sure if the girl heard it too. He no longer trusted his senses.

He'd reluctantly entered the battle with sword.

He would have to make the first move—this act caused him reluctance. She parried his first strike and that was when recognition shown in her face.

He was the one that had injured Fox.

She did not attack then. She did not swing wildly in anger. Instead she again stepped back to her stance of defense, barely.

Her eyes pierced him. Her sword would soon follow.

Again he attacked. His heart was not in it. He wanted her to engage. This was not like ranged attacks, and he did not relish it. Again he was parried.

Again the eyes looked at him, though the hair, head still tilted slightly downward.

"Before I kill you—tell me this: why."

He raised himself to his full height and considered, happy that he was given the opportunity to catch his breath.

"I follow the orders of…"

"NO. Why did you kill him?"

Realizing she meant the boy, his mind raced between truth and fear. He had aimed at her but the boy was in the way. He knew nothing of the boy save that he was part of a tribe that…

"He was in the way."

It was the simplest truth possible.

He longed to be back on his horse—at a great distance from this.

"Stop."

It was a new voice, coming from near the building, not the people who'd run away.

It was Fox, and another.

Standing before them was Fox, still holding his blood-soaked tunic, and holding his shoulder was a man they recognized, though his attire was foreign.

It was the visiting shaman. His hand was behind him holding something —possibly a knife as it shined in the sun.

His other hand held him tightly on the shoulder and it was clear he was using him as a shield.

That was when the man facing off with Ana felt the sharpness of Stojan's blade underneath his chin.

"Let him go!"

Ana yelled at the shaman as Stojan's held his man at bay, though he chose not to wield his dagger that day.

"Come with me. Bring him if you like."

The man's eyes went wide with confusion as the shaman slowly backed up towards what looked like the back exit of the great stone building. Looking around Stojan saw no one peer from the small town. Either there were no more people left or they chose safety over peril. Ana walked slowly along with Stojan as the five people made for a very inefficient movement towards the cathedral.

Stojan and Ana traded glances and he was relieved that the blood he saw looked to be from other than her body, save for a few scratches.

“I am fine.”

She confirmed his assessment without him asking.

Ana examined the attire of the shaman. He did not wear any clothing that she’d seen him wear in the cities or while traveling. Instead he wore pants of a thinner material, and a shirt and vest. Upon his head was a wide-brimmed hat and around his waist was a thick belt not unlike her sword belt. Instead of a sword sheath on his right side was a sort of miniature but wide sheath that tapered like a funnel. The belt was decorated with many cylindrical loops that served no purpose. They held no beads, or gems and were too small for anything useful—even a tiny knife wouldn’t fit in them.

That’s when she saw the thing pointed at the back of Fox’s neck. It was shinier than silver—almost like a mirror—and looked heavy. He held it by a handle that was dark. It reminded her of the machinery of the conveyance in its construction. A small rod protruded from a mass of cylinders. It seemed that Fox feared it, though Ana had never seen one operate. She wondered if it was similar to the long rod used by the man Stojan now held at sword-edge.

The shaman looked at her and shook his head. He smiled at them both with a smile of disgust.

His eyes held anxiety and something else.

Carefully maneuvering the door open, Fox was pulled around unceremoniously and each step looked like it brought pain.

When the shaman saw Ana’s concern he glanced at her hair then spoke.

“He will die soon if we do not save him. I cannot save him if you do not help.”

The words of the shaman were confusing to Ana as they entered the building. The room was large and held a few benches and other items—

cloths and folded clothing.

The door slammed behind them as Fox's eyes found her. He saw her own eyes, her now red hair with black highlights, and her sword—covered in the blood of others.

She saw him look upon her with pain, sadness and recognition. He forced a tiny smile to her and she did the same while darting her eyes at the shaman. She could see the device closer now. He grasped the handle while his index finger went through a loop of metal. The thing had a tiny fin of metal pointed back at him. It was an odd device, surely.

The boy's weak smile quickly turned back to a look of pain, accentuating the warning of the shaman.

She wanted to slice the shaman's hand clean off in one strike and then on the upstroke shove the sword through his throat, up into his head.

Her eyes did not go unnoticed.

"Autumn Wind this is not becoming of you."

The shaman smiled.

"You are to be a great warrior."

"Why?"

She asked quietly, and quite disrespectfully.

In response the shaman shoved Fox in their direction and then closed his eyes tightly as he squeezed hard on the handle.

The device exploded in smoke and sparks and a horrible deafening sound which shook all in the room as the shaman pushed himself backwards though the door.

Stojan saw that his eyes opened only once through the door.

Ana heard the wall behind Stojan make an odd sound as if struck hard with something.

She caught Fox before he collapsed and sheathed her sword immediately.

Stojan kept his hold on the man with him as the tiny cloud offended his nostrils. It stunk of something on fire.

Ana and Fox embraced and she kissed him on the cheek. He turned his head slowly as she pulled away. Their lips met briefly as Ana's eyes turned toward the tall man.

"Stojan…?"

Her eyes looked on in horror at his stomach.

It too was now red.

Stojan tried to glance down, releasing the grip on the man slightly.

Sensing this the hostage pushed away and rebounded on a wall as he fumbled for his sword.

He looked up as a smaller sword was inserted into his throat, pinning him to the wall he now leaned on.

Stojan held his side and dropped his own sword.

Ana pulled her sword from the man as he slid down the wall into a seated position, his eyes watching her hair as he died.

Fox stumbled and fell as well, coming into a seated position that was eerily similar to the man Ana had just killed.

Fox remained clinging to life and held his stomach, as did Stojan.

Stojan smiled at Ana.

"They said this was the end of my journey Ana—the red numbers foretold this."

She shook her head and joined him on the floor, dropping her own sword.

"No Stojan. Don't. Leave me…"

She continued to gently shake her head as her words were broken as she spoke them.

He smiled.

Fox looked on weakly as Ana then looked from him to Stojan, searching for a solution. She was ill-prepared for the two men she cared about to leave her within moments. He was many shades whiter than before.

A soft sound came from the direction of the boy. Looking over, Stojan and Ana saw him slump over to the left as he went limp—blood running on the floor from his stomach now.

He closed his eyes and torn between the two Ana leaped to Fox, holding his hand with one hand and running her palm over his face with the other.

"Oh."

She cried.

"Fox."

Her mouth contorted into a sad frown as tears ran from her eyes.

For many moments she held him, and finally with much trepidation she slowly turned her head to look at Stojan. She was not ready for the inevitable but she looked because she had to.

He stood.

His tunic was pulled up to reveal a wound that bled, but was not on his stomach but rather on the side.

He walked to the wall behind him as she continued to crouch on the floor.

With his finger he poked at the wall, inserting his finger into a hole. He turned his head.

"It went through me. I think."

With that he walked over to Ana, applying pressure to his side as he knelt down to Fox. He touched him on his forehead and then touched Ana upon her shoulder.

"He was a good man Ana."

Her arms withdrew to hug Stojan as her blonde and black hair fell upon his shoulder.

Stojan started to move his hand from his side and thought better of it, and winced in pain as she hugged him.

Ana's emotions were torn between elation and sadness as she said goodbye to Fox.

Stojan, it seemed, would not be leaving her just yet.

"I will be alright. We must find him."

Ana pulled away slowly and glanced back at Fox.

"We will come back for him but must find this shaman. We owe much to these people and he has darkness in his heart. And I think he knows more about us than he has told."

"Then we will kill him."

Stojan was taken aback by her ferocity but did not berate her that day.

After all, he agreed.

Composing themselves, they slowly opened the door.

Stojan expected the shaman to be waiting on the other side—pointing the weapon at the door.

In fact it looked like it could expel the projectiles with such force that it could just break through the door to harm the occupants.

The devices seemed fickle though, and the Shaman had clearly been taken aback by the noise and violence of utilizing it.

They made they way through the doorway, then the hall. There were many doors and one by one they experimentally opened them. Each opening provided a tenseness to them as they expected the weapon to be pointed at them on the other side.

Again and again they were greeted with an empty room.

The layout reminded Stojan of the building he had met the bishop within.

And portions of it unsettled him as they also matched his vision.

They proceeded with caution as Stojan continued the pressure on his side as the blood stained his tunic.

Ana's eyes showed her sadness as they eventually found a room that connected to many doors in a row.

They were taller than the others and the antechamber they stood within had an equally taller ceiling.

It seemed like a prelude to a great hall. It was.

They looked at each other.

Stojan took his hand away from his side— sword still out — and pulled on the door. He hoped it didn't change into anything that day and would just remain a handle.

The door opened. Ana peeked into it and Stojan could see the awe in her eyes.

They walked in.

Row upon row of long chairs were present—pointed at the front of the hall. Ana could see the craftsmanship of the seats, which seemed each to be made of a length of seamless wood—polished and varnished beautifully. She could not imagine the woodworker that had the means to produce one, let alone tens of chairs such as this. In front of each were bins to hold items of some sort—perhaps the swords and accoutrements of the visitors. It was all very impressive and easily filled the visitor with reverence.

The windows were lit with the sunlight and beautiful mosaics were shown of people in robes. Some were sad and some looked like they rejoiced. Ana tried hard not to fixate on them and stay aware of what was to happen next.

"Show yourself!"

Stojan yelled and his voice echoed impressively through the room.

That was when they saw him. He stood at the stage at the very end of the rows—lit by sunlight that poured through windows above him from a skylight.

He stood next to another, dressed all in white.

They peered at him as he stood there. His hands were empty. Whatever means to defend himself he possessed, he did not show it openly.

As they approached they saw the silver device in the short sheath at his side.

He stood both triumphantly and nervously.

"I am glad you are well, Autumn Wind. And you too Watchful Raven."

Stojan cared little for his new name but felt disgust at hearing the man use it.

They stopped at thin stairs leading to the raised area.

The shaman was bathed in sunlight now and it was clear what stood next to him.

A statue.

It looked on, in a pose that was noble and defiant. A man, holding a short sword and wearing robes. It looked to be a guard or soldier in an army from long ago and was a half a meter taller than the shaman—about as tall as Stojan.

The shaman spoke again.

"I've learned many things today and almost made a terrible mistake. I have seen the light on this matter and am grateful."

He glanced at the statue and smiled, then looked back at them.

He seemed as if his sensibility had left him.

"What do you mean?" asked Ana.

"Oh it would not serve things for you or Watchful Raven to die at the hands of others."

He looked at Stojan's stained shirt.

Stojan looked at him as Ana sneered her contempt.

"So beautiful!"

The shaman looked upon her hair; now mostly red with just a few blonde highlights.

"And amazing. I am so fortunate to witness this, and have served to be a part of it from the beginning. It makes me valuable."

Again he glanced at the statue. To Anastazja it was as if someone chose to talk to a tree. It did not talk back either.

"You can put your swords away. You're in no danger from me. I promise that I will not harm you. I cannot."

His request went unheeded as they looked at him with suspicion.

Again he glanced up at the statue and the action irritated Ana. His insanity annoyed her.

Why was he defenseless now?

She glanced around her, thinking many bows were now trained on her. Perhaps someone held one of the rods that could expel a projectile with great accuracy. Perhaps they were surrounded with them. She and Stojan had walked into a trap. He was clever, and brave to draw them out like this.

He moved forward slowly and cautiously, holding his hands out with his palms towards them. He stepped in front of the statue, its head still visible behind him.

"Please. Put those away. As I said…"

Ana glanced at the head behind her. She thought she saw movement.

She did now, in the center of the shaman's chest.

A red object erupted from it—sword point, made entirely of marble. Streaks of red and white ran along the length as the shaman's blood came with it as it exited his body.

“No?”

His only word was a question, as he grabbed the blade with his hands and looked down at it. It quickly exited his hands and withdrew back into the body.

He looked at them.

“I am betrayed.”

He fell to the side, like a pendulum.

Behind him was the statue. It looked at them. It held the sword—soaked with red of the shaman’s blood. The stark contrast of red was stunning on the all white figure.

It blinked.

AN END

It looked at Stojan with a sickly smile—a contortion of the face that seemed impossible, let alone the fact that it was made of marble.

Stojan looked back into the eyes that were simply carved indentations. It blinked nonetheless.

"He brought you to me. For that he was useful. Unlike you Stojan—he talked too much."

Ana's shock at hearing Stojan's name was obvious.

"How do you know us?"

"I know of you and…"

"You are a Saint?!"

Ana was awestruck, and the visible emotion made Stojan ill. Her awe of this thing disturbed him. He'd seen it in his vision—and now in reality. He was over the awe, and it was an evil selfish thing. The entity before him matched his expectations nicely.

It smiled at Ana and almost bowed, accepting her amazement.

"Yes. You stand before a Saint. You are truly blessed."

Ana looked at it—wide eyed still. The voice echoed in the chamber made specifically to enhance the acoustics of any who stood on the dais.

Stojan looked at the solemn form of the shaman to the side, and considered the statement of the statue. He did not believe him to be so blessed.

"I know why you are here."

The voice was hollow and cold—a trick of sound and the air. It made one shiver.

"I know many things." It spread it hands, one still holding a small sword. Ana wondered if it could drop the sword, or if it was forever bonded to its hand. A few drops of red left the tip and made their way to the carpet.

"Does she know, Stojan?"

Stojan did not take his eyes off of the talking statue and just stared.

It continued the sickly, sinister smile.

"Does she know what you did—why you are here?"

It shook its head at Ana, and the smile turned to an expression of sadness, and mock shame. She looked at it with fear, her hair a mix of blonde and black streaks.

"Oh Stojan, Stojan the Butcher of Budziszyn, the murderer of over 50 poor souls in one day."

It swung its sword around in mock combat, drops of the shaman's blood departed from the weapon as it continued the taunt.

"The captain of the guard, with such a promising future, *if they just hadn't taken his little girl from him.*"

Anastazja gasped almost imperceptibly at the sing-song way the statue had revealed this, and it seemed Stojan was going for his sword—his hand moving slowly and almost imperceptibly. He moved between the statue and Ana.

Could it leave its pedestal? He knew not.

"Captain turned assassin. Does she know?" It gestured with the sword toward Anastazja, pointing at her.

"Does she know who you came to kill that day? She doesn't, does she?"

It smiled again, the sickly smile with upturned edges that would be impossible on a human, but apparently possible on a statue.

"All this time and you haven't told her? And you *travel* with her? This is remarkable."

"I already know he was sent to kill my father, he told me himself!"

Ana shouted at the taunting statue, her hand on her own hilt. She stood only a meter behind Stojan. He still hadn't looked back at her, even with the outburst. Had he done so he'd seen the unusual mixture of black, blonde and red her hair displayed that moment.

"He told me himself…" she said quietly, some uncertainty showing in her voice.

The statue looked from Ana to Stojan.

"*Did* he? Tell her Stojan." It remarked playfully, as if in a guessing game.

Stojan remained silent as Ana continued. speaking to the face of the statue, and the back of Stojan's head.

"I said I know that he came to kill my father, and that nature took him instead."

It looked at Stojan, then back to Anastazja without moving its head. It drank in the tension and was moulding it as one moulds clay.

"Oh, *I* will tell her then, and not be robbed of this pleasure. He did not come to kill your father… He came to kill…"

At that Stojan's head slowly turned to Ana, left shoulder facing her, right shoulder towards the thing that spoke.

"You."

Wide-eyed she stared back at the man that stood before her, head hung low. She had never seen him brought so low with shame.

Ana's mouth formed only the beginning of a question. He looked down at no one, standing an arm's length from both the statue and Ana.

"I did not know it at the time. I thought I was agreeing to take the life of a warrior that would to come to kill the bishop. A great warrior. I know now who that warrior is.

"It is you, Ana." He lifted his head after speaking to the floor.

Then he smiled—a genuine smile of pride and love. He raised his head and turned it towards her, his body still frozen at the odd angle, as if he was trying to keep the statue from getting near her.

"You have become a great warrior, Anastazja. You are a humble learner —willing to learn whatever skill is taught. You have such natural ability, such energy and light. I am so proud of you."

She looked at Stojan, her eyes wide. She herself seemed at once both proud and afraid. At some point she had unsheathed her sword like Stojan.

"But."

It was the statue again.

"But there is a problem Stojan. If you destroy my vessel I cannot help you."

He turned back to face him, to hear his elaboration.

"You cannot strike me, for I am the way to set things right. For I can help you undo what has yet to happen."

Stojan's own sword arm dropped slowly.

"Yes. You know what is about to happen…"

"It's too late!"

"No Stojan, it is not too late for me. I do not see this world the way you do. Things are not in a simple line for us. We see it all and are not bound by your rules."

Softly, Stojan asked, "What… do you mean? You can undo it?"

"Yes. Imagine that you will no longer be forever on the road—always running, filled with so much shame.

It shook its head.

"You have yet to murder all those souls. Because…"

Stojan's sword arm dropped to his side, his fist touching his thigh.

"She has yet to die."

Ana looked at the back of Stojan's head, trying to imagine his expression, she then settled on the face of the demon in a statue.

It looked at Ana.

"It in fact happens this very day."

Ana wished she could see Stojan's face.

"Today Stojan. You were sent back past her death and have now caught up to it."

It laughed.

"Your task was to take mere minutes and you overstayed by more than three years. But you are too far away in Amira to rush to prevent it. You could not make it back to Poliska to prevent it in time by normal means. You have arrived to see me on the very day of her death. Imagine that."

It glanced at Ana and then looked back at Stojan.

"I can make it so that you arrive in time—to prevent her death. No, I cannot move you in time—only one could do that. I can move you in distance. You will have your daughter, and no one will have to die. Isn't that wonderful?"

"But..?" Again Stojan's voice was just a whisper.

"Oh." It put its own sword down—at its side—and it was clear to Ana it could not let go of it.

"By setting this in motion you will have never agreed to the bishop's plan, and would not have been sent here."

"And Ana?"

Ana felt tears in her eyes as she listened to Stojan's voice—so little life in it, so weak now.

"I think you know. And that is really none of your concern isn't it?"

Stojan turned to Ana, turning his back to the statue. He had tears in his eyes. They seemed to look at her and yet their focus was somewhere else.

"You don't belong here." The statue continued—reprimanding Stojan as he looked at Ana—prodding him along. Stojan was in slow motion, frozen with emotion.

"Stojan, your window of opportunity is small. This is your chance to undo what has happened. The likes of you does not deserve such a gift, and I make it available to you freely. You know what you need to do. It is, after all, what you *agreed* to."

Stojan continued to look into Ana's blue eyes. Her hair was of amber and she nodded ever so slightly. Tears began to run down her cheeks, slowly, as she reserved herself to the inevitable. The man who had been like a father to her for these past years would leave her. She cherished the time they'd spent together, the training, the moments, the teaching, everything had been with love. Love for her.

"I love you Stojan."

That was when he swung—so quickly, so violently, so absolutely. The big man's sword and sword arm had considerable reach, and in one powerful arc it was done.

It had to be done, and it was the only decision. Though it broke his heart it was the right thing to do, and since he'd arrived that was all he had done.

Though it was not made of flesh, his sword decapitated it nonetheless. In one turn he'd swung and struck—a backhanded movement. It was of utter surprise to both Ana and the statue, as Stojan hadn't even turned his head. He looked at Ana the entire time and let his arm fly—with precision he'd found its neck. The difference was that Ana's face would change, but the statue's head—now in pieces on the floor—would forever show the surprise.

Ana ran to Stojan and hugged him.

"But why?"

He took a deep breath and hugged her back.

"What's done is done. I am who am because of that. I have little wisdom but what I have tells me I am in the right place—with you."

And in the Cathedral of St. John, a statue did fall, and a creature of great power did dissipate that day. With nowhere to go, with no proper vessel to contain it and with a door closed forever it had but one option.

To die.

That fall day in Amira Stojan remained an assassin and a father, and chose to take the second chance he was given, rather than the life of a blonde haired girl that loved him as much as he did her.

And with that he did indeed set something in motion. After 1,000 years an interloper died. The great land of Amira was now influenced less by Saints.

But more still lived.

ABOUT THE AUTHOR

Mark Bradford is an author, speaker, podcast host, coach and builder. He invests a great deal of time and effort researching a subject to come up with an explanation for it that everyone can understand. His podcast interviews as well as his experiences have taught him what life's made of, time management tricks, what multitasking really is, and even how both order and chaos benefit our lives. 15+ year business owner, he also is a full stack web developer.

It is in his nature to build things that fix, augment or create a solution. The fruits of his labors have been a role playing game with three custom 12-sided dice, a writing site, a dating site, five books and a card game.

Mark speaks to professional associations, groups and businesses about status, time, energy and resources, and how we all connect.

Mark produces and hosts a weekly podcast about Time, Energy and Resources that also features interviews with amazing people. Listen to ***The Alchemy for Life*** podcast for more insight, on iTunes and most other podcast providers. Subscribe and you won't miss them.

www.alchemyfor.life

Mark produces ***The Status Game*** series of books and card game that helps demonstrate, educate and enlighten people about an invisible but very real aspect on how we connect, and what we like.

His answers have almost two million answer views on Quora—a question and answer community.

Follow Mark on Instagram for announcements and things related to his content—books, podcasts, etc.

@authormarkbradford

Books by Mark Bradford

Nonfiction:

The Status Game
Navigating the perilous waters of dating and online dating. With a sense of humor.

The Status Game II
How status is the key to all relationships—business and personal.

OneSelf
Faith of a simpler, more direct kind. Or just nonsense.

Alchemy for Life
Everything you need to know about Life Coaching in one book. And 16 formulas for success.

Fiction:

The Sword and the Sunflower

Coming soon:

Fiction:

Amira
Book two of The Sword and the Sunflower.

Thank you for reading this. It means a lot to me that you did. If you liked this book I would appreciate if you took a minute to review it. Your input really helps and is valuable.

Made in the USA
Columbia, SC
22 March 2022